Chuck, C,

Hey Guys! It is great to see you! Thanks for your support. We miss seeing you. Enjoy the book!

Love always,
Timothy [signature]

THE MAJESTIC
OF PURPLE MOUNTAIN

Letters from the Greenskeeper

Copyright © 2012 by Arlington Alan

Published by: Arlington Alan Publishing, LTD

ISBN 978-0-9884270-0-6

www.Arlingtonalan.com

All rights reserved. No part of this publication may be reproduced or transmitted in any form or by any means, electronic or mechanical, including photocopy, recording, or any information storage and retrieval system, without the permission in writing from the copyright holder.

This is a work of fiction. Names, characters, businesses, places, events and incidents are either the products of the author's imagination or used in a fictitious manner. Any resemblance to actual persons, living or dead, or actual events is purely coincidental.

Cover photo 'Shenandoah Mountains' provided by Brandon Atkinson.

THE MAJESTIC
OF PURPLE MOUNTAIN

Letters from the Greenskeeper

Chapter 1

There are times when individuals of the kingdoms of plant, animal and man, although exceedingly rare and excessively brief, while together striving for the greater good, find a common thread of uncommon faith, hidden deep within each, whose exercise, if dared, would move even heaven itself. This is such a time as that.

It is the nineteenth day of April, in the year two thousand and twelve. However, it is not just any day. For it is not just any day when one learns the number of his seasons on earth. To date, my seasons are sixteen-hundred, as seasons are reckoned by man, and this is to be my last. Not only my last, but also the last for a number of others that live here on the mountain with me. For this mountain top, and everything on it, will soon be leveled and swept into the valley below. Purple Mountain, with all its mystery, will be no more. I received this word by way of my friend, Isaiah, having received it directly from the King. Upon receiving it, he hastened to make his way to Purple Mountain despite the long journey.

How does one respond to such a message? Oftentimes we look to the example set by others in similar circumstances. Consider king Hezekiah, who when told his days were numbered, prayed that his days would be extended then wept bitterly. The man Job, when faced with challenges in his life said, "The Lord giveth, and the Lord taketh away; blessed be the name of the Lord." Each man trusting in his Divine Creator, yet each responding differently, with one man requesting and the other accepting. In response, God granted to the one extension of life and to the other restoration of life. However, these are stories of individual men.

What of entire cities facing destruction? Nineveh, that city of old, was told by Jonah the prophet 'in forty days this city will be destroyed.' In another example, Abraham was told of the impending destruction of Sodom. To each a man was sent, with one city receiving an itinerate, yet reluctant, prophet the other a nomadic, yet eager, intercessor. Each city deserving, in equal measure, the fruits of its labor. To each a call was made. For one an outward call was heard and the other an inward. From each a response was required. The people of Nineveh repented and the city along with its inhabitants was spared. In disparity, the people of Sodom continued in their ways. Would the city of Sodom, with all its inhabitants, have been spared from destruction by fire, for the sake of one more righteous citizen added to its number?

It is true, in His omniscience, God knows the times and places of his creation and his prefect purposes for each. In addition, we know that all things work to the good of those that love him. Yes, all things. Our inability to remotely understand these truths by no means invalidates them. Accept these things, do we, not on blind faith but rather with mind faith. We are creatures of reason and have the ability to use our senses. Unto men were given two great lights. Although neither am I allowed to view directly, yet I know of their existence due to the lingering shadows cast by man. These are the lights of conscience and creation. These, together, bear witness to the existence and greatness of God. It was said by the King "faith the size of a mustard seed could move a mountain." However, could such faith keep a mountain from being moved? It is this hypothesis, now set in motion, we intend to prove.

In summary, it is not so much a concern for my seasons being shortened as it is a concern for those whose fate is also tied to that of this mountain. Has each completed the tasks, prepared from ages ago, assigned them? For some I fear, despite the number of seasons already past, be they few or many, have yet to live them to their full extent. That these, given yet a season more of opportunity, to properly exercise their faith will choose to do so. In this way, kingdoms will be made more perfect. This is their story more than it is mine.

Let me introduce myself. My name is Anson, the White Oak of Purple Mountain. My height and span are the same at six score and seven feet. Ten men, standing shoulder to shoulder at my base, it takes to surround me. My bark is white and highly unusual for a tree of my type. In early spring, I have a misty look as young leaves, with their downy texture, begin to develop. As spring gives way, my leaves grow five to eight inches in length and three to four inches in width. They are oblong and seven to nine lobed. In season, my leaves are yellow green and finally turn purple in color during autumn. As winter sets in, down to earth, fall my leaves.

I took root here in Southwestern Virginia, on the side of Purple Mountain where the last rays of the setting sun are seen, just a few years after the first settlements were made in Jamestown. My youth was quite uneventful. I have developed kinships over the years with other trees, plants and the various animals that inhabit this mountain. Some are more personal than others. Yet none are more personal than the kinship I share with the people that settled this land. This kinship is a gift. In creation, I was gifted with the ability to bond with those that have touched the bark of my trunk and with those that have walked Purple Mountain. With these have I bonded. This bond allows me to know their thoughts and feelings. Their stories become part of me. Like a living scroll am I, with their stories rolled within the protective coating of my bark.

They are a resilient people yet soft at heart. They are not a perfect people, as if perfection could be attained by men, and are capable of grievous error. They are willing to admit fault, seek forgiveness and accept responsibility. They have demonstrated a capacity for great sacrifice when called upon. Their warriors are prone to gallantry, fidelity and service. It is with these that I feel the greatest kinship. As I grew, so too did the settlers to this land. We grew together, this nation and I. In the course of life, I found myself involved in two significant military conflicts.

The first was the American War of Independence. My involvement in the American Revolutionary War was limited to one engagement. My spirits soared, as a people strived for independence from tyranny and in so doing brought forth a new nation. However, a nation would not be gained without sacrifice, struggle and faith in God's divine providence. Although many battles were fought in Virginia, not many were fought in this area of the commonwealth. However, there was one incident. A young American revolutionary took refuge behind me during a minor skirmish. A Red Coat fired on his position but the shot hit me instead of the young soldier. The bullet lodged in my trunk and it is with me even to this day. The soldier escaped without injury and lived to fight another day for the cause of freedom.

The second conflict was the Civil War. During this conflict, I experienced the deepest of sorrows, as I watched, from a distance, brother fight against brother. As the war progressed, in late June 1862, a young soldier named Oliver, happened to spend the night beneath my canopy. He was a bugler in the Army of the Potomac and on his way to Harrison's Landing to join his regiment. He arrived in the late afternoon, a few hours before sunset. He practiced with his bugle for quite some time before he settled upon one particular tune. Just before sundown, he walked a distance away, to the spot where the flagpole pedestal now stands. He took up a position there and stood erect facing the setting sun. Just as the sun slipped over the horizon, he played a short but memorable tune. Afterwards, he silently made his way back to my canopy and took his rest. The next morning he left at first light and I would not enjoy the pleasure of his company again. I was proud to stand watch over him for just one night.

These wars, and others, helped shape a nation and a people. Each conflict adding a color to the threads woven into the fabric of a nation; the Revolutionary War added liberty; while the Civil War added humility. Over time, a great tapestry began to emerge, each conflict, foreign or domestic, adding new colors with each strand. As a nation matured so too did its tapestry. This nation became great among the nations of the world. However, the world recognized that it was not the tapestry that made the nation great but that greatness came through the skilled craftsmanship of the divine weaver.

Many changes have I witnessed over the past four centuries. However, some things have remained the same. Man has a desire still, to maintain his awkward lead, in a dance with love and hatred, creativity and destruction, gallantry and cowardice, fidelity and betrayal, fear and faith. All the while believing the dance will bring him peace. Peace, to these, would not come. Some, although feeling the same desires, succumbed to a different dance. They chose to dance with God, accepting His lead, and in His steps they followed. It is these that will find peace.

Sometime in the not so distant past, as a tree measures time, a golf course was laid here upon the slopes of Purple Mountain. The origins of 'the Majestic of Purple Mountain' have long been forgotten by men. Legend has it being spoken into existence or that it fell from heaven itself. But I remember the mysterious circumstances surrounding its creation and the majestic purpose it was created to serve. For it is here, that some who chose to dance with God, yes, those who danced to the song of self sacrifice, who danced in the darkest of places yet with the Light, come to finish the dance of faith and find peace. Should this mountain be removed, where will these go to find peace?

It is on this night, in the year two thousand and twelve, April and nineteen days, that I have dispatched a message back to the King, by way of my friend, Isaiah. It is a fortnight flight and fraught with danger. I realize the King need not receive the message for he knows of its contents already. But, in its faithful dispatch, over a fortnight, I trust that uncommon faith will give call to action and that heaven will be moved to grant my request.

Chapter 2

"Hoo-hoo hoooooo hoo-hoo, may I ask are you talking too-too toooooo too-too General?" asked Tiger, the great horned owl, his bright yellow eyes piercing the darkness of the moonless night just setting in. He took roost on one of my branches. He is a youthful owl, large for his age, standing two feet tall with a wingspan of five feet, his ear tufts though are rather small. Tiger, serves on the night watch. Nightly, he reports on the activities, or lack there of, happening, or not happening, about the course. Of most importance, is his report on the activities of the greenskeeper, John.

"I have been talking with a friend and I have sent him on his way. Also, please call me Anson," I answered quickly, as I did not want to draw attention to Isaiah's visit. Tiger is a respectful owl and almost always calls me by my official title. He accepted the answer and began his report.

"Mr. Anson, sir, here is the nightly report: all visitors have left the course; the clubhouse is empty; all employees have gone home for the day; the service entrance gates are closed. As usual, the greenskeeper has retired too-too toooooo too-too his cabin. All is secure and quiet. That is the nightly report, sir!" he said eagerly.

"Thank you, Tiger, for the detailed report," I said, acknowledging his efforts, "good work. May I ask, to what part of the cabin has the greenskeeper retired?" I asked with expectancy.

"During the last flyover, he was located in the reserve library section of the cabin, sir," he whispered, as if to keep the information between us.

"At what stage was he engaged in his usual nightly routine?" I questioned. Tiger is keenly aware of the nightly routine of the greenskeeper. On most nights, I will ask him for a detailed report on the greenskeeper.

"Nearing completion. The books have been shelved. He was writing the letters and finishing the first one, sir," he ventured.

"I suppose you meant to say 'finishing his first cigar'?" I speculated. John is known to have a Cuban cigar from time to time, although it is a terrible habit and one he should abandon.

"Yes, sir," he divulged. Tiger has a certain fondness for John and knows of my disapproval regarding the cigar smoking.

"Thank you, Tiger. That is all for now. Please update me on the status of the grounds after your next survey," I asked, feeling somewhat uneasy about the unfolding events for the moment. However, my thoughts were beginning to focus on John and his writing, as they often do at this time in the evening.

It is his practice, John that is, to write letters in the evening, except on Sundays. On Sunday evenings he does something else. He has been writing them for one hundred and sixty seasons now, less one, forty years as a man would count them. So many letters, that even I have lost count of their number. However, John knows the exact count. He keeps a record of each in the *Books of Merit* that are meticulously maintained in the reserve library. The original *Book of Merit* is thought, by most historians, to have been lost to the ages. The letters, yes, the letters. Let me explain briefly about the letters. The explanation may be a difficult one to accept. However, I am confident that some will have the faith to believe and that even those without such faith will consider it. For mystery wrapped in majesty is uncommonly beheld.

John has served as greenskeeper here at the Majestic of Purple Mountain for nearly one hundred and sixty seasons. From his dawning on the course, his duties as greenskeeper have been different from what one would expect. Although, this has never concerned him nor his supervisors. Like a husband caring for his wife, is the relationship between the greenskeeper and the Majestic. There is a unique bond between them, John and the Majestic of Purple Mountain, almost sacred.

An introduction, to the Majestic of Purple Mountain, is called for at this juncture. From the first tee through the eighteenth green, she is perfection. The tee boxes present an altar like appearance, elevated and ornate, with their smooth horizontal surfaces exposed to the heavens. The fairways, like an emerald sea with long rolling waves of shimmering color, flow effortlessly into deep pools of jade. Engagingly exquisite, she is, with each green presenting a paradox of beautifully difficult design. Meticulously manicured throughout are the grasses, trees, shrubs and plants with each one adorning the course as jewel set in its mounting. Like a bride in all of her splendor, is the Majestic of Purple Mountain under the care of the greenskeeper. Yet how she maintains this beauty through the seasons is a mystery. It is this mystery that allows the greenskeeper to perform his most sacred duties.

In comparison to what lies ahead, these are elementary concepts. The letters, yes, the letters. One of the greenskeeper's sacred duties is the writing of letters. Letters to whom? Tonight, John is writing to the families of three individuals. These three individuals were in the last group to play the course for the day. He creates two letters for each individual. The introductory letter follows a set pattern, while the second letter is always unique to the individual player.

Wove paper, devoid of any markings, pure white in color, is used for letter and envelope stock. Centered across the top margin of the first page of the first letter, debossed personally by the greenskeeper, are the words 'The Majestic of Purple Mountain'. The second letter has no such marking. The writing is penned by the fountain; the fountain with a heart shaped breather hole. The onyx black ink he uses is kept in an inkwell made from old rag granite. He writes with the steady and skilled hand of an artful calligrapher.

Once the ink, on the pages, has dried, the second letter is bi-folded and receives an applied wax seal. It is then placed onto the first letter and wrapped within it through a single folding of the first letter. The letters are then placed into the envelope whose only writing is the address of the recipient. A postage stamp, in the likeness of a Purple Heart, is affixed to the envelope in the proper place. The envelopes are deposited for mailing the morning after they are written. The unsuspecting recipients, to whom the envelopes are addressed, will receive them within a few days time.

Before his era as the greenskeeper began, he was a freelance writer. Writing the letters is a labor of love for John, for he is a writer at heart. As he writes, the vibration, of the ruby tipped three tined nib, on the wove paper, creates a symphony of characters, combining into words that serenade the intended reader. Sometimes a letter will be like a song written to be played by a single instrument, sometimes a quartet, other times an orchestra. Yet, all share a common melody. Regularly, he finishes the letters in the early evening. Although, on some occasions, he labors late into the night.

Tonight, John was finishing a letter to the parents of a young man. The contents of the first letter were as follows:

> Dear Mr. & Mrs. Johnson,
>
> Please indulge me with a few moments of your time. My name is John and I am the greenskeeper of the Majestic of Purple Mountain. What is to follow will be hard to accept at first. However, you will find comfort in what has been sent to you. The enclosed sealed letter is authentic and contains details that will validate this premise.
>
> Today, your son played the Majestic of Purple Mountain. He carded a score of par 72 with the help of his caddie The Babe, George Herman Ruth, Jr. Your son claimed it was the round of a lifetime. We spent some time together today and he asked that I send the enclosed letter. It has been sealed and is addressed specifically to each of you.
>
> Please feel free to contact me any time.
>
> Regards,
>
> the Greenskeeper

This is one example of the introductory letter that he sends. The art of composing and sending handwritten letters has been lost to the modern age, I suspect. However, to these that receive them, it is as if a lost treasure had been recovered from the depths of a dark void. The introductory letter is placed into the envelope, in such a way, as to make its opening first, a natural first motion. As the first letter is unfolded, the second letter gently slides out and into the hand of the reader. Being sealed, the second letter projects an air of mystery and importance about it. Upon reading the first letter, only breaking the seal of the second letter remains to be done. In all of the years of letters being sent, neither has one been returned; nor a complaint made in response to their receipt. Yet, there are some seals, even to this day, that remain unbroken.

"General, sir!" breaking the silence, announced Tiger, upon his return from his second survey. There was nothing unusual in his second report. However, there remained an unsettling feeling and it refused to depart from me. The evening was coming to a close and a new day would come tomorrow and with it new hope.

Chapter 3

As the sun rises on a new day, a restless town rests in the morning shadow of Purple Mountain. From this side of the mountain, hours will pass before the town receives light directly from the sun. In a daily parade, direct light marches methodically to form a jagged line that advances from the northwest. It marches, pushing back the darkness and halting its advance only upon reaching the mountain peaks where darkness is defeated momentarily. In a seemingly endless battle between night and day, the glorious light of another day shines directly on Worthington. However, a feeling of restlessness still remains despite the presence of the light.

"Good Morning, Anson!" chirped Monk, the Quaker Parrot, interrupting my chain of thought. "Time for the morning report," she said, taking position on one of my branches. Monk is a middle aged, highly intelligent, comical, banded and registered Monk Parakeet. Her owner is the day jailor, at the Worthington police station. This arrangement allows Monk to escape from her cage each weekday, except on holidays, and visit with us here on Purple Mountain without being detected. Riding the morning valley breeze, she ascends the mountain. She provides me with insightful information about the happenings within the city.

"Good Morning to you. Please proceed with your report," I replied.

"Today is... Friday, April... twentieth...; sunrise is at... seven... zero... one AM; moonrise is at... six... zero... eight AM; moon phase is... morning crescent; sunset is at... eight... zero... six PM, eastern daylight time; Today's weather is... sunny; with a... zero... percent chance of rain," mimicked Monk. Living in the home of a police officer, Monk has been exposed to a life of listening to various police scanners and other radios. One of her first recollections of speaking involves reciting the daily weather report from a local AM band radio station. It was an automated voice that she can clearly mimic to this day. On most days, she will mimic this voice and the exact cadence when she gives her report. Over time it has become rather amusing to us.

"Thank you, Monk, for this insightful report!" I quipped, "is there more?"

"Yes, of course there is more. Did you think I would fly all of the way up here to deliver the daily weather report? ... don't answer that," she said jokingly. "It is the talk of the town that there will be a parade tomorrow at noon. It is a parade to welcome home our Iraq war soldiers. Rumor has it that Her Honor, the mayor, will deliver a speech from the portico of the old court house. A rarity that will be and in an election year too. Also, there is a fundraising dinner tonight, at the VFW Post, for the mayor. It is to raise funds for the upcoming reelection campaign. The invitation list includes, among others, Michael and Mr. Garnet from Axis Energy. And one last thought, there are murmurs of a new mining project that may start in the near future. This sounds extremely encouraging for our local economy," answered Monk.

"A new mining project?" I asked. Mr. Garnet is a hard one to read even though he has walked Purple Mountain. Michael, on the other hand, is usually easy to read. Although, he has been somewhat distant since his return from Iraq late last fall. "What time is the fundraiser?" I added.

"Yes, that is what I am hearing. I will follow-up with my sources and garner what information I can on this. Also, the dinner is set for eight o'clock," responded Monk.

"Thank you, I am not sure how I would know what is happening in town without you!" I said. As Monk took flight for town, my thoughts were turning toward Jessica.

Jessica's first appearance in the scroll dates back to the spring of nineteen hundred and eighty-seven. It was late afternoon, the first time she walked Purple Mountain with her father. However, the elements were against them and the walk was interrupted by rain shower causing a delay until nearly sundown. Her father thought it too late to finish the round, as he never expected what was about to happen that evening. Although many might hope for such a thing, exceedingly few would expect such a thing and virtually none would believe it could happen. The faith of a child is a powerful force. A scorecard, lacking but one score for completion, she holds.

Nearly one hundred seasons to the day now have passed and yet she holds that unfinished scorecard. It was the last evening she would ever spend with her father. Somewhere deep within, her hope is to capture that beautiful fleeting moment once again. When the faith of a child caused the sun to reverse its course. She often thinks of that day and wonders if such faith still exists.

Since the year two thousand and nine, Jessica has served as mayor of Worthington, Virginia. Her ascent into public office coincided with a significant economic descent experienced within the community. Challenging economic conditions continue to exist throughout the nation and this town has not been sheltered from them. Not since the great depression has a recession been this severe and long lasting. The resiliency of a people continues to be tested with increasing economic strain pulling at each person. To many, the size of the challenge appeared to be like that of a mountain and it needed to be moved.

The mayor is uniquely aware of the challenges facing the people. Evidence of the strain on the town is everywhere to be seen with generational family businesses closing; lines at the soup kitchen increasing; shelves at the food bank emptying, financial institutions foreclosing; and news of city tax and service revenues decreasing. Heartbreaking conditions for anyone that would look at them. How much more for a mayor that calls this town home one might ask. Although she is young in years, her hallmark is perseverance. This is a trait many believe she inherited from her father. If moving a mountain would save the town, as some believe the size of the challenge to be, she would see to it that it was moved given proper time and opportunity.

Prior to serving as mayor, Jessica was the deputy general counsel for Axis Energy; the single largest employer in the town. She earned her law degree from the University of Virginia and a Bachelor degree from the same. She is a graduate of Worthington High School; Worthington Junior High; and Worthington Elementary school. Life long residents of Virginia we have been. This is our home. Her roots too, like mine, are planted deep in this town.

She works in the mayoral office in town. The structure was completed in 1850 and its architectural style is that of Greek Revival. This style of architecture was a favorite of Thomas Jefferson, as it reminded him of the Greek influences within our system of government. It is a two story rectangular structure, constructed with red brick, with each floor measuring 16 feet in height. Each floor has five equally spaced windows, measuring eight feet in height with each having eighteen glass panes of rectangular shape, fashioned into the sides of the building. The structure has a gable roof with one window in each tympanum. The building is topped with a red roofed octagonal cupola. The eight facings of the cupola resemble the head and torso of a man. Like watchmen looking over the city in all directions, these facings appear. Greek influences are evident when the structure is viewed from the front elevation. Four fluted Doric columns adorn the front of the structure and they support the portico that stands two stories tall. Each column has a rectangular pediment. A double door measuring 12 feet in height and six feet in width is centered across the width of the first floor. It is the main access point of the building. The windows, doors and all trim are white in color. To gain access form the street level one must traverse two sets of stairs. Each set has seven steps with each step not of equal breadth, so that those ascending must give thought to each step.

The mayoral office is located in the back of the old county courthouse. The office walls are covered, from floor to ceiling, in White Oak panels. The room receives ample sunlight through two eight foot windows that sit perpendicular to each other. The wood floor planking is of red oak, unfinished, knotty and varied in coloration, appearing seasoned yet handsome in appearance. The operating fireplace is almost a room to itself. An antique red oak desk is the centerpiece of the office. Handcrafted in another era, it exudes an ideal of permanence in a temporal world.

On this particular morning, she is in her office. The last embers of a morning fire are slowly burning, alternately glowing red to white, from the hearth of the fireplace measuring six feet tall by eight feet wide. Arriving hours before sunrise, she has been at her desk methodically processing the more mundane tasks assigned to a mayor. She is not the type of mayor that enjoys the ceremonial or civic pomp and circumstance that accompanies the position she holds. Those are the type of tasks she considers mundane and even more mundane is the planning of them. However, there is at least one exception to this thought.

A parade will grace the town tomorrow and not just any parade. For there have been a host of parades during her term and each of these have been of the mundane sort. A parade for each and every holiday and special occasion one could think of. Of course, in her official capacity, she is expected to participate in some fashion or another. For some she is a direct participant and others an official dignitary. Although, this one was different.

This parade is to welcome home our war heroes that have been serving in a foreign land. She believes it a fitting tribute to those that have performed their duties with gallantry, fidelity and dedication to service. There is an excitement in the town, related to this event, that for the moment seems to calm the anxieties of day to day living. Perhaps it is due to a return to the familiar with families being reunited. Perhaps it is due to the end of the war and the closure it brings. Perhaps it is all of these things and more; or none of these things at all that accounts for the current excitement. Undoubtedly, there are some that do not feel this sense of excitement. For some there is a lingering sense of loss.

Of this I am certain, she knows the name of each soldier lost in war during the time she has served as mayor. Being the daughter of a soldier declared missing in action, she knows the search for closure and peace is a difficult one indeed. To those that have felt the sting of war, she hopes the parade will move them closer to finding peace.

The parade is set for tomorrow, Saturday, April and twenty-one days, the year two thousand and twelve at noon. The parade route will commence from the south end of Main Street and proceed north until it terminates just beyond the old court house. She will observe the parade from a viewing area located on the portico of the old courthouse. Directly following the parade, she is scheduled to address the participants and viewers. She is not given to speeches but this one is different. This one would be like talking with an old friend after a long absence.

Old friends are on her mind. The morning fire has turned completely to ash on the hearth floor. Tonight, a fundraising dinner is to be held in her honor. Another of her dislikes is the never ceasing activity of fundraising that has become a necessary evil in the modern political experience. What a joy it would be, if a person could rely on an unbiased press to present the candidates, in such a way, as to make an informed decision about them. The power of the press has been replaced by the purchasing power of the candidates. She will not be deterred by the current political climate. Her desire is to have a positive effect on the community and she believes her service as mayor accomplishes that end.

Many old acquaintances will undoubtedly attend the event with each expecting a personal audience. Neither time, nor circumstance will permit such occurrences. Rather, she will politely work her way through the crowd, seemingly everywhere, thanking each. This, while old acquaintances become preoccupied in the recurring ritual of reacquainting themselves. However, there are a few invitees that are of significance to note. One such person is Mr. Alexander Garnet or "Red" as most would call him.

As CEO of Axis Energy, the single largest employer in town, he is a person of significant power and influence. Additionally, he is President of Almandine Mining Co. a joint venture that has various land holdings in the local area. Being the former deputy general counsel for Axis Energy, Jessica is quite familiar with Mr. Garnet and his various interests. Her college education was funded by a scholarship from Axis Energy. As I have mentioned, Red is an unusually difficult person for me to read despite his having walked Purple Mountain. I know that others often refer to him as 'the emperor of a vast mining empire' and that he spends most of his days, sequestered, within the safe confines of the Axis headquarters. He rarely visits with family and does not appear in town often. Of interest to Jessica are rumors of a significant project in the works for Axis and what effect this project might have on the local economy.

Another person that is scheduled to attend is Michael. Michael and Jessica have known each other since attending Worthington Elementary School. At times, over the years, they have been extremely close and at times extremely distant. From the time they were about eight years old, Michael has been protective of her. She feels a deep connection with Michael but has never shared these feelings directly with him.

They also were coworkers at Axis Energy. As the vice president of public relations for Axis Energy, Michael's job is to promote the interests of the company and improve public perception of its operations. Red noticed him at an early age and was impressed with his skills. His college was funded, just like that of Jessica, through a scholarship from Axis Energy. On many occasions, Red has told Michael that he must 'feed the beast'. The 'beast' in the mind of Red is the entire mining operation. Michael, through his communication skills, makes it easier for Axis to obtain the rights to mine and 'feed the beast' the coal that it desires. Michael and his natural abilities in communication serve Red well.

However, Michael recently experienced the loss of his brother who was serving in the Iraq war. An eye witness to the death of his brother he was, being in Iraq at that time. He has been able to conceal his profound sense of loss from the public but not from Jessica. She identifies with Michael and his sense of loss.

The clock is rapidly approaching the noon day mark. Her custom on each Friday, weather permitting, is to eat lunch in the park at town square. Today, being no exception, she heads out of her office and across the street into town square. This is her weekly opportunity to meet with the townspeople and listen.

The square has changed little since she was a girl. There is a sense of continuity here. In the square, the willow trees are mature and the crocus is the first flower to bloom. Perhaps the town would emerge early from this economic downturn, she thought, as she admired the flower in early bloom. This singular flower, whose stem being as tall as a coffee cup, is purple in color and its six cupped petals have yet to open. It looked like two hands touching at the base of the palm and at the fingertips, pointing toward heaven, as if in prayer. She sits quietly but expectantly on the same park bench each week. After lunch, she will return to her office and faithfully execute the remaining duties of the day.

"Anson, I am back and you need to listen to this!" called Monk, as she carefully landed in the midst of my branches. Her bright green feathers were being ruffled by the slight breeze blowing on the mountain today. She was returning from a trip back into the city to obtain information about the possible mining operation. This should prove to be interesting.

Chapter 4

"Monk, you have returned so soon?" I questioned.

"Why ever yes! Now we must find out what is going on in this town of ours. Besides, I needed the exercise. Mr. Loche has been giving me too many treats lately. 'Polly want a cracker?' He is a wonderful human you know. I think I will keep him," she responded.

"Indeed he is," I continued, "a good provider. What were you able to learn about the mining project?" I asked.

"Anson, when I left here I had every intention of going straight back into town. All of my usual sources are in town. However, it occurred to me that a beautiful spring day, like today, brings with it opportunity. It is an opportunity for humans to open their windows for maybe the first time since winter began. Where there is an open window, there is opportunity!" said Monk, as she inched further inward on the branch moving closer to my trunk.

"Perfectly sound reasoning. So, where did your travels take you instead?" I asked.

"Not so fast! Riddle me this: Where the chital deer powerfully bounds and it is black as night in the midst of the day, to this place I went?" she amused.

"A riddle?" I mused.

"Yes, a riddle. Think Genus!" she laughed.

"Monk, I thought you were a parrot not a mocking bird!" I remarked.

"Anson, G– E– N– U– S," she spelled, "not, G– E– N– I– U– S! Maybe, my pronunciation was not clear the first time," she said almost wryly.

"Yes, now that you have spelled it out for me, let me consider your riddle," I replied, thinking out loud, "Genus, a term used in biology signifying a low level ranking of biological organisms," I declared.

"That is correct," she answered.

"Chital deer. Let me think. Oh yes, they are common to Asia. Not exactly near to us here. However, they are of the genus axis. Yes, part of the answer is axis?" I questioned.

"Correct again! You are catching on to this. Continue," she suggested.

"The next clue in the riddle was powerfully bounds. Let me consider this for a moment. Powerfully, powerfully, ability comes to mind. No. Strength. No. Let me think . . . energetic. Yes, energetic is what you are looking for?" I said.

"Maybe, but why?" she responded.

"Let's move on to the last part of the riddle. You said, 'It is black as night in the midst of the day.' What could be the meaning of that? Let's see, you were talking about windows. Where are windows? In buildings. Yes, buildings have windows. How does that fit into the riddle? Oh, yes! I have it now!" I said confidently.

"Okay, Genius! Please unravel the riddle for me," said Monk expectantly.

"The corporate offices of Axis Energy! A chital deer is of the genus axis. Powerfully bounds represented the word energy. Finally, the polished black granite walls of the Axis corporate headquarters appear as night in the middle of the day. Correct?" I ventured.

"Well done my friend! Well done! I went to the headquarters of Axis Energy. If there is mining, then there Axis will be," said Monk.

"A wise diversion in your flight path this was. So tell me, what did you learn from your travels?" I asked, thinking about the building known as the monolith. It is a square structure with polished black granite walls and is a most mysterious structure. It was the first, and largest, of three square structures planned, by Red for the site. A botanical garden, featuring red and white roses, was planned, by Alexander, for the open space between the facilities. Upon completion, it would appear, from above, as the Bride's Chair, from Euclid's proof, adorned with red and white roses.

"As I suspected, there was an open window; of course, humans are so predictable sometimes. Anyway, I found the closest place to perch and listen. From his second floor office, I heard the vice president of public relations, Michael, speaking to someone over the desk telephone. He was talking with Red," she reported.

"This should be an interesting conversation. Please continue," I responded.

"As it turned out, Red was calling him into his office. Of course, those predictable humans, they became predictable again. Red's office is on the other side of the building. When I moved there, guess what? Yes, you guessed it. The window was closed! After all of this, the window was closed! I did not hear anything!" she revealed.

"How long did you wait there?" I asked.

"I waited until their conversation was completed and a while longer after that," she replied.

"Perhaps your trip was still useful in some manner. Did you happen to see anything unusual?" I asked.

"Unusual..., unusual..., yes unusual. From where I watched, I had a clear view of Red sitting behind his desk. He was facing away from me. After Michael left Red's office, Red opened the upper right hand drawer of his desk. He removed three items and placed each on the center of his desk. Individually, he held and examined each one before carefully placing them back into the drawer," she noted.

"Odd behavior possibly. What were these items? Did you see them clearly enough to identify them?" I asked.

"Yes, I saw them clearly from where I was perched. The first was a baseball with some type of sheen on it. It is kept inside a crystal case. The second item was a necklace. It had a red stone attached to the end of a gold chain. The last item was a sealed letter with a small purple stamp. It was mostly white but appeared to be yellowing as if it had been there for a long time," she presumed.

"Anything else of an unusual nature did you witness?" I asked.

"No. Nothing else unusual. After he placed the items back into his desk, I left my perch and started my way back here. I thought I was on to something about this rumored project; then I found nothing. Tomorrow is a new day. When I come to the mountain again, I promise to have some additional information for you," she responded.

"Thank you, Monk. I appreciate that," I replied.

"Anson, I am always glad to help you! Now, I am headed back to town. I must return to my cage before Mr. Loche discovers my disappearance. We can't have the town jailor with a bird on the loose, you know. Have a good weekend. Bye," declared Monk, as she flew toward town.

I appreciate the help of my friend, Monk. However, my thoughts have turned to Michael, the vice president of public relations for Axis Energy. Michael, in his younger years, spent a great amount of time here on Purple Mountain. He not only walked the course, he spent time with me. He has touched my bark and we have a bond.

Although the stories, of both those that have touched me and those that have walked Purple Mountain, are within me, they are at times difficult to access. Each of their stories are like a scroll. Some, like Red's, are nearly impossible to unravel. His stories are like rolls of steel, hardened, needing the application of heat and force to be unrolled. However some, like John's, are easily unrolled. His stories are like a bolt of fine cloth, soft, needing only a slight push to unroll. The reasons for these differences are more a matter of the subject than of the subject matter. However, I consider all of them to be gifts and hope that these gifts would serve a greater purpose than being the memories of an old tree.

These stories are much like memories, I suppose. Each differing in ease of accessibility. Each differing in depth of details accessible. Although, I would prefer to access them at will, they do not respond, to such commands, much of the time. Rather, they become opened to me as individuals are talked about by others in the course of daily living.

Many who have walked the mountain, neither will be mentioned nor will be thought of again; this despite their stories being part of me. Much like a book, having been read and placed upon a shelf, these stories are. Although an interesting read they were, once the pages are closed they will never be reopened. Not that they can't be reopened; just that they won't be. Perhaps other copies of these books exist, as I suppose they do. I am confident that these stories once read and placed on shelves are brought down on occasion and read again.

Said another way, it is my hope that, this attribute of mine, is not unique in this creation. That there are other, living libraries, like myself. Together, we hold the stories of a people and a nation. Each story, being important to the whole, is recorded. Each story ultimately being judged, as to meeting its intended purpose, by the Creator of all stories. From our perspective, these stories seem hopelessly intertwined and impossible to comprehend. Unraveling them appears hopeless but it is not so. For, the Creator of all stories has a perspective above and beyond ours. So, our duty is not in their comprehension, but rather, in their retention.

Speaking of retention, many stories of Michael are accessible to me today. As I talked with Monk, Michael's stories began to unroll within me. At first, the stories were of today's conversations with Red. Those led into recent accounts of work related experiences. At last, the stories settled on his recent trip to Iraq and the loss of his brother Christopher. By the time Monk left, these stories were all unrolled for me. However, had she not taken the diversion in flight, I am certain these memories would escape me for this moment. But, there was the diversion.

Although Monk could not hear the conversation Michael had with Red, I can hear the echoes of it. Michael has been assigned by Red to a sensitive mining project for some time now. The project is nearing a decision point and will be made public soon. However, it is lacking the support that Red believes it should garner. The challenge of gaining the support, Red desires, rests upon Michael.

Red has known Michael for nearly a quarter century. Red offered Michael a college education and job security, in exchange, for his excellent skills as a communicator. Red, over the years, has relied on Michael to, in the words of Red, 'feed the beast'. Red uses Michael's communications skills to secure the trust of the people. Once they trust Michael, it is easy for him to sell the idea of mining to the people. It is not that Red needs their approval, which he doesn't, rather it is that he desires their approval. Michael, 'feeds the beast', by providing a constant diet of support for Axis Energy and approval of its mining operations.

I sense a close relationship between Michael and those he must sway to support this project. However, I can't identify them by name. Perhaps in time I may. I also detect a sense of unease about the project from Michael. Unease is an unusual response from Michael and especially in a work environment. Unusual indeed. This sense of unease, I believe, does not find its source in the happenings of the recent trip to Iraq. However, that particular trip is the subject matter of great unease in his life and with good reason.

Allow me to briefly explain the Iraq trip. Michael was sent by Red to Iraq last fall. He was sent, as an official reporter of Axis Energy, to write a story about the return of Michaels' brother Christopher. Axis Energy was set to employ Christopher upon his return to the states. This story was intend to be used, at a later date, by Axis in its public relations materials. Michael arrived in Iraq in early November of last year.

Michael arrived, in Iraq, as U.S. forces were on the verge of exiting the country. With hostilities at a low point, the mission seemed nearly routine. There is nothing routine about war zone, as Michael was soon to discover. This was Christopher's fourth tour in Iraq and his last. Michael had not seen him personally in over a year, although they had occasionally communicated with each other. When Michael arrived, Christopher was in the final phases of preparing his unit for departure. Michael documented these preparations over the course of a few days and completed the necessary tasks for the related story. Michael finished early, with two days to spare. All that remained for Michael, in his view, was two days of doing nothing and the trip back home. Unknown to him, there was something special planned.

With departure preparations completed, Christopher had something special in mind for their last full day in Iraq. There was a certain golf course that had been reconstructed over the past two years. Overseeing some of the reconstruction himself, he was quite familiar with the course and those that were to operate it. It is known as, the Babylonian at the Hanging Gardens. This course was not quite one of the seven wonders of the golf world. Although, it was a wonder that a course existed in the Iraqi desert during a war. Arrangements were made so that Christopher and Michael could play a round before they were to depart for home. He told Michael there was something he had to see before they left for home and he took him to the course.

When they arrived at the course, the plans had changed. Apparently, Christopher had been outranked. His established tee time had been given to a pair of U.S. Army Generals. Furthermore, being of lower rank, he was conscripted into service as a caddie. Compliance was not optional. Michael was a good sport about this situation. He wanted to see the course up close and spend time with Christopher. So, he volunteered to caddie for the remaining General. It was set then, they would caddie the round. Certainly not the way Christopher intended to end his Iraqi tour but it could be worse. It was a temperate, cloudless, nearly perfect fall day. A perfect day for golf, even for a caddie.

The two brothers were together again. Not since the late eighties had they been on a course together. During the round, they spent some time reminiscing about those days, that summer, on Purple Mountain. That year was, a coming of age, for both of them and each recognized it for the first time. The trajectory of their lives were set that summer and it carried them here, to this moment, nearly twenty-five years later. The round passed by like a morning mist on a mountain side, there one moment and gone in the next. With one hole remaining to be played, the round was nearing an end.

As they approached the eighteenth green, both Generals hit shots into the same sand trap on the left side of the green. Both played up and out of the sand with the help of their caddies. While the Generals made their way to the green, Christopher and Michael lagged behind, like good soldiers they were performing their duty by raking the trap. They did not realize the trap they were actually in. There were no warnings, no clues, no indications of what was about to happen except for one; this was a war zone.

The transition, from coalition forces, to Iraqi security forces, was a long and dangerous journey for those involved. It was always a matter of trust but trust in whom. There remained a loyal remnant, of the Iraqi Republican Guard, that was indistinguishable from the general population. Some of these individuals infiltrated the new security forces. Their plan, in time, was the overthrow of the installed government and destruction of its security force. However, some were impatient and desired to impart harm on the coalition while an opportunity existed. These attacks had mostly subsided over the past few months and were expected to reemerge targeting security forces, after the departure of the coalition. There was one attack remaining.

Michael, pulled the flag stick on the eighteenth green, as the General was lining up his putt. The General started to fall over, as the first shot rang out. He was shot in the upper torso and falling to the ground. Just then, the other General was hit in the legs, as two more shots rang out. Then a fourth shot and a fifth were heard. Christopher was hit. Then silence. It seemed like an eternity, before the final shot rang out, killing the Iraqi security guard that accompanied them during the round.

Christopher, despite being hit, had the presence of mind to pull a sidearm from the golf bag nearest the trap. One shot was all he needed. The Iraqi knew his mission was suicidal and that was part of the plan of attack. Christopher had a slight wound on his leg but the Generals were in much worse shape. Christopher knew they needed immediate medical attention and he called, for an air evacuation, to the local base. There was a surgical unit there and Christopher knew that they were still operational. The immediate area was secured by loyal Iraqi forces and a few coalition forces.

Michael was stunned by all of this. Christopher settled him down and talked with him. He assured him that he would keep him safe. Michael did not speak for some time. After composing himself, he asked Christopher if he had seen them from the sand trap. Christopher said no, he had not seen it coming. But Michael was not speaking of the attack. Michael was speaking of a time back on Purple Mountain. Michael then clearly described the situation he was speaking of. It happened that summer on Purple Mountain, back in nineteen hundred and eighty-seven, and Christopher was there. Michael again asked Christopher, point blank, "did you see them?" As Christopher began his reply, the noise of the approaching helicopter drowned out his words.

The next few moments, being almost like a dream, seem surreal to Michael. Christopher helped load the Generals into the chopper and then boarded himself. He told Michael to meet him at the base. The chopper lifted off and rose above the Palm trees, hovering, before slowly advancing forward. Then the unthinkable happened before his eyes. Another attacker stepped out, from seemingly nowhere, to fire a rocket. The chopper exploded in midair and went crashing to the ground. There were no survivors. All of the souls on board were lost.

"General... General... General Anson, sir!" said Tiger the great horned owl, "too-too toooooo too-too duty, I am reporting early today, sir!"

Chapter 5

"General Anson, sir. Tiger, sir, reporting for duty," repeated Tiger.

"Tiger, my dear Tiger. It is good to hear from you so early today," I responded. My heart was heavy from thinking about Michael. Even though he is on my mind, I must carry on. There are concerns here on this mountain and we must attend to them.

"General, sir. On my way here, I noticed a meeting happening at the main hall of the clubhouse. Permission to return to the location and perform reconnaissance, sir?" said Tiger eagerly.

"Tiger, approximately how many were attending the meeting?" I asked.

"Sir, there were at least four and possibly a few more in attendance," he replied confidently.

"As for your request, permission is not granted. I will accept responsibility for the meeting. As for you, I have a more pressing assignment. You are needed to provide reconnaissance for the mayoral fundraiser being held tonight. A dangerous mission into the city this will require. Prepared for this mission are you?" I asked.

"Yes, sir! I am prepared too-too toooooo too-too complete this mission. What are the mission objectives, sir?" he replied.

"Your mission is to maintain direct visual contact with the mayor during this event. I am especially interested knowing her interactions with Mr. Garnet and Michael. Be particularly mindful to listen for conversations that these individuals may have with one another," I asked. If there is a mining project planned, this would provide a great opportunity for Red to discuss it with the mayor.

"Yes, sir. What time does the event begin?" he asked.

"It begins at zero one hundred Zulu," I responded.

"Yes, sir. I will leave soon, so that I can take up a position before sundown," he said.

"Please plan on being patient during this mission. The event may last late into the evening. Don't let your guard down as the night wears on. Oftentimes, the best information is communicated near the end of the event. There is a strong mountain breeze developing tonight, and with it turbulence in the air. Please proceed with caution," I said.

"Understood, sir," he replied. He appeared genuinely excited about the mission, as he usually is.

The sun was getting lower, in the sky, as evening drew near. Soon darkness would sweep across the town and parade up the mountain driving out the light. Night would soon rule again.

From where I stand, the clubhouse is up the mountain. On some nights with a gentle mountain breeze, when my leaves and twigs are in constant motion, sounds from the clubhouse carry straight through my branches and down the mountain. Tonight is such a night. This is why I could send Tiger down the mountain and yet gain access to the meeting in the clubhouse.

If my suspicions are correct, the annual meeting of the Minutemen Management Group is being held at this moment. They are the management company responsible for the operation of the Majestic of Purple Mountain golf course. Although the course is city owned, its operation is managed by this group. This mutually beneficial arrangement has existed for many years.

The structure of the Minutemen Management Group is a partnership. It is owned and operated by a group of five retired U.S. military officers. Each branch of the military has a representative. A partnership position within the group is currently open. As the mountain breeze gains strength, so do the carrying voices.

"Our new reservations system is now up and running and just in time for use this season. It is accessible through the internet too. This system will help us to manage the day to day play and keep track of future reservations," said Joshua.

"Look into the future and see what, I ask? Look and see who isn't playing!" commented Samson.

"True, things are not the best lately. Our rounds played figures have declined each year over the past four years. They have reached an all time low this year. I realize this is a disappointment for each of us. We must remain resolute in the face of current economic conditions. We must have faith things will improve," said Joshua. Joshua is the lead partner. There is not an elected leader but rather a leader that all feel comfortable following. Joshua is that person.

"Joshua, I lived through great depression. We didn't have nuthin back then. Them was tough times. How bad can things be?" asked Caleb. Caleb is the ranking member of the group and the eldest. He is respected for his wisdom, among this group. When he gets excited, his speech has a tendency to return to a less refined dialect.

"As each of you are familiar, our fiscal year ended on March 31. Financially it was our worst year on record," reported Joshua.

"I guess the finances are bad, now that I think of it we didn't get to make many relief trips last year," Caleb said.

"That is true Caleb," Joshua started, "last year marked the fewest relief trips we have ever recorded. Just like our finances, they have dwindled down, as well, over the past few years. Just four years ago, our group made a total of twenty trips during that fiscal year. We had teams going out every month that year. Last year we recorded eight and Caleb, with his MOH privileges, accounted for three of them. During the year he assisted in the aftermath of the April 25 Little Rock Air Force Base tornado and the May 22 Joplin tornado. Then, he volunteered close to home during the days following the August 23 Louisa County earthquake here in Virginia. Our last effort of the year was assisting those that had been hit with the Halloween nor'easter. There were many relief efforts that we just couldn't help with last year."

"There are considerations more important than those of finances?" Gideon said timidly. Gideon is the least tenured member and the youngest. He has a certain uncertainty about him. He is certainly quiet and holds back in offering his opinions. However, in this instance he spoke up. To gain his support, it usually requires three strong arguments.

"There are not many issues greater than financial," interjected Samson,"yet there are some. Before we speak of those, perhaps we should focus on the financial? Joshua?" said Samson. Samson is the second eldest ranking member. He was once the lead partner and has no interest in leading it again. He has been known to break a rule every now and again.

"Yes, back to the financial. We have discussed the financial situation at length already. Undoubtedly the most important issue facing the course is. . .," Joshua paused,"the possible closure of the Majestic of Purple Mountain–"

"Never!" Gideon protested.

"Not if I have anything to say about it!" Samson interjected.

"May it never be so! During the great depression many places closed and were gone forever. I don't want to see that happen here. I couldn't bear it. No," Caleb remarked.

Silence. The moderate mountain breeze, that swayed my small sized branches, was empty of the sound of voices. What I heard was not unexpected. I continued to listen.

"Gentlemen," breaking the long silence was Joshua, "we all know what is being said of late. There are murmurings of a possible mining project. It is not clear where the project is planned but it is somewhere near Worthington and Purple Mountain. Also, the city leaders are under pressure to tighten their belts. That means cutting back on nonessential spending. Public recreation is not viewed as an essential service by most. Basically, the city pays us to manage the course and some believe any amount is too much to pay. Also, the city could raise a large sum of money from the sale of the Majestic and the sacred ground it rests upon. Our goal must be to show the city and its leaders the essential value of the Majestic to our community. The Majestic is a special place that could never be replaced once lost. The Majestic is an essential component of our community and must be preserved," said Joshua.

"That is the spirit!" interjected Caleb.

"In need of convincing are they? I can be quite persuading when I need to be!" declared Samson.

"So, how do we go about convincing them? Not in the way Samson would prefer but in way that is, shall I say, nonviolent. There are so many things the public does not know about the Majestic. They don't realize how the community is effected by it in such a positive way–" remarked Gideon.

"They don't know much about the Minutemen. And they don't know us and what we do either. Maybe it is time they know the truth!" interrupted Samson.

"Gideon, there are a few ways I see us attacking this. They both involve faith. First, we really can't lower what we ask the city to pay us. We have already reduced our outlays as much as we are able. The course practically takes care of itself and requires little by way of expense to maintain. This is a blessing that remains unknown to the general public. But, any further reductions in what we receive from the city will only jeopardize the programs we support. Remember, we do not make public the fact that this is a volunteer organization. Also, we do not publicize the causes we support nor the trips we make or the dollar amounts of the support we provide. And no, Samson, we won't make things a matter of public record. So what do we do? We continue to support the causes we believe in and have faith that God will honor us with His support," proposed Joshua.

"What do they say, 'the definition of insanity is doing the same thing over and over again and expecting a different result?', yes, that is it. That sounds like a formula for failure! We have got to try something new," insisted Samson.

"I think Samson is on to something here. We need to change the dynamics of the conversation. I believe the people will understand and support what we do up here. But only if we allow them the chance. They won't see it on faith alone," added Gideon.

"We need to tell them about the Final Foursomes. We need to tell them how we started them and what they have become. It is time!" declared Samson.

"How we started them, eh? I want to hear that one! Did the Mississippi begin flowing when Lewis and Clark first saw it? Did Ben Franklin start the flow of electricity with a kite string and a key? Tell them what we discovered here not what we created, shall we?" offered Caleb.

"Tell me Caleb, how was it discovered?" asked Gideon.

"I will tell you–" started Samson before being interrupted by Joshua.

"Him nothing," interjected Joshua, "let Caleb speak of this."

"Where were we . . ., yes, yes the Final Foursomes. It is not that we discovered them as much as they discovered us! We thought it the honorable thing to do you see. Setting a daily tee time, the last one of the day, for a group of killed in action soldiers. We pay for their rounds, you know. Someone must pay because no one plays for free. If we didn't it would be the same as stealing and no honor comes from that. Now does it?" answered Caleb confidently.

"No, Caleb, it doesn't. Tell me, why is it a 'Final Foursome' when only three are listed for the tee time?" asked Gideon.

"Unknown," replied Caleb, smiling.

"Unknown? Unknown? What is that supposed to mean?" asked Gideon.

"Let me take this one," Samson proceeded, "unknown is for an unknown soldier. We always leave a spot for an unknown soldier. Sometimes, a fourth player will show but not always. When they do, John adds them to the scorecard."

"John the greenskeeper. Since I came here, I have always wanted to know about John. As much as we talk about keeping this a secret it really isn't much of a secret. For years, there have been rumors of him seeing ghosts or spirits up here. Some think he is insane. Some think it is an honorable gesture. Some would like to believe, while others have no doubt that it is real. I must ask, does he really see them?" asked

Gideon, as the fresh mountain breeze began to sway my medium sized branches.

"Gideon, my dear Gideon, have you not been here long enough with us to know these things? Have you not seen with your heart what goes on here at the Majestic? Grasses at perfect length yet never mowed? Greens and fairways stay perfectly colored and healthy, yet they are never fertilized? Shrubs and plants stay perfectly manicured, yet they are never tended? Fairway divots that disappear, as if there were never a scar, before the next group plays through? Greens that heal themselves of ball marks? A greenskeeper that walks and talks with the dead? And the letters he sends to the families? Have you so little faith?" responded Joshua.

"I . . ., I . . ., I want to believe. Help me with my unbelief?" asked Gideon.

"John, the greenskeeper, has sent tens of thousands of letters to the families of those that have played in the Final Foursomes. To my knowledge, we have never received even one complaint," replied Joshua.

"Hard to know what a person will believe. Some will believe this and others that. It is much easier to know what God has already promised. Remember, 'blessed is he who does not see and yet believes.' Will the Majestic still be majestic if her mysteries are laid out for all to see?" asked Caleb.

"Gideon, the second thing we can do is pray. Pray that we will have the faith to follow His will, no matter where it seems to be leading us. More often than not, His will defies common convention," said Joshua.

"Waiting and praying are my strong suits. I especially like to wait," added Samson wryly.

"Yeah. Praying gets easier for me as I get older. It has been really easy lately!" Caleb said.

"I like waiting, it gives me time to confirm things. I always have been like that. I like praying too! So much to think about," said Gideon.

"We must move along. I propose a vote. That we approve the financial report as delivered. Second, that we delay, by two weeks, any decision on making public announcements about the mysteries of the Majestic of Purple Mountain and that we pray during this period for faith. Do I have a second to this motion?" Announced Joshua.

"I second that!" said Caleb.

"All in favor?" asked Joshua.

"Aye," said Caleb.

"Aye," said Gideon.

"Two weeks and only two weeks . . . Aye," replied Samson.

"Motion carried," commented Joshua.

'The next item on our agenda is that of taking on a new partner. The time has come for us to fill our open partnership position. Gideon, would you please read the membership criteria?" announced Joshua.

"Per the partnership agreement, admission into the partnership requires the candidate to be: a retired US military officer; the recipient of the Navy Cross, or Air Force Cross or the Distinguished Service Cross; the approval of all partners; acceptance of a lifetime commitment to a position of service. This position offers not the benefit of financial compensation but rather a higher form of satisfaction," pronounced Gideon.

"Thank you, Gideon. We are all quite familiar with Deborah. She was presented to us at our last meeting for questioning. After her presentation, we discussed her qualifications and other issues related to her admission as a partner. Our rules state that we are to take a vote, at this meeting, regarding her admission into the partnership. Due to a prior engagement, she could not attend our meeting this evening.

"All in favor of admitting Deborah as a partner please respond?" inquired Joshua.

"Aye," answered Gideon.

"Aye," answered Samson.

"Aye," answered Caleb.

"The Ayes have it. Deborah is now a partner in the Minutemen Management Group. We welcome her and know she will be a valuable member of our team. Let the records show, the current membership has a record of military service spanning eight decades, beginning with World War II. Each of us were honored to serve our country and each of us finds honor in serving the families of the fallen. We will continue this practice, so long as we have the Majestic of Purple Mountain," resounded Joshua.

"Well, said!" added Caleb.

"Most definitely!" said Gideon.

"Agreed and long live the Majestic of Purple Mountain!" said Samson.

"I make a motion to conclude this meeting. Do I have a second?" asked Joshua.

"What is that? Great timing Joshua! I don't believe it! "Taps" is being played right on cue?" asked Gideon.

We could all hear it. From beneath the flagpole the beginning notes of G– G– C— G– C– E–. . ., were ringing out. John was playing "Taps" as he does every evening. He plays it just as the sun sets each night, except on Sunday. It is played in part to signify the close of activities for the day. It is also played, as a memorial, for those that have fallen in military service. The short tune never fails to evoke emotions that are not easily described.

"Sunset is at exactly eight-o-six pm today and it is exactly that time. John has been called 'Old Faithful' by some, as he is like that old predictable geyser. For over a quarter century, he has played that tune at sunset without fail. Today is no exception. Some say, 'timing is everything', and we timed it perfectly tonight. Do I have a second?" replied Joshua.

"I second that motion . . .," said Caleb, his voice trailing off into the strong mountain breeze.

As they finished their meeting, the strong mountain breeze changed. A near gale force mountain wind made me sway. Thoughts were swirling in my mind. Thoughts of financial realities, recovery strategies, mining possibilities and the threatened closure of the Majestic blew through my mind. Weak financial results were not unexpected. Fewer and fewer people walk Purple Mountain these days. These are difficult economic times we are walking through. Rumors of closure and a mining project cast a dark shadow over the future of the Majestic. Will her mysteries be made known? Will there be an end to the Final Foursomes and the peace she brings to these gallant golfers? Will this deepening darkness forever douse the light of the Majestic?

Yet there is hope, as these Minutemen exemplify a people of faith and courage. They recognize the challenges facing them and have not adopted a fallback position. Prayer and patience are never fallback positions. Like soldiers protecting a valuable treasure are these Minutemen. In a demonstration of faith, they named a new partner, Deborah. She has never walked Purple Mountain. What plans God has for her, in this current struggle, will remain a mystery for now. Her coming is not accidental, this I know. For these Minutemen serve not the god of accidents but rather serve the God of providence. From the perspective of man, and the rest of God's Earthly creation, seeing the difference is a matter of faith.

Finally, we need more information about this mining project. Shrouded in mystery this project is. Paradoxically, it seems as though everyone knows something about it, yet no one knows anything about it. Both Tiger and Monk are working diligently to discover information on this mining project. However, will they find an answer in time? What is to become of the Majestic of Purple Mountain?

My thoughts now turned to John the greenskeeper. After playing "Taps", his routine is to return to his cabin and begin work on the letters.

Since I sent Tiger into town, there will be no first report tonight.

Chapter 6

The greenskeeper's cabin sits, hidden away, a few dozen yards from the eighteenth hole. The cabin, of eighty feet by sixty feet, is of Pythagorean dimension. It is a stone structure made from grade one Winnsboro Blue Granite block imported from South Carolina. The blocks are twelve inches thick and vary in height and length. The stones, all being from the same quarry, are of similar color, shade and cut. Its blocks were laid in place by skilled stone masons. The cabin has a slate roof. The wide and thick stone near the bottom section of the roof gives way to a more narrow and thinner stone above. These stones are in shades of blue, red and gray. There are three gable fronted dormers on the back side roof. Viewed from a distance, the structure appears off white with a streaked purple roof. There is a wide porch, made of wood, that runs along the front and sides of the structure. A wide stairway, made of the same granite block, provides access to the porch. Stone fire places adorn both ends and the center of the structure.

Its beauty lies in its simplicity. The stone structure intuitively blends with the rock outcroppings behind it. It exudes a sense of stewardship in its design and workmanship. It is a nearly perfect example of man and nature existing together, as it was intended from the beginning. This was the home of the greenskeeper.

After playing "Taps", John headed down the path that leads to the cabin. On his way there he passes me and I can sense his presence. As John enters the cabin, he immediately places the bugle in its case. The gold plated bugle in B flat was made by Stradivarius in 1962. It was fashioned after the M1892 model field trumpet. He carefully stows it away for use again tomorrow.

He then starts a fire in the hearth and prepares his evening coffee for brewing. During this time, he reflects on the events of the day in preparation for his writing of the letters. Each player from the Final Foursome group flashes across his mind. Jack, a Seaman Apprentice from the USS Arizona, hull number BB-39, killed in action on December seventh of the year nineteen hundred and forty-one. Donald, an army Corporal of the XXIV Corps, killed in action on February seventh of the year nineteen hundred and seventy. Troy, a USAF BTZ Senior Airman, killed in action on January third of the year two thousand and ten. And an unknown soldier that chooses to remain nameless. These are the individuals, filtering through his thoughts on this particular evening, as his coffee brews over the coals.

The smell of fresh coffee permeates the cabin. Tonight he brewed more than his usual amount, as if he were expecting company. As John prepares to begin writing the letters, he enters the reserve library through the secret entryway. A fire is burning in the fireplace as John enters the room. Before he takes his seat at the desk, he carefully removes the necessary *Books of Merit* from the book shelves. Before sitting, he pulls a cigar from the humidor. He then sits at the desk and reaches for his reading glasses. From the top desk drawer he removes his writing supplies for the evening. A few pieces of paper and three envelops is all he will need this evening. He smells his cigar before cutting it. Then lighting it, he leans back in his chair before he begins writing for the evening. Coughing as he draws his first puff from the cigar, he places it in the ash tray, where it will remain untouched until it burns out.

This is his last box of cigars, as his inventory is almost exhausted. Cigar smoking began for him back in Vietnam. It is a habit he was unable to break entirely. Over the years he attempted to quit but the desire, that began in Vietnam, never completely left him. One of the caddies, a cigar aficionado himself, until a few years ago, regularly brought John a box of cigars. These were no ordinary cigars, as Babe would only bring the best. They were Bolivar Inmensas. Each Lonsdale, in the box, measured six and three quarters inches with a ring gauge of forty-three. However, he stopped bringing them, over a year ago, when he noticed the cough John had developed. In the box, there remained two cigars.

On this evening, John quickly penned letters to the families of Jack and Donald. Within an hour, the wax was set and the two letters were sealed. The envelopes were addressed and ready for mailing. The third letter remained to be written and was more difficult than the others.

On some occasions, the letters flow from his hand quickly and wildly. Like the rapids of the Gauley River, from deep within the Monongahela, flow some of his letters. On other occasions, they flow slowly and powerfully from his hand. These are like the mighty and methodically meandering Mississippi River gracefully flowing across the plains. These letters, whose headwaters originate from within the heart of the greenskeeper, eventually flow in their own way and time.

John then penned the introductory letter to the family of Airman Jones. It reads as follows:

Dear Mr. & Mrs. Jones,

> *Please indulge me with a few moments of your time. My name is John and I am the greenskeeper of the Majestic of Purple Mountain. What is to follow will be hard to accept at first. However, you will find comfort in the pages that follow. The enclosed sealed letter is from your son and contains details that will validate its authenticity.*
>
> *Today, your son played the Majestic of Purple Mountain. He carded a two under par score of 70 with the help of his caddie Dale, the Intimidator. Your son enjoyed the company more than the golf itself. We spent some time together today and he asked that I send the enclosed letter. It is written in my hand. It has been sealed and is addressed specifically to each of you.*
>
> *Please feel free to contact me any time.*
>
> *Regards,*
>
> *the Greenskeeper*

John slid the letter to the side of the desk and lowered his head. He began to think of the time he spent with Troy. From the first tee box through the fairway on the eighteenth, John reflected on the events of the day. At the first tee, he met each player. He watched in solemness as each was awarded the Badge of Merit by the Major General himself. Then he watched as each player was introduced to his caddie for the round. As John settled his thoughts, he began to focus on the encounter he had with Troy between the twelfth green and thirteenth tee. For it was there, under the Water Oak, that Troy gave John the substance of the letter he was to send. So it is there, that John has focused his thoughts for the moment.

Not quite reliving the moment but recalling it with perfect clarity.

After finishing the twelfth hole, Troy and his caddie Dale walked the path that led to the thirteenth hole. Troy decided to stop for a moment and take in the beautiful scenery. He sent Dale ahead to the tee at thirteen. Troy happened to pause under the Water Oak tree and its shade. It was strangely appealing to him in some way. It was as if he were a child realizing, for the first time, that his body cast a shadow. John happened to be there also.

The Water Oak is known for its shade. In season, it has a canopy full of leaves. It casts a grand shadow that the sun does not penetrate except for one small area. Some years ago, this tree was damaged by fire. There is a small section of the canopy that remains damaged to this day. Despite their name sake, these trees are easily damaged by fire. This Water Oak is eighty feet tall. Six men standing shoulder to shoulder would circle the tree at its base. However, the most important attribute of the oak tree, here on Purple Mountain, has yet to be mentioned.

The most important attribute of Purple Mountain oaks, some of them at least, is their ability to act as portals in time. There are a few oaks, spread over Purple Mountain within the footprint of the Majestic, that possess this ability. Accessing these portals is a matter of faith and faith alone. Each member of a Final Foursome possess this type of faith. John the greenskeeper has it also.

The individual golfer determines when this faith will be exercised. For some early in the round and for others later. With the tree as a portal, John and the golfer are taken back in time within a spiritual dimension. They are allowed to visit any two settings that occurred during the lifetime of the golfer. Invariably the golfers choose, as their first, those settings that upon reflection carry with them great significance. They revisit those brief, mostly obscure, yet powerful moments where they walked though destiny's door. Then, as their second choice, they are carried back into the setting where each soldier decided to give their last full measure of devotion.

This portal provides an opportunity to see the innerworking of prayer and the power of faith. Into the moment, where gallantry and fidelity were in harmony, they are taken. Into the moment, where faith was tested and found true, they are taken. Into the moment, where the prayers of the faithful were answered, they are taken.

Only the golfer and the greenskeeper are allowed entry into the portal. Golfers are not allowed to take their caddies with them. However, they are allowed to take with them one attribute of their caddie. Additionally, each golfer is allowed to use this attribute once during their lifetime. How this works is as much a mystery as prayer itself. It is one of the greatest mysteries of the Majestic of Purple Mountain. I will not attempt to explain it here. However, telling the story, of Troy being taken through the portal, may shed some light upon this mystery.

"Great shade isn't it?" asked John, seeming to appear out of nowhere.

"Oh, I thought I was here alone. Yes, something drew my attention to it. To the shade that is. Now here I am within it. My name is Troy. We met on the first tee didn't we?" queried Troy.

"Yes, we did," he replied.

"Are you God?" Troy inquired.

"No, I am the greenskeeper," responded John.

"This course is heavenly. Are you more than a greenskeeper?" asked Troy.

"Before I answer, let me introduce myself, my name is John. You asked, 'are you more than a greenskeeper?' Being a greenskeeper is plenty enough to keep me busy and enough responsibility too. What more could I possibly want to be? You are quite direct. Now the real question is this: why would you think that I am God?" asked John.

"I am aware of what is happening here. Today..., this course..., the merit badge ceremony..., Dale the caddie..., Jack and Donald my playing partners..., it all seemed so dreamlike at first. Somewhere, after the turn following the ninth hole, it came to me but I can't place where. This is no dream. Just a moment ago, it seems like it was just this morning, I was with my unit in Afghanistan. Now, I am here playing golf with Dale Earnhardt, my boyhood hero, as my caddie! He was killed in an accident at Daytona nearly nine years ago. The caddies for Jack and Donald have been gone longer than that. More than that, there is an anticipation of something even more spectacular that awaits. I can sense it. As I see things, you are the only person that seems out of place when compared to all the others. So, I drew the logical conclusion," responded Troy.

"So, I am, 'the logical conclusion', you say. Our logic is not of much use here you will learn. You mentioned the 'spectacular'. I hope you are ready for the spectacular!" he said.

With that the leaves rustled as a cool light breeze passed by them. In an instant, in the twinkling of an eye, they were transported into Afghanistan to a date in early July in the year two thousand and nine. They were now looking down on Kandahar Airfield from a nearby hillside.

"Do you recognize where we are?" asked John.

"Yes, we are in the hills near Kandahar Airfield in Afghanistan. That is where I was stationed," a stunned Troy responded.

"Do you know what is happening over there?" inquired John, pointing to an area where vehicles were operating.

"I do. It is a HMMWV 'High Mobility Multipurpose Wheeled Vehicle', Humvee for short, being used in a training exercise," said Troy with a grin.

"Not just an ordinary training exercise, I suppose? As you may have guessed, we are taken back to pivotal moments," John conveyed.

"Yeah. Actually, this is not really a training exercise. It is a race and what a race it was! The commander was none to happy about it when he got wind of it. We were lucky, all of us, getting only a verbal warning. Anyway, no one expected the move I made going into the last turn. I nudged that guy just like my mentor, Dale, would have . . . " his voice trailing off.

"I am guessing somewhere along the way before the race you said a short prayer. I am not a believer in God's divine intervention into sporting events. However, at times it would appear His intervention was obvious. Anyway, I figure you prayed for some NASCAR skills to come your way to help you in this race?" John ventured.

"In fact, I did. More than anything, I desired to show them that I couldn't be intimidated and that I could dish it out, when it was called for, to win. You see, the officers had this race setup to their advantage. We were not supposed to win. Looking back on it now, what a silly request it was. I could have asked for so much more . . .," Troy explained.

"Troy, don't be too quick now to rethink it. Actually, it was this race that put you at the top of the list for the BTZ (Below The Zone). The senior leadership saw a tenacity that they were looking for in a Senior Airman. You needed some polishing but your total package met with their approval. Your promotion to Senior Airman was set for January and would be six months earlier than your normal promotion date," commented John.

"A few days after the race, our unit was given a new assignment. We were assigned to train a group of four Afghan National Security Forces (ANSF) under the NATO Training Mission - Afghanistan (NTM-A). These Afghans were assigned to us. They basically lived and trained with us, twenty-four hours a day, for about six months. Our first field operations were set for early January.

We were assigned two sets of brothers. Their names were Farzam ibn Atash, Feda ibn Atash, Awrang ibn Shabaz and Hamasa ibn Shabaz. They were from the Jalalabad area and were ethnic Pashtun's from the Khogiani tribe. From what I understand, their fathers worked with the Mujahideen during the Soviet-Afghan war, in the late nineteen-eighties. The families were trusted and that was important in their culture. These families were respected by our leadership too," Troy said.

"Troy, step back into the shade of the Water Oak with me," John asked. They walked about ten paces into the shade of the tree and stopped. As they did, the airport scene faded from their view. They stood silently for a few moments and then Troy began to walk. As he did, his appearance changed and his clothing was changed into his battle fatigues.

As they emerged from the shade of the tree, they were standing on a hilltop several kilometers outside of Kandahar. They were watching a developing scene on the next hilltop closer to town. There were two Humvees cautiously approaching a stopped vehicle.

"Troy, do you recognize this scene?" asked John.

"Yes, that is the Kandahar-Bamiyan Highway. Where we are stopped is about two kilometers outside Chawnay. Kan-

the Majestic of Purple Mountain

dahar is about six kilometers south of there. I never should have trusted those ANSF guys!

This was our third patrol together with the ANSF trainees. We pulled up over that hill and saw that car and stopped right away. We were riding in pairs with two U.S. troops and two ANSF troops in each Humvee. Farzam and Feta leaped out of the back of the first Humvee and went in way too quickly. Cars like this one are prone to be a trap. We were fortunate that we didn't trip an IED (improvised explosive device) before we got that far. Anyway, it was too late to stop them but they knew better. It was a suspicious action. I think everyone, if they really were honest about it, is suspicious of the Afghans working with us side by side.

The four of us talked strategy and protocol with Awrang and Hamasa while the other two talked with the occupants of the vehicle. We were about thirty yards from their position and they signaled us to come to them. We devised a plan. My partner and I would go in with Awrang and Hamasa while the other two in our unit held the point position at the Humvees. I had a bad feeling about it.

When we came to within about ten yards of them, there was a commotion at the car. Farzam backed away from the car and opened his jacket revealing a buff colored vest. He was a homicide bomber! What I know now is that he was working with the Haqqani network and the Pakistani ISI. Pakistan is a problem that our political leadership just won't address. I am a soldier and not a politician. It seems like politicians never have the backbone to deal with the real issues! How can we ever know that the ANSF forces are our on our side? I don't think we can. Afghanistan has never been a good place for foreign forces to wage war.

When he detonated his explosives, a section of his vest did not explode and we were shielded from part of the blast.

Awrang, who stood beside me, was killed instantly. I took a few hits of shrapnel but nothing too bad. My partner had the same and Hamasa went untouched. How we were all not taken out by that blast, even considering the malfunction, I will never know.

Farzam was killed instantly as were the occupants of the car. However, Feda lay wounded. We made our way back to the Humvees. Our plan was to retrieve Feda using a Humvee but it was dangerous. There could still be an IED in play. As we prepared, we saw a vehicle headed toward the village. We called for air support and a medical evacuation but they were a least five minutes away. There was no Predator drone in the area.

Hamasa told us that he had heard 'chatter' about a strike on the girls school that was in the village. Why he didn't tell us before was now a huge problem. Tempers flared, for a few seconds, before I stepped in and settled things down. There was no time for that now. We would have to deal with him later.

I had a plan! It took thirty-seconds to present it while using my finger to draw it in the sand. Then we decided to split into two teams. Alpha team would stay and recover Feda and Bravo team would take out the vehicle headed for the school in the village. I volunteered for Bravo team and Hamasa volunteered to go with me, so I took him. I thought it better to have him with me than with my unit. Hamasa was not the enemy, but he did use some extremely bad judgement in not telling us about the 'chatter'. It was highly likely that the vehicle we were headed to intercept was loaded with explosives.

We implemented the plan and drove the Humvee, by the burned out car, without incident. Our first hurdle was behind us. Hamasa rode behind me and was the gunner. As we approached the other vehicle they fired upon us when we were about one hundred yards from them. We engaged them. Hamasa took out at least two of the four insurgents before he was hit and killed.

I felt a large explosion and it had come from the hill where my unit was. They had taken a direct mortar hit. This was an insurgent set-up. However, I was not going to let them get to those girls in that school. I put the Humvee on a direct intercept course and took fire all the way in. I remember thinking that God gave me the courage to outdrive our commanders. Why not outdrive these guys? The last thing I remember is broadsiding that truck when we were about a hundred yards away from the school," Troy said.

Troy and John watched as a large flash appeared in the village below. Troy had saved the girls from certain death. They watched for a short time. As air support arrived on the scene, Troy turned and saluted toward his fallen friends. Then he headed back to the shade of the Water Oak with John following him. Under the tree the leaves stopped rustling and the cool light breeze had stopped blowing. They talked for a few more minutes under the tree. Troy began to walk, still under the shade, back toward the golf course. As he did, his clothing changed into proper golfing attire. Then he started to walk toward the next tee. But he stopped walking and turned around to face John.

"My mom always thought I would do something spectacular. She would tell me that, from the time, when I was a child. If you see her, could you tell her that she was right?" asked Troy.

"Sure thing kid. You can count on it," replied John.

John could feel the coldness of the room as he sat at his desk. The fire, in the reserve library, had nearly burned out as he was thinking of the time he spent with Troy. He stoked the fire in the hearth and returned to his desk. He then penned the following:

> *Dear Mom and Dad,*
>
> *From the time I was a child, mom always believed I would do something spectacular . . .*

John finished the letter and sealed it with the wax seal. He placed it in the envelope and put it with the others to be mailed on Saturday.

Then he opened the *Books of Merit*. In the books he located the names of Jack, Donald and Troy. In the margin, he noted today's date and the score carded by each golfer. Before closing the books, he located the names of the next three to play the Majestic of Purple Mountain. He wrote the names on a new scorecard dated for Saturday. Closing the books, he placed them back on the shelf and then filed away the completed scorecard. He then retrieved a sketch book from a book shelf and placed it on his desk. From his top right desk drawer, he removed a small box and placed it on the desk along side the sketch book.

He pulled his chair up to the fire and poured a cup of hot coffee. Then he waited.

Chapter 7

The fundraising dinner is in full caucus by nine o'clock in the evening. Tiger, on a reconnaissance mission, has taken a position outside the local VFW post. The facility has many windows and they are all open for this occasion. There is a cool gentle breeze coming down off of Purple Mountain this evening. The room would ordinarily be too cold with the windows open at this time of the year. However, with the large crowd assembled, for the fundraiser, the open windows were needed to keep the temperature levels comfortable. This provided Tiger with ample opportunity to perform surveillance.

    The VFW post is an older structure. Measuring one hundred and twenty feet by sixty feet it is a rather small structure for its kind. It is constructed of cinderblock walls inside and out and has a typical shingled roof. Although it is showing its age, it is fastidiously cared for by its members. They take a certain pride in their facility even though they lack the funds to perform renovations. It is in need of updating. The facility has a banquet section, a members only bar area and a kitchen. The banquet section is setup with long rows of tables having chairs placed on either side. The tables are packed so tightly that there is barely enough space between chairs to walk. There is a large open area in front of the bar area used as a make shift dance floor. This is where most people congregate.

Despite Jessica's dislike for campaigning, this event was almost enjoyable for her. It was more like a wedding reception than a fundraiser. In attendance were family and friends and friends of family and friends. Basically, people you knew and didn't know but were expected to know all the same. All that was missing from this affair to make it a wedding reception, were a few 'wear them once' bridesmaid dresses and a few poorly fitted rental tuxedos. The menu was basic wedding reception fare: fried chicken, green beans, mashed potatoes, mostaccioli, salad with choice of dressing. This was Thelma Mae's fried chicken and the best fried chicken in Worthington. There was also a cake made in the likeness of the park at the center of the town square. The cake was decorated with miniature flowers and trees of the types found around the town square. It was a wonderful setting for a working class fundraiser.

She remembers this hall with fondness from her childhood, as do many others in attendance. Jessica attended a few events here with her father years ago. They are precious memories and for a moment she was carried away in them. She remembers laughing with him in this banquet hall. Like an echo, in a mountain valley, she could hear the laughter in her mind. However, that was a long time ago and before he went missing in action. Her thoughts quickly returned to the events of this evening.

Jessica was not one given to making speeches. One was planned for the next day, after the parade, so she decided to not address the crowd with a lengthy speech. Instead, she stood up on a table and made a short statement. She told the crowd she would be near the bar area if they wanted to talk with her and she thanked them for their support. This was received attentively by the crowd as they laughed, whistled and clapped in support.

Over the course of the evening, supporters stopped by to talk with Jessica. She was a natural politician, although she would never admit to such a thing. Like the bright light of day, her charm warmed the room. She knew these people and they knew her. Most were people she had known from childhood. Many spoke of her father, Doug, and of their respect and admiration for both of them. However, despite her charm, her roots, and the history of her family, none of it could completely mask the sense of anxiety in the room. For behind the laughter and the roar of the voices was a feeling of fear.

The citizens of Worthington are a hardworking and proud people. However, the current economy has tested their faith. In times past, these people believed they could overcome anything brought their way if they just had faith. For faith is believing in what can't be seen. But these were tough times and people didn't see a way out. People were hurting financially and looking for answers. Although everyone had eaten, they were still hungry. Not all hunger is physical. They hungered, in their spirit, for a vision of a future they could believe in.

As the evening progressed, the crowd began to thin out and Jessica took a seat at one of the banquet tables. It was not long before she was joined by Mr. Garnet, the CEO of Axis Energy and her former employer.

To the untrained eye, Red was dressed in what appeared to be a standard blue suit with white pinstripes, white shirt and striped neck tie of the colors red, white and blue. He wore a white Amosu bespoke shirt with platinum cufflinks. Alexander's shoes were loafers and he wore no socks. However, his suit was no ordinary suit. It was a Brioni Vanquish II and one of only a gross made world wide last year. Its speciality fabric, of pashmina, qiviuk and vicuna, is woven together by skilled craftsman at the Dormeuil fabric company. The pinstripes are constructed of platinum threads. Only by touching it, would anyone become aware of its silky smoothness and its sartorial brilliance. No one ever touched Red. The suit fit him well. He was pleased that his hard earned wealth allowed him an opportunity to surround himself in such secretive softness. It was as if he were wearing an invisible cocoon.

    His watch was most interesting. Jessica caught a glimpse of it and remembered seeing him wear it a few times before. In that brief glance, she saw the constellation Draco with its tail seemingly wrapped around Polaris. One remembers a watch of this type. It was a Patek Philippe Sky Moon Tourbillon 5002 P. It is a two sided watch housed within one case and has a crocodilian band. The green band looked as if it were made from the skin of a dragon. The dial of one side contains hour, minute and second hands anchored to the center. Around the perimeter of the white face, are Roman numerals I through XII in their natural positions. Just inside this perimeter, beginning at the two o'clock position and ending at the ten o'clock position, are numbers, red in color, one through thirty-one, odd numbers only, separated by red dots, representing the day of the month, displayed in retrograde. There are four smaller dials within the larger with each having a single hand. At the three o'clock position is a dial that details the month of the year. At the nine o'clock position the small dial displays the days of the week. At the six o'clock position is a small dial representing the moon phases. The last of the smaller dials sits at the twelve o'clock position and has the Roman numerals I, II, III and IV measuring the day, in quarter day increments. Time is a valuable commodity. With this watch, Red knew the time in multi-dimensions with just a glance. Red viewed time, as if it were a commodity traded on the floor of a great exchange. To him, it was a force to be reckoned with. Red loved this side of the watch.

The rarely seen side of the watch is the other face, where a back lid would normally occupy the space, and the one on display this evening. It is a unique face. Majestic celestial objects of the heavens, with their God given intricately orchestrated movements, are displayed in their full glory on the sky blue face of this side of the watch. There are two silver hands, resembling miniature conductor's wands, tethered to the center of the dial. They individually rotate and point to the gold numbers, one through twenty-four adorning the perimeter of the face, according to an Earthly tempo. Three other times are displayed on this face. The tri-faced disk spins counterclockwise with each disk moving in its own canon. These distinct yet intricately choreographed faces display Lunar time, Lunar month and Sidereal time. With this watch, it was if the glory of the heavens, with its predestined and perfect timing, could be held in the hand of man. It felt as if the effects of gravity, on his soul, were suspended when he gazed into Deus' dial. Alexander perceived time, as if it were layers of harmony within a redeemed performance of the music of the spheres. He loved this side of the watch.

"Nice to see you, Ms. Mayor," said Mr. Garnet, introducing himself.

"It is nice to see you too Mr. Garnet. May I call you Red? Thank you for coming to support my campaign. I appreciate it. And please call me Jessica," responded Jessica.

"Please, call me Red. It has been a great evening. This event has provided me with an opportunity to meet with the people of Worthington. Yes, to meet with people I ordinarily don't talk with. Not that I don't like to talk with them. It is more that I just don't have the opportunity to talk with them. Michael usually does that for me," he said.

"Yes, Michael is a talker. We both know that. Have you seen him here, at the fundraiser tonight?" she asked.

"In fact, no I have not. He was supposed to be here but since it started I have not seen anything of him. I wonder where he is?" Red questioned.

"Perhaps he will show? There is still some time before it is over. Although, he missed out on some really good food!" She said.

"Surprising, that he is not here. Anyway, he was to speak with you tonight, officially, on my behalf. Since he is not here, I suppose I will speak with you personally then. Do you have a few moments?" asked Red.

"Of course I do. Please," responded Jessica. She sensed something of significance was to be divulged by Red. He has a flair for the dramatic she remembered.

"Jessica, you are aware of the difficult economic times that face our community. People are losing their homes. Businesses are closing their doors. Unemployment is up and tax revenues are down. Basically, times are extremely difficult for the ordinary person and for city government. Wouldn't you agree?" Red asked.

"Red, I must agree. These are indeed difficult times for the people of Worthington and for the city government also. We are working on solutions but they will take time before their impact is felt on the community as a whole," she replied.

"That is interesting. In fact, we have been working on something too. Something you may be quite familiar with when you hear of it," interjected Red.

"I am intrigued. Please continue," she replied.

"Before we get to that. You do know that your presence is greatly missed by the executive team at Axis?" Red remarked.

"Thank you Red, I am honored to know that my colleagues think of me in that way. It was a difficult decision to leave Axis, as you know," she responded.

"Yes, I remember. Should the reelection campaign not prove successful, please come and talk with us. There are openings in our legal department from time to time. No promises though. You understand," commented Red.

"With your support and the support of others, I hope to be mayor for another four years. However, it is gracious of you to extend the opportunity. So, what was that something we were going to discuss?" she said.

"Right, back to the subject at hand. Are you familiar with the case Naboth's Orchard vs. the Virginia Mining Consortium?" Red asked, as he leaned back in his chair and looked away.

"Red, have you forgotten? Surely not? I was the lead researcher on our team when we filed an amicus brief on behalf of the consortium. Axis was the amicus curiae in that action. The brief was filed just as I left Axis to take the mayoral position. Surely you remember this?" Jessica questioned.

"That is right, I remember now. That was just as you left Axis and the case was still before the court. So tell me, what obscure point of law was resolved so eloquently in that case?" Red probed.

"It has been a few years," said Jessica stalling for time to think, "since I handled that brief. I believe it dealt with eminent domain and the consortium prevailed over the environmentalists in the case heard by the Supreme Court of Virginia?" She said quietly.

"Yes, eminent domain. Most would say that your brief, on behalf of Axis, sealed the case for the Mining Consortium. It has become almost legendary in mining industry circles. This case has singlehandedly enabled the mining industry to implement MTM wherever they choose. Quite an impressive accomplishment I would say. Have you not heard?" asked Red.

"Red, since becoming mayor, I have not kept up with case law. I wasn't aware of the impact this case had on the industry here in Virginia. So, how is that case important to our discussion here?" Jessica asked directly.

"Without this case we couldn't proceed with our plans. You made this possible. Has Michael spoken with you about this?" Red inquired, fully aware of the answer.

"I am not sure he has. Actually, I think he hasn't. Really though, I am unsure since I don't know the subject matter in question here!" Jessica protested.

"I must speak with him about this. He was supposed to prepare you for our conversation. You really don't know do you? I am extremely sorry," declared Red.

"No apology needed, Mr. Garnet," changing the tone to a more formal style, "please just tell me what is planned here?" demanded Jessica, in a polite manner.

"Ms. Mayor," Red was now standing and reaching for his coat, "tomorrow, following the parade, we have called a press conference to make an announcement. I am sorry but I must be leaving now," and with no further comment Red turned and left the banquet hall.

Jessica was stunned. Red is notorious for his lack of both politeness and subtleness. In fact, he is referred to as Mr. Freeze by the office employees at Axis. In the mornings, before Red arrives at the office, laughter and a sense of camaraderie exists in the building. The mood is warm and the people are content and working diligently. However, all of that changes once Red arrives. It is as if a frost covers everything in his wake as he moves through the halls on the way to his office.

Yet, there was something sad about him. While working at Axis she could sense his sadness. Her office was just down the hall from his. His sadness was especially evident in the late spring around Memorial Day. Also, she witnessed him placing a few unusual items into his desk drawer on several occasions. They were oddly matched but he handled them with care. Additionally, there was a stack of old newspapers that filled the bottom section of one of his glass plated bookcases. The banding was still attached to the stack but cut, as if they were purchased in bulk. From looking at the length of the banding, it appeared that perhaps half of the stack remained. She never witnessed him open that bookcase. She couldn't place exactly what it was that made him appear sad. But she knew that there was something unresolved about him.

To some extent we all have unresolved issues. However, the length of time they remain unresolved and the severity of the issue in question, vary considerably from person to person and issue to issue. It is an interesting phenomena to witness, the differing responses of people to a similar set of circumstances. Remember, the same sun that softens the butter also hardens the clay. Often, a response is determined more by the composition of the material effected than by the agent of the effect.

The fundraiser was officially over. Jessica remained at the VFW long after the event was over. She stayed and assisted the catering crew with cleanup duties: folding chairs, stowing tables, sweeping, mopping. The duties of a servant she performed. Of the evening's events, this one provided her with the most sense of joy. This was not unusual for her. Unusual for her would have been to leave the work for someone else.

As she worked, she talked with Thelma Mae. Thelma Mae owned the catering company that provided the meal and setup services for the event. She also owns a diner at the edge of town.

"Miss Jessica, Mayor ma'am, you didn't havs'ta stay ands helps us! But, I am sure glads you wuz here til the end!" Thelma Mae said, laughing and smiling as she finished mopping.

"I wouldn't have it any other way! You and your folks did a wonderful job tonight! Thank you so much!" said Jessica.

"Miss Jessica, Mayor ma'am, it wuz our pleasure! This sure been a nite for helpin. Yes, sure wuz," said Thelma Mae.

"What do you mean?" asked Jessica.

"Miss Jessica, Mayor ma'am, may I call you Miss Jessica?" asked Thelma Mae.

"Why yes! I am sorry I didn't say to already! Goodness!" exclaimed Jessica.

"Miss Jessica, we'ves had some helping tonight. Earlier, when we wuz settin up things we didn't haves all the helps we needs. Cuz uncle Gus wuz sick and couldn't helps us tonite. I didn't knows how we wuz goin to do this party. Then he came and helps us. He does everything uncle Gus was going to do. He saves us he did. He sure wuz a looker too!" recalled Thelma Mae with a smile.

"Did you get his name?" asked Jessica.

"Miss Jessica, now it aint right for a girl to go askin for a name like that. But, it ok for a girl to listens for it. Now aint it?" asked Thelma Mae.

"Thelma Mae, now yes it is. Of course it is! So do tell!" replied Jessica.

"Miss Jessica, that ol' man Red–" Thelma Mae was interrupted mid sentence.

"Mr. Garnet... Red... helped you?" asked Jessica quickly.

the Majestic of Purple Mountain

"Miss Jessica, Miss Jessica, listens to me this time please! I saw that ol' man Red talkin with him. I gots close and listened real good like. But they didn't knows I wuz listening. Ol' man Red calls him Michael. Yes, Michael wuz his name. Sure wuz," said Thelma Mae proudly.

"Where did he go?" asked Jessica.

"Miss Jessica, ol' man Red sent him ups into the nite Breeze," said Thelma Mae, looking toward the mountain.

"The night breeze?" inquired Jessica.

"Miss Jessica, 'nite breeze' you say," laughing and shaking her head, "how long you lived here? Ol' man Red done sent him up Purple Mountain and at nite too. I hopes he tooks that owl withs him when he went too. I hearz him out there tonite you knows, hooting and spyin on us over here. Anyway, he wents up there to see the greenskeeper," reported Thelma Mae.

"Thelma Mae, thank you. Thank you. I need to head home now" said Jessica as she slowly walked out of the VFW hall. She was quite confused at this point. She wondered why Red would send Michael to see John. Michael had not been to the Majestic in years. She felt that Red was up to something and something big.

"General Anson, sir! Tiger reporting sir!" said Tiger, returning from his evening at the fundraiser.

"Tiger, please report," I said. Tiger proceeded to give an account of the fundraiser. He detailed the conversations between Jessica and Red. He also mentioned that Michael was meeting with John tonight at the cabin. After completing the report, I sent him on a mission to the greenskeeper's cabin. Perhaps we will finally discover what Axis Energy has planned for this mountain.

68

Chapter 8

From the rearview mirror, Michael saw her silhouette pass in front of the VFW's main entrance. It was just a glimpse but he knew her in an instant. There has been a bond between them since they were eight years old, since the summer when they first met. No matter how far apart these two were, this bond always remained.

Michael was prepared to talk with her. He had rehearsed it over and over in his mind. He knew exactly what he was going to say and how he was going to say it. Near the end of the evening he planned to talk with her, after the crowds had gone. Despite not knowing what her reaction would be, the time had come. He owed her that. This was a talk twenty-five years past its due. Time heals nothing he realized. For healing to begin, the wounds must be opened, examined and cleaned. He was going to tell her this time. She needed to hear the truth, all of it, before healing could begin.

In an instant, it all changed. This time something other than himself stood in the way; it was Red. Red had other plans for Michael and now he was headed up the mountain. Michael was not prepared for this diversion, although he knew it was coming someday. Now he was thrust into it.

This too, was a talk that had been twenty-five years in the making. It was the summer of nineteen hundred and eighty-seven when he and the greenskeeper had last spoken. At the time, Michael was a quite mature eight year old (odd as it sounds it is true). Responsibilities were placed on him that most grown men would find difficult to handle, if they could manage them at all. However, it all flowed so naturally with him.

At the time, it seemed as though he would inherit the mantle of the greenskeeper someday. Then it happened. That summer, in nineteen hundred and eighty-seven, he was confronted by a dilemma of faith. He, like the greenskeeper, could see the unseen. The Final Foursomes were visible to him. However, on this singular occasion Michael did not want to see nor hear with the faith of a greenskeeper. It was too much to ask of him he thought. So he left and never returned. Until tonight.

Michael knew it was too late to catch the mountain tram up to the Majestic. Also, the main service entrance was closed by this time of evening. To open the gate after hours was nearly impossible and time consuming if approved. This left just one way to reach the greenskeeper tonight, the 'you-ee'.

Michael was unsure if the 'you-ee' still existed. The 'you-ee' is the name that Michael and Christopher used when talking about the utility easement. This utility easement was a reserve entrance up the mountain used by the local electric company for its service vehicles. It was almost a path twenty-five years ago and who knows what it was now. Michael knew exactly where it began and hoped it was still passable. He left town and headed straight for it.

Interesting the things a man will remember from his youth; the sting, in the hand, from catching a well thrown baseball; the smell, in the nose, from grandmother's freshly baked apple pie; the sight, in the eye, of a comet streaking across a moonless night sky. Some memories never seem to fade away despite the time that has passed since our last visiting of them. This was a place Michael couldn't forget. Like a burning fire in his bones, were his memories of the Majestic.

As he passed by Worthington Cemetery, with its old and new sections, he knew he was getting close. There it was. The entrance tucked between two inconspicuous pine trees. With age they had both grown taller, the trees and Michael. Seeing the entrance he turned in and hoped for the best.

In the darkness of a moonless night, his Jeep sat motionless pointing slightly up the mountain path. The headlamps lit the path like a candle lighting a dark hallway of a long abandoned farm house. It was like he was a grandchild, returning to the long abandoned farmhouse of his grandparents. After being away for such a long time, he vaguely remembered its secrets. From what he could see, the path was virtually unchanged from years ago. With its ruts, rocks, weeds, low overhanging branches and one usable lane, it looked just as he remembered it. Memories flooded his mind like the lights flooded the abyss in front of him. He slowly started his ascent.

He and Chris must have traveled the path a hundred times that summer he thought. It was a long walk up the path, especially carrying golf clubs. However, that was before Chris modified the old golf cart to make the arduous journey. Chris could do magic with anything mechanical. Using parts from several scrapped golf carts, bicycles and a riding lawnmower he constructed a machine. They called it 'the creeper' because it crept up the mountain slowly due to the low gear ratios Chris used for safety. Its singular purpose for existence was to carry them up and down the mountain so that they could golf. Not just any golf; it was free golf.

They were soon to learn that nothing is free in life, especially golf rounds at the Majestic of Purple Mountain. For they were soon to be discovered by the greenskeeper. They had golfed only a few rounds before they were caught. As he continued up the mountain, the memories descended upon him like a light mountain breeze. Each turn of the Jeep on the path brought an old memory, from that summer, to light. It was a summer of adventure. It was the summer when they came of age as brothers, he and Christopher. It was a summer Michael would never forget.

Michael stopped the Jeep just before the bridge. He knew he was getting close to the end of the path. There was a wooden bridge that crossed a mountain stream just near the end of the path. Michael turned off the Jeep's ignition and shut off the lights. It took several minutes for his eyes to adjust to the darkness. While they did, he could hear the rushing of water from the stream below. It was comforting, like a lullaby from his childhood was its sound to him. Once his eyes adjusted, he spotted his favorite celestial images. He found Draco with his tail of stars seemingly wrapped around Polaris. He could see the milky way with its billions of stars arching across the blackened sky. If only he could summon the wisdom of the stars, he thought. He was comfortable up here, on this mountain, even in the dark of night. For here, unlike any other place, he could be at peace. Here, on this mountain, he could be himself. On this mountain, he felt he could write his stories. Stories that were important to him and not the ones that were important to Red and Axis. What if, he thought cautiously. After a while, he took just a few more minutes to collect his thoughts about what brought him on this journey tonight. Perhaps he did have the answer, to his dilemma, after all of these years. The moment passed as quickly as it came. Then, as usual, he returned to thinking about the realities of life; the realities of Axis Energy; the realities of his job; feeding the dragon.

He started the Jeep, turned on the lights and drove across the small wooden bridge. He parked the Jeep at the top of the next ridge. Leaving the Jeep behind, he walked the short distance to the greenskeeper's cabin.

As he approached the cabin, the yellowish red glow of the fireplace illuminated the wooden porch. The stone walls faded from black to gray and back to black again as the fire flickered and light bounced from surface to surface. The front stairway, from the ground to the porch, was throne like in appearance with its large stones and flashing lights. He quickly ascended the stairs and headed straight for the door. Even in the dark, the cabin of the greenskeeper was just as he remembered it.

Michael paused before he knocked on the door of the cabin. The peaceful feeling he experienced just moments ago in the Jeep, down by the bridge, escaped him now. That old dilemma, like a murmur in a demonically still and devilishly dark cathedral, echoed in his mind. Maybe, he thought, John wouldn't recognize him. Perhaps, John would recognize him but forget about the details of his departure so long ago. This was wishful thinking he concluded. He summoned the courage of the eight year old within and he began to knock on the door.

Chapter 9

John sat, in the reserve library, looking directly into the fire. An occasional cracking sound interrupted the hypnotic effect of the dancing flames. In his hand, he held a nearly half full cup of cold coffee. Then it came, the knock on the front door of the cabin. From here it is a faint sound and one must pay attention or it would be missed. The knock was not unexpected. He placed his coffee on the desk and headed for the door. He exited the reserve library and sealed it for the moment. He planned on returning to it later in the evening. Once in the main living area, he rushed to the front door.

Just as Michael began to knock on the door for the second time, it swung open. There they stood face to face. He was moved by the sight of his old friend. Gone for the moment was the feeling of anxiety regarding the dilemma of by gone day. He couldn't think of himself at this moment. The years had not been good to John. Michael could sense the pain that John was in. He was especially concerned for his old friend because of the content of the message he was to deliver to him tonight. All of these thoughts, like water rushing down a mountain stream, swirled through Michael in an instant. Michael, composing himself, smiled and extended his hand to John.

John, like the father of the prodigal son, stepped out quickly onto the porch and embraced Michael. He was not ashamed of his emotional reaction. For the greenskeeper had come home. John knew this to be true. He could feel it in his heart. He turned and positioned himself behind Michael and gently ushered him into the cabin. He closed the wooden door behind them.

Meanwhile, Tiger positioned himself in a tree just a few yards away from the front of the cabin. His bright yellow eyes alternately glowed bright then dim as they reflected the firelight emanating from the cabin. From the low hanging branch his view of the cabin's living area was unobstructed. From this location he was sure to gather prime information for General Anson. He would need to be especially aware of his surroundings for being this close to the ground was dangerous. Hoping to build upon the success of his previous mission he settled into reconnaissance mode with his ear tufts extended.

The cabin always looked smaller on the inside than what Michael envisioned. The westward facing front door opens into the main living area. It is about forty feet square. Two sets of double windows are on either side of the front door and give a clear view to the front porch. The main living area features a vaulted ceiling and a large fireplace at the center of the back wall. All the walls and ceilings are covered with oak paneling. On either side of the fireplace are built in book cases. On either side of the book cases are passageways leading to the two bedroom areas that occupy the east side of the cabin. The south side of the cabin houses the kitchen and dining areas and has a fireplace. The north side houses a study, with a fireplace, and a bath area. French doors, twelve feet in height, provide the entry ways between the main living area and the dining area on the south and the study on the north. The floors are made of hardwood plank. The craftsmanship provides ample decoration. Michael was comfortable in the cabin of the greenskeeper.

John had Michael sit on the couch near the fireplace in the main living area. John placed a few logs on the still burning embers. He sat in the chair that was located perpendicular to the couch. The newly placed logs were glowing red and in need of turning before either of them thought to speak a word. Then they remained quiet for some length of time with both looking into the fire.

In front of both the couch and chair was a three foot by four foot rectangular antique solid oak coffee table. Its top featured an image of a world map circa 1770's. Crests, of each branch of the US military, were carved into each side of the table. On each side of the table there was a center drawer. Each drawer had a small wooden handle in the shape of a heart. The short end of the table faced the chair. Michael gazed intently toward the drawer in front of the chair where John was sitting. It was as if he were looking for something.

"Michael, please accept my sincere condolences on the loss of your brother Christopher," said John. As painful as it was, he knew it was what needed to be said.

"Thank you, John," said Michael. Thinking of Christopher was a regular habit for Michael. Not a day passes when he does not think of his brother and how he was lost.

"How are you doing with it, Michael?" asked John.

"Fine," Michael quickly replied. Michael did not want the conversation to hover around Christopher.

"I am glad to hear that, Michael," responded John, "Michael, it has been a few years since we have seen each other. How many years has it been now?" John asked.

"It has been nearly twenty-five years," responded Michael quickly.

"Twenty-five years! That's right," answered John.

"Yeah," answered Michael.

"Michael, your being here tonight is not an accident. We both know that we need to have a conversation. I won't bore you with small talk," said John.

"John, yes indeed we do need to have a conversation. There are a few items that we need to discuss. There have been some recent developments– things that have brought me here tonight," responded Michael.

"Yes, I agree," said John, "since you are visiting, I will start first then."

"Well—" Michael was interrupted by John as he began to speak.

"Michael, I won't waste your time up here tonight and I will come right to the point. In the last twenty-five years not much has changed here on Purple Mountain. Things work the same way they always have up here. The Majestic is, as alive, as she ever was. The Final Foursomes still play every day except Sundays. I still play "Taps" at sunset each day for them. Letters are still sent to the families of each player. However, things are about to change. God has beautiful plans for this place. I know it," postulated John.

"John, I am aware of the plans for Purple Mountain and for the Majestic–" started Michael.

"Michael, wait, I know what you are going to say" interrupted John, "I have waited patiently all of these years and I am so glad that you have come here tonight. There were times I thought you would never return here but I had faith you always would. You were so young when it happened. You were learning and growing in it so quickly. It was an amazing thing to watch. Then you saw him and it ended as quickly as it had begun. But now here you are!" said John becoming more animated with each word.

"John, let me explain–" started Michael.

"Explain. There is no need to explain!" exclaimed John, "you have come here tonight for a purpose. So many years ago, you were chosen to become the next greenskeeper. God anointed you as my replacement. So tell me, when are you leaving your public relations position at Axis?" asked John confidently.

"John, John, John. Please slow down! And please let me talk now," said Michael anxiously, "I did come up here tonight for a purpose but it is not for the purpose you have laid out. There are plans for this mountain and this course. This will not be easy for you to hear but you must hear it and hear it from me. I owe you that," said Michael.

"Michael, I apologize. I was excited, caught up in the moment and couldn't hold it back. Now it is your turn to talk," said John.

"John, no apology is necessary. If there is an apology to be made it should come from me. Before I say what I came here to say, let me say this. For years I thought I would never return to this place. Ever. Then things changed and now I am here speaking with you. I wish now that I had come back years ago. It would have made tonight easier. I know that now," said Michael with hesitation, "but I can't change the past. I did not come back until tonight," said Michael.

"Michael, no apology is required. You finally came back! That is the important thing to remember here!" replied John.

"John, I must tell you tonight what is planned for this mountain," said Michael.

Michael, say what you must. I am listening," replied John.

"This mountain and everything on it will be cleared off when the mining project begins in late summer. Everything up here will be gone. The Majestic, the clubhouse, the cabin, the railway, they will all be gone. The plans are already in motion and can't be stopped. Axis Energy has identified this area as a site for a MTM project. Yes, Mountain Top Mining. Many prefer to call it MTR though. That is short for–" said Michael.

"Mountain Top Removal," said John finishing the sentence for Michael, "and yes I have heard of it. But, what you must understand is that this is not a surprise to me. This MTR or MTM project, whatever you prefer to call it, is not going to happen. And yes, you will be the greenskeeper. I have faith in this," replied John.

"I knew this would be difficult for you to accept. I understand that, I do. John, look around you. The Majestic has not performed economically for the past several years. It is a drain on the city and on the taxpayers. The city will receive fair compensation for the property. They need the money. They do.

Axis has a job for you at their corporate office. You will run the grounds maintenance department. The pay will be right and there are medical insurance benefits too. I have been there for a few years now and it is a great place to work. You will like it there.

As for the project, once the mining is complete an economic development zone will be established on the old mountain top site. An office park and a shopping mall are planned, at first, with more development to follow. This entire project will bring much needed jobs to our area and additional economic development as well. It is the only way to pull this city and our people out of the trouble we are in economically. It is the only way to save our way of life," Michael stated. He was cognizant of how quickly he returned to being a company man and the vice president of public relations. He was on a mission and he needed to meet the objectives that were laid out for him. However, just minutes ago he was full of compassion for his old friend and now this. It was difficult for him to reconcile this in his mind and he was conflicted. He sat silently there with John and neither spoke a word.

Michael couldn't help but notice that John seemed to look better now than when he first arrived. It was not that he wanted to see his old friend upset, quite the contrary. However, this was an upsetting conversation. John's overall look and demeanor defied common logic. He found it puzzling.

After a few minutes, John quietly stood up from his chair and put four more logs on the fire. Then he hung a cast iron pot on the swivel arm of the fireplace crane and swung it out over the flames. He walked into the kitchen and returned a few minutes later with a ceramic canister, two coffee cups and a cafeolette. The cafeolette was a nineteen thirties vintage, glass bodied, two cup press with a stainless steel filter. He sat them down on the table between the couch and chair. He walked back into the kitchen and returned with a small walnut colored box. The box had a small stainless steel bowl mounted on the top with a crank handle. It was a coffee mill. He brought it to the table and set it alongside the other items.

The water in the cast iron pot was boiling. John walked over to the fireplace and swung the pot away from the burning embers on the hearth stone. As he moved in front of the fireplace, his body cast a long shadow across the room. After removing the pot from the swivel arm, he brought it to the table and placed it on a well worn pot holder.

Michael was intrigued by the ceramic canister, as it was of an unusual design. It was conical in shape with a base of six inches and a peak of eight inches. An air tight lid was cut three inches from the top of the canister and was held tightly in place with a spring loaded clasp that recessed into the side. Upon closer examination, he noticed it was a miniature representation of the peaks of Purple Mountain. He wondered where such a piece would have been made and how John came to possess it.

John popped the clasp of the canister and laid open the top. To Michael, it looked as if the top of the mountain were hanging upside down and suspended in space. Black coffee beans filled the space where the top of the canister had been and some of them rolled down the sides and onto the table below. John quarried into the mound of beans with a metal scoop as more beans tumbled down the sides. One scoop, then two and three until the mound of beans was reduced to a level below the cap. With each scoop he began to fill the coffee mill. He ground the coffee by spinning the handle in a clockwise direction. The mill, on a corse setting, transformed beans into large uniform coffee chunks. The intermittent grinding sound echoed off of the interior walls and compounded the sound effect. The coffee grounds collected in the wooden drawer of the mill. He removed the drawer and carefully poured the contents into the press. The coffee aroma began to fill the area. He slowly added the steaming water to the press. First covering the grounds before a small bloom appeared. As he steadily added water, the grounds became fully saturated. He stirred the mixture with a small stick about six times until the water became as black as coal. Then he waited.

After a four minute steep, he inserted the plunger and with an absolutely straight single push, pressed the pot. As he held the lid tightly, he poured the hot coffee into the two cups and slid one in front of Michael. The cups sat on the table with vapor slowly rising into the air before vanishing from view. Like a morning mountain mist, it was there one moment and gone the next. The aroma was almost intoxicating.

"Drink," said John after what seemed like an eternity.

Michael lifted the cup and took a sip. The coffee was stronger than what he was used to drinking but not bitter. He thought it to be a bold and balanced blend. Also, it had texture from using the press. It was impressive, all of the effort that was put into making two cups of coffee. The experience seemed to take the focus off of the prior conversation.

"Good coffee..., hot..., bold...," Michael commented before taking another sip, "has texture..., I approve. Thank you," said Michael.

"Good. I am glad you like it. I have been making it this way for years now and it is almost down to a science for me now. But science is not the responsible party. The beans were roasted only a few days ago and the water is straight from the stream. However, the key to good coffee is good company. Anyone can keep freshly roasted coffee on hand and grind it as needed. Just as, anyone can keep filtered water ready for brewing. But, it never tastes as good alone as it does with a friend," said John.

"Agreed," responded Michael with appreciation in his voice.

"General Anson, sir! Tiger reporting, sir!" said Tiger, as he landed on one of my branches. Tiger had departed from his location at the cabin about the time that John began pouring the coffee from the cafeolette.

"Tiger, please report on your reconnaissance mission to the cabin," I replied.

"General Anson, sir. Michael did arrive at the cabin as we suspected. He and John had a lengthy conversation about the future of Purple Mountain. I have two scenarios to report. The first: John believes that Michael will become the next greenskeeper of Purple Mountain," Tiger said pausing, "the second: Michael believes that a mining project will take place here on the mountain. It will cause the destruction of everything up here on Purple Mountain! Everything we know will be destroyed . . . even you General. I won't allow this too-too toooooo too-too happen, sir. We will fight for this mountain, sir!" reported Tiger with passion and resolve in his voice.

"Excellent reconnaissance work, Tiger. Now that we know of their plans we may now develop our defensive strategies," I responded confidently.

Chapter 10

They were finishing their cup of coffee as the fire in the hearth died down. Died down, as well, had the initial shock of his visit and the news he brought. With the coffee finished, it seemed as though the night was wrapping up. Then a sudden flareup in the hearth began. There remained an unburned section on two of the logs where they had been resting on each other. As the fire burned down, the logs shifted and exposed these sections to heat and oxygen. The logs began to burn brightly again.

"So, what did you do with the letter?" asked John breaking the silence. John was not sure of the answer to the question he asked. However, he had every reason to believe that Michael had not read it. He got up from his chair and went to the fireplace. He placed two fresh logs on the fire and sat back down.

"Letter? What letter?" responded Michael. Instinctively his eyes slowly moved down and to the left bringing into focus the drawer at the end of the table. Michael knew exactly what letter John was inquiring about.

"Do you expect me to believe that you don't know 'what letter' I am talking about?" responded John. He was almost parental in his tone.

"Yes, that about sums it up," said Michael in a tone that was almost childlike.

"I see. You are taking that route are you?" said John as he began to clean up from making coffee. He cleared the items from the table and took them into the kitchen. He returned and sat down in the chair. He then leaned forward and placed his hand on the heart shaped handle. He paused and looked at Michael before he gave the drawer a pull. It was difficult to open, as if it had been sealed for some time. With a little force it finally slid open. From the drawer he removed an old letter. Without looking at it, he placed in on the table and slid it toward Michael. "Maybe this looks familiar?" asked John finally looking at the letter that was now on the table in front of them.

"Just where I left it . . .," said Michael as he leaned in and over the table looking directly at the letter, "how long has it been in there?" asked Michael in amazement.

"Since the day you," said John looking up from the letter and now looking at Michael directly, "put it in there. I wondered for years what had happened to it; if you had it; if you burned it; if you left it here maybe. I didn't know until just a while ago where it was,"

"You haven't opened that drawer in twenty-five years? And tonight, while I am sitting right here, you open it? You must have known it was in there?" asked Michael.

"It is a wonderful old coffee table but I really have no need for the drawer space. I don't put things in those drawers and never have. When you first sat down tonight, I noticed you looking at the table. Only later did it become obvious that you were really looking at it. I had no idea it had been here all of these years," responded John.

"Was it that obvious?" asked Michael.

"Yes, it was 'that obvious'," John said smiling.

"So, after twenty-five years it is still a mystery," said Michael as he picked up the letter from off of the table, "what is in this letter anyway? Why don't you tell me?" asked Michael as he examined the letter.

"As you can see, it is addressed to you," said John looking directly at Michael holding the letter. "Why not open it up and see for yourself?"

"You say 'it is addressed to me' but I don't see that. I do see that it says, to the greenskeeper of the Majestic of Purple Mountain. Since I am not the greenskeeper, then it is not my letter. You remember word for word what is in here don't you?" asked Michael.

"At the time you received the letter, you were the greenskeeper. Well, in my absence you were the acting greenskeeper anyway. Before I left, I wrote this letter to you. There were things I thought you needed to know," replied John.

"I was eight years old! I wasn't ready for the Majestic. This place was different from everything that I knew. But I liked it. What I didn't like, as best I can remember, was your leaving and not telling me where you were going or why you were going," said Michael passionately.

"You are right. I should have told you. I am sorry that I didn't. Perhaps we can set things right. Yes, tonight we can set things right!" said John.

"And how do you propose we 'set things right' tonight?" asked Michael reluctantly.

"As you know, the Majestic is a special place. Things operate a little differently here than other places. Wouldn't you agree?" asked John.

"From what I remember, yes they do. But that was a long time ago. What do you mean by 'operate differently'?" responded Michael timidly.

"Yes, 'operate differently' I did say. The course maintaining itself, you remember that don't you? The Final Foursomes, you remember them don't you? The shade of Southern Red, you remember that don't you?" John paused and saw Michael nodding is ascent. He continued, "you didn't experience everything there is to know about the Majestic that summer. Even the letter you are holding doesn't explain everything. It can't. Some of it must be experienced. It is difficult to explain, but let me try," said John.

"Yes, I remember all of those things. But what else are you trying to communicate here. I am a little confused," said Michael.

"Michael, there are some unresolved issues from that summer. Are there not? Wouldn't you like to see them again. Go back to those moments in time and look at them again but with the perspective you have now?" expressed John.

"What are you saying? Some kind of time travel? We go back into the past and just put things right. And then we wake up and everything is perfect? I don't believe in that kind of nonsense. This place is different, I will give you that. Life flows in one direction and we have to live with the decisions we make. We don't get the luxury of going back and doing it over. No matter how mysterious and special the Majestic is, no one, no place, can do that," declared Michael.

"I am not saying that at all. Going back and looking is different from going back and changing. Changing is not allowed but going back and looking is another matter altogether. It is possible to go back and look. I am not sure if you have this ability but I do. It only seems logical that you would have it also, since you have many of the same abilities that I possess. It is possible to visit that period of time, I am sure of it," contended John.

Michael ventured, "So, why do you believe you have this ability?"

John professed, "You ask 'why'? I don't ask the why questions anymore. What I believe about this ability, I will answer that. Two things," John held up one finger, "first, I believe I have it because I use this ability frequently. I use it to help me remember what the golfers desired for me to communicate to their families," John held up another finger,"second, I believe this gift, to go back and visit the past, was given to me so that I could help soldiers and families find closure. Does that help answer your question?"

"Let's suppose going back is possible, as you say it is. I am not saying that it is possible, only that we suppose it is. How does it work?" asked Michael.

"It works naturally. It is like a moment, wrapped in a memory, sealed in a dream. It is like day dreaming in four dimensions instead of three."

"What is the 'fourth dimension'?" he asked.

"It is time. Let me ask you something, ok?" proposed John.

"All right, ask away," said Michael as he leaned back on the couch, "do I need to close my eyes or do anything special?" responded Michael snickering.

"No nothing special. Just relax. Think about the time this evening when I was making coffee. Think about what you saw . . ., what you heard . . .,what you smelled . . .. Go back to that moment in time this evening. Now tell me about it?" asked John.

"Of course I can tell you about it! It just happened. I remember it. What is so special about that? And what is the fourth dimension? That bothers me," responded Michael quickly.

"Michael, bear with me here for a minute. All I ask is that you give it a try. You will be on your way soon enough. Just try this for me. One time is all that I ask of you," pleaded John. "And the fourth dimension is that of time,"

"All right, I'll give you one more shot at this. I know this is important to you, so I will do it. But, if it doesn't work this time, I am calling it a night," said Michael with respect, "ok, what do we do now?"

"We are going to meditate for a moment–" said John as he was interrupted by Michael.

"Do I need to clear my thoughts?" asked Michael beginning to become more serious.

"No. Quite the contrary. We will not empty our minds but rather we are going to fill our minds with thoughts," said John in a calming voice. "I want you to think about the first time we met."

Michael began to focus on the past. It was difficult for him at first. So many thoughts were going through his mind tonight. But he promised John he would try. He settled the thoughts of the day in his mind and set them aside like a magazine. As he focused on the past, people and places flashed across his mind. He thought about Jessica and the time they spent together at Axis. He pushed further back. He thought about his college and high school days. He pushed further back. He thought about his brother Christopher. Yes, Christopher was with him that day.

"Think about what season it was; where you were;" said John in a firm voice after a slight pause.

Michael began to picture a mid spring day. He pictured the utility easement in his mind. The trees were beginning to bud out but were still mostly bare. This allowed him to see through the sides of the path and view the mountain. Grass had not yet grown in the center of the path and wildflowers were just beginning to blossom. He felt a sensation of movement.

"Who were you with; what time of day it was;" John continued after another pause.

Michael could see him now. It was Christopher driving 'the creeper' up the mountain. He could see that old converted golf cart carrying them, an eight year old Mike and his older brother Christopher, up the mountain. It was midday as the sun was directly overhead and 'the creeper's' shadow fell straight beneath it. It was as if he were standing at the side of the path watching them drive by.

"What sounds you heard;" said John breaking into the silence, "what smells there were in the air;"

Michael couldn't hear the creeper like he thought he would. Instead he heard the sound of rustling leaves and clanking iron. He had a musty scent in his mind. The smell of old leaves being turned over after a long winter on the ground. They were walking through the woods and kicking up leaves as they moved along. In his mind, he could hear the sound of the golf clubs hitting each other as they were being carried in the bags thrown over their shoulders. He could hear muffled giggles and an occasional shush.

"What you felt on your skin; use all of your senses and focus your being on that particular moment in time," said John with a sense of finality.

Michael could no longer hear the rustling of leaves nor the clanking of clubs. It was quiet now. He could sense coldness on his skin and a feeling of anxiousness. Then a feeling of warmth came over him and the anxiousness departed. It was as if he had passed from darkness into a bright light.

Chapter 11

A few moments passed before his senses adjusted and then he was able to see clearly. He could barely believe his senses but he held on to the moment. It was as if they were transported from in front of the fireplace at the cabin to this point and place in time. Michael and John were now standing together on the edge of the eleventh fairway at the Majestic of Purple Mountain.

The date was Saturday, May 2, 1987. It was mid afternoon. From where they stood, they watched as an eight year old Mike and a sixteen year old Christopher played their first illegal shots of the day. The boys were teeing off at the eleventh hole. The tee shots landed in the center of the fairway about thirty yards from where Michael and John stood. The boys picked up their golf bags and started to walk.

"What are you doing here?" whispered Michael.

"I am the greenskeeper. I work here. This is what I do," replied John in a hushed voice.

"Oh, all right. So this is it? That wasn't so difficult!" said Michael confidently but softly.

"I never said it was difficult to get here. The real question is what are you two doing down there?" responded John as he pointed at the two boys in the fairway. His voice now growing louder and almost at normal pitch.

"Yeah right, 'what are we doing' you asked," said a confused Michael, "I believe we are playing golf. Can they see us up here?" Michael asked while lowering his voice, "can they hear us talking?"

"No, they can't hear us. So, you don't need to whisper," said John in a normal tone of voice.

"Then why were you whispering earlier?" asked Michael still in lower tone than usual.

"I was following your lead. You brought us here," responded John with a smile.

"You still have not answered the question. Are they able to see us up here?" asked Michael again. The eleventh hole is a par 4 with a slight dogleg to the right. The fairway is sloped from side to side and Michael and John stood on the high side at the apex.

"No. Not exactly," responded John shaking his head from side to side.

"That doesn't sound good. What do you mean by 'not exactly' and that head shake?" asked Michael with a hint of concern in his voice.

"Just what I said, 'not exactly'. Although they can't see us standing up here watching, you are experiencing something down there. As best I can describe it, it would be called déjà vu," declared John. "The strength of the feeling of déjà vu down there, is directly proportional to the number of times you view the experience from up here. The feeling increases with each time you come to this particular moment."

They both watched as the two boys, Mike and Christopher, hit their shots up toward the green. As Mike put his club back into the bag he seemed to pause and look directly where Michael and John were standing. Then Mike turned and ran to catch up with Christopher who was already walking up the fairway toward the eleventh green. Michael and John walked along in the rough following them.

"Nice shot, eh?" said Michael jokingly, "that déjà vu thing is interesting. I will have to remember that. By the way, how much of this will I remember anyway? I mean to say, what will I remember of this when we return to the cabin? We do go back to the cabin don't we?" asked Michael stopping in his tracks.

"Yes, we go back to the cabin. Don't concern yourself with that. Just play along for now," said John as he continued to walk along, "let's see where this takes us? Are you ok with that?" asked John.

"Sure. I think I know where this goes from here," said Michael.

"All right, take me there," asked John as he looked away from Michael and toward the thirteenth hole.

Michael began to focus on the sights, sounds and sensations of the next location. He thought of his brother. The faint smell of apples was in the air and he could hear the rustling of leaves in the woods. Instantly, Michael felt a coldness replace the warmth on his skin. It was like dark clouds suddenly blocking out the sun on a bright clear day. That anxious feeling had returned again. He knew exactly where he was going. He was taking them to the thirteenth green.

There was only one path in and out of the thirteenth green. The slightly elevated thirteenth green sits in the midst of a grove of trees. The path to the fourteenth fairway is cut forty yards in front of the green on thirteen. So after playing the green, the golfers must retrace their steps back down the fairway to reach the path to the next hole.

It was the perfect place for an ambush. Perhaps ambush is not the correct word to use here. The boys had set their own trap by sneaking on the course in the first place. Now they would meet the greenskeeper just after they putted out on thirteen and began the walk to fourteen.

John and Michael stood together and watched as the two boys lined up their putts on the thirteenth green. The boys were so engrossed in their game that they had no idea they had been discovered. John and Michael watched from the far side of the fairway directly across from the cutoff to the fourteenth.

Then they saw the greenskeeper appear as if from out of nowhere. There he was, standing in the cutoff, juggling three golf balls and an apple. Catching and tossing in smooth motions, like a juggler in a circus act. He kept the balls in the air and managed to take bites from the apple while doing so. All of this, while remaining silent. As he continued to juggle and eat, he slowly walked toward the opening to the thirteenth fairway.

As the boys approached to within eight yards of the entrance to the cutoff, he threw a ball into the woods just ahead of where the boys were walking. He continued walking and juggling now only with two balls and a partially eaten apple. The boys stopped and quickly turned their heads in unison to look into the deep woods. Then he threw a second ball into the woods. It made knocking noises as it hit trees before resting on the leaves. He continued to walk. He tossed a ball in one hand and ate the apple with the other. The boys set down their clubs in the fringe of the fairway. They hunched over and with curiosity approached the tree line. Like flies headed into a web they were. Finally, he threw the last ball even deeper into the woods and with one more step he cleared the tree line and was on the fringe of the fairway. He was now in plain sight of the boys but they were not looking.

The diversion made their capture easy work for John. He came in from behind them and gathered up their golf bags without their even hearing him. He finished the apple and tossed it toward the boys. The apple, or what was left of it, slowly rolled to a stop just a few feet in front of the boys as they stood looking into the woods. In unison, they slowly looked down at the apple. Then they looked at each other and they turned around and saw him. There was no where to go. "OK fellas, follow me," the Greenskeeper said to the boys as he turned away from them and started to walk toward the greenskeeper's cabin with golf bags on each shoulder. The boys followed in silence with heads down. They alternately gave each other an occasional slap to the back of the head and a gentle push on the shoulder. They were brothers. Brothers in trouble but brothers in trouble together.

John and Michael watched the three of them walk past. They were close enough to count buttons on the boy's shirts as they walked past. Christopher looked so young Michael thought to himself. Michael for the first time wanted to warn Christopher about Iraq. But the thought passed as quickly as it formed. Then the three of them were over the hill and gone out of sight.

"Congratulations, you win the prize!" announced John with a laugh.

"Not exactly my most shining moment," reckoned Michael.

"Not exactly. But you got us here didn't you?" suggested John.

"I am confused. You said 'got us here' but where and . . . when is 'here'?" asked Michael looking puzzled.

"When we started this exercise back in the cabin, I asked you to take us back to where we first met. That is the 'here' I am speaking of. You have done well for your first time at this," John observed.

"When they walked past us a few minutes ago, I wanted to stop Christopher and tell him about Iraq. I wanted to tell him not to go. I must tell him not to go!" divulged Michael passionately.

"That is not why we are here. Anyway, it doesn't work like that. Trust me, I know this," John contended.

"We can do all of this but we can't change anything? Why not?" Michael expressed with a growing sense of agitation.

"It's not that we 'can't change anything; it's just that we can't change the past. As for 'why', I can't answer that one. Those 'why' questions are the toughest ones," responded John in a calming voice.

"If we can't change the past," Michael said growing more frustrated,"then what can we change? Maybe I am better off as the vice president of public relations any way? From there at least I have some influence."

"You said 'influence'? We are conduits of change in the present and influence change in the future. We take what we learn from here and share it in the present. That is what the greenskeeper is called to do. There are people that need to hear the stories that we can tell them about their loved ones. Stories from their loved ones who came here and played the Majestic while on their way to their final home. We help those that come and play in the Final Foursomes too. We help each of them see how their faith made a difference in life and help them find peace. Then we help the loved ones, of those that come, find closure. You want to have 'influence'? You will have it here," John opined.

"So, I can't help Christopher?" Michael surmised.

"Perhaps, in time you will. If he comes here to play, then you will have an opportunity to help him," John contended.

"But when he comes it will be after the helicopter crash in Iraq? Right?" Michael postulated.

"Yes, That does not mean that you can't help him though. If he comes here, he will come for a reason," asserted John.

"So, when is he scheduled to come? You know don't you?" Michael hypothesized.

"Think of it like this," John began to look around the course and extend his arm with an open palm, "those that come here to play are near the end of a journey. Playing the majestic is like riding the Orient Express from Strasbourg to Paris–"

"What does riding an old closed down railway, like the Orient Express, from Strasbourg to Paris have to do with this place?" Michael interrupted John in mid sentence with his question.

"From eighteen hundred and eighty-three until nineteen hundred and sixty-two, the Orient Express provided rail service between Paris and Istanbul; between Europe and Asia; between East and West. Strasbourg to Paris was the last leg on the return trip from Istanbul to Paris," John declaimed.

"So, the Final Foursomes come here to the Majestic as the last leg of their journey?" Michael summarized.

"That is the idea. Imagine taking a journey to the Far East and using the Orient Express to get there. Imagine the adventures one would have there in Asia and the stories one would have to tell about them. Then the time comes to return home. The trip back is a long journey by way of the Orient Express. Excitement would give way to boredom as the trip home wore on. However, that changes when the journey back nears the end. Excitement once again comes to life as preparations are made to recount the adventures to family and friends. Imagine how many stories were told to conductors on the west side of Strasbourg while headed to Paris. Now, the greenskeeper is like the conductor on the Orient Express," John posited.

"How is the greenskeeper like a conductor?" inquired Michael now playing along.

"The conductor is responsible for keeping a log of the journey, checking passenger tickets against the manifest and attending the needs of passengers among other things. However, he does not choose the passengers nor when they ride. But he is made aware of the passenger manifest before they arrive," John declared.

"So, as the greenskeeper of the Majestic you do all of these things?" surmised Michael.

"Yes, That is part of the job description," declared John.

"You said 'keeping a log of the journey'?" asked Michael.

"There are records, yes. They are kept in various formats. I will show you when the time comes," John ventured confidently.

"And, 'attending the needs of the passengers', what does that entail?" Michael asked.

"Yes, 'attending the needs of the passengers', that 'entails' listening," responded John.

"'Checking passenger tickets', now how does that work?" asked Michael.

"It works by asking them their names and checking them against the scorecard for the round," remarked John.

"How many days in advance does he receive the passenger manifest?" asked Michael.

"One typically but at the most two days," John conveyed.

"Again, when is Christopher coming to play?" insisted Michael.

"Not tomorrow. Beyond that I only know one thing," said John confidently.

"And what is that 'one thing' you know?" asked Michael.

"According to you, he needs to come soon if he is ever to play the Majestic again," responded John.

"Yeah. I guess he does. You know, he didn't believe in this greenskeeper thing," Michael remarked.

"That doesn't surprise me. Most people don't believe what they can't see. They are like doubting Thomas," John said pointing in the direction of where Mike and Christopher had just been walking. "Quite easy is it for you and I to believe it, as we can see them play. I hold no grudge against those that can't see them. However, I have a special admiration for those that believe but yet don't see. Those are the ones with childlike faith. That kind of faith keeps mountains from moving."

"Didn't you mean to say move mountains," Michael said pointing to the mountain peaks above, "not 'keep mountains from moving'? Faith the size of a mustard seed can move mountains, the King once said. That is what you were quoting?"

"I said what I meant to say. But there is a more important question. What did you say about it?" John said returning question with question.

"Say about what?" asked a confused Michael.

"What did you say to Christopher, the doubting Thomas? Somehow you knew he didn't believe. So, I assume that you spoke with him about what we see up here at the Majestic? You did tell him didn't you? You told him you could see the Final Foursomes?" John inquired.

"Well, you have to understand Christopher. He must have been born in Missouri!" Michael conveyed.

"'Missouri, the show me state! That doesn't answer the question. Explain?" asked John.

"Christopher was the quintessential 'doubting Thomas'. If he couldn't see it he wouldn't believe it. You couldn't convince him to believe. But, when he did see and when he did believe, you could find no more ardent supporter for the cause. He would give his life for the cause he believed in. That was Christopher!" declared Michael passionately.

"That explains Christopher," said John folding his arms and looking at Michael, "so, what did you tell him? Out with it."

"Of course I told him!" said Michael looking away.

"Told him what? You are going to answer this question," expressed a determined John.

"I told him that I couldn't see anything! There, I said it. I looked up to Christopher. I just knew he would think I was crazy or something. It was just easier that way," revealed Michael.

"Let me see if I understand. You told Christopher that you couldn't see the golfers in the Final Foursomes. However only a few moments ago, you were asking me when will he come and play," John observed asking, "you do see the irony here don't you?"

"No, I think I took the other train," declared Michael wanting to avoid the answer.

"Let me help you get back on the right track then. You are asking me when your brother, who doesn't believe in Final Foursomes, is going to come here and play. Do I have that part right?" posed John.

"Yes, that is right," responded Michael with head down in a small voice.

"Also, you believe that the Majestic will be scraped away by some mining project in the near future. Do I have that right?" continued John with his questioning.

"Yeah, that is what I said earlier," observed Michael in an even smaller voice.

"One more thing. If I understand it correctly, the greenskeeper, me, will soon be working at Axis and no longer working as the greenskeeper. Do I have that right?" asked John again.

"Yeah, you have it right," uttered Michael barely audible.

"So, let me summarize for you. Or better still, you summarize for me?" insisted John.

"My doubting Thomas brother is coming to play a course that doesn't exist so that he can tell a story to a greenskeeper that doesn't work there any longer. Do I have it right?" asked Michael in summary.

"Yes, you do. That about sums it up. Although, I still have a question for you," John maintained.

"What question do you have for me?" Michael asked.

"Setting aside all the irony, what possible reason do you have for thinking that Christopher would come here to play the Majestic in a Final Foursome?" John asked.

"It is really quite simple, I think. It comes down to faith," Michael revealed.

"Faith. Interesting," said John.

"Well, where do we go now?" asked Michael.

"That is up to you. You brought us here but at my request. We were going to take a look at some of those 'unresolved issues' from the past. If I remember correctly?" John remarked.

"Right, 'unresolved issues'. I think we should follow them,"declared Michael as he pointed up the fairway on thirteen where the boys and the greenskeeper had just been walking.

Michael and John began the short walk from the thirteenth fairway to the cabin of the greenskeeper. The sky grew dark and the temperature began to drop. A storm was coming.

Chapter 12

"It's in the hole! It's in the hole! It's in the hole!" she screamed as she scampered over to the cup to remove the ball that had just gone in.

"Yes, it is, caddie. Thanks to your great advice on how to putt this one! I haven't made a long putt all day until now. Great job! Oh, please remember to put the flag stick back in the hole after you remove the ball," he said as he put the putter back in the golf bag. As he began to lift the bag he felt it suddenly become heavy.

"Not so fast. That is my bag to carry today! I am your caddie, remember?" she said as she gently pulled on the shoulder strap.

"No, I didn't forget. I just thought you may want to take a break from carrying this old golf bag. It can be a heavy burden after fourteen holes. You have carried it all day and I am so proud of you! I can carry it the rest of the way and you can enjoy the afternoon," he suggested.

"That was not the deal and you know it! The deal was that I would be your caddie today. I am not tired and I can do this! Anyway, I know you already cheated me out of some of it!" she surmised, smiling.

"Cheated! Cheated! Now, now, how have I 'cheated' as you say?" he asked laughingly.

"Look at the bag," she suggested as she sat it down and pointed to it.

"What about it? It is a golf bag isn't it? And a nice one at that," he proposed.

"Is it your usual Saturday golf bag? Or is it perhaps something say . . . smaller!" she alleged as she hoisted the bag on her shoulder and began to walk.

"Now that you mention it . . . it is smaller than my normal Saturday golf bag. Now how ever did that happen?" he suggested as he followed her.

"Humph . . . I wonder?" she mused.

"Mom!" they said in unison after a short pause looking at one another. Then they laughed together, as only a father and daughter can laugh. They continued to walk together. With the caddie just a few steps ahead of the golfer.

"Then there are the golf clubs. The shafts are not shiny. Are these your normal Saturday clubs?" she remarked.

"The 'shafts are not shiny' you don't say. How did these get in here? These are my graphite irons," he pondered as he pulled a five iron from the bag. They both stopped and examined the club carefully. She gently took the club and placed it back in the bag.

"Mom!" they said again in unison. Again laughing and shaking their heads. They stopped on the fifteenth tee box.

"What do you say caddie? What should I go with here on this one?" he asked.

"Hmmm . . . let me see; par 4; straight away; no water; fairway trap at one hundred and sixty yards. I suggest the big stick on this one," she proposed.

"Good choice! Club please!" he voiced.

Doug pulled a pink golf ball from his pocket and placed it on the tee. Jessica found humor in having her father play with a pink golf ball. She was happy that her father played along with her attempt to get him off of his game. As best she could tell, it did not effect his game. He hit the ball splitting the fairway perfectly and they walked after it, father and daughter, golfer and caddie.

"Nice hit. You only have a little work left on this one. I think you are about one hundred yards away," she speculated as they continued to walk.

"How do you know that?" he asked.

"Because, your ball is even with the pine trees. That is how I know," she revealed.

"Who told you that?" he asked.

"The Majestic. It says it right here on the scorecard, see?" she expressed as she pointed to the wording on the scorecard.

"I should have brought you here a long time ago! Do you know how much I have learned from you?" he stated.

"Really! You have learned something from me? I thought you knew everything!" she asserted as they came up to where the ball sat.

"I know that I need a club! Any suggestions for a shot of exactly . . . one hundred yards!" he replied laughing.

"Let me see . . . one moment while I look at the book," she said as she held the guide, "one hundred yards; slightly up a hill; the pin is on the back tier and left of center; wind is in our face. I say a firm nine iron with a little movement from right to left. Start at right edge of the green," she proposed with confidence pulling the club from the bag.

"I was thinking . . . my pitching wedge; hit hard; right at the middle. But the wind is picking up. Yes, a firm nine iron and right edge is the shot!" he commented as he took the club from her hand. He lined it up and struck the ball perfectly.

"Putter?" she assumed pulling it from the bag. She took his nine iron and handed him the putter in the same motion. She loved to spend time with her father. She loved the confidence that he showed in her decisions about the club selections.

While other girls played with dolls, she spent her time learning about the game of golf. During her father's long deployments, she would study his collection of golf magazines. She read articles about the greats like Jack, Arnold, Tom and Gary and how they played the game. She read articles about the future greats like Payne, Fred, Seve and Bernhard and admired each for their individual style. Many of the stories said that the game was changing and that a new era was beginning. However, she didn't see it that way. She saw the game as a child.

For her, the game was simple. First, it was a game played in the great outdoors in mythical settings. St. Andrews with its wind swept scenery, castles and the Royal & Ancient carried her off to a far away land. Spyglass Hill with the pounding surf and deep forest settings seemed enchanted to her. However, The Majestic of Purple Mountain was the most mysterious of all the courses she knew. Local stories regarding it were legendary. These places seemed to draw her closer to her father while he was on deployment. Second, it was a game played with a ball and a few clubs. The objective was to get the ball into the hole in the least amount of strokes possible. After eighteen holes you added the scores. The person with the lowest total score was the winner in tournament play. When playing alone, the objective was the same. Except, there was no winner to declare. It was just the golfer against the course. To her the game was the same as it ever was.

Instead of watching cartoons on Saturdays, she watched golf tournaments. Her personality fit well with the game. She possessed attributes of independence, patience and attention to detail combined with a competitive spirit. At the age of eight, she knew more about the game than most men would know in their lifetime.

Knowledge of her father's love for the game drove her interest in the game. She thought that her knowing the game better would help her get to know her father better. Since he spent time on the course between deployments, she thought what better way to have a chance to spend more time with him than to learn the game. Knowing the game helped her to gain the caddie spot. So, she concluded that the plan was working.

"Thank you, I think the putter is a fine selection for the next shot. I am thinking . . . birdie!" he stated with a wink.

"You know what they say," she said smiling, "they say 'drive for show and putt for Dough'!"

"They do, do they. And who are 'they'?" he asked.

"Oh . . . I don't know! But it does rhyme and sounds funny to me," she remarked as she continued to walk toward the green.

"I think it is a straight putt?" he said walking around the hole from various angles. "What do you say, caddie?"

"I say . . . distance and direction are key to making any putt. Let me think . . . fifteen footer; uphill; against the grain and wind. I recommend . . . half a cup to the right; firm grip; head down and keep it down until you here it fall into the cup," she contended.

"Aye, Aye, captain!" he replied as he leaned over the ball. He executed the shot just as she suggested. They both watched as it raced toward the hole.

"Birdie! Birdie! Birdie! You did it! Just like I said it. You didn't even look up to see it go in. How did you know?" she asked.

"I had faith in you! I could see the ball go in before I hit it. I just knew you had it right!" he declared as he went to her and picked her up and hugged her. He knew his daughter was growing up and that she would grow even more during his next deployment.

"We did it!" she said with arms raised in the air as her father lifted her up. It was a simple gesture and almost went unnoticed. That was the moment when she knew. She knew she had the approval of her father. Not because of what she had done but because of who she was and who she would become. For her father, acknowledgement of faith and trust did not come lightly.

They finished the celebration and put the flag stick back into the hole. Then they went on to the sixteenth tee. However, in all the excitement of the day neither of them noticed the approaching storm.

"Jessica, have you ever heard the legend of the sixteenth?" he mentioned as they continued to walk toward the sixteenth tee.

"No daddy, what is it. Tell me. You know I love a good story!" she responded as she continued to walk along.

"The sixteenth hole is the Lincoln hole," he said pointing to the tee marker. "Do you know who he is?"

"Yes, Abraham Lincoln was our sixteenth President of these United States. He was from Illinois and served during our nations' darkest hour, the Civil War. He believed that 'all men were created equal' and helped win freedom for the slaves. He had four sons but three of them died before they became adults. He was assassinated and then his funeral was held in the U.S. Capitol rotunda and his casket was placed on a catafalque. He was taken by train to Illinois where he is buried," she declared.

"Wow! You are quite the history buff. I am proud of you for knowing so much about him. What made you mention a 'catafalque' and do you know what that is?" he asked.

"I like the word 'catafalque'. It sounds funny! Catafalque! Anyway, it is the thing that they put under the casket to hold it up in the air," she answered.

"That is right. You must pay attention to the details in school! We should go to Washington D.C. and see the Lincoln Catafalque someday. It is kept in the Crypt of the U.S. Capitol. Even to this day it is used to hold the caskets of those that lay in state in the U.S. Capitol Rotunda. I have seen it," he responded.

"When did you see it? Tell me!" she said with excitement.

"I was in D.C. on May 28, 1984, for the ceremonies related to the Unknown Soldier of the Vietnam Era. I went to the public viewing in the Rotunda and then to the ceremony held at Arlington National Cemetery at the Tomb of the Unknowns. It was an honor to attend that event and I will never forget it," he declared.

"I agree and we should go there some day," she responded.

"Yes, I must take you to Arlington," he solemnly paused, "So, do you know why this hole is named after President Lincoln?"

"They named the hole in honor of him didn't they?" she assumed.

"That is right–" he began to say.

"But how is that 'legendary'? And I am sorry for interrupting you," she observed while handing him his driver from out of the golf bag.

"Good question," he said as he took the driver from her outreached arm. "Although Lincoln's presidency is considered 'legendary', in American history, that is not the 'legend of the sixteenth'. This hole is also known as the blue and the gray. When this course was originally planned, Lincoln was to have two holes. One hole for each complete term he served as President. But, before the course could be constructed the president's life was cut short by an assassin and he only served as President for five years. To honor the president the course was redesigned. Two par fours became a par five and a par three. But the story doesn't end there," He declared, as he stood on the tee box with his club outstretched and pointing toward the split fairway.

"So, how does it end?" she asked.

"The course was constructed and the Lincoln became the par five sixteenth. However, God himself was not pleased with this hole. Some say, it was not challenging enough to represent such a great President. Others say, the sixteenth hole was too pristine and wasn't reflective of the Republic during the Lincoln years. So, God sent a powerful earthquake and it split the Lincoln fairway into two. After the earthquake, a north fairway and a south fairway were created. Course rules were developed to read that the golfer has to choose one fairway to play; he can't play both; nor can he crossover after he has begun play. So to this day, the north fairway is called the blue and the south fairway is called the gray. Regardless of the fairway one chooses, all players end the hole playing on the same green," he declared. Then he lined up his shot and teed off. It was a perfectly executed tee shot and it split the fairway.

"That is a neat story daddy. Daddy, why do you go off and fight in wars?" Jessica asked looking directly at him while taking the driver from his hand.

"Jessica, I go and fight to protect you and mom. I also go to protect and serve our country. Someone has to protect our way of life and our values. There are people out there that don't want us to live the way we do. They don't like freedom or liberty. They don't want us to have them," He declared still standing on the sixteenth tee.

"What freedoms daddy? What liberties?" she questioned.

"Our Declaration of Independence says 'all men are created equal, that they are endowed by their creator with certain unalienable rights, that among these are life, liberty and the pursuit of happiness.' Liberty is being free to choose what you want to do," he said.

"OK. Like choosing to be a doctor, golfer or a soldier when I grow up?" she posed.

"Yes, That is the idea. But don't tell mom about the soldier part in that. Now, let me tell you about those 'freedoms' I spoke of. We have the freedom to go to church and worship God; to say what we want to say; to choose our friends; to choose our form of government; to protect ourselves; to own a gun; all of these and more. It requires sacrifice to keep our freedoms. It requires eternal vigilance also. When I go and fight, I sacrifice time, that could be spent with you and mom. You and mom sacrifice the time you could spend with me by letting me go. Our family has a history of producing warriors. It is what I do. But when I am home, I am home with both of you!" he again declared.

"I understand, I think. But I don't like it. Why does it have to be this way?" she questioned, as she hoisted the clubs on her back and took the first step toward the fairway. The storm was rapidly closing in on them from behind but the winds had yet to pickup, so it remained unnoticed.

"Jessica, that is a tough question," he said as he began to walk with her. "The Bible says it is because man rebelled against God. We didn't follow his rules and chose to make our own. Since then, there has been trouble in the world."

"Why do you believe in what the Bible says, daddy?" she asked as they continued to walk.

"I believe it because it is true. I also believe it, because it can be proven to be true. The places mentioned in the Bible all exist and archeologists have proven it. There are many copies of the Bible from the time when it was first written, so we know it hasn't been changed. It tells a consistent story from beginning to end, even though, it was written over the course of thousands of years by many different writers. It predicted the future of the known world correctly many times over. And finally, there is Jesus. He rose from the dead like he said he would. That is why I believe," he opined.

"So, have you always believed?" she asked as she pulled a three iron from his bag.

"No. There came a time, in my life, when I had to choose. Just like I chose what fairway to play earlier. But it was a little more important than that. You understand?" he said as he lined up his fairway shot. He struck the ball solidly and it flew perfectly straight toward the target. As they began to walk, he handed her the club. She took it from him and cleaned it before placing it back in the bag.

"I understand. So like this hole, despite the fairway you choose everyone plays the same green in the end. So, religions are like different paths that people take to reach heaven?" she asked.

"No. That is not what the Bible says. The Bible says there is just one way to heaven. Confess that Jesus is Lord and believe that God raised Him from the dead. You can't earn your way in and religions won't get you in either. The only way in, is to repent of your sins and have faith in Jesus and what he did for you on the cross. This is a gift from God, a gift of faith. That is what I believe," he said to her as they stopped in the fairway where the ball had landed and come to rest.

"Does he force people to believe?" she asked as she handed him his pitching wedge.

"No. We are free to choose. But those that have been given faith desire to choose Him," he answered as he surveyed the green before making his approach shot. He knocked the ball up on the green and had another birdie attempt before him.

"Nicely played, daddy," she said while exchanging the wedge for a putter. Talking with her father was comfortable. He treated her with respect. Sure he demanded a lot when it came to chores around the house and being respectful of the elders and all of that, she thought. But even at her age, she knew he respected her as a person and not just as his daughter. They went on to the green and two putted for a par.

"So, how did I shoot Lincoln?" her dad asked wryly.

"You don't shoot the president dad!" she said with a laugh in her voice, "I think you were on par with the president!" she shot back.

"I like that!" he said laughing as he handed her the putter. They walked the short distance to the next tee.

They came to the par three seventeenth. It takes a mid iron to reach the three tiered green. They were in the sand off of the tee but got up and down for a par three score on the hole.

"What do we have next on the scorecard?" he asked her as they began the walk to the eighteenth tee.

"Eighteen, it is the number one handicap on the course. And it is the finishing hole! I think," she said in a high pitched voice, "we are going to get wet!" she said as it began to rain, just a few drops at first.

"Don't worry, I think we will be able to finish before the heavy stuff moves in. Go ahead and grab the umbrella and let me carry the clubs from here," He took a driver from the bag and teed off. He hit the shot up and over the crest of the fairway. Then they began to walk. As they walked down the fairway, the skies grew darker and the rain began to fall. By the time they were one hundred yards out into the fairway the storm hit. The winds kicked up and the temperature dropped.

"Jessica, come with me!" yelled Doug, leaving his clubs behind, he grabbed Jessica and headed for the lowest part of the fairway. They huddled together, crouching down low to the ground, under the umbrella and decided to wait it out there.

Chapter 13

The storm hit just as they were stepping onto the porch of the cabin. Michael and John timed their walk perfectly. They were now peering through the front window. Inside were Mike, Christopher and the Greenskeeper. Mike and Christopher were sitting on the couch and the Greenskeeper was sitting in the chair.

"What are we doing out here? Can we go in?" Michael proposed as he motioned toward the door with his hand.

"I don't see why we can't?" John remarked.

"OK, follow me but keep it quiet," Michael insisted instinctively. He grabbed the handle of the door and it was warm to the touch. It felt like the warmth one would have from a hand shake with an old friend. He paused at the feeling then pushed the door open and went inside.

"If you say so!" John uttered, seemingly blowing their cover, as he followed Michael in through the door.

"Shush . . . or they will hear us!" Michael asserted.

"No, they won't. Remember, they can't hear us or see us!" John reminded Michael. The experience was so life like, to Michael, that he forgot the rules that quickly.

"All right! You are right. But keep it down anyway. I want to listen," Michael said.

"OK boys, it is time we had a talk," the Greenskeeper announced. "What are your names?" The Greenskeeper, with the boys in tow, had arrived here a short while ago. Their discussion was just beginning. He kept a close watch on the time, for he knew that "Taps" must be played at sunset.

"My name is Christopher. Can we go now?" he insisted, as he began to stand up from his seated position on the couch. Christopher was quick to respond, thinking he could quickly negotiate their way out of this mess they were in.

"Kris-toh-fer . . . yes. Christopher . . ., your name is of Greek origin and means 'Christ bearing'. And have a seat. It took some effort on your part to get all the way up here today. No need to leave so soon. Besides, it is raining outside. Do you prefer Chris or Christopher? Are you boys thirsty?" the Greenskeeper asked in succession.

"I'd prefer to leave but call me Christopher. You can't keep us locked up in here you know. There are rules," he demanded.

"Did you say 'Rules' . . . hmmm" the Greenskeeper mused,"an interesting appeal coming from you. Wouldn't you say? Anyway, the door is not locked. You are free to go at any time," said the Greenskeeper motioning toward the door. "But, your clubs stay with me. Also, you may want to start walking now. The golf cart you brought will be staying here as well. Your property will be returned once we settle these matters."

"My name is–" started Mike, after a long silence before being cutoff by Christopher.

"Be quiet. You don't have to tell him anything," commanded Christopher asserting his authority as the older brother. Christopher was trying to shield Mike from the situation. Christopher felt responsible for getting his brother into this mess. He remained seated knowing that the Greenskeeper held the tactical advantage.

"Christopher, it is ok. My name is Michael and we are brothers. But, most people call me Mike," he declared.

"Mai-kel . . . yes. Michael . . ., your name is of Hebrew origin and means 'who is like God'. Are you thirsty, Michael?" asked the Greenskeeper.

"Yes, I am. Do you have any water?" Mike asked.

"OK. I am going into the kitchen over there," said the Greenskeeper pointing to the kitchen area. "I will be right back. Make yourselves comfortable. We will talk when I return," he got up from the chair and went into the kitchen leaving the boys alone for the moment.

"Mike, listen up," Christopher said as he turned to face him, "let me handle this. I will do the talking. Just sit there and don't say anything. Understand!" Christopher commanded. His brother's cooperation was not optional.

"I'll try," responded Mike.

"Here you are boys. Two glasses of mountain spring water with ice," he placed the two glasses on the table in front of them. He then sat down in his chair. "Well, go ahead and drink."

"Thank you for the water, sir," Mike began to say as his brother looked crossways at him,"may I ask you a question?"

"Sure Mike. Ask away," the Greenskeeper replied.

"What is you name, sir?" asked Mike.

"My name is John. I am the greenskeeper," he stated.

"May I ask one–" he started to ask another question but was elbowed by Christopher before he was able to finish.

"One more question it is then. And Christopher, please stop hitting the young man," he insisted.

"What does the name John mean?" Michael queried.

"That is a great question, Mike. John is an English name that has its roots in a Hebrew name that means 'Yahweh is generous'. Names are interesting. Perhaps we are like their descriptions in a way?" he answered.

"Mr. John, sir. What is it that you want from us?" Christopher interjected trying to move the discussion back to negotiating their way out.

"A few more answers to start with. Christopher, where are you?" he queried looking directly at him.

"I am in your cabin I suppose? This is your cabin isn't it?" He paused, "we really don't belong here."

"Yes, it is my cabin. Most of the people I invite here find this place comforting. It has a soft couch and a soft chair for visiting. It has a large fireplace to keep them warm and the company is good. Some people feel like they are right at home, like they belong here. Now why is it that you don't feel that way?" he asserted?

"Because I wasn't invited here like the people you spoke of. You made us come here with you," Christopher contended.

"True. You were not invited. You came up here as uninvited guests. You were not guests of the Majestic today. Perhaps, that is why you are feeling as you are?" he proposed.

"You are right, we are not guests. Now may we leave with our things?" Christopher asked.

"Christopher, I really don't think you understand where you are. You are at a crossroads in your life. That is where you really are. This cabin and the Majestic are not the 'where' I asked about. You will decide soon what kind of person you will become. Will you choose a path that reflects your namesake and become Christ bearing? The game of golf is a game that builds character and perseverance in the player. The game is built upon the principles of honesty, integrity and personal responsibility. You can decide to take responsibility for your actions or you can choose to walk away from them.

Either way, there will be consequences for your actions. But, you will be the better man for choosing the path of responsibility. It is your choice?" he declared.

"So . . ., how do we make this right? What do you want from us?" Christopher conceded after a noticeably long pause.

"Here is what I propose: You two work under my direction every Saturday until the first week in June. This is your punishment for breaking the rules. I will pay for the rounds you have stolen from the people that operate the Majestic. Someone has to pay for the rounds, as golfing is not free at the Majestic of Purple Mountain. And you will have your equipment returned to you. I will give you a little time to think this over among yourselves. I have something to attend to and I need to leave now. I will return in about thirty minutes. Please have an answer for me then," John proposed as he got up from his chair and moved toward the cabin door. Before he left, he stopped at the door and opened a case that was sitting there on a small table. From the case he removed a bugle, tucked it under his arm, and went out the door.

"I am not going to make it!" he said as he stood on the porch looking in the direction of the setting sun. "The sun is too low in the sky!" They heard him say to himself as he quickly walked away. He did not close the door behind him but left it wide open.

Chapter 14

"Daddy, I think the rain is letting up now. We still have time to finish," Jessica exclaimed.

"It is too late to finish the round today. The course closes at sunset. Sunset today is at eight sixteen and it is just past eight eleven now. We were rained out," he responded sadly. He knew this was the last opportunity to play before his deployment and wanted her to finish her first round as a caddie.

"But daddy! The clouds are clearing and I see the sun just barely peeking out. Why can't we try?" she asked, as she strained to see the setting sun under the clearing clouds. She bounced up and down, attempting to get a better look at the sunset.

"The rules are that the course closes at sunset. I can't change the rules, Jess. It is time to pack it in," he said as he started to walk and pickup the ball in the fairway.

"But daddy!" she continued, "we can finish this. I know it! We can finish this one round before you leave tomorrow for deployment."

"Jessica, look at the horizon. The sun is almost gone now, in just the short time we have been talking. It is over for today. We can't change the rules. Next time I am home we will finish this round. Here is the scorecard. Keep it in a safe place for me until I get back. Let's get going now," he declared faithfully.

"Daddy, I know we can't change the rules. Maybe we can change the sunset? Then we could finish our first round as golfer and caddie! What do you think?" she proposed with childlike faith.

"Jessica my daughter, that would take a miracle. Now let's get moving," he contended.

"Daddy, you do believe in miracles?" she speculated.

"Jessica, look across the way toward the clubhouse. At sunset everyday, a song is played here. It is one that honors all the people that have given their lives in service of this country. The Greenskeeper plays it everyday just as the sun sets in the sky, except on Sundays. The song is called "Taps". He stands under the flagpole while he plays it. It also serves as the signal that the course is closed for the day," he declared as he stood with her in the fairway straining to see the flagpole area.

"Daddy, the sun has already set . . . see. Why has he not played the song? What happens if he doesn't?" she questioned. But the flagpole area was not viewable from their position.

"I am not sure if he has ever, not played it. Something is wrong. Let's go up by the green and take a closer look for him," he said, as he started to quickly walk up the fairway. After a few paces, he noticed she was not following him. He stopped and looked back at her. Her hands were just unclasping and her head raising. It was as if she had been praying. She smiled and ran to catch up with him.

"Daddy, everything is going to be ok! You will see! You will see!" she said with childlike faith. They continued their walk up the fairway toward the eighteenth green. He quickly walked as she skipped along beside him.

"We shouldn't be here!" said Mike in a whisper, "we need to go back to the cabin and wait for him! We are in enough trouble already! I don't like this."

"Shush . . . or someone will hear us. We will go back soon enough and get there before he does. I have got to know where he went in such a hurry," Christopher revealed. The boys were hunched behind a large White Oak tree near the eighteenth green. It was a large tree, with whitish bark, but it wasn't the tallest of the trees. Christopher figured it was nearly five feet in diameter and a perfect tree to hide behind. From here they could see the clubhouse and maybe spot the Greenskeeper.

"Who are those people over there?" Mike expressed with hesitation looking at the green.

"I don't know. It looks like a dad and a daughter walking up the fairway. I think they are going to walk close by. Stay down and stay close enough to hug this tree. We don't need them to see us here," Christopher commanded.

"I wasn't talking about them. I was—" he was cutoff mid sentence as he tried to communicate what he had seen.

"Be quiet! Would you!" Christopher barked in a muffled voice. He was concerned about being discovered and really didn't pay attention to what Mike had said. They crouched low behind the tree and waited.

"Jessica, come stand over here with me. The sun is down! Where is he?" Doug said as he stood near the green where he had a good view of the clubhouse and flagpole area. Doug was standing about twenty-five yards from where Mike and Christopher were hiding.

"There he is! Don't you see him? He is standing by the flagpole!" Jessica announced as everyone looked in that direction.

the Majestic of Purple Mountain

What everyone saw was the Greenskeeper standing at the flagpole. He was facing west and at attention with his bugle in playing position. However, no sound was being made. But yet he continued to stand there, it was as if he were frozen in time. Then it happened.

From out of nowhere, a shadow appeared behind the Greenskeeper. Everyone focused on the darkening shadow appearing behind the Greenskeeper. Just as his shadow fully formed, it started. They could all hear it now. From beneath the flagpole beginning notes of G– G– C— G– C– E–. . ., were ringing out. John was playing "Taps", as he does every evening at sunset. The song seemed to echo off of the mountain and even off of the sky, if that were possible.

Then they noticed it. Sometimes the miraculous happens right in front of our eyes and we don't see it. While each had been focused on the shadow appearing behind the Greenskeeper they missed seeing the sunrise in the western sky. Everyone, except Jessica and the Greenskeeper, looked on in disbelief, as the sun set again in the sky. Some saw it as a Novaya Zemlya effect. Yet others saw it as a true second sunset.

Each witness viewed it from a unique and individual perspective. Doug stood at attention facing the flagpole in remembrance of fallen friends. His thoughts turned to his next deployment beginning at zero six hundred tomorrow morning. He had received his orders a few weeks earlier from his commander, D. Sparks. Hearing these notes convinced him, in his heart, that the sacrifices made by him and his family, to defend the Republic, were not made in vain.

Christopher watched, in amazement, as the notes of the song hit a chord deep within him. As the flag gently waved in the sky, he could feel a stirring within his spirit. This stirring quickly became a calling to serve his country. He admired the steadfastness of the Greenskeeper, as he stood at attention. He saw a man of faith and conviction. He stood alone. Christopher, decided in that moment to make his life worthy, someday, of that song being played for him.

While standing at her fathers' side, Jessica focused her attention upon four heart shaped purple leafs that were laying on the fringe of the green. The leaves looked as if they had passed through a fire. They were delicate and almost ashen in appearance. She bent down to touch them. Upon touching them, she felt a slight shock. It was a gentle shock, like one feels when pulling on a sweater on a dry winter day. As she touched each one, they disintegrated before her eyes. Only an outline, of the heart shape, remained where each leaf had rested. She wanted to show them to her father but now they were gone.

Mike intently looked, at the peak of the eighteenth green. It was as if he saw ghosts. He saw the outlines, of four men, standing shoulder to shoulder and facing to the west. As the song progressed, each man, in turn, began to walk off the green and over the hill. Mike watched, as each faded into glory and out of sight.

The Greenskeeper stood, beneath the flagpole, waiting, with bugle in playing position. He felt the warmth of the sun, as it lit his face. He felt a chill, in his arms, as goose bumps began to form. When he opened his eyes, the sun was beginning to set. In faithful execution of his duties, he began to play, giving praise to God through his faithfulness in waiting for the miraculous.

Then the moment was gone as quickly as it appeared. The last note faded away, as if it were chasing the sunset over the horizon. For each, this moment crystalized in their minds and was never to be forgotten.

John and Michael watched the entire event from the patio of the clubhouse. They had left the cabin shortly after Mike and Christopher had gone to find the Greenskeeper. For a brief moment, Michael remembered the uniqueness of being the greenskeeper of the Majestic. It felt like an old pair of jeans. The kind of jeans that one never wants to lose nor outgrow. It was the feeling of a relaxed and comfortable fit.

"Now that is something you just don't see everyday! I love to see the reactions, on their faces, as they begin to realize what has just happened," John confessed.

"Yes, I will never forget that moment. The moment that I realized a Novaya Zemlya effect had happened. This was also the first time that I noticed Jessica. And the trouble Christopher and I were in, at that moment, couldn't escape my mind either," Michael reminisced with a hint of melancholy.

"I noted a hint of heavy-heartedness in your voice. What is it?" John commented.

"I am not exactly sure. It seems like I missed something in that moment?" Michael supposed.

"Perhaps you did 'miss something' as you say. Do you know what caused the second sunset?" John queried of Michael.

"I believe it had something to do with an optical effect? An elongated inversion layer, in the atmosphere, having a special air temperature may cause a mirage when viewing the sun from a low angle. Normally, it only happens in colder climates. Its first recording was by a person named, Gerrit de Veer, during a failed polar expedition, in the late sixteenth century. The expedition witnessed the effect while they were on the Island of Novaya Zemlya. That is how it was named. Does that sound right?" he asked.

"Wow! You said 'does that sound right'. Now, I have to ask you, where did all of that detail come from?" asked a surprised John.

"I remember doing a little research about it sometime in high school. I think it was a science paper or something like that. I am surprised that I remembered that much," responded Michael.

"I believe you are over thinking this second sunset question. If it can be completely explained, where is the miracle in that?" John reckoned.

"OK. Suppose I go along with the second sunset being a miracle and that line of thinking. What answers do we have to explain the 'cause'?" Michael ventured.

"I think you are looking for questions and not answers. The questions will lead you to the answers," John suggested.

"Right. Questions . . . what questions?" Michael asked.

"Start with the easy ones first. I'll give you a hint. Who stood to benefit directly from the miracle?" said John.

"Let me think . . . I would say, the Greenskeeper, Jessica and Doug stood to gain the most," he presumed.

"What makes you think that?" John asked.

"The Greenskeeper was late and missed the playing of "Taps" at sunset. Jessica and Doug needed only a few more minutes together, in the sunlight, before Doug went on deployment. How does that sound for starters?" Michael speculated.

"And what of the others that were there?" John proposed.

"I am not sure," Michael remarked.

"Maybe it was an answer to some and a prelude for others?" John articulated.

"How do you propose to answer that one?" Michael observed.

"There were two groups of people there. One group needed a miracle and the other needed to see a miracle," he claimed.

"And into what group did I belong?" Michael asked.

"You fit into the latter. Witnesses of miraculous events are the recipients of great expectations. The size of the expectations are directly proportional to the miraculousness of the event," John opined.

"So, let me understand this. First, you are saying that the event was a miracle and not an effect? You are saying that the sun actually set a second time that day? Second, you are saying that the miracle directly benefited some in that exact moment? Third, you are saying that others witnessed it and are 'recipients of great expectations'? Have I summed it up correctly?" Michael postulated.

"Yes, that sums it up nicely," John said with a smile.

"So, why is it that 'great expectations' were not placed upon you as well then? We were all witnesses of the same miracle that day?" Michael insisted.

"Now, that is a great question! Think it through, Michael. What was the Greenskeeper doing before the miracle happened?" John encouraged.

"You arrived at the flagpole just after sunset. But you took up your position and you stood your ground, at attention, and waited? Why not just play it? What did it matter?" Michael proposed.

"For the Greenskeeper, playing "Taps", at sunset, is a covenant. If the covenant is broken then the privileges are lost," John declared as he surveyed the Majestic from his location on the patio of the clubhouse.

"What privileges would be lost?" asked Michael inquisitively.

"The ability, of the Greenskeeper, to see the Final Foursomes among other things," he declared.

"How long were you going to stand there waiting?" he asked, as he looked in the direction of the flagpole.

"Until the sun rose in the west to set again. Until the covenant was restored or remade," John responded confidently. He was now looking westward and out beyond the deep purple horizon.

"But it wasn't your fault that you missed the sunset! You were dealing with me and Christopher. You were trying to help us. Set us straight. We made you late. It was our fault and not yours. Doesn't that matter?" Michael pleaded looking directly at John now.

"No. A covenant was broken. Here, at the Majestic of all places, the rules are important. How could the Greenskeeper lecture you and Christopher about the rules and not abide by them himself? Yet, there is a place for mercy and the possibility of new covenants, in this creation," said John still looking out to the horizon.

"Perhaps I see the answer to the 'expectations' question now," Michael revealed, as he turned from John and looked out into the deep purple horizon, "at the Majestic, seeing requires faith."

"Each greenskeeper, of the Majestic of Purple Mountain, has been tasked with 'great expectations'. Each different from the other. On that day, the Greenskeeper met face to face with one of those 'great expectations'. However, fulfilling these expectations in our humanity is impossible; fulfilling these expectations requires a miracle. The miracle of faith," John opined.

Chapter 15

There they stood, John and Michael on the porch of the clubhouse looking westward. They watched, as the purple twilight was swallowed up by star lit blackness. The moon, in an evening crescent, hung in the western sky at sixty degrees. To view it they would need to tilt their heads and slightly lift their eyes and look to the southwest sky.

The crowd on the eighteenth green had dispersed. Jessica, with scorecard tightly gripped, and her father Doug were already taking the tram down the south side of the mountain. The Greenskeeper lingered at the flagpole longer than normal before heading back to the cabin. The boys, Mike and Christopher, hurriedly returned to the cabin in hopes of getting there before the Greenskeeper.

As John and Michael stood on the porch of the clubhouse, they could hear the sound of voices carrying out of the main meeting room. Tonight was the annual meeting of the Minutemen Management Group. This group is under contract, with the city, to manage the course and its operations. It was unusual for them to conduct business after the playing of "Taps" but not unheard of. They decided to linger and listen to the discussion for just a few moments.

"Joshua, this is your first meeting with us as a partner. It is customary that the newest member describe, for the record, his view of the Majestic of Purple Mountain Golf Course. This description should include descriptions of the clubhouse, the course layout, and any other information that you deem important. Your descriptions will become part of our permanent records. Please begin when you are ready," declared Caleb.

"The Majestic is the living crown jewel of Purple Mountain. Her natural beauty is unequaled, her design unparalleled, her difficulty unmatched, her origins unknown, her secrets unimaginable and her reign unrivaled. She was created with a grand purpose; a purpose more grand than herself, more grand than her adornments or the mountain she rests upon. Despite her challenging demeanor, she was created to bring peace to those that have a conquering faith.

From a distance, the clubhouse appears as a sculpture cut from the mountain itself. This would be true, if it were not for the fact that it is made from sandstone imported from Aquia, Virginia. The clubhouse area marks the eastern most boundary of the Majestic of Purple Mountain. Its highest peak stands one hundred and forty-four feet above the highest playing surface of the course. As viewed from the west, it appears as the head of the course.

The three sectioned structure is of Corinthian order. A domed topped center section measuring one hundred feet square is connected to northern and southern sections measuring sixty feet by eighty feet each. The northern and southern structures are recessed by twenty feet on the west elevation. All three sections are flush across when viewed from the east elevation. The basement of the three floored structure is exposed on the west. In total the basement measures two hundred forty feet by three hundred and twenty feet. Portions of the roof of the basement section serve as the patio area. The patio area is outlined with a forty-eight inch wrought iron railing. The railing is made into ten foot sections. Each section has two parallel bars spaced three inches apart at the top. In the center area of each section are three hearts that are equally spaced and attached at two points to the lower of the top railings and at one point on the bottom railing. The railing sections are connected by vertical posts at the ends. The railings and posts are painted black. Staircases, northern and southern, descend from the midpoint of the western porch edge to reach a shared, ground level landing area. Viewed from the east, the stair cases form into the outline of a heart.

A walkway extending from the landing area of the staircase leads down a slope to the circular shaped flagpole pedestal. The pedestal is thirty-six feet in diameter with the flagpole set into the center. The flagpole reaches thirty-six feet into the air. The walkway and the pedestal are lined with thirty-six inch sandstone railings.

The entire complex is constructed with sandstone. The central dome, measuring fifty-four feet in diameter, has an iron skeleton and is clad in sandstone. It has a total of seventy-two windows. Small wooden domes are set into the center of the northern and southern structures. If it were not for changes made during the construction, the structure would have been a scaled down version of Thornton's Capitol.

The center section of the clubhouse serves as the main service and administrative section. The first floor houses the pro-shop and restaurant. A large circular area, known as the crypt, with eighteen Doric columns, each fluted with thirty-six parallel concave grooves, supports the floor of the rotunda.

The second floor houses administrative offices adjacent to the rotunda area. The walls of the rotunda are curved and made of sandstone. There are four entry ways, one each north, south, east and west. There are five framed niches between the north and east doorways. There are four framed niches between the east and south doorways. There are five framed niches between the south and west doorways. There are four framed niches between the west and north doorways. Fluted Doric pilasters, each with eighteen parallel concave grooves, separate the niches and doorways. Above the niches and doorways, carved into the sandstone, are representations of local flora. A fresco, the Apotheosis of Anson, adorns the eye of the rotunda. The belt of the rotunda, located thirty-six feet above the floor, has a circumference of one hundred and sixty-nine feet and remains unpainted to this day.

The third floor has been closed off since the late nineteen sixties. The original design called for the basement catacomb space to be used as a gallery. The floors of the basement are covered with inlaid encaustic tiles purchased from H&R Johnson Tiles Ltd., located at Stoke-on-Trent, England.

The north and south structures are like fraternal twins. They are similar in design and complementary in function. The first floors serve as locker room facilities. The upper floors were designed as meeting rooms and to accommodate banquets. Seventy-two sandstone columns adorn the perimeter of the structure and serve as supports for the entablatures. Were I to describe every detail of the structure, our meeting would never end.

Being a public course, all are welcome to play regardless of creed, color or gender. The same rules of golf apply to everyone without partiality. However, accessing the course grounds is controlled. There are three access routes to the course but only one is open to the public. When one chooses to come to the Majestic, they are confronted with its challenging approachability. All who play here are brought here by the same means.

The tram route is open to the public. The tram runs on the south side of the mountain. It is a descendant of the Locher rack system. It was selected for its stability in use with steep gradients and high winds. The three rail system uses a center rail with notches cut into the sides instead of on the top. These notches are engaged by gear teeth on two horizontally mounted cog wheels located under the drive engine. There is a single track and one tram. The tram runs up the mountain on the hour and half hour. It is a five minute ride from bottom to top and a ten minute wait at either end.

There is a controlled access service road that runs along the northern slope of the course. This second route is used for resupply and service of the clubhouse and maintenance facilities. The third access route is a restricted use utility easement that runs through the northern arm of the course.

Now for the course itself. Her left arm, the southern nine, measures three thousand six hundred and twenty yards. One is allowed thirty-six strokes over the first nine holes for a par score. The southern is composed of five par fours, two par threes and two par fives. Hole number one, the Washington, is the western most hole. From there the holes run southeast in direction until they pivot northeast on hole number five. On hole number eight the course changes directions again and finishes in a northwest direction. The holes sit atop three distinct ridges. From above, the holes would appear to run in a counter clockwise direction. Although this arm is slightly shorter than the other, it is challenging in its own right. This arm is a shot makers dream. Landing areas for tee shots are small but well defined. Players are greatly rewarded for hitting these areas and severely punished for missing them. Where the greens are generous in size, they are onerous in scoring. The player remaining faithful, to the execution of shot planning and placement, will be generously rewarded.

Her right arm, the northern nine, is the longer of the pair. Although nearly symmetrical with the southern arm, it measures three thousand seven hundred and twenty yards and has a par of thirty-six. The northern is composed of five par fours, two par threes and two par fives. Hole number ten is the western most hole of the north arm and is symmetrical with hole number one. From there the holes run northeast in direction until they pivot southeast on hole number fourteen. On hole number seventeen the course changes directions again and finishes in a southwest direction. The holes sit atop three distinct ridges. From above, the holes would appear to run in a clockwise direction. This arm is a risk takers dream. Landing areas for shot makers make for tempting targets from the tee but leave exceptionally difficult approach shots. Players are rewarded generously for hitting the stretch shot off of the tee. A successful stretch shot leaves the player with an exceptional scoring opportunity. Although its length is greater, its greens are smaller than those of the southern arm. They require a steadfast hand to ground their lightning speed. To be generously rewarded on the northern arm, one must add gallantry to the fidelity demonstrated on the southern arm.

It is not that one arm is stronger than the other. Rather, each arm compliments the other. Each arm has characteristics that challenge the best qualities of each individual player. Players demonstrating fidelity and gallantry will be well served by them. For here, at the Majestic of Purple Mountain, they will discover that their faith has been brought to fruition. When these finish their rounds, they will likely hear the words 'well done' and echoes of a familiar tune ringing in their ears," Joshua opined.

"Well, said!" declared Samson.

"I agree," said another Minuteman.

"Spoken as one who knows the mysteries of this mountain," said another.

"Apparently you know the Majestic quite well already. Wonderfully stated. Welcome!" Caleb commented.

"Thank you," said Joshua.

"Samson, please update us on our financial status," Caleb asked.

"Our financial position is strong. The facilities are operating normally and are in need of nothing from a maintenance perspective. Our rounds played are increasing year after year. We have an open relationship with the city leadership and they are pleased with our management of the course. We are in position to experience a long and prosperous future," Samson declared.

"Michael, I believe we should be moving along now?" John proposed as he began to walk in the direction of the cabin.

"This is fascinating! How is it possible that we are able to listen to these discussions? I wasn't here when they took place so long ago," Michael articulated still standing on western edge of the clubhouse porch.

"I am not entirely sure. Perhaps, the voices carried the short distance to the cabin and you actually heard them? It is another mystery," John supposed.

"Hmmm... possibly. Let's go to the cabin and listen then! Shall we?" Michael declared.

In an instant they were back at the cabin of the greenskeeper. The ice in the glasses had melted in the cups. Sweat ran down the sides of the glasses and began to collect in pools around the bottom of the two glasses sitting on the table. The boys had not yet returned.

"Whew . . . ok, looks like we made it," said Christopher, as he ran through the cabin door, panting from the run back from the eighteenth green, "hurry up and sit down!"

"OK! We did it! We made it back before he did. I knew it!" Mike asserted.

"You knew what? Oh, forget it. Just straighten up and try to look like we have been sitting here all this time," Christopher declared.

"How do I do that?" Mike asked.

"I don't know. Just act normal. Well, kinda normal anyway. Oh, just sit there and be quiet. I will handle this!" Christopher replied.

"I can hear him. He is coming!" Mike insisted.

"Well, . . . I see you are still here," John said as he entered the cabin. He placed the bugle back in the case and set it on the table by the door.

"Yes, we are," Christopher declared.

"Have you prepared an answer for me?" John asked the boys.

"Yes, we have," Christopher responded quickly, "we have decided to accept your offer,"

"Good . . . Good . . . A wise choice given the circumstances. Now I need to get you boys home," John stated.

"That is ok. We can manage the trip home but thank you for the offer," Christopher explained.

"No. It is too dangerous and too dark to use the utility easement. I have something else in mind. Come with me," John insisted, as he motioned to the boys to come to the front door.

The boys followed him down a path that led to the terminal point of the service road. This area is just a short distance from the cabin and is located near the north end of the clubhouse. To their surprise, they found their equipment loaded on the truck. However, this was not just any truck.

"Wow! A genuine W200 Dodge Power Wagon Crew cab? A 1967 with a big block 383 cubic inch V8, two speed transfer case with a four speed transmission? An eight foot cargo box on a three quarter ton chassis? Really?" Christopher ventured in amazement. This truck was everything he dreamed of. He had seen them in books but never had the honor of seeing one in person.

"Really! Now get in and I will get you boys home," John insisted. The boys excitedly jumped into the cab of the truck and headed for home.

Michael and John watched them load up from a distance. The truck headed down the mountain and the boys were beginning a new adventure. The lives of Mike and Christopher were now on a path that passed through this mountain and the home they left earlier that afternoon would never be the same for them again.

"Where are we off to now?" John asked as he watched the tail lights of the Power Wagon disappear into the blackness.

"Not sure. I am thinking about it. But I think I have an exceptionally good idea of 'when' we are going to!" Michael asserted, as he watched the Power Wagon drive off and into the blackness of the mountain night.

Chapter 16

Michael and John arrived at the morning of May 9, 1987, like a train arriving at the station right on schedule.

A light frost dusted the windows of the tram, as it sat warming for its first run of the day. The tram was painted deep blue on the exterior with red trim. The inside of the tram was solid white. Boarding the tram at the base station was always awkward. Due to the steep incline the seats inside the tram face down the mountain. It was a short ride to the clubhouse of the Majestic from the base station. The first tram was the least traveled but most enjoyable tram of them all. The mountain seemed more alive in the morning. In the morning, bright flowers seemed brighter, green grasses seemed greener, blue skies seemed bluer, puffy white clouds seemed whiter and wildlife seemed wilder. As one traveled up the mountain, the old world seemed to fade away, as the frost melted from the windows of the tram. A new world was revealed, no longer seen as through darkened glass, rather, as through crystal.

"So, this is what it looks like from the other end of the mountain in the morning?" John commented as he stood on the platform of the tram station. "I have never caught the morning Majestic."

"Well, then, this will be a treat. Somehow I thought there was nothing you hadn't done here?" Michael postulated as he entered the tram door. "Come and sit with me. We are ascending the mountain!"

"Believe it or not, there are many things that I haven't done here on this mountain," John declared as he boarded the tram and took a seat at a window.

"The boys, Christopher and Mike, will be here soon. This is their first time riding the tram," Michael added, as he sat a seat above where John was sitting. From here they would have a panoramic view during the short ride up the mountain.

"Here they come," John announced as they watched them.

The boys waved, to their mother, as she slowly pulled her car away from the drop-off area of the station. The boys ran directly to the tram and climbed aboard. They were quickly seated.

"Are you ready for this?" Mike asked his older brother.

"Not really. I could think of a lot of things I would rather be doing than going up there to work today. But we made a promise and we are going to keep it. That doesn't mean I have to like it," Christopher stated as he looked out the window.

"I don't know how I feel about it yet. I will wait and see. I hope he doesn't work us too hard? I guess he won't," Mike said, as he too looked out the window.

"Who knows? Probably not. A guy with a Dodge Power Wagon can't be all that bad?" Christopher reckoned, as he smiled at his younger brother.

"I am sorry that I got us into this mess," said Mike looking at Christopher.

"You? We got into it together and together we will work our way through it! Now stop it and I don't want to hear that anymore! Got it?" Christopher insisted.

"All right, no more of that. Got it. That 'Power Wagon' is the coolest though," Mike said smiling, as the tram began to lurch forward. "Here we go!"

"Hey," Christopher nudged Mike, "wanna take a look through these?" he suggested laughing. He was holding a pair of binoculars, backwards, up to his eyes and looking out the window.

"What are you doing! Let me see!" Mike insisted as he grabbed at them.

"Vertigo!" Christopher yelled, before he removed them from his face and handed them to Mike.

"Seriously, weird! I never knew the world could look like that! Cool!" Mike said as he looked out the window and down the mountain while alternating the focus of the glasses. He stopped suddenly as he felt a sense of déjà vu. "Here, you can have them back now."

The tram reached the mountain station and came to a quick stop. The boys hopped down and off of the tram. They began their short walk to the cabin of the greenskeeper.

Michael and John were already waiting at the cabin when the boys arrived. Although the door was open, the boys stood outside and waited. They dared not enter without permission.

"Mr. John, sir," Christopher called through the open doorway, "it is Christopher and Mike and we are here to work today. Are you here?"

"Come on in boys. The door is open," John insisted while calling to them from the kitchen, "I will be out there in a few minutes."

Mike and Christopher gingerly walked through the doorway. It was as if they expected someone to jump out at them. They found themselves sitting again in the same places

139

where they had sat during their first visit. This despite trying to avoid the memory of it.

There was a copy of the Worthington Times laying on the table between them. Mike moved to take a closer look.

"Saturday, May 9, 1987, . . . Sunset is at 8:22 PM . . . moon phase" Mike hesitated, "waxing gibbous . . . headline . . . Almendine Mining company . . . purchases land on the east side of Purple Mountain . . . former location of St. Margaret Mary's Industrial School for boys that has been shuttered . . .," Mike read from the front page aloud and then stopped reading.

"Hey, 'Paul Harvey' what's the 'Rest of The Story'?" Christopher grinned as he asked Mike.

"What? Who is 'Paul Harvey'?" asked Mike with a perplexed look.

"Never mind who he is. What does the article say?" Christopher asked.

"Let me see," Mike said as he put his face into the newspaper, "Axis Energy . . . largest employer in Worthington . . . plans to build headquarters . . . promises to bring more jobs to area . . . says Alexander Garnet, President of Axis Energy."

"Well, now gentlemen, it is good to see you here so bright and early today. Perhaps you are hungry and would like to eat some breakfast? It will be a long morning before we break for lunch," the Greenskeeper asked while standing in the doorway to the kitchen area.

"Sure, thank you!" Mike spoke up before Christopher could stop him.

"That is kind of you, Mr. John. Yes, we would," Christopher replied feeling pushed into acceptance by his brother's remark.

"Please come into the kitchen and we will eat," he announced.

The kitchen was on the southwest corner of the cabin. The boys walked through the dining area to access it. Eating in a kitchen is informal. It gives one the impression of closeness and the feeling of being family. In this case, it served to relieve the tension of the moment.

They sat in the breakfast nook area between the kitchen and dining room. The chairs were wooden and painted red. The table was small. It measured three feet by four feet and was made of wood. Its top was painted blue and the legs white. Three plates, loaded with breakfast staples, were sitting on the table. There were pancakes, eggs, bacon, butter milk biscuits, sausage gravy, apple butter and maple syrup. It was the kind of breakfast one would have back at grandmas house.

"Let us give thanks," the Greenskeeper said bowing his head, "Lord, we ask your blessing on this day and on this food. I ask that you would lead and guide us through this day and that our actions would be pleasing to you. In the name of your son, Jesus, I pray these things. Amen."

"Amen," Christopher and Mike said, in the same breath, before they started to eat.

"Thank you for this meal. We appreciate your making it for us. So, what will we be doing today?" Christopher asked, breaking the silence.

"Your welcome," he said with a smile looking at the boys, "we will take some time and get to know the course. After that, I will have an assignment for each of you to complete. When the assignments are finished it will be getting close to lunch time. We will come back here for lunch and then head out for our afternoon activities," John declared as he poured coffee from a coffee press into his cup. It had been sitting there, steeping, since they entered the room.

"That sounds good to me," said Mike as he took a bite out of the sandwich he made out of the biscuit and some of the items on his plate.

"May I ask, when will we finish for the day?" Christopher probed. He nearly didn't ask, considering the amount of work the Greenskeeper put into making breakfast for them. But it didn't stop him from asking.

"You may leave whenever you feel it is time to go. I will consider your obligation complete for the day once we finish our lunch," he said.

"But you said we had 'afternoon' activities'?" asked Mike with his plate nearly empty.

"Yes, I did. You will have to wait until then for the details," the Greenskeeper responded.

"That sounds fair enough!" Christopher announced with a smile. He was finished eating. He was counting the hours in his head and planned on a quick exit after lunch. This was going to be easier than he thought.

Michael and John watched them eat from the dining room. Michael was enjoying his trip down memory lane. They watched as the boys helped the Greenskeeper clear the table. Then the boys and the Greenskeeper left the room and headed out the cabin door. They were headed to the first tee, so they could walk the course.

"When did you get that coffee canister? The one shaped like Purple Mountain," Michael asked John. He saw it sitting on the counter in the kitchen and remembered seeing it long ago.

"It was a gift from a friend," John replied casually, "don't you think we should be following them? They just left!"

"Not just yet. So, how did you know that we were hungry? What gave it away?" Michael confided in asking the question.

"All teenage boys and their younger brothers are always hungry! Even I knew that. Besides, I wanted to see what kind of manners I was going to be dealing with. I must say that I was impressed," John commented with a smile.

"You expect me to believe that, I suppose?" Michael responded.

"Of course I do. Speaking of course, we need to be headed out. They will reach the first hole soon," John stated as he headed out of the dining room and toward the front door.

"All right. It is time to catch up with them now," said Michael, as he slowly walked from the kitchen. As he walked, he looked around the room taking in every detail. He did the same visual inspection of the main room of the cabin on his way out the front door. He joined John, and they headed off to the first tee.

Chapter 17

"Boys, I hope you have your walking shoes on today!" the Greenskeeper remarked as they walked across the patio of the clubhouse.

"Wow! What a view!" yelled Mike as he looked out westward from the western edge of the clubhouse patio. The three of them stopped there together.

Mike, Christopher and the Greenskeeper were standing at the railing between the two staircases. They were at the exact midpoint of the back wall of the patio. The boys stood on either side of him. To the west, out to the horizon, they could see rolling foothills. To the west and down the slopes, of Purple Mountain, they could see part of the city of Worthington. From here it was easy to survey the entire course. To their left was the south arm of the course and the north arm was to their right. At a fifty-three degree angle to their right and one hundred yards away sat the center of the eighteenth green. Sixty yards directly in front of them was the flagpole. It sat in the center of the circular flagpole pedestal. They could hear the flag as it whipped in the moderate morning breeze. At a fifty-three degree angle and one hundred yards to their left sat the center of the ninth green.

The course sits on six distinct ridges with each arm, of the course, having three. There are two each of lower, middle and upper ridges. Each ridge on the north arm is symmetrical in elevation, slope and direction with its twin on the south arm.

"The Majestic of Purple Mountain, quite a sight isn't it?" the Greenskeeper suggested.

"It is almost heart shaped? But it looks upside down from here," Christopher commented.

"It looks like an opened heart shaped locket. You know, the kind mom has. When it is closed it looks like a half of a heart. But when opened, it becomes heart shaped. Too bad it is upside down though," Mike insisted.

"I am not sure I ever saw it that way from here. Well, we need to keep moving," The Greenskeeper declared, as he moved toward the stairs.

They descended the stair case, at the west side, of the clubhouse patio. Mike took the stairs to the left and Christopher the right stairs. At the bottom of the stairs is a landing area. There are three pathways that one may choose from. The pathway headed due west leads to the flagpole area. It is the center pathway and the one with the thirty-six inch tall sandstone railings. The pathway to the right, leads to the tenth hole and the north arm of the course. The pathway to the left, leads to the first hole and the south arm of the course. They walked down the left pathway. It was neither a long nor a short walk. They would arrive at the first tee box shortly. Christopher led the way with Mike and the Greenskeeper following.

"What is that? A hoof print?" Mike said, as he bent down to look at something just off of the pathway.

"Nelson!" the Greenskeeper groaned, as he passed by the scene, "I asked him to keep that mischievous creature on the pathways. I will have to talk with him about it again. Let's keep moving, Mike."

"Who is Nelson?" Mike asked.

"Never mind. Let's keep moving. We will be at the first tee shortly," he said.

Michael and John were waiting for them to arrive at the first tee. They were standing near the back of the center tee box. From this vantage point they had a great view of the pathway leading to the hole from the clubhouse.

"I had nearly forgotten how breathtaking the view is here on the first tee," Michael declared as he surveyed the setting.

"Yes, the Washington hole is a special place and beautiful as well. Of all the places on the course, I have probably spent the most time here on this one tee box," John commented, as he turned to look at the upper tee box. "What is he doing up there?"

"Who? Where?" asked Michael?

"On the gold tee! I don't believe it. I didn't see him back there, back then? I couldn't have missed it?" John questioned himself, as he looked intently at the gold tee box area.

"It looks like a man and he has some equipment with him. Who is he and what is he doing?" Michael questioned as he too looked in that direction.

"I know who it is and exactly what he is doing!" John announced, as he continued to look in that direction. "It is George Washington! He is here earlier than expected today."

"What does he have with him? Why is he here so early today?" Michael asked, conceding the fact that seeing him wasn't a surprise. Michael was not just repeating John's words. He was remembering the events of the summer of 1987. These events had been buried in his mind for a long time.

"He has a compass, transit and a Gunter's chain," John identified the items and continued, "not much is known of his early childhood. During his adolescence, he went on a surveying journeys through Virginia's Western territories plotting land. He was required to keep surveyors notes but they have been lost to the ages. However, his surveying exercises made him stronger in mind and body. It also led to his having an interest in the colonization of the West."

"Thanks for the history lesson, 'Christopher'," Michael said with a smile, "sometimes you sound like him, you know. Anyway, what is he doing back there?" Michael asked, in amazement.

"It looks as if he is surveying the hole," John replied watching Washington's every move. He was using the compass and then the transit. He then made some notes in a small book. He collected his things and put them into a duffle that laid on the ground by his feet. Then he pulled out the Gunter's chain. A Gunter's chain was the main tool of the surveyor. It was used to measure distance. Eighty of them strung end to end would equal a mile, more or less. This one appeared to be made of brass. The chain was 22 yards long and was made of one hundred interconnected lengths. The beginning and ending lengths had large rings attached. These were used as an aid in carrying the apparatus and in keeping it in place during use. He then staked one end of the Gunter's chain into the ground and began to walk toward the fairway.

"Why?" Michael asked again.

"I am not sure. He has been known to show up here from time to time apart from his official duties. This one is unusual, I will give you that!" John said with a bewildered look about him, as the surveyor walked past them. "Don't worry, we will see him again."

"Have you ever seen him doing this before?" Michael asked.

"No. Can't say that I have," John said as he watched George continue to walk down toward the fairway. "I have

the Majestic of Purple Mountain

seen many things but not this one. I am still amazed by what goes on up here at the Majestic!"

"OK. This is a bit unusual. It is not every day that I see our first president surveying a golf course! But, I will go along with it for now. Why not. What can it hurt?" Michael said, in bewilderment, being just a few chain lengths away from disbelief. "OK, setting the survey crew aside, why did you spend so much time here on the first tee?" Michael asked, keeping the conversation going until the boys arrived.

"You will remember soon enough," John replied softly, knowing that Michael would soon turn his attention to the boys.

"Here they come," Michael announced. He was getting the hang of visiting these places now and was feeling increasingly comfortable with each site they visited. "I always thought I looked bad at that age. I just never realized how bad. I was a husky kid with long straight hair parted in the middle. At least my mom had the sense to cut my bangs short. Look at those clothes!"

"True!" John confirmed, with a grin on his face.

"You didn't have to agree so quickly you know," Michael replied while continuing to watch the boys. "I did idolize him, didn't I? It is so obvious, as I watch it now. I even tried to walk like him. Look at that."

"I believe you did– 'idolize him' and with good reason. What eight year old doesn't look up to his sixteen year old brother? He was learning too. This was a turning point for him," John observed, as he watched the boys approach.

"A turning point? How so? This punishment turned him around or something?" Michael asked.

"A good father chastens his son. Not to benefit the father but for the benefit of the son. For we all go astray but chastening can lead us home. It is our response, to it, that builds character. Sometimes the character built is honorable and sometimes dishonorable," John asserted as he intently watched the boys.

"Why is honor the result in some and dishonor in others?" Michael asked.

"You said 'why' but that why question is always a tough one for me. Perhaps we will see the answer somewhere along the way," John remarked, continuing to focus on the boys. The boys were intently watching the Greenskeeper.

The Greenskeeper was delivering his training monologue to the boys. He seemed more like a drill sergeant now than a greenskeeper. This was not the first group of mischiefs to be put to work nor would it be the last. However, something was different about these two. The Greenskeeper could sense it.

"Now gentlemen, do you understand the rules?" the Greenskeeper pronounced.

"Yes, sir," the boys said in unison.

"Christopher, what is your assignment this morning?" he asked.

"My assignment is to determine a new location for the gold tee markers on each tee box. They must be moved at least two club lengths from their current position. However, they must be no closer than two yards from the back or front edges of the tee box," Christopher recited.

"Great! Now Mike, what is your assignment?" he asked.

"My assignment is to move the gold tees to their new place. Christopher will tell me where to put them," Mike repeated.

"That is it exactly. While you are adjusting your tee markers, I will handle the blue, white and red tees that require adjustment. All right then, lets start working," the Greenskeeper declared.

All three adjusted their markers. The Greenskeeper gave each of the boys a few small pointers but they followed the instructions quite well. They knew the game enough to know the basics of tee marker placement. However, the Greenskeeper talked with them about the importance of tee marker placement and the impact it had on the play of the game. He called each of the boys to the white tee markers after they were finished.

"Gentlemen, this is the Washington hole. It is the first hole of the Majestic of Purple Mountain. What do either of you know about George Washington?" the Greenskeeper asked as he stood in the middle of the tee box.

"He was our first President! His picture is on the dollar bill!" said Mike confidently.

"How about you?" the Greenskeeper asked looking at Christopher.

"Not much is known of his childhood, except that he spent time in Western Virginia on a survey crew. I think he was about sixteen then. As a major in the Virginia militia, in his early twenties, he was a leader at a young age. At this young age, he led men into battle in the French and Indian War. He was a farmer and cattle owner and owned an estate called Mt. Vernon. He was a member of the Virginia House of Burgesses and was appointed Commander-in Chief of the colonial army during our war with the British. He helped us gain our independence from Britain and he was elected to serve as our first president," Christopher said with a straight face knowing that he had just impressed the drill sergeant. "I wrote a report about him in school this year."

"That is a great biography, Christopher. I can picture him at about your age. Imagine him being right over there," the Greenskeeper now pointing his finger at the gold tee box, "can't you just see him with his surveyors tools? Imagine him holding a compass, transit and Gunter's chain in his hands? Perhaps he was here, on one of those surveying missions he took in Western Virginia? Anyway, what did you find most interesting about him?" the Greenskeeper queried.

"First would have to be his indomitable spirit," Christopher proposed.

"You say 'indomitable'. Now that is a good word choice," the Greenskeeper replied with eyebrow lifted. "What does it mean?"

"The Latin root word means to tame. When you add the prefix of 'in' the root word is changed to a negative. So, it means not to tame," Christopher contended. "Again, part of the school assignment. We were required to choose a word to best describe him."

"What made you choose that word to describe him?" he asked.

"I probably read it somewhere along the way and liked it? I am not sure," Christopher replied shrugging his shoulders, "but, he never gave up. Some of his first military experiences ended in failure. He was defeated a few times early in his military career and he learned from it. He didn't quit!"

"Interesting. Most people focus on his successes in the Revolutionary War or as our first president. What else did you find interesting about him?" the Greenskeeper asked.

"He respected the common soldier. He respected the little guy. So much so, that he created a special medal. It was the Badge of Military Merit. In the British army, lower ranks were not awarded such things. Washington said with this award that 'the road to glory in a patriot army is thus open to all'," Christopher declared.

"Tell me more about this 'Badge of Military Merit'?" the Greenskeeper asked.

"The award was given, to a soldier, in recognition of a single act of merit. It was made of purple cloth and was cut in the shape of a heart. It had the word 'merit' sewn into it. It was pinned to the uniform coat just above the left breast. When a rank and file soldier wore one, he was allowed into places reserved for officers only and allowed in without question. His name and regiment were written in the *Book of Merit* maintained by George Washington himself," Christopher maintained while looking at the Greenskeeper.

"What happened to this award? Does it still exist? And what of that *Book of Merit* you speak of? What happened to it?" the Greenskeeper replied full well knowing the answers.

"The award is now known as the Purple Heart. A few of the original badges still exist and are in museums I think. The *Book of Merit* was lost and has never been found. At least that is what I remember from doing the report," Christopher remarked, running out of things to say about his report.

"You stole his report! I can't believe you! Do you have no shame?" Michael asserted, after listening to the entire exchange between Christopher and the Greenskeeper.

"I don't know what you are talking about!" John said, as he looked away laughing.

"Well, at least he got you that day! You had no idea Christopher knew that much about George Washington. Now did you?" Michael said.

"Keep watching and listening. The best is yet to come," John stated with a grin. John and Michael would follow them through the first green, watching and listening.

"Impressive!" the Greenskeeper lauded Christopher as he began to walk toward the fairway. The boys kept pace on either side. "Now about this first hole. The player with an indomitable spirit will score well on this invincible hole. It measures four hundred yards from the gold tees and is a par four. The hole is practically straight from tee through green. The fairway is generally sloped from right to left. There is a level landing area two hundred and thirty yards out and on the right side of the fairway. Hitting the landing area leaves the golfer with a level approach shot into the green. Missing that landing area is costly to the player. If he is left of the target he will face a side hill lie. If he is long he is faced with a downhill lie."

"I guess it is a hard hole to play then?" Mike commented.

"Yes, it is," The Greenskeeper answered.

"I don't understand. You said an 'indomitable spirit' can score well on an 'invincible hole'. Isn't that a contradiction?" Christopher questioned as he walked along side the Greenskeeper.

"The Majestic of Purple Mountain, you will find, is full of paradoxes and mysteries. Although she is intriguing, she is nonetheless true. You will find no contradictions in her," the Greenskeeper stated as he continued to walk.

"I still don't understand?" Christopher responded as Mike continued to walk with them and listen intently to the conversation. They had passed the landing area and were walking down the sloped fairway. A few dozen yards ahead it sloped back up and eventually led to an elevated green.

"OK. Let's work through a contradiction then," the Greenskeeper proposed as they continued to walk. "Look around you. You see this beautiful mountain, the grass, trees, flowers and the blue skies? All of nature was created by God. Wouldn't you agree?"

"Yes, God is the creator," Christopher answered.

"God is omnipotent. He is all powerful and able to do anything. Nothing is more powerful than God. Wouldn't you agree?" the Greenskeeper asked.

"Yes, that is what I have been taught to think about God. I would agree," Christopher responded as the three approached the first green.

"Then answer this riddle. Can God create a rock, so heavy, that he can't lift?" the Greenskeeper proposed as he stopped beside the first green.

"Well, . . . yes I think he could. He can create anything. But then . . . he wouldn't be all powerful any longer? But, if he can't create something then is he still all powerful? Oh . . . I don't know. This is confusing!" Christopher answered, shaking his head from side to side.

"Why would he want to?" Mike interjected, after remaining silent during the conversation.

"Precisely!" the Greenskeeper announced. "The problem is in the question itself! God is not the author of confusion. My riddle was not a riddle after all. It was a contradictory statement. Contradictions can't be solved or reconciled."

"So, where does that leave us with your 'indomitable spirit' and 'invincible hole' statement? That is what we were talking about," Christopher reminded them.

"My statement was a 'hyperbole'. It was not a contradiction," the Greenskeeper answered with a smile.

"A 'hy—perb— a— what? I don't understand?" Mike said looking at the Greenskeeper.

"A hyperbole. It means an exaggeration," he replied.

"I still don't understand?" Mike replied.

"It is like something you say to get a point across. OK, suppose your brother hits long tee shots. What do you say to describe that to me?" the Greenskeeper asked Mike.

"I might say he 'hits the ball a long way'?" Mike responded.

"Something else maybe? This time tell me how 'long' a long way is," the Greenskeeper asked.

"I might say 'he can hit the ball a . . . mile'?" he said shrugging his shoulders and whispering, "but he really can't you know! Is that better?"

"Yes! So in your example, does the ball really go a 'mile'?" the Greenskeeper hypothesized.

"No. It is just a saying," Mike responded.

"Exactly!" the Greenskeeper observed.

"Mr. John, sir, are you teaching us writing and debating skills? Or, are we here to work the course?" Christopher asked directly, wanting to move the day along.

"Neither," he responded, as he began to walk toward the second tee. "Let's keep moving."

The boys followed him for the remainder of the morning. They adjusted the tees on every gold tee box working together as brothers. As the morning progressed, the Greenskeeper introduced them to the Majestic of Purple Mountain.

After all of the tee markers had been adjusted, the Greenskeeper assigned the boys their individual tasks. Christopher was assigned sand trap duties from the Lincoln through the eighteenth green. Mike was assigned mowing duties on the same. The Greenskeeper escorted them back to the Lincoln hole where their tools were waiting for them. These were basic tools and consisted of a rake and a push rotary mower.

"I can't believe you made me push that old mower! It was probably a violation of some child labor laws or something," Michael declared as he and John stood on the Lincoln tee box. They had been waiting for the group to arrive here and begin their work.

"I will agree with 'or something' as you put it!" John commented, as he looked at the mower sitting across the fairway. "The way I see it, you needed to mow more than the course needed mowing."

155

"Explain this to me. How is it that the first cut of the rough looked fine on our first pass through and only twenty minutes later was in need of mowing? Also, how in the world could you expect me to cut all of that?" Michael questioned.

"Like we have heard already today, the Majestic is full of mysteries!" John claimed with a smile. Michael and John moved out and into the south fairway of the sixteenth, for a better view.

"I have to rake all of these?" Christopher said to the Greenskeeper, while pointing to the various traps that lined the south Lincoln fairway.

"No," the Greenskeeper answered.

"Whew, that is good," Christopher remarked, taking the rake in hand and entering the first trap.

"No. Not only these, but when you are finished with the traps on the south fairway please rake the ones on the north fairway as well," the Greenskeeper disclosed, while he pointed to the north fairway. Don't miss a one of them."

"I'll be lucky if I don't die in a sand trap!" Christopher muttered under his breath, as he kept raking.

"Now as for you, let me introduce you to Silens Messor," the Greenskeeper said, looking in the direction of where Mike stood.

"Who is 'Silens Messor'?" Mike asked.

"This is Silens Messor" the Greenskeeper said, pointing to the reel mower sitting in the first cut of the rough.

"Why call it that. It is just a mower?" Mike asked, looking at the apparatus he was expected to push.

"He likes being called that because it sounds better than silent cutter," the Greenskeeper explained.

"How does it work?" Mike asked, while continuing to look at the mower.

"You push and he cuts," the Greenskeeper continued, "as you push, the bar in the back turns and drives a chain that is connected to the cutting reel. As you push harder the blades spin quicker. Remember this, quicker blades cut the grass easier than slower blades."

"It looks kinda old? Does it even work?" Mike commented, as he looked at the mower.

"He may be old, but he will help you get the job done," the Greenskeeper replied.

This mower, Silens Messor, was like scissors in the hands of a barber. The mower had a T-shaped wooden handle that led down to a bracket that attached to the axel of the mower. The wheels were twelve inches in diameter and it cut a path eighteen inches wide. It had seven curved cutting blades. Three blades were painted red and the others blue. The shaft and discs that connected them were painted white. When in operation and viewed from a distance, it looked like a barber's pole turned on its side. When the blades spun fast enough, the cutting reel took on a purple hue.

Despite its antique appearance, it held several advantages over other, more modern, mowers. Firstly, its design produced less stress on the grass being cut and produced a more uniform cut. Secondly, it was nearly silent and created no distractions for the players. Lastly, it was inexpensive to operate, as it required no fuel and was powered by a renewable resource.

"Mr. John, sir. Where am I cutting with this . . . 'Silens Messor'?" Mike asked looking at the Greenskeeper.

"Start here," the Greenskeeper took the mower, in hand, while standing on the fringe of the south Lincoln fairway, "and keep the inside wheel, the one facing the fairway, just outside the line where the grass gets shorter. And then push it a mile!"

"Mr. John, sir," Mike paused looking up at him after they had stopped. The Greenskeeper pushed the mower for a few yards as an example.

"Yes, What is it? Do you understand?" he replied.

"Please tell me that you just used one of those 'hyperboles'?" Mike said, with a smile, as he took the mower in hand and began to push.

"Wait! You will need these," the Greenskeeper announced.

"Why do I need glasses, gloves and an orange hat?" Mike asked as he stopped mowing.

"Safety!" the Greenskeeper replied, while he placed the items on Mike. "The glasses will protect your eyes, the gloves your hands and the orange hat will make you noticeable to anyone playing the course that may come along."

"So, how long are we going to stand here and watch?" John asked Michael as they stood on the Lincoln tee box watching the two boys working.

"Until Christopher rakes all the sand in the Arabian desert and until Mike pushes that mower a million miles!" Michael mused in hyperbole.

Chapter 18

"So, how long are we going to stay with this first day of the program? Have you seen enough? Have you seen what you are looking for? Are you ready to head back to the cabin? Then you can call it a night and jump in that Jeep and drive back to town? And never come back?" John questioned Michael.

"I am not quite ready for that just yet. There are a few things I need to see before we leave this place," Michael responded, as he walked through the opened barn doors.

A few yards away from the greenskeeper's cabin was a barn. It is the only structure, located on the grounds of the Majestic, made entirely from wood. It is almost unnoticeable and is tucked into a grove of trees. It is twenty-four feet wide by thirty-two feet long. Standing thirty-two feet tall, it has two stories. The structure is painted white and trimmed in red and blue. There are two main doors measuring six feet wide by eight feet tall cut into the western wall. There are six windows, three feet wide by four feet tall, cut into the north and south walls each. There are three on the first floor and three on the second. Each wooden window frame contained four panes of wavy glass. There is a single door on the east end of similar size to those on the west.

The surface of the ground floor is made of timbers and is nearly impervious to moisture. The timbers are black as coal, in color, and have a semi smooth surface. It looks as if someone stripped away the soil and uncovered anthracite coal. It was as if someone etched its surface to make it look like inlaid timbers. However, anthracite coal was not common to this area.

The first floor area looked like a car garage. The kind of garage where old cars were restored and given new life. It was organized and well kept. In the back of the barn was a single horse stall. The worn name plate affixed to the door read 'N LSN'. The second floor loft area covered the back half of the structure. It was accessed using a stairway that was on the north side of the barn. It wasn't like a garage at all. It was more like the studio of an artist.

"This is just how I remembered it! Look at it! It is still in pieces!" Michael remarked as he looked around the barn.

"Yes, every piece needed to put it back together is here. The barn hasn't looked like this in years. It was so full of life back then," John observed, as he leaned on the frame of the barn door.

"Yeah. I think we are about to witness some of that 'life' in a few minutes. Assuming I timed it right?" Michael presumed as he began to walk up the stairs to take a position in the loft.

"Have you ever been up there before?" John asked while still standing in the doorway.

"I don't remember. What I do remember is working on finding the pieces needed to put that thing together. Is there something I should know about the loft?" Michael queried. To Michael, John appeared as a perfect silhouette of a man. Perhaps it was due to the lighting conditions of the moment. But he looked more like a painting at the moment than an actual person. Well, as much as a person can look like an actual person from within a memory or from within whatever this was.

"There is plenty you should know. I am just not sure you want to know this part of it now. Perhaps it would be better if you went up there later. Besides, the view will be better from down here. Your view will be obstructed from up there," John maintained, still standing at the doorway.

"Intriguing," Michael hesitated at the bottom of the stairs considering what John had said, "I think the view will be better from down here," Michael stated as he backed away from the stairs. He made a mental note to come back and visit the loft.

"I can hear them coming," John warned Michael. They moved to the rear of the first floor and stood under the loft overhang.

"Now gentlemen. Your official duties are complete for the day. You are free to leave and head home now," the Greenskeeper told them while standing just outside the open barn doors.

"Mr. John, sir. I thought that you said we had 'afternoon activities'?" Mike insisted as he tried to look into the dimly lit barn.

"Yes, I did. Didn't I?" the Greenskeeper replied, as he looked at the boys. He continued, "would you like to know what they are?"

"Yes, I would!" Mike announced excitedly.

"Christopher?" the Greenskeeper asked, while looking directly at him.

"What can it hurt to listen now?" he responded. This arrangement, working the course on Saturdays, had a serious effect on Christopher and his plans. He had a summer job lined up but he had lost it. He knew it was his fault but that was no consolation. He planned on saving money for a car. But that plan was gone now.

"Good. Follow me," the Greenskeeper replied as he turned and walked through the open barn doors. It was dark, as the shutters over the windows were closed. The open barn doors provided the only light. The boys funneled in behind him.

"Is that what I think it is?" Christopher observed, as his eyes surveyed the room.

"And what do you 'think it is'?" the Greenskeeper asked.

"A 1941 Willys MB?" Christopher uttered. He slowly walked around the disassembled relic of a vehicle that was sitting on jack stands. There were pieces of the vehicle, spread out, all over the room. There was an engine on an engine stand and a transmission was sitting, in a corner, on the floor. The hood was standing up against the wall. It was lettered with white paint. The letters were 'U S A'. Below the 'U S A' was a partial serial number of 'W 2 0 1 8 9' that was barely visible beneath the dust. On the opposite side of the room, from the hood, was the split window windshield. A neatly organized pile of parts sat on the floor just under the loft. There were tires, a bumper, gas can, seats and too many other items to mention or identify in that pile. It was just the stuff that an enterprising mechanic would need.

"Good eye, Christopher. I thought you might know. Not many sixteen year olds would have known what a Power Wagon is but you knew it the other night. That tipped me off," the Greenskeeper divulged.

Christopher quickly fired off the questions, "how did it get here? Who owns it? What are you going to do with it?" He began to circle the Jeep and make mental notes of its status and what it would take to repair it. Everything is here he thought.

The Greenskeeper, as he looked at the disassembled Jeep, began to explain, "it is mine and I got it from my father. He got it after World War II and used it for a while. Then he parked it out at the farm in a barn. It sat there for years until I brought it here. I always planned on restoring it. I started the project once. The engine and transmission work are complete. But I have never found the time to finish it."

"Wow. That looks really old. Do you think you can fix it?" Mike uttered his first words since entering the barn.

"Ye–" Christopher began to respond before being interrupted by the Greenskeeper.

"I don't know? It has been a long time since I have worked on a project like this," the Greenskeeper responded.

"Yes . . . Mike. I know I can fix it!" Christopher announced as he stood next to the Jeep with his hand on the fender. The fender was not attached and quickly gave way under his weight and fell to the ground. "I can fix that too!"

"Now, about those afternoon activities–" the Greenskeeper began to say but was interrupted by Christopher.

"I will stay! Where are the tools? When can I start?" Christopher exclaimed as he scurried about the room picking up various parts then setting them back down.

"Wait! You have not heard what the activities are yet," the Greenskeeper cautioned.

"OK," Christopher stopped where he stood with steering wheel in hand, "what do you have in mind?"

"This is what I propose. You stay here and work on the Jeep after our morning sessions. If you can have this thing running by the time school starts in the fall, it is yours to keep. I will get anything you need in parts or supplies and you can use my tools. But you must have it running before school starts up. Oh, and your mom must agree with your keeping it," the Greenskeeper proposed.

"Mr. John, sir. You are being serious? Do you really mean it?" Christopher asked in a small voice.

"Yes, I really mean it," he replied.

"Why would you do this for me? Especially after what I had done. With sneaking on the course and all of that," Christopher asked.

The Greenskeeper declared, "you were forgiven for your offense and you accepted the consequences for your actions. Christopher, I have faith in you and your abilities. You have a special gift for fixing things. So, fix it already!"

"What about Mike? What is his assignment?" Christopher asked now thinking of his brother.

"I have something special in mind for you! I didn't think you would be too interested in fixing up the old Jeep. Anyway, I have been looking for an apprentice?" the Greenskeeper asked Mike.

"Christopher is really good at fixing things and he does need a car soon. He planned on buying one someday. I am happy for him," he said looking at Christopher. "So, what is an 'apprentice'?" Mike asked.

"You will do everything that I do. You will come with me in the afternoons and learn what it is to be the greenskeeper of the Majestic of Purple Mountain. Does this sound interesting to you?" he asked.

"As long as I don't have to push that mower all afternoon, it does! When do we start?" Mike replied.

The Greenskeeper answered, "we will start right away. Once we get Christopher settled here, we will hit the course."

Still viewing this memory, were Michael and John. They were watching from the shadows underneath the loft.

Michael began, "he loved that Jeep you know! This exact moment was a turning point for him. He loved fixing things and this just ignited his passion for it. But he needed someone to believe in him. He needed someone to give him a chance and a challenge. He never quit fixing Jeeps after this. Yeah, the name has changed to a Humvee but it is still the same. He would enlist in the military after high school. Then he spent his career in the military fixing equipment like this. He was good at it and he earned the respect of his unit. It was his passion and he wouldn't have lived it any other way," Michael commented from his position under the loft. He missed his brother dearly.

"As much as that moment was a turning point for Christopher, what happened during the course of this one afternoon was a turning point for you," John commented.

the Majestic of Purple Mountain

Chapter 19

In an instant, in the twinkling of an eye, Michael drove his memory like a Jeep through a jungle, and arrived at his desired location. He brought his passenger, John, with him. Michael asked John, as they stood on the western most edge of flagpole pedestal, "tell me, when did you become the greenskeeper?"

Thirty-six feet above them a flag, with thirteen horizontal stripes, alternate red and white, and the union having fifty white stars set in a blue field, unwavering waved. It was the time of day when the warm westerly valley breeze reached its zenith and the mountain breeze its nadir. In an afternoon sky, the soft spring sun slowly slipped past the pinnacle of its warming power. It was as if continuity and change were simultaneously seeking complete reconciliation. But friends need not be reconciled.

"I am not sure I ever, as you say, 'became' the greenskeeper. When did Babe Ruth become a baseball player? When did Harry Houdini become a magician? When did Amelia Earhart become an adventurer. When did Fred Astaire become a dancer?" John replied.

"I don't know. However, those are some rather larger than life comparisons wouldn't you agree? Michael asked.

"You should ask them that question," he responded.

"Sure enough. I will ask them the next time I see any of them," Michael insisted in jest.

"Good," he replied, "I'll hold you to that."

"Let me see if I can phrase this question correctly," Michael uttered as he continued to think, "how did you come to work here as the greenskeeper?"

"It was the year 1972, and I responded to an ad in the Worthington Times. It read 'Needed: Greenskeeper. Prior experience required. Apply in person at the Majestic of Purple Mountain'. I decided to respond to it. I decided that I had prior experience but just not prior experience in greens keeping. The advertisement had a period between greenskeeper and prior experience. So, that is how I reconciled it in my mind. I had faith that this position was waiting for me, somehow," John recounted.

"How did you come up here?" Michael continued in his questioning.

"I drove the Power Wagon up the service road," John recalled.

"Who did you meet with and where did you meet with them? What did you say during the interview?" Michael asked with his curiosity growing.

"I met with Caleb. He was the one tasked with finding the greenskeeper. We sat," John turned and pointed to the patio area of the clubhouse just between the stairs, "right up there. I wouldn't really call it an interview. It was more like a conversation with an old friend. I told him right away about my lack of greens keeping experience but it didn't seem to concern him. His eyes seemed to light up when I introduced myself but I didn't know him.

He explained the requirements of the position. Basically, it was to maintain the course in its current state and to attend to the details of maintaining course playability. He never asked a direct question of me about greens keeping. He asked me to tell him 'what I liked to do' and said to 'forget about the greens keeping job' for the moment. I told him that I liked the outdoors and nature and that I loved to write and paint. He asked me what I thought about on my journey up the mountain on the service road. I told him that a million stories, written about the Majestic, would only scratch the surface of the secrets it holds. I told him that if the secret scenes of the Majestic were painted on canvas, I doubted there existed a gallery large enough to contain them. I finished by telling him that I felt a curious calling to write some of the stories and paint some of the scenes. Although I knew nothing of the Majestic, I wanted to know everything about the Majestic.

He asked me what jobs I had held in the past few years. I told him that I worked off and on for a local catering company that had just started operation and that he could contact Thelma Mae, the owner, about me and my work ethic. I told him, prior to that work, I was a writer. I was stationed in a hot and wet climate but loved my work. I wrote what I had witnessed with truthfulness but that my editors had let me go. They told me that I had lost my, in their words, 'objectivity', and that my writing was viewed as supporting the conflict I was assigned to cover. The editors said to me that 'they wanted their readers to know their truth not the truth'. I replied to them that it was they who had lost their, in their words, 'objectivity'.

Caleb told me he had faith that the right person would come. He told me to remember that this position was 'greenskeeper' and not 'greens keeping'. He said that the Majestic needed a 'greenskeeper that operates from the heart'. The next thing I know, he is telling me how much the position will pay. He told me that the greenskeeper position required on campus living and that there was a small cabin that came with the position. He told me that I didn't have to leave and that I could stay the night in the cabin to get acquainted with the Majestic of Purple Mountain. He would accept an answer in the morning. I told him that I had decided to accept the offer and that I could start immediately. We never looked back."

"So, how long was it before you knew? I mean, when did you see them for the first time? The Final Foursomes, when did you first see them?" Michael got straight to the point.

"I was standing right at this exact spot about forty years ago," he remarked.

"Right here? Why here?" Michael asked.

"Yes, right here on this pedestal. I can't answer the 'why' question you posed. Those why questions are tough. However, I can answer the what questions. Questions like what I saw and what I was doing. Those I can answer," he insisted, as he looked out over the Majestic of Purple Mountain.

"I keep forgetting about those why questions. So, what were you doing at the time?" Michael asked, as he too looked out over the course absorbing its beauty.

"After I accepted the position, Caleb and I continued to talk. I believe he would call it my orientation session. After all, it was my first day on the course. He described the course to me by reading various selections from the minutes of their Minutemen Management Group meetings. Partner after partner described the Majestic of Purple Mountain. Like jewelers describing the 'Le bleu de France', each individual described it from their unique, yet qualified, perspective. It is said that the Majestic like the 'Le bleu de France' has a violet hue that is imperceptible to normal vision. Each description, given by a partner, only added to the mystique of the Majestic.

He then explained the Final Foursome concept to me and how important it was to them. He asked if I would be interested in being involved in it. However, he said that it 'was not a job requirement' to participate in it," John explained, as he continued to look out over the course.

"What explanation did he give for the Final Foursomes?" Michael probed

"The members of the Minutemen Management Group, that operate the course, have a strong commitment to supporting military families. Especially those families that have lost a loved one on the battle field. So, to honor those members of our military that have given their, to quote Lincoln, 'last full measure of devotion' they instituted the Final Foursome concept," John explained as his gaze shifted to the eighteenth green.

"Please continue," Michael asked as he listened intently.

"So, they took it upon themselves to establish a tee time everyday except Sundays. This tee time was reserved and paid for by the Minutemen Management Group. There were four honorary positions reserved for this tee time. Players names filled the first three positions on the scorecard with the final position being listed as unknown soldier. The last tee time of the day was reserved for a Final Foursome. The term, Final Foursome, flowed naturally and has been used to describe it ever since," John stated as he continued to face the eighteenth green.

"That explains the concept but when did you first see them?" Michael insisted.

"I am getting to that. After my orientation session, I was encouraged to walk the course. Caleb asked that I return to the clubhouse in the late afternoon but before sunset. He would show me the cabin at that time. He told me that the course closes at sunset.

I walked the southern arm of the course beginning at about five o'clock. I spent so much time there that I didn't have enough time to walk the north arm before meeting again with Caleb. We met and went to the cabin. He gave me a quick tour and said he would see me again in the morning. Then he left and it was just me and the Majestic.

I was impressed with everything I had seen and experienced. I wondered how I could ever live up to the task ahead of me. I knew nothing of greens keeping and this was a beautifully manicured course. But I remembered what Caleb had said earlier, that the Majestic needed a 'greenskeeper that operated from the heart' and not a keeper of the greens. But what did that mean? So, I began to unpack what few things I had in the Dodge. And there it was–" John was cutoff by Michael mid-sentence.

"There what was?" he interjected.

"My bugle!" John said as he lifted his hands into playing position.

"Your bugle? And then what happened?" Michael asked.

"I carried it into the cabin with me and set it down on the table just inside the front door. I was still contemplating what it meant to 'operate from the heart'. Then it came to me. I knew exactly how I could contribute to the Final Foursome concept. If only it were not too late, I thought. I grabbed the bugle and headed to the flagpole pedestal.

When I arrived at the flagpole, the sun was a few minutes from setting. It was a great orange disk on the western horizon, the kind of sun you could look at briefly without damage to the eyes. I stood at the western most point of the pedestal against the railing. To my left was the ninth green but I saw movement out of the corner of my eye to the right. There was a group of golfers on the eighteenth green. This group was late I thought, by at least twenty minutes.

Then the thought occurred to me. It couldn't be, I thought to myself. It can't be real. The Final Foursome was just a concept. With the approaching darkness, all I could see were silhouettes and there were four of them. They appeared to be watching the sunset. I quickly looked back to the horizon and the sun was partially set over the horizon. It was time.

In one motion, I turned to face the setting sun and lifted the bugle into playing position. Then, from the heart, I played "Taps". The last note carried in a majestic echo throughout the course. As I looked to the eighteenth, it was as if I could see silhouetted soldiers complete their salute and fade away into glory," John opined as he looked at the eighteenth green.

"You saw them for the first time on the eighteenth green? You are sure about this?" Michael insisted.

"I am absolutely certain of it. At that exact moment, I decided that faith had come to fruition. My era as greenskeeper of the Majestic of Purple Mountain had begun. So, why is this eighteenth green of such importance to you in the story?" John asked revealing his curiosity.

"As you say, those 'why' questions are the tough ones. Perhaps you should ask what interests me about the subject or how is this important?" Michael commented with a smile.

"So then, what interests you about my seeing them, for the first time, on the eighteenth green?" John rephrased the question also smiling.

"Oh, it is nothing really. Yes, nothing of concern," Michael said as he looked at the eighteenth.

"Now let me ask you a question. Where did you first see a Final Foursome?" John asked him directly.

"Not where you would expect me to have seen them," Michael responded.

"Yes, I remember it well. Actually it surprised me that you brought us here instead of there," John commented.

"Perhaps you should define what you call 'here' and 'there' for me. I am a bit confused by them," Michael stated.

"I did not expect you to bring us 'here' to the flagpole pedestal. Rather, I expected you to take us to the first tee box. I thought you would take us to where, I thought, you had first encountered a Final Foursome. I thought we would leave the barn and go directly to the first tee," John revealed.

"You were right when you assumed that I would take us to where I had my first 'encounter' with a Final Foursome. However, you were wrong about the time and place," Michael maintained as he sat on the railing of the flagpole pedestal.

"Wrong? How could that be? You acted so surprised when we saw them for the first time together on the first tee. When could you have possibly seen them before that?" John proposed, as he swiveled his head from side to side in disbelief.

"You are the greenskeeper of the Majestic of Purple Mountain. Think with your heart and not with your head," Michael challenged him.

"You saw them there didn't you? When we went back to the miracle scene, the 'Novaya Zemlya effect', the second sunset, you focused me in on the miracle. However, you saw them standing on the eighteenth! What a revelation!" John hypothesized enthusiastically.

"The heart wins out over the head again. Yes, you are correct. I saw their silhouettes. Christopher and I took up a position behind a White Oak tree. From there, I saw the soldiers standing at attention on the eighteenth. As "Taps" played, I saw a second sunset. I witnessed a miracle! Without knowing it, I witnessed a man of faith put faith to the test. Then, I watched as the soldiers walked off of the green and into glory," Michael disclosed, as he looked out over the Majestic and beyond.

Michael wondered if he were wrong about what his brother had seen in that moment. It was his hope that Christopher had actually seen the Final Foursome. Then he brought his focus back to the Majestic and the area near the first tee.

Chapter 20

"Here we are again. It seems like we were here earlier today?" John remarked as he nudged Michael in the side with his elbow.

"You knew we would be back here. We couldn't miss this one. Could we?" Michael declared, as he stepped to the side to avoid another nudging from John.

"Mike and the Greenskeeper will arrive soon. As I remember, it took a little more time than I thought to get Christopher started on that Jeep project. But, it was time well spent in the planning phase of the project. Now that they have the project mapped out, he will be able to complete it before the start of school in the fall. Without the planning session, I am not sure what would have become of the project," John contended, as he looked for any signs of Mike or a Final Foursome.

"Christopher was beside himself that day. He was so excited he didn't know where to start. You did a great job of setting him down the right trail on the project," Michael suggested, as he also scanned the area for any movement. "What is that sound? It sounds like the beating of horse hooves?"

"I know that sound— Nelson! That is who is making that sound," John said, as he looked to the tree line a few yards to the southwest.

"Who is Nelson anyway!" Michael asked, as he looked to the tree line also.

"They have stopped now. I hear something down there. He will be here any minute now," John stated confidently.

"Who will be here 'any minute now'?" Michael said, as he squinted to see the tree line more closely.

"Who else but the Major General and the commander-in-chief of the Continental Army, none other than, George Washington himself!" John announced, as he watched the Major General appear from out of the tree line. The Major General stopped and adjusted his regimentals to their proper fitting, before he continued any further in his advance.

The Major General appeared in his regimentals that were made in 1789. The long coat has an exterior made of blue wool, a buff lined interior, and its length stops just below the knees. The coat has a buff wool rise and fall collar about the neck, buff cuffs at the end of the sleeves and buff lapels. There are ten equally spaced half-dollar sized yellow metal buttons on either lapel. These buttons begin just below the collar and run the length of the lapel stopping parallel with the buttons on the cuff of the sleeve. Affixed to the cuff of the sleeves are six buttons matching those of the lapel. The inner buff waist coat has fourteen equally spaced quarter sized yellow metal buttons. The bottom ten were buttoned. The buff breeches were tucked into his black leather boots. They stopped just above the calf but below the knees. The breeches have five, equally spaced, nickel sized buttons. They begin just below the knee and run down the outside of the leg. His hair was light brown in color and pulled into a short braid at the back. This was the regimental, of his choosing, for the performance of awarding the Badge of Military Merit. Proper military attire was important, to Major General Washington. He valued military dress. It relayed a sense of professionalism amongst the ranks and to adversaries alike. He believed that proper dress was important to effective leadership.

"He looks different from when we saw him this morning, when he was surveying. Now he looks like the person I saw in the history books. Is this how he normally dresses?" Michael asked quietly.

"Yes, this is how he always dresses for the Merit Badge ceremonies. They are replicas of the regimentals, that he wore, when he first awarded the Badge of Military Merit on May 3, 1783. These regimentals are close to the ones, that he wore, when he received his commission as commander in chief of the Continental Army. He prefers the title of Major General Washington for this activity. Although his other titles may confer greater significance, President of the United States or General of the Armies of the United States, the title of Major General is his choice when he visits the Majestic," John remarked. They both stood in awe, of the Major General, as he resolutely strode his way toward the tee box.

"Where did they come from?" Michael asked, as he looked to the back of the gold tee box.

"They assembled there before the Major General arrived. I can't tell you how many times I have missed their arrival, due to watching the Major General stride his way up here," John commented, as he looked toward the back section of the gold tee box.

They were both looking at the Fife and Drum Corps of the third U.S. Infantry Regiment. There were thirteen members in all. One drum major carrying an espontoon and wearing a light-infantry cap. One bass drummer, three snare drummers, four each of ten hole fifes and single-valve bugles. Each member of the corps wore a black tricorn hat. Their uniforms were fashioned after the regimentals of the Major General, with a few minor exceptions. The coats were red and lined in blue. The lapels, collars and cuffs were blue. The buttons were of the same number and size but were silver in color. The waist coat was white as well as the breeches. The corps wore leather shoes with socks pulled to the knee. They stood at attention and in formation flanking the Major General's position.

"Where did they come from? Where are all of these people coming from?" Michael asked again. Then he watched, as another group approached.

"Just wait. There are a few more that need to show up!" John commented and then he smiled at Michael.

"I am surprised that I don't remember this. The Major General, the corps and who knows who else that will show up soon. I have remembered so many things from the times and settings we have already visited. It is not this one particular first tee event that I am talking about. I am sure we arrived, on a few other days, with plenty of time to witness what we have seen here, right now. Why is this first tee setting so different?' Michael proposed. He continued to look about in disbelief.

"Sometimes, the events that our minds remember our hearts choose to forget," John speculated, as he absorbed the setting.

A group of four soldiers were ascending the stairs. These stairs led to the gold tee box, of the first hole. The stairs were located at the center of the east side of the tee box. John and Michael were standing on the tee box just south of the stairs. They turned to the east to watch the soldiers ascend the last few stairs. The soldiers were marching single file and wore military dress from their period of service. They were ordered in line according to the date in which they gave their final sacrifice. The soldier having the oldest date was leading the line. As the first soldier set foot on the tee box, the Fife and

Drum Corps began to march in place and play the tune 'Chester' the anthem for the Colonial Army. When the soldiers stopped, they formed a line running north and south and they faced to west. This placed them just across the tee box from the Major General. The Fife and Drum Corps, standing at the southern edge of the tee box, were to the left of the soldiers.

"Mike, we need to hurry up now," the Greenskeeper insisted, as they walked down the path toward the first tee box. They had just left Christopher, in the barn, to work on the Jeep. The two of them were nearly to the first tee when the Fife and Drum Corps started to play.

"What is that sound? Are those drums and flutes that I hear?" Mike asked. He hurriedly walked beside the Greenskeeper.

"You hear that?" he said stopping dead in his tracks, "you hear that noise? Tell me again, what do you hear?"

"It sounds like drums and flutes. It sounds like it is coming from just over there," Mike said, as he pointed in the direction of the first tee.

"That is what I thought you said," the Greenskeeper replied and he began to walk again. "We need to get down there! They are about to start."

"Who is about to start what and where?" Mike said, as they neared the last turn before the tee box came into view.

"Good. We made it. They are just about to start," the Greenskeeper panted. He stopped just a few yards away from the stairs leading to the first tee box. "Do you see them up there?" he asked Mike.

"Yes, who are those people? They don't look like golfers to me," Mike replied, as he looked up at the tee box.

"I will explain who they are later. For now, I need you to do me a favor. Please maintain an attitude of silence and respect, because this is a special time for those soldiers up there. You will know when it is safe to talk again," the Greenskeeper declared as he watched the ceremony begin. The ceremony was happening on the gold tee box. It was to their left and slightly above their position near the bottom of the stairs.

The Fife and Drum Corps completed the playing of 'Chester' and the drum major silently signaled them to stop marching. Upon issuing another silent signal, a snare drum roll commenced.

"Helen, Staff Sergeant, U.S. Army, Nurse Corps., please step forward," the drum major commanded as he issued a silent signal to the snare drummer to cease the drum roll. "For unusual gallantry while serving on the HMS Newfoundland and during the battle of Hanau, Germany in April, nineteen hundred and forty-five; for extraordinary fidelity; and for essential service; you are hereby awarded the Badge of Military Merit. Your name and regiment will be enrolled in the *Book of Merit.*"

"Well done, Helen," Major General Washington proclaimed, as he stepped forward. He reached into his coat pocket and pulled out a small purple heart shaped cloth. On its surface, embroidered in white, was the word MERIT. It was surrounded by eighteen embroidered leaves, nine on either side, connected by a thin line resembling a branch. He pinned the badge above the left breast pocket of her uniform. She saluted and stepped back in formation. As she stepped back, the drum major sent another silent signal to begin a drum roll.

"Wally, Lance Corporal, U.S. Marines, 1st Marine Division, please step forward," the drum major commanded as he issued a silent signal to the snare drummer to cease the drum roll. "For unusual gallantry during the battle of Pusan, Korea, in September, nineteen hundred and fifty; for extraordinary fidelity; and for essential service; you are hereby awarded the Badge of Military Merit. Your name and regiment will be enrolled in the *Book of Merit*."

"Well done, Wally," Major General Washington proclaimed as he stepped forward. He reached into his coat pocket and pulled out another small purple heart shaped cloth. On its surface, embroidered in white, was the word MERIT. It was surrounded by eighteen embroidered leaves, nine on either side, connected by a thin line resembling a branch. He pinned the badge above the left breast pocket of his uniform. Wally saluted and stepped back in formation. As Wally stepped back, the drum major sent another silent signal to begin a drum roll.

"Kyle, Gunnery Sergeant, U.S. Marines, 1st Marine Division, please step forward," the drum major commanded as he issued a silent signal to the snare drummer to cease the drum roll. "For unusual gallantry during Operation Starlight, South Vietnam, in August, nineteen hundred and sixty-five; for extraordinary fidelity; and for essential service; you are hereby awarded the Badge of Military Merit. Your name and regiment will be enrolled in the *Book of Merit*."

"Well done, Kyle," Major General Washington proclaimed as he stepped forward. He reached into his coat pocket and pulled out another small purple heart shaped cloth. On its surface, embroidered in white, was the word MERIT. It was surrounded by eighteen embroidered leaves, nine on either side, connected by a thin line resembling a branch. He pinned the badge above the left breast pocket of his uniform. Kyle saluted and stepped back in formation. As Kyle stepped back the drum major sent another silent signal and the drum corps began to march in place.

"Deron, Staff Sergeant, U.S. Army, 82nd Airborne, please step forward," the drum major commanded as he issued a silent signal to the snare drummer to cease the drum roll. "For unusual gallantry during the Tet Offensive, Vietnam, in August, nineteen hundred and sixty-eight; for extraordinary fidelity; and for essential service; you are hereby awarded the Badge of Military Merit. Your name and regiment will be enrolled in the *Book of Merit*."

"Well done, Deron," Major General Washington proclaimed as he stepped forward. He reached into his coat pocket and pulled out another small purple heart shaped cloth. On its surface, embroidered in white, was the word MERIT. It was surrounded by eighteen embroidered leaves, nine on either side, connected by a thin line resembling a branch. He pinned the badge above the left breast pocket of his uniform. Deron saluted and stepped back in formation. As Deron stepped back the drum major sent another silent signal to begin a drum roll.

"At ease soldiers. You are hereby dismissed," Major General Washington commanded. Then he pivoted one hundred and eighty degrees and began to march his way toward the woods. The Fife and Drum Corps pivoted ninety degrees and began to march toward the woods. As they marched, they were playing 'Yankee Doodle'. Into the woods, went the Major General and then the corps disappeared into it as well.

"What happens next?" Mike asked the Greenskeeper.

"We go up there and talk with them for a few minutes. Their caddies will be here soon and we will send them on their way. They will be teeing off in just a few minutes. By the way, I think your tee placements from earlier today are exceptional. I caught the Major General admiring them during the ceremony," the Greenskeeper commented as he began to walk

up the stairs leading to the first tee. Mike followed closely behind.
"When they were dismissed, I noticed that their clothes had changed. They were no longer in the military uniforms but were in golfing clothes. How did they do that?" Mike asked.
"There are many mysteries at the Majestic of Purple Mountain and this is one of them. I still don't know how they do that," the Greenskeeper responded.
"Maybe we could ask a magician?" Mike proposed as he stood by the Greenskeeper.
"That is a wonderful idea. We will ask Harry the next time he is here," the Greenskeeper responded.
"Who is Harry?" Mike asked.
"You will see. He is a frequent visitor here. He gets lots of requests to caddie. All right, Mike, I need you to stay quiet for a few minutes while I talk with our guests," the Greenskeeper insisted.
"All right, I will. But may I ask one last question?" Mike replied as he stood on the gold tee box.
"Yes, but make it quick. We have a tee time to make," the Greenskeeper remarked.
"Who are those people down there?" Mike turned and pointed down the stairs, "the people in the white jumpsuits standing next to the golf bags."
"I have been waiting on them! Good eye Mike! You are really getting the hang of this," the Greenskeeper said. He turned to look at the caddie selections for the day.
"Your welcome. I will be quiet now," Mike responded.
Deron, Wally and Helen were introducing themselves, as the Greenskeeper approached them. It appeared as though they were enjoying the occasion already. Before the Green-

skeeper could get to them, he was stopped by Kyle who had broken away from the group.

"Excuse me sir. This may sound a bit unusual but this is already unusual. You see, I am a Marine, a jarhead, as some would call us. The way I see it some things appear to be in place. The Fife and Drum Corps, Deron, Wally and Helen, even the Major General, they are not unusual given the circumstances here. They seem to fit. The golf course setting is a bit off but I can live with that. However, what seems out of place is— you!" Kyle contended.

"Yes, Kyle, I can only imagine how odd this all must seem to you. However, it will all fit together soon," the Greenskeeper assured him.

"I mean, this place is beautiful and all of that. Hell— oh sorry. Heck, I just saw President Washington pin a Merit Badge on me and talk about Vietnam. There is a nurse here that fought in World War II and she looks like she is in her mid-thirties. Granted, I am a Marine but I can think things out. We are trained in situational awareness.

This is not what most people would picture Heaven to be. Some I suppose, picture pearly gates and streets of gold. Some I suppose, picture the King on His throne set upon a sea of emeralds. But I figured, when I met God he would be rather unassuming and more like an older brother or an old friend from years past. I figured him to be powerful but in a humble kind of way. You vaguely remind me of that type of figure. I admit, I should probably have a stronger image in mind of what God would look like. So, what is the situation here? Are you God?" Kyle asked.

"No. I am the greenskeeper."

Chapter 21

"Good afternoon to everyone! Let me be the first to welcome you here to the Majestic of Purple Mountain. We are honored to have you visit with us here today. I personally thank each of you for your dedicated service to our Republic. An anonymous donor has paid for your round here today, as a small token of their appreciation.

You have chosen an extremely beautiful but unusually challenging course to play. However, you have the benefit of using a caddie during your round today. I must warn you though, as your caddie selection may seem odd at first–" the Greenskeeper began with his introductory speech but was interrupted.

"'Odd'! Do you think this is just a game for men? Have you never seen a woman caddie before?" Amelia retorted.

"'Odd'! How can you say I look 'odd'?" Bobby proposed while he tipped his Tam o'Shanter and smiled politely.

"Odd! It will be 'odd' if you can dance your way out of this one!" Fred added.

"'Odd'! Hand me a paint brush and I show you 'odd'!" Pablo declared.

"Now, now, please let me finish!" the Greenskeeper said chuckling, "each of you have selected your caddie for the round today. I know, this whole setup is hard to believe. But, I ask that you have just a little faith in me on this one. With the

the Majestic of Purple Mountain

Major General having just been here, I don't think it is asking too much.

These caddie selections are of extreme importance to you. They are responsible for seven things during your round today. First, they carry your clubs for you. They will help you with club selection and put the club back in the bag after you have used it. Second, they clean your clubs after you use them. Third, they rake the sand traps and bunkers after you have played from one. Fourth, they measure yardages for you. Fifth, they replace divots and ball marks for you. Sixth, they tend the pin for you.

The seventh responsibility is unique. Your caddie is allowed to share, with you, one attribute that they possess. Working together, you and your caddie will decide what this attribute is. You will be allowed to use their attribute one time during your lifetime.

One last item of housekeeping. "Taps" is played at sunset. Please finish the round before then. I will be working the course for the remainder of the afternoon. Should you require anything, please contact me. This is a stroke play competition and the USGA rules of golf apply. Now that you know the rules, it is time to begin play. Players, please introduce yourselves to your caddie," the Greenskeeper announced. Then the golfers met with their caddies and again with one another.

The pairings of player and caddie were as follows: Helen and Amelia Earhart; Wally and Pablo Picasso; Deron and Fred Astaire; Kyle and Bobby Jones. Each player knew their caddie choice before the Greenskeeper uttered a word. One might expect an air of infatuation or a smell of idolatry, on the part of the players, in respect to their caddie. However, quite the contrary was the reality. For the players, despite their knowledge of the qualities possessed by their caddie, viewed them, as fellow soldiers in the battle of life. Their caddie was neither to be revered nor reviled, venerated nor vilified but was to be loved, as another person, like themselves, passing through this phase of existence. Each player had faith in their selection of their caddie. Now, their faith would be tested in battling the Majestic of Purple Mountain.

"All right Mike, it is time for us to begin our afternoon duties," the Greenskeeper said to him as they walked down the stairs.

"So, who are those caddies? I think I have seen some of them before in my school books. That lady, Amelia, looked like someone. Someone I have seen before. And the guy with the funny pants who is he?" Mike asked, as they walked together.

"You will learn more about them today, as we watch them help the golfers. We will spend much of the afternoon following them about the course and will have time to talk with them along the way. The lady, the one with the white leather jacket and white leather flying cap is Amelia Earhart. She was a great adventurer, writer and aviator. The man in classic golf attire wearing all white knickers, a white long sleeve buttoned collared shirt with a tie tucked in, and with the slicked back hair, is Bobby Jones. He was the best amateur golfer ever to play the game. He beat the best pro golfers of his day and retired from playing at the age of twenty-eight. He remained an amateur for his entire golf career. He made his living as a lawyer. He went on to build one of the most famous golf courses ever built, Augusta National." the Greenskeeper commented. Then he and Mike watched each player tee off on the first hole.

"Who are the other caddies?" Mike continued as he watched the tee shots soar into the air and softly land and roll to a stop on the fairway.

"The tall slender man, in the all white tuxedo, is Fred Astaire. He was a showman, dancer, and a movie maker. He believed that dance was to be woven into the plot of each of the movies he made. The other man in white slacks and a white Bahama shirt is Pablo Picasso. He was a visionary, artist and a Cubist some would say. He had a special way of looking at things and considered things from many angles and then painted them that way," he said, as he watched the soaring tee shots.

"I think I understand. Each caddie has a special talent and no two caddies are alike. We can learn from them and they can learn from us," Mike concluded. He hid the words of the Greenskeeper in his heart.

"How can they learn from us?" the Greenskeeper asked him as he was caught off guard by the statement.

"I am thinking about Picasso. He looks at us and sees something different in us. He learns something about us, as he views us from different angles. Then he paints it and we are here to look at what he has painted. So, we help him and he helps us," Mike concluded as he began to walk down the fairway.

"Mike, that is a wonderfully impressive observation. The player caddie relationship is mutually beneficial," he said as they walked.

"What does 'mutually beneficial' mean?" he asked.

"It means that both people are better for having the relationship," he told him.

"Like us, right?" Mike asked him.

"Yes, Like us," the Greenskeeper replied as they walked down the first fairway just past the landing area on the right side. They stopped in the rough just off of the fairway.

"Where do we go from here?" Mike asked him as they stood just outside the landing area on the right side of the fairway.

"As they play their round, we follow them. Sometimes we will jump a few holes ahead and other times we will be a few holes behind them. Typically, I split my time evenly between the players," he told Mike.

"What do you do when you spend time with them?" he asked as they watched the players taking their second shots on the first hole.

"I talk with them and find out about their lives. I love to hear their stories. So, I have a routine that I use to make sure that I have enough time to talk to each golfer," he said as he watched Helen hit her second shot. "Great shot Helen!"

"What is a 'routine'?" Mike asked him.

"Do you remember watching the Major General, as he pinned the awards on the soldiers?" he queried of him.

"Yes, he did the same thing over and over. And he did it the same way each time. But he did use a different name for each person," Mike declared, as he remembered the awards ceremony.

"That is right. There were many routines displayed during the awards ceremony. The drum major of the Fife and Drum Corps had one. The drum major sent signals, to the members of the corps, with his espontoon. But the Major General had the best one of all if you ask me," the Greenskeeper said.

"I thought so too," he said as he watched Deron hit his second shot, "so, what is your routine?"

"Well, I spend about two or three holes with each golfer during their round. That leaves me with enough time to visit with the players and still tend to anything that the course may need. I like to finish by the time they hit the thirteenth green, if at all possible," he stated.

"Why there? You must like hanging out at that hole or something!" Mike asked him with a slight grin on his face.

"Leaving from there allows me time to prepare for the close of the course for the day. But you will see all of this soon enough. And no, I don't necessarily 'like hanging out at that hole'. Although, on one particular day I did!" the Greenskeeper declared, with a smile, as they followed the group toward the green.

Chapter 22

"There they go," Michael observed. He and John watched the groups make their way to the first green. They had been slowly shadowing them since they teed off on the first hole. Now they were standing on the east side of the first fairway just across from the ideal tee shot landing area. They were standing near the stump of the Carolina Cherry Tree. The stump is quite legendary but that is another story.

"Quite a sight isn't it?" he asked. "The Final Foursome, their caddies, the Greenskeeper and Mike all of them walking toward the first green. We looked so young back then."

"Yes it is. However, there is something though," Michael said to John.

"What is it?" John replied.

"In all the excitement, I missed something back then. A small nuance, but a nuance just the same," Michael admitted still watching the groupings who were on the green putting.

"So, what is this nuance? What is it that you have discovered?" John questioned him after a long silence. The silence was quite long. So long, that the golfers were close to finishing putting out the first hole.

"You didn't seem surprised that I could see the Final Foursomes, the caddies, the Fife and Drum Corps and the Major General. How could that be?" Michael asked him.

"Simple. I had faith in you as my apprentice," John maintained, as he watched the groups head off to the second tee.

"Simple as that?" Michael said.

"Yes, Simple as that. It was by faith and faith alone," John opined.

"It is obvious now. Obvious that you had faith in me back then," Michael commented. Then they walked toward the second hole keeping the group in view.

"I still have that same faith in you!" John declared while walking with Michael.

"Now, we will stay close to the Greenskeeper and Mike for a while. Things are about to get interesting with all of them headed into the next few holes," Michael said, as he changed the topic away from faith.

"Things are always interesting in the past. But remember, we can go back to the cabin at any time. Remember, you brought us here and you can take us back at any time," John reminded him.

"Not yet, this is fascinating. There are so many details that I have nearly forgotten. There are a few more memories that I want to visit," Michael said, as he continued to walk. "When do we have to go back?"

"We can visit these memories for as long as you feel we need to be here within them. When we go back, the Jeep will be parked just where you left it. Then you can head back down the mountain and into town. The world remains just as we left it," John remarked.

"It is settled then. We will stay a little longer in the year 1987. The year 2012 can wait a little longer for our return," Michael announced. Then they arrived at the second hole.

"All right, then lets get a good viewing position for what is to come. I suggest we stake out a spot near Southern Red, that old oak tree, that sits between the third green and the fourth tee," John suggested to Michael.

"Well, then. It is decided and that is where I will take us to wait," Michael announced. Then he began to think about sights and sounds underneath the Southern Red Oak tree.

the Majestic of Purple Mountain

Chapter 23

"Where are we headed now?" Mike asked the Greenskeeper as they walked along in the high rough of the second fairway. The Final Foursome group of Helen, Deron, Wally and Kyle were all walking to hit their second shots on the second hole. The Greenskeeper and Mike were keeping pace with them but were having their own discussion for the moment.

"We are going to say hello to the pink dogwoods and the daisies. They line the fairway of the second hole and I haven't said anything to them today," the Greenskeeper stated as they continued to walk.

"Why are 'we' going to talk to trees and flowers? They won't answer us," Mike insisted.

"Perhaps it is not an 'answer' we are looking for?" the Greenskeeper proposed.

"Why would we talk to them then?" Mike asked as they came upon a a row of dogwoods with daisies interspersed between them.

"You do like your 'why' questions don't you? Some scientists say that just the carbon dioxide gas alone, from our breath, provides the plants with something they need. Others, like Dr. Fechner from Germany in the eighteen hundreds, believed that plants were capable of emotions just like we are. They can be happy and sad; joyful and sorrowful; peaceful and angry," the Greenskeeper remarked as he walked under a dogwood tree.

"What do you believe about the plants? Do you think they hear us?" Mike asked him as he bent down to smell the daisies.

"I am not sure it matters much what I believe about them. They either hear what I say or they don't. My believing one way or another won't change that. However, when I talk to them they seem to grow better than when I don't," the Greenskeeper commented.

"How long have you been talking to the plants anyway?" Mike asked him.

"Since the early 1970s. It took years of talking with those Azaleas, on thirteen, before they would bloom in the proper season. They are a deciduous shrub and they lose their flowers once they have served their intended purpose," the Greenskeeper maintained.

"What is deciduous?" Mike asked him.

"It means that they are not permanent. The flowers will fall away once their season has past. But they will return again in their proper season. Although, they might return quicker and fuller if they are talked with!" the Greenskeeper stated with a laugh.

"I think— I will let you do the talking for me. If that is ok with you for now?" Mike proposed.

"That is perfectly fine. It took me a long time to become comfortable talking to them. I am not sure that anyone knows about it except for you and the plants, of course," the Greenskeeper said with a smile.

"Thanks, I hoped you would understand," Mike said with a sense of relief. "Are people deciduous?"

"Sometimes it appears that way," the Greenskeeper claimed.

"How does it 'appear' that way?" Mike asked.

"People are granted the gift of seasons here on earth but the seasons eventually come to an end," the Greenskeeper remarked.

"What are 'seasons'? Do you mean 'seasons' like spring, summer, winter and fall?" Mike asked.

"Yes, four seasons to a year. But also, seasons of like childhood, adolescence and adulthood to name a few," the Greenskeeper said.

"I understand. Why are our seasons 'limited'?" Mike asked.

"It was not intended, to be that way, from the beginning. However, from our perspective, here on earth, it may seem that a person's purpose has been fulfilled when they die and their seasons come to an end. But not from a heavenly perspective. We are evergreens and not deciduous creatures when it comes to the heavenly perspective," The Greenskeeper opined as he walked with Mike toward the third hole amongst the dogwoods and daisies.

"An 'evergreen' like a pine tree?" Mike supposed as he walked along.

"Yes, Evergreens have their 'green leaves' through the seasons. We are creatures of eternal life not creatures of seasons. However, where we live that eternal life is dependent upon the choices we make during our seasons here," The Greenskeeper explained.

"So, people are really evergreens but sometimes look deciduous?" Mike concluded after reflecting on the conversation.

"Yes, that is a good way of thinking about it," the Greenskeeper encouraged him.

"Where are we going next?" Mike asked him.

"We are going to the third tee box," the Greenskeeper announced.

"An uphill par three, if I remember it correctly from earlier today?" Mike replied as he stopped to smell the daisies.

"Yes, you do. There, we will meet up with our golfers and caddies and see how they are doing. But, I have a few more plants to talk with before we get there!" the Greenskeeper said. They continued to walk along the second fairway among the blossoming dogwoods and daisies.

Chapter 24

The Kennedy hole is the third hole of the Majestic of Purple Mountain. When one approaches it, their round is yet young and full of promise. The third hole is vibrant and strikingly beautiful. Although it is the shortest of holes, a player should not be fooled into thinking that length is directly proportional to difficulty. The hole plays, on a good day, two clubs uphill. Also, it is nearly a blind shot into a stunningly small green.

"Impossible! I couldn't fly a ball up there and drop it close to the pin!" Amelia declared, as she searched through Helen's bag for the impossible club.

"It might take two to tango on this one! I am not sure we can get there in one shot?" rummaging through Deron's bag, Fred expressed his reservations, while looking for the perfect partner for this shot.

"Just swing smooth and hold your finish. You will look good even if we don't make it up there. If we are left with an up and down scenario, so be it!" Bobby recommended. He peered into Kyle's bag to pluck out the perfect club.

"No matter the angle, I don't see us making the shot," Pablo professed to Wally. He looked for the club that best fit the perceived reality of distance required to hit the green. Not finding it, he pulled a club at random.

"Some golfers see a two club uphill, one hundred and eighty yard, into a crosswind, par three and ask 'why'? The great golfers see a two club uphill, one hundred and eighty yard, into a crosswind, par three and ask 'why not'!" the Greenskeeper announced. He walked up and onto the third tee box with Mike following.

"Time to re-chart our flight path! I flew a plane across the Atlantic once. I know we can make it up on that green with what we have in that bag!" Amelia stated, as she confidently pulled another club from the bag.

"Hold this club in the closed position and just waltz on up there!" Fred suggested to Deron, as he introduced him to his new dance partner.

"The jury is in and the verdict is unanimous! Let's use one less club but take a big cut at it!" Bobby announced. He took out the next highest numbered club in the bag and handed it to Kyle.

"Marine, I need your best sniper shot! No disrespect to the former President intended," Pablo told Wally, as he pulled a one iron from his bag.

Each, of the players, reached the green with their tee shot. The players and their caddies went up to the green to finish the hole. Meanwhile, the Greenskeeper and Mike walked toward the fourth hole.

"Why are we stopping here," Mike asked? He and the Greenskeeper stopped under an oak tree. This oak tree stood just off the path between the third green and the fourth tee.

"This is Southern Red. We will wait here until the group catches up with us," the Greenskeeper said.

Southern Red is an eighty foot tall oak tree with a trunk measuring two and a half feet wide. It stands alone, just a little off the path between the third green and the fourth tee. It has deep green bristled leaves that are bell shaped at the base. Its leaves are deeply lobed and have three or five lobes per leaf. It is an acorn bearing tree. Each has a dark reddish brown colored cap covering sitting atop its light green fruit. The acorns are a favorite treat for the local wildlife. It is faster growing than most oak trees and is corse grained. Its bark is thick and brownish black in color. The tree has a broad canopy of eighty-two feet at the lowest branches and is good for shade.

"Amelia, wait here for me please. I am going over there, to that tree, just down the way. Oh, and please tell the others that I will only be delayed a few moments here. There is something about the shade of that tree," Helen said. Then she left her caddie, at the path, and headed for the shade of the Southern Oak.

"Helen, please come join us," the Greenskeeper beckoned to her from within the shade of Southern Red.

Helen walked up to the edge of the shade and hesitated. Her mind drifted to thoughts about her childhood and then of her grandfather. Her grandfather had been a pilot in the Great War. He was a member of the 94th Fighter Squadron and was awarded the Distinguished Service Cross in 1918. After the war he continued to fly. When he was home, between barnstorming journeys, he spent many a night in his study. He kept it dark except for a reading light and a small fire in the fireplace. The fire was more for ambiance than for anything else. He liked the light it put off and the sounds it made. On occasion, he smoked a pipe packed with a small amount of peppermint tobacco. She was standing, in the light of day, while peering into the shade of Southern Red. This reminded her of standing in the doorway of her grandfather's study. She could almost smell the peppermint, hear the cracklings of the fire and see its glow in the darkness.

With childlike faith, she stepped into the shade of the tree. In the twinkling of an eye, her appearance changed into that of a twelve year old girl. She was wearing an oversized, but worn, brown leather bomber jacket with a 'hat in the ring' patch sewn on to it. She wore new blue jeans and a pair of brown lace up leather boots. On her head was a leather flying cap with goggles pulled to her forehead. Her raven black hair was pulled back and into a pony tail. It protruded from the back of the cap and hung down past her shoulders. She had a warm smile and her blue eyes pierced the darkness of the shade. She walked nearly forty feet into the shade to reach the trunk of the tree. And then, just on the other side of the trunk she saw familiar sights. She continued to walk just a few feet further. Underneath the Southern Oak, the year was now nineteen hundred and twenty-six.

"Are you God?" Helen asked the Greenskeeper as she approached him.

"No. I am the greenskeeper," he replied with a smile as he continued, "let me introduce myself. My name is John and I am the greenskeeper here at the Majestic. I am pleased to meet you. I am sorry that there was not more time for introductions on the first tee," the Greenskeeper said as he extended his hand to her.

"I am pleased to meet you, John. This is a beautiful course, I must say. But it does appear that we have left it behind for the moment," she said as she looked back over her shoulder to where she had entered the shade of the tree. "May I ask, who is your friend there?"

"His name is Mike and he is my apprentice," the Greenskeeper answered as Mike stepped forward with his hand extended.

"I am pleased to meet you ma'am," Mike announced as he shook her hand.

"Please call me Helen. I am pleased to meet you, Mike, the apprentice. What have you learned today as an apprentice" Helen politely asked.

"I have learned that the Majestic of Purple Mountain is a unique place," Mike replied.

"Oh, I must agree. Indeed, it is a unique and beautiful place. Even this tree for example, its shade drew me to it. Now here we stand," Helen observed as she stood with them under the cool shade of the Southern Oak.

"Unique, I must agree," the Greenskeeper commented, "behind you, where you came in, is the Majestic of Purple Mountain. Where you stand and in front of you lies the year nineteen hundred and twenty-six."

It was as if the shade of the tree was a short hallway. On one end was the golf course and on the other end was her childhood. They exited the hallway and stepped into the light of her childhood. As they did, they were now standing in a Midwestern wheat field just after early summer harvest.

"So, here we are! It has been a long time, since I have seen this place," Helen commented as she looked about.

"Exactly where is here?" Mike asked her.

"Oh, yes! We are in rural southeast Kansas and just southwest of Riverton," Helen declared.

"Why here? And what are all of those people doing over there?" Mike asked politely. Across the field, he could see numerous vehicles parked in a single file line with a few people standing by each vehicle. There was a Duesenberg Model A Phaeton, a Chrysler Imperial, a Studebaker Big Six, a Studebaker President, a Ford Model T truck, a Desoto and too many others to mention here. The people were all looking up and out, into the bright blue sky.

"Just wait a few minutes and you will see," Helen advised as she looked up and into the bright blue sky. However, she was not looking in the same direction as the others.

"Who is that walking past all of those cars over there?" the Greenskeeper asked, as they looked across the field. The person was dressed exactly like Helen and was of the same build. "She is walking toward the end of the line. I wonder where she is going and who she is talking with? Don't you wonder what they are talking about?"

"I will tell you, if you really want to know. For that person over there is me!" Helen announced.

"Please, tell us!" Mike insisted.

"Oh, yes that is me over there all right. At this moment, I am talking with an older wealthy man. He drove the Duesenberg and made sure everyone knew it. He was commenting to me about how much I reminded him of Amelia Earhart. I think he said something like 'who do you think you are, Amelia Earhart?'. Well, I stopped dead in my tracks on hearing that. You see, I was a huge Amelia fan! I wasn't about to let some old man kid me about her! He said something about living in Atchison, where she was born, and knowing her personally. I didn't believe a word of it. Except that maybe he lived there," she recounted, continuing to look skyward.

"Why Amelia Earhart?" Mike asked her.

"Amelia was the greatest female pilot of my time and possibly ever. She was a pioneer, a writer, an aviatrix and an adventurer. And best of all, I was just about to meet her. You see, not much is recorded about her flying activities between 1924, when she sold the Canary, a second hand Kinner Airster biplane, and when she was believed to have begun flying again in 1927.

Yes, this was the day that I met her. For years, I had asked God in prayer that I could have the courage of Amelia. I didn't ask it for myself you see, although I expected to receive it. Rather, I wanted to use that kind of courage to do courageous things for others. I wanted other girls to know that we girls had value and that we could do anything we girls set our minds and hearts to do!" Helen opined as any twelve year old could opine.

Just then, from behind the clouds, opposite from where the crowds were looking, it roared into view. It came from the direction in which Helen was looking. There it was, the Canary, the bright yellow Kinner Airster biplane. That old second hand biplane was flying again and Amelia was at the stick. Amelia had borrowed it from the new owners and was out spreading her wings over the early summer wheat fields of Kansas. It was still down wind and the crowds were yet to notice it. However, Helen knew where to look. On this particular day, during mid flight, Amelia joined up with another biplane.

And then, the people saw what they were looking for. In the direction they were looking, came a biplane. It was the barnstormer that had been giving rides and putting on aerobatic displays. It was a Jenny, a Curtiss JN-4HT, two seat, dual control trainer version biplane. Thousands of these JN-4 planes were sold to the public after the Great War ended. Some of them were used by barnstormers, former Great War pilots, to make a living by performing aerobatic stunts and giving rides. Helen's grandfather was one of them. And not just any one of them, but particularly, this one of them.

Minutes earlier, the Jenny had disappeared into a bank of clouds but now had reemerged and was headed in for a landing. As it approached, it came in low and did a 180 degree turn and quickly landed. The plane almost came to a rolling stop just in front of the Duesenberg and where the young girl, dressed like Amelia Earhart, stood waiting with head tilted. The young girl pulled her goggles over her eyes. Then the plane pivoted and turned ninety degrees. The propeller kicked straw up and on to the Duesenberg and on the people standing near it. Then the plane came to a complete stop. As the propeller quit its spinning, the girl removed her glasses, brushed the chaff from her coat and hat and winked at the older gentleman who was covered in straw and chaff.

Then to the astonishment of the crowds, another plane came in for a landing. Only one plane was billed for this event in the fliers. Helen had dropped the fliers from the Jenny, as they flew over the town the day before. The fliers advertised the arrival of the barnstormer and gave directions to the site where the townspeople could come out to participate. For a nominal fee, of course, they could watch the barnstormer perform. For a more significant fee, they could fly with him. But this arrival was a new and unexpected development. It was the Canary and it came straight on in and touched down. It gently rolled to a stop along side the Jenny.

"Now do you see why we came here, Mike?" Helen asked as the Greenskeeper and Mike looked on is amazement.

"That was really cool! Who is flying those old planes? I really like the blue one! Who is in the blue one?" Mike insisted, as he looked on, examining every detail of the biplanes.

"Then blue one, Jenny is piloted by Captain David, my grandfather. The Canary is piloted by none other than–" Helen began to reply but was interrupted by Mike.

"Amelia Earhart! She is the pilot isn't she! Isn't she!" Mike screamed in the excitement of the moment.

"Yes, Mike you are insightful. Please don't lose that excitement as you get older. Don't lose the ability to see what others can't see. Don't lose faith in the story that is your life," Helen encouraged him as from one child to another.

"Don't worry. I won't. I promise," Mike declared solemnly.

"You see, this was his last season as a barnstormer. It was the last season for barnstorming as a whole. The world was changing. Soon Route 66 would find its first completely paved state roadway, all twelve miles of it, right here in this little corner of Kansas. Times were changing. The government would enact laws, governing the use of small planes, like these, forcing the barnstormers out of business. They said that Jennies and other biplanes like her were unsafe and unfit to fly. The pilots that flew them were pilots from the Great War. They served their country with honor. This is how their service would be rewarded? My grandfather was never the same after that.

He loved to fly. He loved to take people for rides in the Jenny. Sure he charged a few dollars but a man has to make a living. Right? It was an honorable profession you know. He never put anyone at risk. Well, never anyone he wasn't related to. Please don't tell my mother!

I hate when seasons end. But there was nothing I could do about it. This giant was too big for David to conquer. Not even Amelia could stop it," Helen remarked. Then, she looked at the planes sitting side by side on the plains of a golden Kansas wheat field.

"What happened next? Tell us please? Maybe this season didn't have to end?" Mike contended looking at Helen.

"Sometimes, God saves the best things for last. Her grandfather had just landed with his last passenger for the day. This was to be his last flight as a barnstormer, but we didn't know it at the time. We thought there would be a next season. Who doesn't think there will be a next season? Sometimes, we don't see it coming. Sometimes, we just won't see it coming even though we see it coming. But this time there wasn't another season in the wind for us. I was there, when the seasons came to an end. I was there, when the wind beneath their wings was taken and the barnstormers, with their grand biplanes, were grounded for good. But there was one last performance to be given. The best performance of all!" Helen declared.

The Greenskeeper had been quiet for some time now. He was comfortable with Mike asking the questions. The Greenskeeper had been to thousands of scenes just like this one, during his reign, as greenskeeper of the Majestic. Each person has a story of faith to tell him. Each story being different yet each having similar themes. Each story as exciting and fresh as the last. He never tired of them, rather they gave him life. These were the types of stories he recounted in his letters to the families of the Final Foursomes. For it was here, that the soldiers shared details that only family or close friends would know or understand. It did not escape him that the Majestic may have its seasons end one day. He couldn't bear the thought.

However, if seasons were to end for the Majestic, they should end with honor. He hoped that there would be no more KIA's added to the *Books of Merit* and that there would be an end to wars. Yet he knew from the scriptures, that there would be wars until this epoch had ended and the world was remade. Until then, on this side of heaven, people will die and seasons will end. Until then, he purposed to live by faith, keep courage, and love those sent his way. Until then, he would be the greenskeeper of the Majestic of Purple Mountain.

"Well, tell us about it!" the Greenskeeper insisted after a long pause.

"Sorry my friends but this is a story that can't be told!" Helen maintained. She stood looking across the golden wheat fields, some bearded and some shaved, of southeastern Kansas.

"What? Oh, come on. You have to finish the story for us? You can't leave it like this can you? What happens next?" Mike protested with arms extended and palms facing the sky.

"That is right. I can't tell you . . . But I can show you! We will watch it from here. I can even narrate, if you would like me to?" Helen said with a smile.

"Helen, who are those two people over there?" Mike said as he looked west. There were two people watching the happenings but from quite a distance away.

"I am not sure. I don't remember them being here. Anyway, the show is about to start," Helen stated. Now Helen, Mike and the Greenskeeper all turned their attention to the barnstormers.

Chapter 25

A large crowd had amassed, in a shaved wheat field, just outside of a small town, in southeastern Kansas. The local farmer, owner of the property, had collected his money in advance and was enjoying the performance. He would use the money to complete the construction of a barn. The people had come for a barnstorming performance and had been pleased with the aerobatics of the show. Some had even taken rides with the pilot. Although it wasn't planned, there was going to be an encore to this performance. The crowd yelled and clapped and even honked car horns in a show of appreciation and encouragement for one last act. This crowd was a little more worked up than a normal crowd. This was due to the unexpected arrival of the Canary and its pilot, Amelia Earhart.

The two biplanes sat parked next to each other. They were wingtip to wingtip. The three of them, Captain David, granddaughter Helen and Amelia Earhart, stood in front of and between the two beautiful flying machines. Captain David began to address the crowd.

"Everyone, I want to thank you for being here today. You have been witnesses of flying maneuver's that were developed, during the Great War, by extremely skilled pilots. It has been my pleasure to perform them for you today and to take several of you up for a view of the great state of Kansas.

We are extremely blessed to have another aviator with us here today. She holds the altitude record for a female flier and was the sixteenth woman to receive a pilot's license from The Federation Aeronautique. Please give Amelia Earhart, a Kansas native and a flying phenomena, a warm welcome.

Our final performance, will be a reenactment of the most famous of the Great War's aerial battles. Of all of the fighter pilots, in the Great War, one soared above them all. His name was Manfred Albrecht von Richthofen. In an age when fighter pilots that achieved just a few kills were considered aces, he was the ace of aces. During his career, he is credited with eighty kills. Normally, a pilot wanted to maintain a level of obscurity during flight. This would allow him an element of surprise when confronting his adversaries, be they on the ground or in the air. No, not this pilot. He flew in a bright red plane, though not at first. This plane and its pilot became the object of great respect and much fear. He was none other than, the 'Red Baron'.

Our reenactment will be of the final flight of the Red Baron. That flight took place nearly eight years ago. The Red Baron was twenty-five years of age when he was shot down and met his death. Although he was the enemy, there are many things we can learn from his life. He overcame his fears, he persevered and he led his men into battle with confidence and courage. I encourage you to read about him sometime.

For our exercise today, I will play the part of the Red Baron. Amelia will play the part of Captain Arthur Brown of the Canadian Air Corps. He is credited with shooting down the Red Baron. I leave you with this one question: Who is the greater pilot, the ace of aces or the ace that shot him down?"

With that, the pilots headed to their planes. Captain David to the Jenny and Amelia and Helen to the Canary. Unknown to Helen, David and Amelia had already conversed about this arrangement. David was confident in Amelia's ability as an aviator. So confident in fact, that he would allow Helen to fly with her. Amelia was honored to have her as her apprentice. There was only one stipulation. Helen's mother was never to hear of this arrangement. Ever.

The excitement, of the arrangement, was evident when looking at Helen's face. She was all smiles. Before Amelia turned the engine, she spoke with Helen. She told her that the plane was outfitted to fly from either seating position and that Helen should hold on to the controls gently and follow her lead. Amelia told her, 'you control the plane with the stick and foot pedals but that you fly from the heart'. Despite flying with her grandfather on numerous occasions, Helen felt a twinge of fear. She silently asked God for courage during this reenactment.

The two biplanes started their engines and headed down the makeshift runway. The Jenny was first in flight and then the Canary. The dog fight was on. The Red Baron headed east and Captain Brown west. Then the planes turned and headed toward one another on a direct course, at about 2,000 feet in elevation.

Amelia and Helen started with a simple Aileron Roll. The plane turned 360 degrees on its longitudinal axis. Picture the rotation of a football thrown in tight spiral and you have the idea. They did this several times in a row for the effect. Helen watched, as the world seemed to spin before her eyes. She nearly lost her flying cap but managed to button it down before it blew away.

Captain David, with his beard blowing in the wind, flew toward them and then started the classic loop the loop. He executed it, to perfection, making a perfect circle in the sky and at the end of the maneuver he was headed in the same direction as when he started the maneuver. During this time Amelia and Helen went past his position by flying underneath him.

Both planes made wide banking turns and again headed into battle. The Red Baron began with a Barrel Roll. It is a combination of a loop and an Aileron Roll. Amelia and Helen flew straight into it performing a tight Aileron Roll. The planes passed one another. It looked like a football being thrown through the open ends of a whiskey barrel turned on its side. They once again passed each other in mid flight.

The Red Baron made another wide banking turn for another run at his adversary. Rather than making a wide turn, Amelia pulled the plane into a Hammerhead maneuver. She flew the plane straight up into the sky, at a ninety degree angle to the ground below. Helen looked out to the sides of the plane in amazement. The plane climbed higher and higher. And just when it was about to lose all airspeed, Amelia pushed a full left rudder. The Canary cartwheeled, one half turn, in the sky and was now in a nose dive position. Amelia pulled up at twenty-five hundred feet and was now flying directly toward the Red Baron. They passed again but then Amelia executed a maneuver that David had never witnessed. In later times it would be called, the half Cuban.

The half Cuban is basically a modified loop the loop. The modification is made near the top of the loop. After reaching the top of the loop, in the classic loop the loop, the plane is upside down. In the half Cuban, the pilot turns the plane right side up, at this point, and dives down the back side of the loop and finishes the loop headed one hundred and eighty degrees from its previous heading going into the loop. A basic turn around procedure, in a tight space. This move placed Amelia and Helen directly behind the Red Baron for the kill shot.

The Red Baron knew this and immediately pulled into the Hammerhead maneuver. Amelia and Helen followed directly behind. The Red Baron, spitting smoke from behind, disappeared into a cloud during the maneuver and Amelia and Helen pulled out of the Hammerhead before they went into the cloud. They cartwheeled and came down.

The Red Baron was never seen again by the crowd. In the words of the poet John Gillespie, 'I have slipped the surly bonds of earth and touched the face of God'.

Amelia and Helen performed a low pass flyby of the crowd at about one hundred feet above the golden wheat field. As they passed, Amelia waved her hands above her head for nearly eighteen-seconds leaving Helen with the controls. The crowds cheered as they passed. Then one last Aileron Roll. It was her first solo.

Amelia and Helen made a long banking turn and headed up and into the cloud cover at five thousand feet. The crowd never saw them again. As the shaven wheat fields of gold gave notice of the changing of the seasons, so to did the disappearance of these biplanes. The seasons of the barnstormer were complete and these would never return to the golden age of flight.

Chapter 26

The three of them, Helen, Mike and the Greenskeeper, stood near Southern Red looking across that golden wheat field in southeast Kansas. There were a line of automobiles now leaving that wheat field, where the barnstormers had just performed. Each automobile pulled on to the dusty rock road that, in just a short while, would become the Kansas leg of Route 66. The spectators were on their way home. A new season, that of travel by automobile, was beginning with the creation of Route 66. Just like the barnstormers, it too would have its seasons. But that is another story.

Helen commented, "We met up with the Jenny over southeastern Kansas after the dog fight. It was as if we flew for an eternity in a day's time. We landed somewhere amongst the golden bearded wheat of western Kansas. Amelia delivered me unruffled to my grandfathers wing. She was not much for words. We exchanged gifts. I gave her a jar of Dr. C. H. Berry's Freckle Ointment that I kept in my travel duffel. She gave me a square, black makeup compact with a single mirror. We hugged, shook hands and my grandfather and I watched as she took to flight. She flew the Canary in a northeastern direction and disappeared into the clouds. We never saw her again.

Some months later, a letter arrived at the home of my grandfather. It was addressed to 'Amelia, Jr.'. Thankfully, grandfather got the mail that day. The postmark, on the letter with the unusual stamp, was from Riverton, Kansas. Within the envelope were two small pictures. The pictures were of the three of us standing between the planes and a picture of me standing in front of the Duesenberg. On the backs, of the dated pictures, were written short incriminating notes and they were signed by a 'Mr. Duesenberg'.

Oh, how I wanted to show off those pictures. But mother would find out and that couldn't be allowed. So, I hid the pictures in the safest place I could find. They were hidden, in a place, where neither grandma nor my mom would ever look. They were hidden in the tinderbox that held my grandfathers peppermint tobacco. My sister, Leona, called it the 'peppermint pipe box'. They would never look for anything in there, I calculated."

"Well, I believe our time here is complete. We should be going. The group will be waiting for you on the fourth tee of the Majestic. Don't you agree?" the Greenskeeper announced, as he turned and headed for the shade of Southern Red. He was followed by Helen and Mike and they all disappeared from the season that was 1926.

Amelia, the caddie, stood on the path looking into the shade of Southern Red, "Come on now Helen. The others are waiting for us on the tee."

Helen appeared from out of the shade of Southern Red and went to Amelia, "So, tell me about the Canary, barnstorming and the Red Baron!"

"I thought you would never ask! Somewhere in the wheat fields of southeastern Kansas . . . " Amelia began as they walked toward the fourth tee.

"Wow! That was the coolest thing ever! Do we get to do that again?" Mike asked as he stepped out from under the shade of Southern Red.

The Greenskeeper, stepping out from beneath the shade of Southern Red, said, "Yes we will. You see, each golfer that comes here has a story to tell. Then, I am allowed to tell it to someone else. Someone that was close to them."

"I think I understand. So, now where are we going?" Mike asked.

"We are going to follow the golfers. We need to meet with the rest of them just like we did with Helen. Each one has a story to tell us," the Greenskeeper informed him as they walked toward the fourth tee.

Mike asked, "Is that all that Helen has to tell us? Will we spend some more time with her before she completes the round?"

"She does indeed have more to tell us. We will spend a little more time with her later. Do you remember what the Major General pinned on her at the first tee?" the Greenskeeper asked him.

"I think it was the Badge of Merit?" Mike supposed.

"You are correct! It was the Badge of Merit. When we meet with Helen again she will tell us about how she earned it," the Greenskeeper remarked as they watched the golfers walk down the fourth fairway. Mike and the Greenskeeper followed them closely.

During the course of the afternoon, Mike and the Greenskeeper were given first hand accounts of the seasons that were of importance to Wally, Kyle and Deron. Typically, these stories are all told before the groups reach the seventh tee box. Stories about how the Badges of Merit were earned are typically reserved for the back nine. These stories, typically, are recounted after the ninth hole and finish before the thirteenth hole begins. This is the natural flow of communication between the greenskeeper and members of the Final Foursomes.

Chapter 27

John and Michael emerged from underneath Southern Red who stands between the third green and fourth tee. They had returned from a trip back to the year 1926. There they watched, from a distance, the aerobatic performance of the barnstormer and the reenactment of the last flight of the Red Baron.

John and Michael, together, were still visiting Michael's memories. This particular memory was of the summer of 1987. They were still visiting the memory of May 9, 1987. For that was the day, when Michael became the apprentice of the Greenskeeper.

"Well, what did you take away from that experience?" John probed him.

"I didn't realize that the barnstormers era was drawing to a close. I was so wrapped up in the excitement of it all, the biplanes, Amelia Earhart, and the old automobiles that I missed it. Did you see it? The changing of the seasons?" Michael inquired.

John responded, "it is not that I didn't notice it. The changing of seasons, in the lives of those that come through here, is the one constant, in all of these stories. So, I choose to enjoy the moment with them. Later, after the moment has passed, I mine the experience for its valuable mineral. Then I tuck that mineral away for later use."

"So, what was the 'valuable mineral' that you 'mined' out of that experience?" Michael insisted of him.

"Courage," he replied.

"You say one word after all of that! You say 'courage'? How did you come away with that?" Michael questioned.

John began his reply, "Simple. That is what she asked God for during her prayers. She asked for courage. It was something she felt she lacked. It was something she felt she needed. Listen to what they are asking for in their prayers. It is there, in their prayers, that you will find your nuggets of truth."

"From prayers? You get your information by listening to their prayers?" Michael commented.

"Yes, if God listens to the prayers of his children, then why shouldn't I listen as well?" John explained.

"Who made you God that you should listen in?" Michael retorted with a growing sense of frustration.

"Michael, my dear son. You have missed the point," John said softly.

"How so? What is the point actually?" Michael responded.

John responded, "as the greenskeeper, we have been given a special gift. We are allowed to witness the means by which God chose to fulfill the prayers of a few of his faithful. We are allowed, to see, behind the prayer curtain. We help these, the faithful, that come here to the Majestic, to see how God chose to answer their prayers."

"Where did courage come into it? She was flying with two great pilots," Michael responded easing up after John's response.

"Remember even the ace of aces, the Red Baron, recorded being fearful before his first solo. He says so in his writings. Even Amelia had much to fear, being a woman competing in a man's world. Each of them refused to submit to fear and experienced courage as a result. In the case of Helen and her request for courage, God could have silently and mysteriously answered. Were we to record these, answered prayers, there would not be enough room in the world to store the books.

But we serve a grand God who is gracious and loves to shower his faithful with answered prayer. And on special occasions, He goes out of the way to confirm an answer. Thus, with Helen, He sends none other than Amelia Earhart. She comes riding in on the clouds, like an angel, and the faithful prayers of a little girl are answered," John declared.

Michael responded, "Why was courage so important to Helen?"

"You and those 'why' questions. Do you not remember her story? Remember, she asked for courage not for herself but so that she could use it to help others," John remarked.

"I remember, she became a nurse. The Major General, at the ceremony, called her a nurse. Perhaps she used it during her nursing duties?" Michael supposed.

"Yes, She did become a nurse. If you don't remember her story, then I propose that you take us to where we can hear about how she used her courage on the field of battle," John challenged him as they stood on the path between the third green and the fourth tee at the Majestic of Purple Mountain.

"All right, then it is off to find out more about the courage of Helen," Michael replied as he began to walk but stopped abruptly, "I'm afraid that I may have forgotten. Now, just where would that be that we are going?"

"Have you truly forgotten?" John asked him as they stood on the path, "Remember, being the greenskeeper comes from the heart. Follow your heart. Where we go from here is up to you. I cannot take us there. Only you can take us there. Be courageous, Michael, and take us where we need to go."

In an instant, in the twinkling of an eye, they were transported to another location on the course. They found themselves under the shade of a Northern Red Oak tree. This tree sits alone, just a ways off the path before one comes to the tenth tee box. It has a short trunk, rounded top and is about ninety feet tall. Its leaves are from five to eight inches long. They are oblong in shape and have seven to eleven lobes. The tops of its acorns are nearly flat and resemble small brown berets. Its bark is red and is laced with short white furrows that when viewed from a distance form an almost recognizable argyle pattern.

In the fall, it is a brilliantly colorful and bright tree. It is the kind of tree that people love to go and see during the autumn leaf season. Of the many trees at the Majestic, this is one of the signature trees. It has a prestigious location, being on the extreme western boundary of the course. It has a twin, just as prestigious, that is planted in the same location by the first tee box. They are perfectly symmetrical and nearly indistinguishable. Like reflections, on a glassy smooth pond, they mirror one another.

Together, they courageously guard the western most boundary of the Majestic of Purple Mountain. Their bright red leaves would instill fear and respect, in the heart of any enemy, were there an enemy. Together, when viewed from the flagpole pedestal during the peak of autumn, they are stunning.

"And here we are! Was there ever any doubt?" Michael asserted.

"None whatsoever," said John from underneath the beautiful shade of the Northern Red, "I had faith you would bring us here."

"They will be here any moment now," Michael insisted, as he looked toward the path. He was standing next to John under the shade of the Northern Red.

"I see them now. The Final Foursome with their caddies behind them. Yes, and there are Mike and the Greenskeeper just ahead of them. They will be here soon," John commented while standing in the deep shade of the tree.

"We will stay right here and get a glimpse of 'courage'," Michael declared.

Chapter 28

"We are going right over there, under that Northern Red Oak tree," the Greenskeeper said, as he pointed to the strikingly beautiful tree just to the west of the tenth tee box. He and Mike went and stood underneath its shade.

"Oh, there it is again!" she said to her caddie Amelia, "I must go over there and experience the shade of that tree."

"I will tell the group that you will be right there to tee off on the tenth. I will have them wait for you. Just like last time," Amelia yelled, as she continued on to the tenth hole, not stopping this time.

Helen confidently entered the shade of Northern Red. As she walked through the shade, her appearance began to change. She was no longer in golfing attire, but now in U.S. Army fatigues. As she exited the shade, on the other side of the tree, she found herself in southwestern Germany. The date was Easter Sunday, in the month of April, in the year 1945.

"Where are we?" Mike asked, as he stood next to the Greenskeeper.

"We are in Europe, in southwestern Germany. The date is sometime near the end of World War II," the Greenskeeper declared. Then he turned and addressed Helen, "where are we?"

"We are at war. That is where we are. And we were on the move," she stated.

Mike asked, "where were you going?"

"My Nursing unit was stationed near the front lines. Our troops were advancing almost daily. They were pushing, the battle front, north and east. We were moving our medical support unit along with them but just a few miles behind the fighting. The war was going well, as far as wars could be said to be going well," she recalled.

"What town are we in— exactly?" Mike asked again.

Helen responded, "we are just south of a town called Darmstadt, Germany. This is an abandoned German airfield. We were using it, as a base, for our medical operation. Some of the team would remain here but I was moving northeast with the advancing war front."

"Why are you dressed differently from the rest of the nurses? That is you standing over there by that airplane isn't it?" Mike questioned as he looked across the airfield.

"Yes, that is me over there. I am wearing the uniform of an enlisted nurse, my old uniform. I chose not to wear the officer's uniform that had become the standard dress," Helen declared proudly.

"Why? Did it matter what uniform you wore?" Mike asked her.

"Well, that depends on who you ask. Congress passed a law making all nurses officers in the army. Before they did that, many soldiers wouldn't take directions from a nurse. They thought they were above us and that we were just women. We didn't get the respect we deserved. So, Congress cleared it up and we were all given field promotions. This happened just after my incident on the HMS Newfoundland when I earned the Purple Heart. But that is another story.

I chose to remain an enlisted nurse. I refused the promotion and all that came with it. There were other women, in the service, at the time that were not promoted to officer ranks. I decided that I would wait until things were made right for all women in the service," She recalled while touching the places on her uniform where officers insignias would have been.

"How did that go over with your fellow officers and soldiers?" the Greenskeeper asked.

"It was a mixed bag. Most did not understand but really did not say much about it. Others strongly disagreed. They thought it was disrespectful to refuse the promotion on those grounds. Some sneered at me. Some said I thought I was 'Amelia Earhart' or some other 'women's rights supporter'. I didn't like that much. A few, supported the position I had taken," she recalled painfully.

"So, what happened? That wasn't fair. You were a nurse and helped people get better. Why couldn't they help you?" Mike asked.

"It is not that they couldn't. It is that most wouldn't," she again recalled, "this day was a good example. My unit left me behind. I was tending to a serious patient issue and missed the departure time. No one even came to check on me."

"Where were they going?" the Greenskeeper asked.

"We were just south of Darmstadt and we were moving to the northeast. We were headed to a town called Gelnhausen. The road left Darmstadt and went northeast, bypassing Frankfurt. The road passed through Hanau a few miles before it reached Gelnhausen. What we are witnessing, is the moment when I learned they had left without me," she winced as she looked on.

"Now that looks familiar," Mike said pointing in the directions of the hangar, "that is one of those biplanes!"

The Greenskeeper added, "that looks like a JN-4HT. You are right Mike. But they were not used during World War II. The season for biplanes being used in battle was over by then. I wonder what it is doing there? Helen, any ideas?"

"Oh, I know all about this one. This is where things start to get interesting! Oh, how I wished Amelia would drop on in from the clouds. Like she did that day, over the golden wheat fields, of southeastern Kansas. But her seasons were cut short. We just never know when our seasons will end. She was lost in the South Pacific, some say near Nikumaroro Island, during her circumnavigation flight. That hurt me so, when I found out she had been lost," Helen recounted and gave pause, "anyway, the war continued as wars do. This plane was a relic from the last war and had been preserved by the Germans for some reason. I think it was used for war reenactments, perhaps. They painted it red and gave it German markings. It was strikingly similar to the Red Baron's color scheme. They left it behind, when they abandoned the airbase. It was here when we arrived and in perfect operating condition."

"How did you meet up with the people that left you behind? Or did you meet up with them?" Mike asked.

"That is where things got interesting," Helen said. Then she turned her gaze toward the hangar, where the Jenny sat waiting, "there was this one pilot. The kind of pilot that respects a nurse, when she passes up a promotion. So, he said he would fly me to Gelnhausen. He also promised that we would beat them there!"

"Did you beat them there? Did you? Tell us please?" Mike insisted.

"In a Jenny? Wasn't that dangerous? The Allies still didn't have all of Germany under control, at this point in the war," the Greenskeeper commented.

"You bet it was and that pilot knew it. He made sure the Jenny was armed and ready for battle. We had a machine gun, cockpit mounted rifles and one gravity bomb. However, it would probably not go well, if we encountered any German aircraft or ground fire. We were just too slow for the modern age of warfare. But I needed to get to Hanau and get there before my unit did! Oh, and he covered over those German markings with U.S. insignias," Helen recalled with a new sense of confidence.

"What happened next?" Mike asked her, now being engrossed in the story.

"I will tell you what happened! Midwestern American barnstorming was in season above midwestern Germany," Helen exclaimed. They all watched the Jenny roll down the runway and take to flight.

"There they go! How long did it take to meet up with your unit?" Mike asked.

"It wasn't supposed to be a long flight. We decided to follow the main roads, as they were to have been cleared in advance of the unit convoy. Things were going well ten minutes into the flight. We had another ten minutes in the air before landing in Gelnhausen. The scenery was beautiful. It was spring and the world was coming to life again after a hard winter. It was a great day to fly. There were sporadic clouds at three thousand feet. They were all white, thick, and puffy. They looked like cotton candy without the stick. We were almost to Gelnhausen and then we saw it," she said shaking her head.

"What did you see? What was it?" Mike asked quickly.

"Our convoy was under attack! It was the German sixth SS Mountain Division!" She said with a sneer.

"I hate those guys! I never liked the number six anyway!" Mike yelled, "what did you do? Did you turn back or go on to Gelnhausen?"

"Neither," Helen said with a grin.

"Neither? Then what did you do?" Mike replied as he tilted his head.

"We circled for a few minutes. I prayed for courage. I thought about Amelia and the time she flew in on the clouds. Somehow— it felt like she was there with me. Then we decided to fight!" Helen said with fire in her eyes and thunder in her voice. Then she began to recount the battle of Hanau.

"The pilot ascended into the clouds and then prepared to dive bomb their position. He set the plane into a seventy-five degree nose dive. When we came out of the clouds, they started firing at us from the ground. He then started a series of Aileron Rolls, while still diving. The bullets whizzed by us and a few made contact with our wings but the 'Jenny' held together. As we got close to the ground, he stopped the Aileron Rolls and prepared to drop the gravity bomb.

As he released the bomb, one last bullet ripped through the plane. My pilot was fatally wounded and died instantly. The bomb hit its target and destroyed the German personnel carrier and all aboard.

I knew that I should have been afraid but I wasn't. There was no time to think. But I thought back to my flight with Amelia. She told me to 'fly from the heart' and that is what I purposed to do in that moment.

So, I took the stick in my hand and pulled the plane out of the nose dive and back into the sky. Then I executed a banking turn and came back at them again. I put one of their vehicles in my sights and fired the rifle hitting one of them. Then I pulled up and did a wide turn, so that I could see what was happening below. It looked like they were in retreat. I was elated but thinking about how I was going to land the Jenny. Little did I know, landing was the least of my problems!" Helen insisted.

"What problem? You got 'em didn't you? They were giving up and you won!" Mike didn't understand.

"Mike, sometimes you win the battle but lose the war," she told him.

"But we won World War II— didn't we?" Mike asked.

"Yes, we did. Please let Helen finish the story," the Greenskeeper interjected.

"German bombers! A pair of JU 87's, the Stuka, were at twelve o'clock. Although most of the German Luftwaffe was destroyed, there were still a few planes out there. Apparently, the SS called in a couple of these guys, to help them out. Or they were just flying by at random. Either way, they were coming after me.

The Stuka was a bomber and not a fighter. They were poorly defended and didn't handle well. This at least made it a fair fight, considering I was in a plane thirty years its senior. I was seriously under powered though. Its top speed was just over two hundred miles per hour. They were almost three times as fast, as the Jenny.

Hopefully, this little red plane would remind them, of another little red plane from another day. Hopefully, they would think about the Red Baron! Maybe they would think he had returned and had switched sides for this war. I was counting on that. The mind can play tricks on us you know!

I leveled off at 2,000 feet and they were straight ahead of me but a long way out. I began a classic barrel roll. The maneuver my grandfather taught me, while we flew over the bearded golden wheat fields of Kansas, that one summer in twenty-six. The world was nicer then. There were no bullets flying past us then. I am sure there were bullets whizzing by, in the mind of my grandfather, as he flew those maneuvers. Oh, how I missed him now! I missed his laugh. I missed his beard blowing in the wind.

Before they got to me, I pulled the Jenny into a half Cuban. It was the trick that Amelia taught me. If it fooled my grandfather, it would fool these guys! They flew underneath me and slowed. When I came out of the clouds, I was just completing the Half Cuban. I dropped in just behind them and they did not know I was behind them. I let go with blasts from the guns and took one of the Stuka's out! The remaining Stuka began to gain speed and went into a banking turn. I didn't like it.

I immediately pulled the Jenny into a Hammerhead maneuver and headed straight up for the clouds. I thought that I could hide in them, if I could just make it to them. The Stuka was not fooled by this and began to follow behind me. The bullets came whizzing by. The engine started smoking about the time I hit the clouds. I climbed and climbed, hoping to reach Heaven. Maybe angels will grab my wings and take me home, I prayed.

Then the Stuka went flying past me. In the clouds, he lost sight of me! We popped out above the clouds and he was almost in my sights. I pulled a hard left rudder and fired, as the plane cartwheeled. I hit the target! Then the Jenny sputtered and died. Together, we fell back into the clouds. The seasons of the barnstormers had truly ended.

It was as if God gently pulled me out of the clouds and placed me upon the grounds of the Majestic. In this one last maneuver, the maneuver of faith, the grace of God conquered the gravity of my sin. The next thing I know, I am marching up the stairs and on to the first tee of the Majestic of Purple Mountain. Then, the Fife and Drum Corps played 'Chester' and the Major General said 'well done soldier'! And as if that wasn't enough, there was Amelia waiting to be my caddie! Dressed in her whites, she looked angelic. I am sure I will leave the Majestic on the wings of angels," Helen smiled, at the thought of it, as she finished her story.

"Are you ready to go back now?" the Greenskeeper asked her.

"Yes, There is nothing more for us here," she said as she turned away from that Easter Sunday in the year 1945. As she walked through the shade of the Northern Red, her clothing changed back into proper golfing attire. As she exited the shade of the tree, the year was again 1987. She confidently marched toward Amelia, her caddie. Then she abruptly stopped and turned back to look at the Greenskeeper.

"Yes, Helen, I will tell your sister about the picture in the box with the peppermint tobacco," he assured her, "I don't think your mother will find out now."

With that Helen turned and walked off with Amelia. They were headed toward the tenth tee.

"What happened to her friends? The ones she was trying to save?" Mike asked him.

"The incident at Hanau, like the HMS Newfoundland, can be found in the history books. It will make for a great school report someday," the Greenskeeper replied.

"Where has Helen been all of these years? It was 1945 when this happened and now it is 1987?" Mike asked him.

"With God, a blink of the eye is as a day and a day is as the blink of an eye," the Greenskeeper said.

"I don't understand," Mike replied.

"Neither do I, but I believe it. We are witnesses to it," the Greenskeeper said.

"How did you know what she was going to say?" Mike asked him.

"Some things will remain a mystery at the Majestic. I knew in my heart that her sister needed to know about the pictures," the Greenskeeper declared, as he began to walk toward the tenth tee. There were more stories to be told that afternoon, before the course closed for the day.

Chapter 29

Michael and John watched, from beneath the Northern Red Oak, as the Greenskeeper and Mike followed Helen and Amelia to the tenth tee. The players in this Final Foursome were turning the corner. They were entering the part of the course where gallantry is put on display. Each of these players would come through and score exceptionally well, on the northern arm, of the Majestic on this day.

"You said we would see courage and we did," Michael confessed.

"Yes, we did at that. Helen was not the typical player. Not at all," John commented.

"How so?" Michael asked.

"We didn't have to explain any of it to her. She pulled it all together. She was of much faith. Soon, her faith will be brought to fruition," he announced.

"What is the 'it' you are referring to?" Michael questioned.

"The 'it' is that her prayers, for courage, were answered by God through faith. Just as she had asked, her courage was used to the benefit of others and not of herself," John replied.

"When will her faith be brought to 'fruition'? During the playing of "Taps"?" Michael hypothesized.

"Yes, a little anticlimactic at this point but yes," John said, "so, where are we off to now?"

"I would suppose that we would want to take a look at the closing ceremonies? Wouldn't we?" Michael suggested.

"We would, indeed," John responded.

In an instant, in the twinkling of an eye, they were transported to the patio of the clubhouse. They were standing at the western edge of the patio, between the staircases. When viewed from the flagpole pedestal, these stairs form a heart shape. This was one of the best areas from which to view the playing of "Taps". They stood there in anticipation of what was to come.

The Final Foursome battled with the Majestic of Purple Mountain, until the sun had nearly set. In their own way, each player demonstrated gallantry, fidelity and service during their collective struggle. Although each played the same course, the course challenged each player in a unique way. These challenges refined, shaped and allowed grand purposes to be displayed. There remained one last challenge before them, the eighteenth green.

Just before the sun began to set on May 9, 1987, the Greenskeeper assumed his position, on the flagpole pedestal. He steadfastly faced to the west, with bugle tucked at his side, being resolutely ready to render his service. His apprentice, at attention, was standing on the walkway just to the east of the pedestal. Above them, an unwavering flag waved briskly in the mountain breeze.

Their rounds now complete, these players faced one last challenge. There was yet one enemy left to defeat, the enemy called death. These, that came here, had faith that death was conquered long ago. These that had given their lives for others had first given their hearts to the One who had conquered death. For these conquerors, all that remained was the final surrender.

As the sun set, "Taps" was softly sounded. The sound reverberated, within the boundaries of the Majestic of Purple Mountain, penetrating the souls of those that heard it. As it played, each soldier surrendered their purple heart shaped Badge of Merit and entered into the majestic grace of God. In solemn silence, the Greenskeeper and his apprentice retreated resolutely. An unwavering flag waved briskly in the mountain breeze over the Majestic of Purple Mountain. The flag would remain illuminated until the dawn of the next day.

Chapter 30

As they walked toward the cabin, the Greenskeeper began talking with his apprentice, "So, what do you think about being my apprentice for the summer?"

"I think it will be an acceptable arrangement," Mike responded, as he walked along the path that led from the clubhouse to the cabin of the greenskeeper.

"Well, then, it is settled. After the morning working sessions, you will join me out on the course and assist with the duties of being the greenskeeper of Purple Mountain," he stated, as they neared the cabin.

Mike ran out ahead of him and toward the barn, "Christopher! Christopher! Where are you?"

"I am in here, working on the Jeep. I lost track of time. Where have you been? It is getting late," Christopher said to him.

"I have been working! Remember? I am the apprentice of the Greenskeeper you should know!" he said while running toward his brother.

"Yeah. I forgot that already— Nah, I didn't! How was it?" he asked him, as he started to cleanup for the day.

"It was really cool. We met some golfers and they told us some old war stories and stuff like that," Mike told him, "so, what have you been doing?"

"What does it look like I have been doing?" he started, "while you were out doing nothing, I have been working on this Jeep of ours! How does it look?"

"Not quite ready to drive home . . . maybe!" Mike said with a smile, "let's get going, huh?"

"Yeah, I called mom and told her we would be running late. I went up to the clubhouse and they let me use the phone. I explained everything to her and she was ok with our staying up here this extra time. I would have come and got you if she weren't," he told him.

"Well, how are we getting home? The tram is closed already. And we can't take that . . . Oops," Mike questioned with a smile.

"Thanks for the support there buddy pal! Somehow, I think the Greenskeeper has it figured out. He has a way, with that kind of thing, I am finding out," Christopher contended.

The Greenskeeper walked into the barn saying, "gentlemen, it is time to head home. Don't worry about putting things away in here. It will all be here, just like this, when you come back next week."

"How are we getting home tonight?" Mike asked him.

"We will take the Dodge. Is that ok with both of you?" he asked them.

"Sounds good to me!" Christopher said.

Mike was nearly in the truck saying, "I like the Power Wagon! Let's go!"

They all loaded into the truck and headed down the mountain using the service entrance. This was not the day that John had expected. He was impressed with these two brothers. He knew that the next month would pass by quickly and that the boys would soon be enjoying the summer season and its offerings. His mind drifted, as he drove them home. He thought about his upcoming mission. He didn't particularly like the idea of being away from the Majestic for an extended period of time. Although, he had permission to be away from his duties. He wondered when and what he would tell the boys of his upcoming trip.

The Greenskeeper drove back to the cabin after taking the boys home. As was his custom, he made coffee in the coffee press, and retired into the reserve library. A small fire burned on the hearth floor. He pulled down the necessary *Books of Merit*, the sketch book and pulled his last Bolivar Inmensas cigar from the humidor. Babe should be coming soon, he thought to himself, as he lit the cigar. Now, there were letters to write, stories to tell, and sketches to draw. He pulled the fountain pen out of the desk drawer. It is the one with the heart shaped breather hole and he prepared to write.

Dear Mrs. Henderson,

Please indulge me with a few moments of your time. My name is John and I am the greenskeeper of the Majestic of Purple Mountain. What is to follow will be hard to accept at first. However, you will find comfort in what has been sent to you. The enclosed sealed letter is authentic and contains details that only you could know.

Today, your father played the Majestic of Purple Mountain. He carded a score of par 72 with the help of his caddie Fred Astaire. Your Father received a warm reception here at the Majestic. I was in the pleasure of his company as we spent some time together today. He asked that I send the enclosed letter. It has been sealed and is addressed specifically to you.

Please feel free to contact me any time.

Regards,

the Greenskeeper

    He sealed the letters in the customary fashion and set them to the side. He continued this process until all of the letters were complete. Letters were sent to family members of Helen, Deron, Wally and Kyle as these were the players that made the Final Foursome for May 9, 1987. He recorded the dates and scores, in the *Books of Merit* beside the names of each of the players. Then his attention turned to the sketch books. By now, it was early Sunday morning, May 10, 1987.

Chapter 31

Michael and John continued their mystical march through Michael's memories of a mid-spring season. Michael decided that they should visit the events of Saturday, May 16, 1987. That date was the second working session for Mike and Christopher, at the Majestic. Each of his work days, during that period in May 1987, would be fairly similar to the previous working session. Each would follow a consistent pattern. Michael realized this, as he continued to walk through his memories of that period.

His heart was opening again, to the Majestic, like a flower in the springtime. To his heart, some memories were like spring time showers. With each word, thought, and sight raining down, on his soul, providing much needed moisture. While others were like soft sunlit spring time days, whose radiant rays, penetrating the eye of his heart, steadily warmed his soul. His heart, like a flower in the spring time, was exposed to the elements that cause growth. Should this flower not bloom, during this one season, then it never would.

Michael and John were waiting on the first tee, as Michael began, "I don't quite remember what task you had us completing for you on this fine morning. However, I am sure that we did not start working on an empty stomach."

John added, "There is no doubt that I fed you boys well. Anyway, what is it that you expect to find here."

"I am not certain about that. At the time, I thought that this working exercise wouldn't ever end. As a child, I had such a limited view of the concept of time," Michael said.

John replied, "time is a difficult concept to grasp for anyone. I am not sure we ever truly understand it. However, now it is time to watch."

The boys, Christopher and Mike, were nearly running down the path toward the first tee with the Greenskeeper following a few yards behind at a brisk pace. A few moments later and they were all assembled at the first tee. It was 8:45 in the morning and tee times would not start until 9:45 AM. Today the Greenskeeper would teach them a new skill.

The Greenskeeper began, "gentlemen, today we are going to learn a new skill. It is the skill of green speed measurement. However, as we walk the course we will relocate tee markers, on an as needed basis."

"How will we determine when the tee markers need to be moved?" Christopher asked him.

"Use what you learned from last week. Remember, I look at them on a daily basis and change their position frequently. Just imagine, how you would like the tee area to look, if you were the player here today. When in doubt, you can always ask me," the Greenskeeper told them.

Mike assessed the first tee areas, "these look ok to me. No need to move any of these."

"Mike, Mike, Mike! Please explain how you can see the red markers" the Greenskeeper now pointing his finger, "all the way down there? We must walk the tee boxes to make a proper assessment. Remember, proper care of the Majestic requires a hearts on approach and paying attention to the details. So, let's start walking the tee boxes."

They walked together, down the fairway of the Washington hole, with the Greenskeeper talking about the various trees, shrubs, grasses and flowers. He knew he had little time left with these boys and wanted to share as much as he could with them. As they passed the stump, of the Carolina Cherry Tree, the Greenskeeper failed to explain the cause of its demise. Some legends defy explanation. There was another one, growing nearby, with its white small flowers in bloom. When they reached the green, a wooden apparatus was laying in the fringe.

"This is a Stimpmeter," the Greenskeeper told them. He lifted the green colored device off of the ground and held it in his left hand. He swung it back and forth several times, as if it were a golf club. This particular Stimpmeter was constructed out of wood. It is basically, a v-shaped track. It is roughly a yard long and is just wide enough to support a golf ball. As a ball sits on the v-shaped piece of wood, only two points of the ball touch the device. There is a groove cut perpendicular to the length of the rail about six inches from the top that holds the ball in place. The other end of the device is fashioned, in such a way, as to prevent a ball from bouncing when rolling off the device. Rather, when rolling off of the device, the ball releases into a smooth roll. This device simulates, in a consistent fashion, a well struck putt.

"What are we going to do with that funny looking thing?" Mike asked him.

"We are going to measure the speed of the greens with it," he told them.

Christopher chimed in, "why is it called a Stimpmeter?"

The Greenskeeper replied while swinging the device from side to side and walking. He stopped in an area of the green that was quite level and said, "it is named after Ed Stimpson.

the Majestic of Purple Mountain

He invented it, back in 1935, after attending the U.S. Open held that year."

"How does it do that?" Mike asked him while taking a closer look at the device.

"Come over here and I will show you," he told him.

"OK," Mike said as he took the Stimpmeter from the Greenskeeper, "now what do I do?"

"Put this ball on the board and slowly lift the end until the ball starts rolling," the Greenskeeper instructed him.

Mike slowly lifted the device until the ball started to roll down the groove and he held it at a 20 degree angle until the ball left the device. "Cool!" The ball came to a stop some distance from him.

"Now what do we do?" Christopher asked the Greenskeeper.

"We measure it, that is what we do! Take this tee and stick it in the green next to the end of the stick," he said as he pulled out a tape measure from his pocket.

"OK. From the spot where the ball left the stick, it measures nine feet and eight inches. So, what now? Are we done?" Christopher asked him.

"No, we are not," the Greenskeeper announced, "we must roll it two more times in that same direction. Then we will measure each of them as well. Each roll must be within eight inches of the others. If they are not, we start the process again at another spot on the green. If they are, we calculate the average distance of the three rolls. Then we go to where those balls stopped. Then we measure back to the tee we placed in the green, using the average distance we just calculated. That is the spot where we will place the end of the Stimpmeter. Then we will roll three balls back toward the tee. We will measure those and calculate the average distance."

Mike protested, "That could take all day!"

"Yeah," Christopher joined in.

"Let's keep them rolling or we will be here all day. Once we get the six rolls we can average them and record the speed of the green," the Greenskeeper told them.

"So, the distance the ball travels, on average, counts for the speed we will give this green?" Christopher ventured a guess.

"That is correct. We will average the two averages and that will be the speed of this green. Now lets keep rolling or we will be here all day!" the Greenskeeper suggested.

Mike asked, "why is it important to know this information. This is an awful lot of work to just measure how far a ball will roll?"

The Greenskeeper replied, "Those why questions are always the hardest! I will answer the 'why' question with a what answer. The more a golfer knows, about the conditions of the course, the better prepared he is to play it."

Christopher asked, "How do they know the speeds when they come to play?"

"As the green speeds are measured they are recorded and those recordings are given to the clubhouse for posting in the golf guide," the Greenskeeper told them.

Mike asked, "will we measure all of the greens? That could take all day!"

"Is there somewhere you need to be?" he asked him.

"Not really, it just seems like this will take forever!" he stated.

"Quit your whining! We can do this and we will do this!" Christopher spoke up.

"OK, Stimpey! Let's get rolling," Mike said laughingly.

"We will only measure six greens today. I typically complete the measurements on six greens every day, except Sunday," the Greenskeeper announced and his words were warmly accepted.

They finished up on the first green and recorded the measurements. Then they began to walk the course from the second tee through the eighteenth green. Along the way, the Greenskeeper stopped at various places to show them the uniqueness of the Majestic of Purple Mountain. He wasn't sure how much, if any, information these boys would remember but that did not stop him from trying.

They walked the entire course in under two hours. After that, they were assigned to their midmorning activities. Christopher had raking duties on the Lincoln hole, again. Mike had grass mowing duties on the same. The Greenskeeper kept a close watch on the boys during this working period. Both of the boys, would develop character and physical strength through the tasks that they were assigned, at the hand of the Greenskeeper.

Upon completion of their duties, it was time for lunch. They ate a quick bite and both boys were ready to start their afternoon activities. Christopher was excited to work on the Jeep and Mike couldn't wait to get down to the first tee.

Michael and John watched the morning activities with light hearts. Michael began to realize the mountainous magnitude of detail contained within his memories. In the span of two weeks, he was exposed to the mystery and majesty of the Majestic in a way that few would ever experience. However, he had not been to the summit. Mike was coming of age, growing taller and stronger, with each passing day, during that period of time in the spring of 1987.

Michael decided that this was the last working session that he would revisit. However, there were two more events he had in mind to visit, while he was scaling the mysterious mountains within his memories. The first, was a medium sized mountain of a memory. It was of an afternoon spent with a KIA soldier. The second, was a monstrous mountain memory of Everest sized proportion. He was not yet prepared to scale such a dangerous slope. However, he knew, that to reach the summit, he must traverse the Hillary Step.

Chapter 32

Michael and John waited, on the first tee, for the arrival of the Greenskeeper and Mike. It was the afternoon of Saturday, May 16, 1987, and the final tee time of the day, a Final Foursome tee time. Michael decided to focus on a particular soldier that had been killed in action in Korea. Michael and John would watch, as the events of the afternoon unfolded before them.

"I love to see the Major General and hear the sounds of the Fife and Drum Corps as they play," Mike said. He watched the Major General and the Fife and Drum Corps walk off of the tee box and into the wooded tree line in the distance. Mike was new to this scene but he was learning quickly.

"Yes, it always brings me chills to watch it. Even after all of these years, each time is as fresh as the last. It is like meeting with old friends, after a long absence. There is an anticipation about it," the Greenskeeper commented.

"Who is that caddie over there and what did he hand you earlier?" Mike asked him.

The Greenskeeper held the box tight, "That is Babe Ruth and only the greatest baseball player ever to play the game."

"I have heard of him. He was a Yankee— right?" Mike ventured.

"Yes, he was. Babe Ruth was part of the 1927 Murderers Row. The Yankees's that year included Earle Combs, Mark Koenig, Lou Gehrig, Bob Meusel and Tony Lazzeri. The Sultan of Swat, Babe Ruth, set the single season home run record with 60 of them. The Yank's finished with 110 victories and won the World Series. Most would say, they were the best team ever to play the game of baseball," the Greenskeeper declared. "When he comes to caddie, and he gets a lot of requests mind you, he always brings me something. He brings me a box of Cuban cigars."

"I don't like those. They smell really bad. You like them?" Mike asked him.

Looking at the box, he responded "Actually, it is a habit that I should give up. They will probably kill me one day. But, once you start something like this it is extremely difficult to quit. So, don't ever start. However, I do find them pleasurable. There is just something about them that is indescribable. I take the box and put it away in the cabin and pull one out every now and then. I am glad to see him, because I was running low on them."

"Please don't smoke them around me!" Mike insisted.

"Since you and Christopher came, I have quit smoking them while I am on the golf course," he commented.

"Thank you," Mike responded, "I like his uniform. Those thin black pinstripes look really neat on his white pants and jersey. Did he always wear the number three?"

"Beginning in 1929 he did. Before that time, the players didn't have numbers on them," the Greenskeeper commented, "we should be moving along now, as they are headed down the first fairway."

They followed the Final Foursome over the next several holes. The Greenskeeper took the opportunity to tell Michael

247

about the Pampas grass with its plume like flowers lining the third hole.

"Pampas grass is a tough shrub and will grow nearly anywhere. It grows fast and thick and is a great refuge for some of the small animals that live here. It also creates an obstacle for the golfers who happen to send an errant tee shot beyond the edges of the fairway," the Greenskeeper explained while they walked along.

Mike listened, as he stroked one of the flower plumes. They were soft and fuzzy to the touch, "at least they can enjoy its flowers when they do."

The Greenskeeper wasted no time with his young apprentice. He purposed to teach him as much as he could before his upcoming trip. They walked ahead of the foursome and settled in the shade of Southern Red who stood between the third green and fourth tee.

"Babe, go on ahead to the fourth and wait for me there. I am going over there, under the shade of that tree." Charles told his caddie. Charles was a corporal in the U.S. Army's I Corps, 7th division. He was killed in action during the Battle of Pork Chop Hill on July 11, 1953. Many lives were courageously given, during this battle, for a location with little or no strategic value.

As he entered the shade of Southern Red, his appearance began to change. He changed from a man of 24 years of age into a teenager of about 16 years in age wearing a well worn baseball uniform. The hat seemed out of place, as it appeared to be new and looked as if it had never been worn. It was a New York Yankee's hat. Around his neck and hanging outside of his jersey was a gold necklace. Attached to the necklace was a garnet stone. As he exited the shade of the tree, he was standing on the east side of Purple Mountain and the year was 1945. Mike and the Greenskeeper stood beside him.

"Hi. My name is Mike!" he said.

"Hello, Mike. My name is Charles. That is my school over there," he said looking out across the field. They were standing behind the school and up the mountain just a bit. There was a baseball field behind the school and he seemed to be focused on the activity around the ball diamond.

"Charles, my name is John and I am the greenskeeper of the Majestic. It is a pleasure to meet you," he said.

"I am pleased to meet you. The Majestic is a wonderful course and I am looking forward to getting back there to play. But there was something about the shade of that tree that drew me and now we are standing here," Charles said.

"Do you know where we are?" the Greenskeeper asked him.

Charles looked around intently, "Yes, we are in Worthington, Virginia. That is St. Margaret-Mary Industrial school over there. That is where I lived before I joined the army."

"What is all of the commotion over there today?" the Greenskeeper asked pointing at the baseball field behind the school.

Charles smiled, "I remember it well. This is the day Babe Ruth visited us and gave us the surprise of our lives!"

"Babe Ruth was in Worthington! How come I never heard of it?" Mike said.

"Sometimes we don't hear about all of the good and wonderful things that people do. Sometimes they want to keep it quiet. Sometimes they don't let their right hand know what their left is doing!" Charles stated.

"Why didn't he want anyone to know?" Mike asked him.

"I am not sure exactly. I know that we were all sworn to secrecy. The nuns told us not to tell anyone or there would be trouble. Babe told us to be quiet about it too. But the nuns knew that we wouldn't listen to him for that. We needed to know that our lives would be taken if we told. We didn't cross the nuns!" he said with a serious tone in his voice.

"What was the Babe doing here?' the Greenskeeper asked him.

"He told us that he went to a school just like this one when he was a kid. He left it when he started playing baseball. He was here to teach us about the game of baseball. He taught us about life. We trusted him immediately. Not only was he the greatest baseball player ever, he was one of us too. The things he did on the baseball field, I think, pale in comparison to the things he did off of it. What he did during his twenty-two seasons playing professional baseball are legendary. What he did for us during that one day was fiduciary. He would die of cancer just three years later. At the age of fifty-three, his seasons came to an end.

Anyway, he spent the entire afternoon with just our team. Our insignificant team, from some old Catholic reform school, on the back side of a lost Virginia mountain, had the Babe for a day! Think of it, just us nine guys and the greatest player ever to play the game!" Charles recounted.

"If I may ask, how did you come to be at the school?" the Greenskeeper asked.

"I wasn't the best behaved kid and I gave my parents a hard time of it. They couldn't do anything with me but they tried. They finally sent me here. My dad gave me this necklace. The stone meant that we would meet again someday, he told me. Anyway, there was family in Worthington too," He recalled.

"So, did you talk to him? The Babe . . .?" Mike asked.

"Yes, I did. It was like he could read me, no matter what I threw at him. When I threw junk, he didn't respond. When I got honest and threw my best stuff at him he stepped in and told it like it was. He had an eye for seeing into the soul. He knew my story and I didn't even have to tell him. He said, I was just like he was as a kid. He said 'I learned early how to drink beer and wine and whiskey' and he said 'I was about five the time I first chewed tobacco'. He also said 'that if it wasn't for baseball, I would be in a penitentiary or in a cemetery'," Charles recounted for them. "Just like the Babe, I was looking for something. I prayed for a place where I could belong and make a difference. The Babe encouraged me to belong to something greater than myself. He reminded me that greatness can come from what appears to be insignificant beginnings."

"So, what happened?" Mike again asked him.

"We played ball! He showed us how to hit and pitch. He was a great pitcher, you know. He told us everything we ever needed to know, all in one afternoon. He signed nine baseballs. Then he handed one of them to each of us. Imagine, nine dirt poor kids with a ball signed by the king," he told them.

"What happened to the ball?" the Greenskeeper asked.

"Funny you should ask that now. It is just about to head our way. I was dumb enough to take the ball he signed for me and pitch it to him! Guess what? Yep . . ., you guessed it. The King of Clout crushed it!" he announced to them. They watched as the pitcher threw the ball and Babe hit it. It flew over the fence, down a slope and into a crevice in the rocks.

Mike watching the ball in flight, "Wow! That was a home run! Now I know why they call him the King of Swing!"

"I'll say it was. He is the High Priest of Swat, you know!" the Greenskeeper added.

They watched as the pitcher ran after the ball. He paused, as the ball flew over the fence, down a hill and gone from sight. He continued his chase by jumping the fence and then heading down the hill.

Mike, Charles and the Greenskeeper moved in for a closer look. They saw the pitcher go down to the bottom of the hill and enter a small rocky area. They watched as he tilted his head and looked intently at the ground. Then, he disappeared from view behind the rocks.

They went in for an even closer look. They came to the place where they last saw him and he was gone.

"Where did he go? Who is he anyway? Houdini?" Mike said in disbelief.

"That is me!" Charles announced to him.

The Greenskeeper looking around, said, "Interesting!"

"Hey, what is that over there?" Mike said, as he looked up the hill just a few yards. There, nearly hidden, was a small crevice in the rocks. It was just wide enough for a youth to slip through.

"It looks like an opening to a cave. I never heard of one being found anywhere close to here though," the Greenskeeper commented, "maybe the ball landed so hard it knocked some rocks loose and exposed a cave entrance?"

Moving toward the cave, Mike said, "I am going to see what is down there!"

"Wait! It could be dangerous!" the Greenskeeper said. However, it was too late as Mike had already gone in.

As he entered the cave, he expected it to be dark. However, he noticed that the walls seemed to have a shimmer. It was like looking up into the sky, on a moonless night, and seeing the Milky Way. He could see the outline of the young pitcher, stooped over and holding something. It was almost round, and shimmered just like the walls of the cave. The pitcher held it up to his face for a few seconds before he turned to leave the cave. Mike quickly exited the cave, ahead of the pitcher. The pitcher exited the cave and stopped. He stood at the entrance. He alternately looked at the ball in his hand and then at the cave entrance. He sat the ball down, on the ground, a safe distance from the entrance.

The pitcher saw a group of loose rocks above the cave entrance. They were slightly covered with dirt and debris. He climbed to that area and began to work the rocks loose until they fell, one after the other. He stopped when he had covered the small entrance completely. Then, he came down and picked up the ball. He walked back up the hill with the Ruth ball in his hand.

The Greenskeeper asked, "What was he doing in there?"

"He went in there to get that baseball. There was something shiny in there and it got on the ball too," Mike told them.

"So, Charles, you have been quiet over there?" the Greenskeeper said to him, "would you like to say something?"

"It has been so long, that I nearly forgot about that. I remember running down the hill to get the ball and finding it. But in the excitement of it all I forgot about the cave." Charles recounted as he watched his younger self disappear up and over the hill.

"What did you see in there, Mike?" the Greenskeeper asked.

"There was some kind of silvery white powder on the walls and on that ball." Mike told them.

"That is right. I remember that now. The walls were shiny in there. I thought that I would cover up the entrance and hide it. Later, I would return and explore its contents," Charles told them, as he looked in the direction of the cave opening.

"Did you ever go back?" Mike asked.

Charles turned away and started up the hill, "not that I can remember. I have seen all that I need to see here."

the Majestic of Purple Mountain

The Greenskeeper and Mike began to follow him up the hill. They walked past the fence of the ball field and back to Southern Red. Charles entered the shade of Southern Red ahead of them and left the year 1945 for the last time.

The Greenskeeper was next to enter the shade of Southern Red. He followed Charles closely, momentarily losing track of Mike.

Mike was last to enter the shade of Southern Red. He loved the game of baseball and meeting the Babe. He took one last long look at the old ball diamond and the school as they were in 1945. Then, as he looked back, it was like watching a time-lapse motion picture. The kind used in a documentary. He noticed the passage of time by the changing of the seasons and the look of the automobiles in the parking lot. The huge rounded sedans of the 1940s gave way to the fin tailed cars of the 1950s and then to the muscle cars of the late 1960s. The cars became sleeker and smaller in the 1980s due to the oil shortages of the late 1970s. But the motion picture didn't end with the year 1987 it continued.

Mike's time lapse movie now became more of a vision. It looked more like a series, of Picasso paintings, than a dry and drab time lapse documentary. Mike saw a great red dragon with a huge tail and black smoke coming from its nostrils. With mighty swings of its tail, it utterly destroyed the old school. Not one brick remained standing on another. Then the dragon unleashed yellow beasts, with each having a single sharp claw. The beasts scraped away the debris, as black smoke billowed from their nostrils. The beasts clawed and clawed, at the earth, with their sharp claws. They suddenly stopped and backed away. The ground, where the school formerly stood, looked as if it had become a solid sheet of black granite. Then rising, along the edges of the sheet, were solid black granite walls. The walls stopped at a height that was about equal to the height of the red dragon. Then the red dragon stomped away. The structure that remained appeared to be a huge black granite castle.

They all exited the shade, of Southern Red, at about the same time and were back in the year 1987. Mike came running out of the shade and headed for the fourth tee. He did not look back. He was running to see the Babe, who happened to be, the biggest guy in the group.

Running up to the Babe, Mike began "Mr. Ruth, please tell me about Murderers' row? I want to know everything!"

Back near the tree, Charles, now in proper golfing attire, started to walk toward the fourth tee. Then mid-stride he paused and looked back at the Greenskeeper.

"I gave that ball to my nephew, Alexander. I wonder what he did with it? Anyway, I always planned on telling him about that place I found back there. His family was involved in mining interests, you know," Charles recalled, as he looked at the Greenskeeper.

"I will write him and tell him about it. Is that ok with you?" he asked.

"I would appreciate that. Alexander was like a younger brother to me. He is a good kid and had it rougher than I did. At least I had my family. He lost his at an early age. Anyway, I think he will know what to do with whatever is down there, if anyone would," Charles said. Then, he turned and headed to the fourth tee.

The Greenskeeper and his apprentice followed the Final Foursome as they played the remaining holes of the front nine. The Greenskeeper and Mike were allowed access into the stories, of the other players, as the round progressed. This was the practice and privilege of the greenskeeper of the Majestic of Purple Mountain.

In the distance and throughout the afternoon, Michael and John followed and watched. Michael was still scaling the mountainous memories of that mystical spring season in 1987.

Chapter 33

The Final Foursome of Saturday, May 16, 1987, had just finished the ninth hole and were headed to the tenth tee. Above them, a strikingly beautiful blue sky was streaked with whispery white cirrostratus clouds. Like the ends of eagles' wings, they soared high in the sky. Completing the heavenly scene, a group of low hanging cumulus clouds leisurely floated in the sky. They were on their way to wherever it is that clouds call home. It was another late afternoon, at the Majestic of Purple Mountain.

The Greenskeeper and Mike waited in the shade of the Northern Red. They were just a short distance from the tenth tee and were waiting for Charles to arrive.

As they neared, the Babe was saying "the way a team plays as a whole determines its success. You may have the greatest bunch of individual stars in the world, but if they don't play together, the club won't be worth a dime." He changed the conversation, as he looked toward the shade of the Northern Red "go ahead now. The shade of that tree over there is calling you. I'll be waiting for you when you get back and we will take our best swing at finishing this round under par."

Charles walked into the deep shade of the Northern Red. As he walked, he transformed into a Korean War era soldier. His U.S. Army issued uniform was constructed of herringbone twill. The standard color was olive drab No. 7. A U.S. Army insignia, gold on black, was sewn above the left jacket pocket. The insignia was partially covered by a small purple cloth cut in the shape of a heart. He wore black double buckle boots made with a leather upper and sole. His laces were tied together in several odd places but were still fit for duty. Charles was now standing on Pork Chop Hill, in Korea. The Greenskeeper and his apprentice, Mike, were at his side. The date was July 11, 1953, and it was a black moonless night.

"Where are we?" Mike asked as he stood, in the darkness, close to the Greenskeeper. The sounds of war reverberated through them and the flashes of exploding bombs bounced off of them.

"We are in hell, if you are asking me and please excuse my French," Charles began, "we are in the final moments of the Battle of Pork Chop Hill."

"What are we looking at?" Mike asked him.

"We are looking at what happens when Generals become politicians, while they are still Generals. We are looking at what happens when soldiers become brothers, while they are still soldiers. We are looking at my unit. They are over there," Charles said pointing to the ridge-top, "underneath that flimsy stack of sandbags the army called a bunker but we called home plate," he finished.

They were looking at a partial sandbag structure cut into the top of Pork Chop Hill. In all its unsung glory, it stood about four feet tall and was shaped in a 'U'. It had sandbags on three sides, was heavily timbered and had a partial rooftop made of scrap tin. There were slots between the sandbag stacks where a gun barrel could poke through. It was a cold, dark, and dirty place and it smelled of war.

Mike continued to question, "What are they doing?"

"They are defending their position from the Chinese Army. They won't let them over that hill!" Charles said.

"What is that red light streaking through the sky? It looks like it came from where your unit was, from over there?" Mike asked him.

"That is a flare, a red star rocket, and it is sending a message that we are under attack!" Charles continued, "the Chinese were advancing on our position and they were getting close. We only needed to hold them off for just a few more minutes."

"You said 'just a few more minutes'? What was going to happen in just a 'few more minutes '?" the Greenskeeper asked.

"In just a few more minutes, the General would give an order to abandon our positions on Pork Chop Hill and end this political exercise and the battle behind it," Charles recounted for them.

"So, what happened?" Mike asked.

Charles began, "Minutes after we sent the flare up, gunfire continued. We hoped the Chinese would stop, knowing that we called in reinforcements but they didn't. My unit continued to return fire and suddenly the shooting stopped.

Suddenly, the entire hill top became illuminated. Our reinforcements had turned on the spot lights and were lighting up the hill. It looked like a baseball field at night. They were trying to expose the Chinese positions for us. But we couldn't see anything of them. We knew they were still there because of the occasional sniper fire. We waited for what seemed like an eternity. I looked through the slits in the sandbags to see the enemy. Nothing.

Then, there was movement, at twelve o'clock. It was a young Chinese soldier holding a grenade. I didn't have a clean shot at him though, as he was behind a short mound.

the Majestic of Purple Mountain

The mound was about sixty feet six inches in front of us. He waited and waited holding that grenade in his hand. He was like a baseball pitcher toying with the batter. I knew just what he had planned, for I had witnessed it a few times already. I knew just what I had to do to protect my brothers. Looking around, I grabbed one of the timbers and prepared for what was to come."

"What was to come? Tell us!" Mike asked Charles.

"I thought about what Babe Ruth had told us, back in 1945. He told us how baseball had saved him. Somehow, I knew that the army had saved me. Saved me from a life that was headed toward insignificance and trouble. I had prayed that God would help me make my life count for something. I had struck out many times, in my short life, but that wasn't going to keep me from swinging again. Every strike had brought me closer to this home run.

This was my team. These were my guys. There was Artie, he was the artillery guy. Back home in Texas, he could hit a cow with a potato-gun from a half-mile out and just tip it over. Arnold was our sniper and lead volunteer. Back home in Tennessee, he could shoot the cap off of a bottle, sitting on a fence post, from 600 yards. Afterwards, he would go and drink from it and not cut his lips on it. Then, there was Doc. He was our unit medic and kept us from falling to pieces. He was from the East Coast and lots of Docs come from up east. These were just a few of my brothers but they were the ones that were there through thick and thin.

Then there was a short burst of gunfire and my guys all ducked down out of instinct. I knew my time had come. I watched, as the young Chinese soldier stood on the small mound sixty feet six inches from our bunker. I swung around the side of the bunker with timber in hand and stood right beside home plate. By the time I took my stance, the Chinese soldier had already released the grenade from his hand and it was whizzing toward us. I watched it spinning and tumbling and finally hanging right out in front of me. With one swing of the timber, I made contact and sent the projectile flying toward the fence. I watched it fly beyond the dim lights of the battlefield and explode when it finally hit the ground. My guys were safe but I was exposed to the final shots of the Battle of Pork Chop Hill," Charles proclaimed, as he turned from the battle field and headed for the shade of Northern Red.

As he walked toward the tree he continued "General Taylor ordered the hill abandoned just moments after that monstrous blast. The Chinese quit firing on our positions and my guys walked out of there without a scratch. I didn't strike out this time. My life counted for something."

Charles was first to enter the shade and he was followed by the Greenskeeper. Mike lingered looking at the battle scene. He heard what sounded as the hoof beats of a thousand horses but he couldn't see what made the noise. The noise seemed to come out of the sky. He looked down and he was standing on sand. When he looked up he saw something strange. It looked like Purple Mountain but with its flowering plants suspended in the air. It looked like a hanging garden. It looked like something Picasso would dream of, he thought. Then he turned and ran into the shade of Northern Red.

They all exited the shade and were standing near the tenth tee of the Majestic of Purple Mountain in the year 1987. Charles was again dressed in proper golf attire. He confidently walked over toward the tee where his brothers were waiting for him. Upon arriving at the tee, he spoke with the Babe for a moment. Before addressing the ball, Charles pointed to the place in the fairway where he intended to place his shot. With a mighty swing, he struck the ball and immediately turned away. He walked over to where the Babe stood, not watching the ball in flight. He handed his club to the Babe and they laughed. Then he and the Babe began the walk down number ten fairway. There was no need to look, they both knew exactly where the ball would be.

The Greenskeeper and Mike followed the golfers as they played the back nine. They visited the stories of the others in the Final Foursome that day. During their walk, the Greenskeeper showed Mike the Firethorns that line part of the fourteenth hole. They are considered an evergreen shrub. In season, they have thorny oval leaves and groups of red berrylike fruits. They have small white leaves in the spring and were in bloom. These Firethorns form a hedge along parts of the fourteenth fairway.

At sunset, the Greenskeeper played "Taps" as is his custom. His apprentice stood by watching. He watched the eighteenth green, as the final notes rang out. The players of the Final Foursome slowly faded in glory.

The Greenskeeper again drove the boys, Christopher and Mike, home after a long day at the Majestic. There were only a few sessions remaining for the boys. His trip was set to begin in early June. John, the greenskeeper, would soon be on his way to Afghanistan.

Before the day was finished, the Greenskeeper sat in the reserve library of his cabin and penned letters to the families of the Final Foursome players. Among them was a letter addressed to a local resident. This letter, from the Greenskeeper, was addressed to Mr. Alexander Garnet.

Chapter 34

The sign at the entrance displayed the words 'Worthington Memorial Cemetery'. The cemetery was located on the western slope of Purple Mountain and a short distance from town. It is a beautiful setting, with large trees and stone benches spread throughout. It has a small reflecting pond with white swans. There is an old section that stopped accepting internments in the late 1950s. Many grave sites were adorned with fresh flowers, flags and other meaningful mementos of love. It was Monday, May 25, 1987, Memorial Day in the late evening just before sunset.

"What are we doing here?" John asked Michael as they stood in the old section of the cemetery.

"I am not really sure myself. I remember coming here with my Mom and we put flowers on grandma's grave. But, I was intrigued with the old part of the cemetery." Michael commented as he looked around.

"What was so intriguing about it?" John inquired.

"The monuments! They are so much larger and detailed. These were handcrafted pieces and each one seemed to tell a different story. Some monuments were tall and reached into the sky. Other monuments were large and looked like boulders and some were even wrapped with angelic looking beings. Each one was unique. In the newer section, the monuments all seem alike. At a glance, they all seem to tell the same story," Michael commented.

"There must be something more?" John contemplated.

"Over there! He is just leaving. We need to go and see what he was looking at," Michael declared as he began to walk in that direction.

They came to the place where a man had previously been standing. They were standing in the the old section of the cemetery. It was an easy place to miss being located behind a tightly grouped grove of gnarly oak trees. It sat on an extreme boundary of the cemetery. In front of them, were five identical sarcophagi. Each had a base that was eight and a half feet long by four and a half feet wide and eighteen inches high. Above the bases sat the burial boxes. Each were six feet high, four feet wide by eight feet long and entirely constructed out of polished black granite. There were no ornamental markings on any of them and their surfaces were as smooth as glass . The only markings to identify these strangely unique structures were the names and dates etched into them.

From left to right the names and dates on the sarcophagi read as follows:

Raymond Garnet
2/17/1910 - 5/25/1953

Eleanor Garnet
2/14/1909 - 5/25/1953

Sylvester Forrester
3/22/1929 - 5/25/1953

William W. Forrester
1/5/1908 - 5/25/1953

Rose Forrester
1/15/1908 - 5/25/1953

Michael and John stood in front of the monolithic looking structures. There was nothing else like them in the entire cemetery. However, they were strangely familiar. On the ground, in front of the middle sarcophagus, was a single piece of folded newspaper. They watched as the young Mike stood looking at these unusual monuments.

Mike bent down and picked up the piece of paper. It was dry and brittle but did not break apart as he unfolded it. It was a page from the Worthington Times printed on May 27, 1953. It read as follows:

> *Tragedy struck a local family two days ago, on May 25. Local residents Raymond Garnet and his wife Eleanor along with William W. Forrester and his wife Rose, the sister of Mrs. Garnet, and their son Sylvester were killed in a head-on collision with another vehicle. The families were on their way home from the train station where they had picked up the younger Forrester. He was on military leave from service in the Korean conflict. The Garnets' son and daughter have been placed in the custody of relatives. The driver and only person in the other vehicle was killed...*

Mike put the paper back on the ground and ran back to catch up with his mother.

"Now do you remember what brought us here?" John asked him.

"I think I do. All these years and I never put it all together. It is strange, that you can work for someone and not know them or their story. This even when they are from the same town," Michael contemplated, as he spoke.

"Interesting indeed. Sometimes I wonder if we know our own story all that well?" John muttered. "So, you work for Red. However, visiting this site never came to mind?" John asked him.

"No, it hasn't. I think this is the only time I ever came to this part of the cemetery. Now I know where the design for the corporate offices came from. Interesting what inspires people, isn't it?" Michael assessed.

"Yes, it is. Some people choose to live in the pain of their experiences and others chose to run from them. Yet, others go through the grieving process and move on with their lives, no matter how difficult that may seem," John declared, as he walked around the tombs touching them. They were cold to the touch and exceptionally smooth. In the distance they heard "Taps" being played. It was sunset.

"I suppose Red chose to live in his pain," Michael said. He walked among the black stone structures. He felt their silky smoothness but he didn't feel their coldness despite their being cold. It was like he was coldblooded, in this situation. He knew these stones, for they were cut from the same quarry as those used to build the Axis Energy headquarters.

John responded, "and how did you reach that conclusion?"

"Just look at the corporate offices of Axis and you will understand," he suggested to his friend.

"Perhaps, I am not the one who needs to look. I suppose you spend more time in the Axis sarcophagus than he does," John surmised, 'Now tell me, where do you chose to live Michael?"

Michael stood among the black granite sarcophagi still as a stone.

Chapter 35

As a child he had recurring dreams. He dreamed of a mountain that had two kingdoms. On one side of the mountain, there was a great castle made of white stone. Its surface was rough but warm to the touch. It was ruled by a mighty king that had left on a long journey. His knights protected the kingdom while he was away. The greatest of the knights was Sir Gallant the brave. Among his many duties, one of them was to write messages to the king. These messages detailed the status of the wars being fought by the knights of the kingdom. The child served as his squire and hoped to be made a knight some day.

On the other side of the mountain was a great castle made of black stone. Its surface was smooth but cold to the touch. It was ruled by a mighty emperor. The emperor always stayed in his kingdom. He did not have any knights, for he said there were no wars to wage in his kingdom. However, he kept a mighty red dragon hidden deep within his kingdom.

As the squire grew, a time of testing came upon him. To be a knight, required sacrifice and hardship but offered great reward. He went to ask advice of Sir Gallant the brave but he was away in battle. The squire remembered the words of the knight. He said 'that a knight fought with his hands but that he served with his heart'. But, the squire considered the sacrifice too great and the hardship to difficult. So, the squire went to the other side of the mountain and inquired of the emperor.

The emperor knew of the squire and had heard of his mighty skills. He advised the squire to stay in his kingdom. In his kingdom, the emperor said, there were no wars or knights, neither sacrifices to be made nor hardships to suffer. The squire, after much consideration, decided to stay with the emperor in his kingdom. The emperor was proud to have him. After a time of training, the emperor assigned the squire to care for the red dragon.

As he grew older, the dreams stopped and they faded from his memory. Or so he thought. Visions of castles and kingdoms and dreams of knights and dragons remained.

Buried deep within his consciousness, were visions that were given to him during the summer of 1987. Contained within his subconscious mind, it was as if there were eighteen individual kaleidoscopes. Each contained an individual picture that had been cut into pieces and tossed into the object chamber.

As best as it can be described, this is what he saw in each kaleidoscope: a ram in a thicket; a white sarcophagus and an eternal sentinel; a red dragon and a cross; a one toothed black dragon with a banded rainbow tail; dogwoods and daisies; the shekinah glory of God; knights with flaming javelins; black monoliths with red and white roses; dragons with hammer and sickle tattoos; knights as pillars of a grand white castle; a jade box and a dragon with a gemstone tail; a monk in a tree with a flying tiger; a damsel and a smiling dragon; a sea serpent at the bottom of a jade sea; stars circling the walls of Jericho; gray, white, black and red horses; a Great White Oak and snow angels; a long tomb with white tigers and blue dragons.

Chapter 36

Michael continued to march through his memories of that season back in the year 1987. He decided that he would move beyond the memories of the time he spent as the greenskeeper's apprentice. The next set of memories would be more challenging to work through. It was something he knew he needed to do. Michael decided to visit the events that transpired while he was the acting greenskeeper of the Majestic of Purple Mountain. These events began on June 8, 1987.

Michael and John stood on the porch of the cabin. They were waiting on the arrival of the boys. "We will follow Mike during this period. This will be a difficult few months for me. I ask that you hold your comments until we return to the cabin and we have left our trip through these memories. Hang on because we are in for a ride now. Now, wherever he goes, we will go," Michael instructed John. And they waited.

Caleb, a member of the Minutemen Management group, was sitting silently on the porch steps waiting on Mike and Christopher to arrive. He was assigned the task of managing the boys during the absence of the Greenskeeper.

"Who is that waiting on the porch? I wonder where the Mr. John is?" Mike uttered, as the boys approached the cabin.

"Hello boys, my name is Caleb. I am here to get you started with your day today," he said beginning to stand, "please have a seat on the stairs. We need to talk for a few minutes."

Christopher had an uneasy feeling as he sat down, saying, "Yes, sir. May I ask, where is Mr. John, the greenskeeper? He usually meets us. We arranged to be here every day this summer. I am working on the old Jeep in the barn and Mike is helping me in the mornings. In the afternoons, Mike was to spend his time as the greenskeeper's apprentice and was to be with Mr. John. Will he be here later, or tomorrow maybe?"

"Is he sick or something, Mr. Caleb, sir?" Mike asked before Caleb could respond.

Caleb responded, "I will answer all of your questions but please give me some time to work through them all. Mr. John has left and he is on a special mission. I expect that he will return by the end of the summer–"

"Awww . . ., he never told us he was leaving!" Mike complained.

"Now boys, please listen to me," Caleb continued, "we have worked out the details and you boys may still come here daily. Christopher, you are to work on the Jeep as planned. Mr. John was insistent upon this. Mike, you will work on the Jeep with your brother in the mornings and spend your afternoons on the course as planned."

About that time, a rather large gentleman rounded the corner. He looked like he may have been a linebacker for the Green Bay Packers, back in his day. That except for the fact that he wore extremely dark glasses and walked using a white cane with a red tip. The cane was not used for balance.

"As I said, Mike will spend his afternoons on the course as was planned. Now, I want to introduce you to someone," Caleb announced, as he pointed to the rather large man who looked like a retired linebacker. "This is Mr. Samson. He will be your chaperone while you are filling in for Mr. John, during his absence. Mr. John was insistent on this arrangement. He can be insistent! Anyway, he wanted you to fulfill his greenskeeper's duties while he is away. In fact, he named you acting greenskeeper of the Majestic of Purple Mountain until his return. He told us of the wonderful work you have done, as his apprentice, over the last month. We agreed with him and believe you are the person for the job. I realize this is all so sudden and that you may need some time to think it over. Just so you know, your mother has agreed, to allow this arrangement, should you decide to accept the position. So, what do you say, Mike? Do we have a deal or do you need time to think this over?"

Christopher interjected, "Mike needs a few minutes to think this over. Don't you Mike!"

"Yeah, that. I need a minute or two . . . I think?" he said as Christopher began to whisper into his ear.

"Look, I need that Jeep. So you and that blind linebacker over there are going to do this 'acting greenskeeper' thing. Understand!" he not so gently whispered into the ear of his brother.

"He accepts. Now, can we go work on the Jeep?" Christopher declared and began to get up and head to the barn.

"I think we need to hear that from your brother, Christopher. But thank you for speaking up for him," Caleb said, as Christopher took a seat on the steps.

"So, how do I know that Mr. John approved this?" Mike replied.

"Interesting question. In fact, he left you a letter. It is on the door of the cabin just behind you, if you would like to read it," Caleb responded.

Mike got up from the steps, retrieved the letter and sat back on the steps. The letter was addressed to 'the greenskeeper of the Majestic of Purple Mountain' and was sealed on the back with a wax seal. He held it in his hand without opening it, "I will accept your terms on one condition," Mike declared without opening the letter.

"Conditions, I wasn't prepared for conditions. All right, what are your conditions?" Caleb asked with a smile. Samson, standing by and listening, was impressed with the spunkiness of the young boy. It reminded him of himself at that age. He thought that he was going to like this kid but he knew he couldn't ever show it to the kid.

"That I am only the acting greenskeeper and that the second that Mr. John returns, I go back to being the apprentice greenskeeper," Mike demanded.

"I believe that those terms are acceptable to us. So, we have an acting greenskeeper until Mr. John returns," Caleb announced with a smile.

"Let's head over to the barn and start working on that Jeep!" Christopher said, as he left the porch running in the directions of the barn.

Mike turned and went back up to the cabin. He went in, through the front door, leaving it open behind him. Samson heard this and followed him. First, he ascended the stairs and then he stood in the doorway. Mike went to the coffee table, the one with the heart shaped drawer handles. He opened the drawer on the short end of the table and gently placed the letter in it and closed the drawer tight.

"Shouldn't you at least read it first?" said Samson breaking the silent stillness of the seconds that swept by them.

"Mr. Samson, sir–" Mike began to respond before being interrupted.

"Mike, there is no need for all of that 'Mr. Samson, sir' stuff. We are going to be spending lots of time together, so just call me Samson," Samson growled in a less growly growl than was usual.

"OK ... Samson ... how did you know I didn't open it?" Mike asked him.

"I may be blind but my hearing is fine! Don't underestimate me kid, that would be a monumental mistake," Samson warned him in a little more growly tone than before.

"OK–" Mike began.

"And knock off the OK stuff too. Just talk like a normal kid, ok?" Samson told him being fully aware of the inconsistency in his response but saying it anyway.

Mike paused for a long while before responding, "Sure thing, Samson. I thought I would just keep it here until I am ready to read it. Just because you get a letter from someone, doesn't mean you have to open it right away."

"I will accept that, for now. But remember, I am watching you kid," Samson said with a stone straight face while smiling inside.

"So, how is this going to work. Am I going to be leading you around the course in the afternoons or something? I don't want to upset you or anything like that. But with you being blind and all ... I just thought we should talk about it?" Mike assumed.

"Like I said kid, 'don't underestimate me'. You just treat me like you would an uncle of yours and I will treat you like a nephew of mine?" Samson proposed.

"I don't have any blind uncles!" Mike responded.

"I don't have any nephews, either. So it looks like we are even on that score. I guess we will figure it out as we go along. Now, don't we have a Jeep to fix or something?" Samson responded. He turned and headed for the stairs.

"Yes, we do. Christopher will love the help. Do you know anything about this Jeep?" Mike asked him as he ran past him and down the stairs.

"I wrote the book on them!" he replied smiling.

Mike stopped in his tracks and turned, saying, "Really, can I read it? Did you bring it? That will really help!"

"Sure you can read it. But only if you can read braille!" Samson said snickering to himself.

Mike already knew that they would hit it off. He knew that Samson had to maintain his outward gruffness and stay in character. It was the wry humor Samson used that gave him away. Just maybe this would workout, he thought. Mr. John will be back in a short while he thought. So, why not give this a try.

The three of them worked on the Jeep for the entire morning. They made good progress on the project and Christopher was seeing the Jeep come together. After lunch, Mike and Samson headed out for the afternoon greens keeping work.

As usual, Mike mowed the first cut of the rough on the sixteenth fairways. Samson, followed the boy as he mowed. The sound of the spinning blades was music to his ears. The smell of the grass reminded him of his football days and fond memories they were. Occasionally, he would yell to the boy 'keep pushing' just to say something. He could hear the boy mutter 'OK' under his breath and he smiled. I am sure my nephew would say that, if I had a nephew, he thought.

Then, the time came for the Final Foursomes. Mike wondered how this would go over with Samson. Did he know about them? If he did, what did he think about them? Could he see them too? These thoughts ran through his mind as the time neared.

"I guess it is time to head over to the first tee. We don't want to be late." Samson commented, as he began to walk in that direction.

Mike calculated his response, "what will we be late for?"

"Now kid, don't you remember what I said?" Samson responded with a short growl.

"You said for me not to 'underestimate you', right?" Mike responded with a smile.

"So, why are we going there?" Samson turned the question back on him.

"Those 'why' questions. I quit asking those a long time ago. Now those what questions, I can answer those," the acting Greenskeeper retorted.

"OK, nephew. For what purpose are we going to the first tee?" Samson responded with all smile and no growl.

"We are going to help the members of the Final Foursome get acquainted with the Majestic of Purple Mountain. You do see them don't you?" the acting Greenskeeper asked him in all solemness.

Samson responded, as he walked along with his walking stick waving from side to side, "I see them perfectly. I feel the beat of the drums and hear the call of the fifes. I smell gallantry, fidelity and service in the air. I see the Major General pinning each of them with a badge of merit. So, sure thing I see them. In my minds eye, I see them with perfect clarity."

"I never doubted it. No, not you Uncle!" the acting Greenskeeper said as he prepared to explain the rules to the members of the Final Foursome of that day.

After explaining the rules to them and watching them tee off, the acting Greenskeeper led Samson down the first fairway. As they walked, the acting Greenskeeper talked with the various plants and trees that lined the course. He told Samson all that he knew about them and explained their every detail.

Samson, having not seen these things in years, was reminded of every minute detail of each plant the young boy spoke of. He explained them in such vivid detail that Samson could visualize them once again. He thought he had lost this ability but the boy breathed life back into his imagination. Samson smiled, on the inside.

    They visited the memories that the players chose to share. They were taken to the Korean and Vietnam wars on this particular day. Samson went right along with the acting Greenskeeper on these missions, although he was quiet and didn't comment on them. He allowed the acting Greenskeeper to perform his duties without interference from himself.

    As the final Foursome finished the thirteenth hole, the acting Greenskeeper knew what he had to do next. He needed to find a bugle. He instructed Samson to follow him to the cabin and they were off. However, when they arrived at the cabin there was no bugle by the door.

    "Samson, we have a problem," said the acting Greenskeeper.

    "What might that be?" he asked him.

    "I need to play "Taps" at sunset and there is nothing to play it with?" he said to him with a saddened tone.

    "Ah, your first challenge as acting Greenskeeper! Now, what do you suppose the Greenskeeper would tell you to do? Maybe, there is an answer in the drawer just over there?" Samson said pointing his walking stick directly at the drawer with the heart shaped handle.

    "I don't need the letter. I need the bugle!" he said, as he tore through the cabin looking for it.

    "A bugle is not what you need. Think back to what the Greenskeeper told you. He did tell you what it was, to be a greenskeeper at the Majestic, didn't he?" he asked.

"He did. But he didn't tell me about this!" he yelled from somewhere in the cabin.

"Think! Search with your heart, not with your hands! How do you think I find things when I lose them?" Samson revealed to him.

Mike stopped immediately, "You are the acting greenskeeper of the Majestic of Purple Mountain! Search with your heart, not with your hands. Come on Samson, we must get to the flagpole pedestal before the sun sets! Hurry!"

Mike ran as fast as he could to get to the flagpole pedestal. Samson followed behind, at a quick pace. When Mike arrived, at the pedestal, he didn't see what he expected to see. He expected to find the M1892 model field trumpet, used by the Greenskeeper, just waiting for him to pick up and start playing. His spirit was nearly crushed. He hung his head over the sandstone railing of the flagpole pedestal.

"Why the sad face?" Samson asked, as he approached the flagpole pedestal, "Don't you see what you were looking for?"

"No. It is not here," he said.

"What is not here?" Samson asked.

"The bugle. It is not here. I thought it would be here!" he complained.

"Sometimes, we overlook the obvious," Samson replied.

"And what would that be?" he retorted.

"You are looking for his instrument. You are not him. Look for your instrument. This is your time," Samson encouraged him.

Mike turned back to face the flagpole and there it was. It was sitting beneath the flagpole. It was a long bore Native American six hole flute made of walnut.

"Where did that come from?" he asked in surprise.

"During my college days, I played football with a Mattaponi native American Indian. His name was Mike Major and he was a descendant of the chief of that tribe. He fought alongside me in Vietnam. He never made it home. He left his flute to me and now I give it to you. It has a deep voice and it should carry well from this spot. Who knows, maybe he will hear it calling him home?" Samson declared.

"It is beautiful. Thank you, Samson!" he said in amazement.

"OK, kid. Enough with all that stuff. The sun is setting and you have a song to play," Samson reminded him.

Above them, an unwavering flag waved briskly in the moderate mountain breeze. The mountain heard an old tune but with a new and mystical voice, as the sun set that day. As he played, the members of the Final Foursome, standing on the eighteenth green, faded into glory. The epoch of the acting greenskeeper had begun.

Chapter 37

The acting Greenskeeper and Samson continued their daily routine through the summer of the year 1987. Mike grew a few inches that summer, hitting an early growth spurt. Pushing the mower, all those days, down the fairway rough of the sixteenth, took care of the pudginess he had carried on his frame earlier in the year. Seasons were changing for him. He was beginning his adolescent years.

During his time as acting Greenskeeper, he had the privilege to work with numerous caddies. These caddies walked with the members of the Final Foursomes as they completed their rounds. He walked with the likes of Christy McAuliffe, a courageous school teacher and space explorer; Branch Rickey, a skilled baseball executive and storyteller; Jim Thorpe, a versatile athlete and Olympian; Jim Elliot, a missionary and Christian visionary; these and too many others to name visited the Majestic of Purple Mountain that summer. Each came representing their legacy and witnessed its having an impact on those that came to play the Majestic.

As the days moved on, the Jeep began to look like a Jeep again. The huge pile of parts had been reduced to a few odds and ends. The hood was mounted and the windshield was back in place. At this point, all that remained was cosmetic work. A few areas needed touchup paint and the bulbs for the lights all needed replaced. And it needed a new battery.

Christopher could have finished a month ago but was timing the project to end with the start of school, next week. He could finish it in thirty minutes if he needed to. He saw the relationship his brother and Samson shared and appreciated it for what it had become. He didn't want this season to end.

The date was Saturday, September 5, 1987, and this was to be the day when the Greenskeeper returned. The boys had been told a week earlier to expect Mr. John to return by about noon on the next Saturday. Mike was excited about his return. He had already forgiven Mr. John for leaving without telling them in advance. He was proud of his accomplishments, as acting Greenskeeper. He had kept every scorecard and written down every name of every player that came through a Final Foursome. The scorecards were stored in a safe place within the cabin.

As the time neared, Mike and Samson headed for the first tee. It was late afternoon, and yet no sign of Mr. John. Mike was getting a little worried but not that worried. However, it was just minutes before the Final Foursome was scheduled to tee off.

There was an unusual development in the Final Foursome of that day. When it was time for the golfers to ascend the stairs only three of them went up and one stayed behind. He looked familiar to Mike but he couldn't identify him. The unknown soldier remained on the path and did not approach the tee box. He didn't have a caddie either. The other players completed the ceremony and after receiving instructions from the acting Greenskeeper, they teed off. The members of the Final Foursome began their round and headed down the fairway. This left Mike, Samson and the unknown soldier behind.

"Hello, my name is Mike and I am the acting greenskeeper here at the Majestic. May I ask your name?" Mike said as he walked down the stairs from the first tee box.

"My name is Doug," he told him, "where is John, the greenskeeper?"

"It is a pleasure to meet you Doug. John was supposed to be here by now but he is running late. You see, he has not been here in months but he is coming back today!" the acting Greenskeeper said.

"Yes, I am aware of that. I thought he would be here. He is supposed to be here by now. But he isn't. So, we are going to have to improvise," Doug told him.

"Improvise? What do you mean by that?" the acting Greenskeeper asked him.

"You will see. Where is the closest tree that will take us back into the past? You do know where they are don't you?" Doug asked him, seeming in a hurry to start moving.

"Yes, I know where they are. The closest is just a few holes away. It is the Southern Red Oak and it is near the fourth tee box. Would you like for me to show you?" Mike asked him.

"Yes, Please," Doug said.

"Before we go, I have a question for you," the acting Greenskeeper said, "What is the reason for your not playing in the final foursome today?

"It is not my time to play," he responded.

"Then what brings you here?" Mike asked him.

"Unfinished business. The Greenskeeper would understand," Doug said to him.

"Is he giving you trouble?" Samson growled sensing the tension in the voice of his nephew.

"No, Samson. It is OK," his nephew replied, "Doug, I am the acting greenskeeper! I will understand," Mike said, as he stood a little taller with his shoulders back.

"That may be, before we are finished today," Doug told him, as the three of them began to walk down the first fairway.

"Do you know the Greenskeeper? I am not sure I have ever met a player in a Final Foursome that has known him before they arrived here," Mike questioned.

"Yes, we are friends. We go way back he and I. Where is he?" Doug probed.

"Like a friend once told me 'don't underestimate me'. Like I said, sir I am the acting greenskeeper and I assure you I can help. Whatever the Greenskeeper could do, I can do also," Mike declared.

"Ah, you are the apprentice he spoke of. I expected someone much older by the description he gave. So, you are the apprentice! Why didn't you say so?" Doug smiled.

"Apprentice or acting greenskeeper, big difference I would say!" Mike told him confidently.

"You are bold, I'll give you that. So, explain this 'big' difference to me then," Doug asked.

"All right, I will. As his apprentice I followed him. I learned what it is to be the greenskeeper of the Majestic of Purple Mountain. But I was not responsible for keeping their stories or keeping the course. I was simply learning," he declared.

"What skills and what stories?" Doug followed up as they walked by the first green.

"There are not many skills to learn. Being a keeper of the greens requires work of the hands. Being the greenskeeper comes from the heart," he said confidently.

"What does that mean exactly?" Doug asked him.

"Anyone could mow the tees and keep the greens, for a while. But not just anyone can talk the Azaleas, on the fifteenth, into blooming at the proper season. Not just anyone can get the Golden Bellflower to ring behind the green on sixteen. Not just anyone can see the members of a Final Foursome through a round and play a song that leads them home at exactly sunset," Mike explained as he walked along the second fairway among the Dogwoods and daisies.

"Wow. That answers the skills question, I think? Now, what of those stories?" Doug asked.

"Stories? Have you looked around this majestic mountain? There are more stories here than books to contain them, were they all told!" Mike declared.

"Exactly what kind of stories? Do you have an example for me?" Doug pressed him.

"Sure, I don't think he would mind me telling you about it. But, I must keep it anonymous. There was a Vietnam War soldier that came through here about a month ago and Harry Houdini was his caddie. Seems he was held prisoner by the Vietcong for some time. He and a few of his soldier brothers that is. So, just like Houdini he planned a great escape. He worked on it for a long time and when the time was right, he performed the escape. It worked. But he had to get his guys set free too," Mike recalled for him.

"What happened to him?" Doug asked.

"He was tired from his escape but he got all of his guys out of their cages. They ran away from their captors and into the jungle. But as they ran, he was too tired and he didn't make it out with them," Mike declared.

"So, now what do you do with the story?" Doug asked him.

"He wanted me to give his daughter a message for him. I was to tell her 'Rosabelle', believe' among a few other things," Mike insisted as they neared the second green.

"Wow. That is an amazing story. How will you find her?" Doug asked as he walked along.

Mike replied as he walked among the Pampas grass, "I am not really sure. But I have faith that I will find out. The Majestic has many mysteries and many mysterious ways."

"So then, you are the acting Greenskeeper?" Doug questioned.

"Yes, I am," he replied as he touched the flower tips of the Pampas grass.

"So then, what am I to expect?" Doug questioned.

"I guess we are 'improvising'? I have not experienced a Final Foursome like this one. Although you are here, you are not part of the group. That has never happened on my watch," Mike declared.

"Thanks. So, what do you think will happen?" Doug asked.

"If it works like the other times, then I think it will happen like this. First, we will visit a story from your past. We will do this before we reach the eighth tee. On the back nine, you will share how you earned your purple heart. At sunset I will play "Taps" and you will go home. That is the typical flow of a Final Foursome," Mike told him with an air of certainty in his voice.

"So, this is all the time I have left? Until sunset?" he asked.

"I am not sure. But I am sure of this one thing," Mike commented.

"You said 'one thing' what do you mean?" he asked.

Mike replied, "No one standing on the eighteenth green when "Taps" is played ever stays past sunset."

"Well then, I will just stay off of the eighteenth green," he responded as they neared Southern Red.

"For what reason?" Mike inquired.

"We are 'improvising' remember?" Doug reminded him, as they approached the shade of Southern Red.

"Remember, I am the acting greenskeeper. When we go in there, you give me your story to tell. As acting greenskeeper, I am bound to tell it. It is one of the reasons you come here. But there are other reasons," Mike said. They stood just outside the shade of the tree.

"I'll trust you then, acting Greenskeeper," he said. Then, he walked into the shade of Southern Red just beyond the third green.

They entered the shade of Southern Red. As they walked, Doug changed in appearance. His closely shaven face slowly became bearded and his hair grew a few inches in length. His military dress changed into what looked like the clothes of a shepherd. A rifle was strapped to his back and a handkerchief covered his face. When they exited out of the shade on the other side of Southern Red they were in Afghanistan. The date was June 20, 1987. Doug was wearing sunglasses.

"Where are we?" Mike asked him as he looked across a range of mountains.

"This is Afghanistan. We are in the mountains just north of Parachinar, Pakistan. We are near the Chapri Forest and a place called Tora Bora." Doug recalled as he surveyed the landscape.

Mike responded, "What are we doing here."

"The Greenskeeper didn't come to us, so we are going to him!" Doug stated. Both the statement and the scene startled and confused the young, although brave, acting Greenskeeper.

Chapter 38

Doug and Mike stood watching a group of men standing on a hillside. The hillside was covered in rocks. In the distance, were a few old run down buildings made of stone, wood and brick construction. The men were handling a long black cylindrical shaped piece of metal with what appeared to be writing on it.

"What is John doing here? And where is he? Over there?" an exasperated and confused Mike asked him. He pointed to the men on the hillside.

Doug passed him the binoculars, "He is the one sitting in the background, just behind those men over there. Take a close look and you will recognize him."

Mike took the glasses and held them to his small face, "Which one? Yes, the one in the back . . . sitting . . . It is him! I see him! What is he doing here? Where is here anyway?"

"We are halfway around the world from the Majestic of Purple Mountain. We are in Asia. You do know geography don't you?" Doug asked him.

"Sure, I know it. Asia is just east of Europe and north of Africa. I think . . ." he answered.

"That is right, you got it!" Doug assured him.

"Why did he come all the way over here?" Mike asked him again.

"What do you know about Mr. John?" Doug asked him as he continued to look across the valley.

"I met him this year. He is the greatest greenskeeper ever and he is my friend . . . but he didn't say goodbye when he left. He did leave a letter though?" Mike answered.

"I am sure he is the greatest greenskeeper, ever. And he is much more. He is my friend too. Let me tell you about him.

John was a writer a long time ago. He wrote stories about the Vietnam war. He went into battle with the soldiers and wrote about what they lived through. He wrote the truth and the people he worked for didn't like that, so they fired him. They sent him away. Then he went to be the greenskeeper at the Majestic.

However, a general knew about John and the great writer he was. The general wanted John to work for him. He wanted him for just a little while. He wanted him for a special project," Doug declared to him.

"So, what was the special project he was asked to do?" Mike asked while continuing to look through the binoculars.

Doug continued, "There is a war going on over here in Afghanistan. We are secretly helping the freedom fighters. Our government issued NSDD 166 (National Security Decision Directive) and it said we were to help the Mujahideen, the freedom fighters over there, win a victory over the Soviet Union.

So, we secretly brought weapons to the Mujahideen. Weapons like that FIM92 stinger missile over there. We taught the Mujahideen how to use the stingers against the Soviet's aircraft.

John is here to write a first hand account of the mission. He will write it, so that people can know the truth, some day, about how we helped the Afghan people."

"Why can't they know now?" Mike asked him.

"Grown-up reasons, I guess. The Soviet's are not our friends and they won't like it if we are helping their enemies. So, we are keeping this 'hush-hush'," Doug told him.

"I see. Grown-up stuff again! I'll trust you on this one," Mike told him, as he put down the binoculars. "So, what is he doing?"

"He is writing the stories, as he watches us train them to use the stinger missiles. But, he has also met friends here. I am sure he will write about their hardships and their fight for freedom. It is good for us to write these things. We can learn from these experiences. I am sure of it!"

"I know we can. I have heard lots of stories, like this one, this summer. I am sure there are many, many more to be told," Mike assured him.

"OK, acting Greenskeeper, I need a promise from you?" Doug asked him in a serious tone.

"A 'promise'? What promise?" Mike replied being intrigued.

"You must keep what you have seen here a secret for the next twenty-five years. You can't tell anyone. What John is writing will stay secret for the next twenty-five years by law. Can I trust you with this?" Doug asked him.

"Yes, I promise. I know this is important to you and to John. So I am in!" Mike solemnly promised with a raised hand.

"Good boy! I thought you would understand," he said. He turned and headed for the shade of Southern Red.

Mike followed him into the shade but stopped to look back as Doug kept walking. Mike saw a vision through the shade. He saw two flying dragons. Each dragon, on its side, had a tattoo of a hammer and sickle. The sound, of their wings, was like that of the hoof beats of a thousand horses. They were looking for Sir Gallant he could sense it. The sky grew dark and Mike turned and ran into the shade of Southern Red and back into the safety of the Majestic.

As Doug walked through the shade, his appearance changed and he was back in his proper military uniform. They were now standing near the fourth tee at the Majestic.

The Greenskeeper was nowhere to be found.

Chapter 39

The acting Greenskeeper preformed his duties as usual with Samson as his chaperone. This was the last day they would walk the Majestic together. The kid had grown on Samson and he would miss him when Mike returned to school. Samson knew that he would be seeing Mike around the course from time to time and that made him smile. Samson had gained a new perspective on the course. He had seen it through the eyes of a child. From the first tee through the eighteenth green, he knew every plant, tree, shrub and grass that grew on this majestic mountain. He especially appreciated the sound of the wood flute as it sang out at sunset.

The acting Greenskeeper and Samson followed the Final Foursome from the twelfth green to the path that leads to the thirteenth tee. As they walked down the path the Water Oak came into view. Doug was waiting for them and standing just outside of its shadow.

"Are you ready, acting Greenskeeper?" Doug asked.

"Where are we going?" Mike replied.

"Follow me and I will show you. However, you are still sworn to secrecy for twenty-five years. Do you understand?" Doug questioned him.

"I understand," Mike replied.

Doug walked into the shade of the Water Oak and Mike followed him. As he walked, his appearance changed into his dress military uniform. Doug wore the traditional blue U.S. Army Dress Uniform and a Green Beret. He served as a Special Forces Intelligence Sergeant. His jacket was laden with awards and patches. On the left pocket flap, were various proficiency badges. Above the left pocket were ribbons that represented various medals and commendations. His name tag was pinned to the upper right pocket flap. His left shoulder had a badge that was covered in black and could not be identified. On his right shoulder were patches that represented his previous deployment.

As they exited the shade of the tree, they immediately found themselves at a military medical center in Europe and it was dark. The date was Saturday, August 8, 1987.

"Where are we," Mike asked.

"We are in Landstuhl, Germany at the LRMC (Landstuhl Regional Medical Center). It is a medical center operated by the U.S. Army," Doug commented, as they walked through the vacant halls. It was zero two hundred local time and the night shift was on staff at the hospital.

"What are we doing here?" Mike asked him, as he walked next to Doug. The corridors were like a maze to him. He did not know where they were headed. He could hear the echoes of their footsteps as they walked down the empty corridors.

"We are going to visit someone," Doug replied. They stopped at a nurses station and Doug looked at the patient charts. He started talking to himself, saying, "Where is it? Ah, there you are my friend— Room 0322. The doctor says your release date is set for early September and you will be state side by September 6."

They began walking down the hallway into the Helen Rehabilitation Center. Various units of the hospital are named after former army nurses. This particular wing was named after a nurse who sacrificed her life to save other nurses in the battle of Hanau, Germany during World War II. Her picture was framed and hanging high above the entryway into the Rehab Center. In the picture, she stood in front of an open hangar door with a biplane in the background. On the picture were written the words: Darmstadt, Easter 1945.

"I knew her. You know, she must have been a great nurse to have this place named after her. But man, could she fly a bi-plane!" Mike said. He stopped for a few seconds and looked up at the picture and smiled. He smelled peppermint in the air.

Doug whispered, loudly, from down the hallway, "Mike! Come on. We must keep moving. I want to catch him while he is sleeping. The chart says he was due for medication over an hour ago. I am betting that he will be back asleep by now."

Mike catching up to him said, "OK, here I am. Where is this room we are looking for?"

"It is right here. Room number 0322. Please be quiet, we don't want to wake him," Doug cautioned him before he opened the door.

"Doug, who ever is in there won't be able to hear us! Trust me on this. I have done this before and I know what I am talking about," Mike reminded him while pushing open the door.

"I wouldn't be so sure about that, acting Greenskeeper! Now keep it quiet, he is a light sleeper. Trust me on this, I spent some time with him recently," Doug declared, as they walked into the room.

The person in the bed was sleeping. He was bandaged about the face and hands and had a bandaged leg that appeared swollen. He was connected to an assortment of medical equipment. The room was dark and quiet except for the occasional noise of the medical equipment. Doug walked right up to the bed with Mike following close behind.

"Mr. John?" Mike whispered, not so quietly, as he recognized his friend, "what is he doing all the way over here? I thought he was with you in Afghanis . . . " Mike said as he dropped to his knees on the floor.

Doug stopped and kneeled by his side, "it is all right, Mike. He is going to be fine. In time, he will be fine. Trust me, OK? You can handle this. I know it."

"OK, he has got to be OK. What happened to him?" Mike asked as he touched John's hand lightly.

"It is a long story," Doug asserted trying to delay the conversation that was to come.

"I didn't realize it earlier. Perhaps I just didn't want to. I visit with dead soldiers all of the time, you know. It is what I do as acting greenskeeper. When I met you, I knew. You know that don't you?" Mike asked him directly.

"Yes, I knew. I came to the Majestic because I knew it was special. And it is even more so, for me, than most," Doug answered.

"You are different from the others. You are the first one that has not taken me to where they gave their last full measure of devotion. Well, at least I don't think you are taking me there," Mike assumed while he looked at Doug.

Doug looked at him, "You are right. We are not visiting there. I brought you here instead."

"So, what happened? I suppose something happened in Afghanistan? When we went there earlier, I saw something just before we left." Mike told him.

"What did you see? I thought we left at about the same time?" Doug responded.

"You didn't see it because you were already in the shade and headed for the Majestic. This happens to me sometimes and I don't understand what I see. I met Picasso once when he came to caddie. After that, I read about him and studied his paintings. They are a little weird but I think I understand them better now. The things I see, when people take me into the shade of the trees, sometimes look like a Picasso painting," Mike said. He was beginning to open up to Doug.

"What did you see this time?" Doug encouraged him.

"Do you want to know? It is a little weird?" Mike said with hesitation in his thoughts.

"Yes, please tell me," he asked him.

"When I looked back, I saw two flying dragons. Each of them, on their side, had a red tattoo of a hammer and sickle! And there was the sound! It was like the sound of a thousand horses running. It was so loud, I could feel it in my chest," Mike revealed, as he looked out the window of the dark room.

"Yes, I understand. It is not weird." Doug assured him.

"What happened over there?" Mike asked him, as he looked at Mr. John laying motionless in the hospital bed.

Doug began, "There once were two knights—"

"Really? I have heard it all over the past few months! I may be young, but I can handle it," Mike insisted.

"That would be too easy. And remember, this was a secret mission too. So, I kinda have to work around the details. Will that work for you?" Doug asked.

"OK, but don't get too far out there and go adding princesses and stuff like that! I am listening," Mike warned. He sat in a chair by the bed.

"Like I said, there once were two knights on a journey to a far away land. Their friends, in this land, had problems with dragons. They wanted the knights to train them in the lost art of dragon slaying. One knight was named Sir Valiant—"

Mike interrupting, "That is you! Nice name, for a knight by the way."

Doug restarted, "Hmm . . . oh yes, where were we? The other knight was Sir True–"

"And that is Mr. John," Mike supposed, as he sat up a little in the chair.

"Yes, Sir True was along to send messages back to the king. These messages detailed our training and our battles with the dragons. Sir Valiant was the knight responsible for training their friends.

One day, before the training was complete, two dragons came unexpectedly. The knight's friends were not yet trained to slay them. These were the dragon's with the hammer and sickle tattoos. So, Sir Valiant and Sir True fought them. They fought courageously and killed one dragon with their flaming javelin. However, the other dragon got too close and they could not use the faming javelin to kill it.

The remaining dragon took aim at Sir True and breathed fire at him. But before the fire could reach him, Sir Valiant stepped in front of Sir True to protect him. Sir True was brave but he was not a dragon slayer. The dragon thought he killed them both and flew away.

Both knights were wounded, but Sir Valiant more so. His wounds were mortal. As they lie there, he made a request of Sir True," Doug paused.

"What was the request?" Mike inquired now intrigued with the story.

Doug continued, "Sir Valiant had a princess daughter, with childlike faith, back in the kingdom—"

He laughingly interrupted, "oh no! Not that princess stuff! I warned you!"

"The princess was beautiful and was his only child. Sir True was asked to look after her. Also, upon approval from the king or after a period of one hundred seasons he was to tell her about her father's bravery.

Sir True wanted to fulfill this request with all of his heart but knew his injuries were grave as well. He told Sir Valiant that he had a squire, with unique skills, that lived on a majestic mountain and that somehow this word must get to him. Sir True knew that the squire would fulfill this request.

Sir Valiant called on the great eagle of the kingdom, Isaiah, to come at once and carry him home. However, Isaiah the great eagle, only carries the souls of fallen knights. So it was, that Sir Valiant breathed his last breath. Then the great eagle carried his soul to the majestic mountain.

On arriving, Sir Valiant hoped to find his friend and looked for Sir True. He found him not. Instead, he found the squire, as Sir True said he would," Doug finished the story and silently waited.

It finally came upon him and his eyes were opened, "you were there, when the sun rose and set a second time in one day, on Purple Mountain. You and her were the ones that walked up the fairway just before it happened. I saw you both from beneath the White Oak tree. It was you! I know you! You are the father of Jessica! Tell me it isn't so?"

"It is as you say," Doug declared.

"This burden will not be mine! Sir True will wake up! You promised he would!" Mike declared standing and releasing the hand of his old friend, "it is time for us to go now," Mike declared, as he began to leave the room with a determined stride. He marched down the hall not even looking at the picture of his dear friend, Helen. He was determined to leave this place and never return. He was determined to leave it all. But there was one last duty to perform at sunset.

He and Doug arrived at the Water Oak at the same time. They entered the shade of the tree and they walked back into the Majestic of Purple Mountain. The date was Saturday, September 5, 1987.

Mike walked away from Doug and headed toward the eighteenth green with Samson following him. Doug did not follow them. Mike and Doug would not speak again.

the Majestic of Purple Mountain

Chapter 40

The acting Greenskeeper stood on the flagpole pedestal for possibly the last time. Over the course of the last few hours, he determined that the burden of being the acting Greenskeeper was too great for him. Earlier, while on his way from the cabin to the flagpole pedestal he stopped by the barn where his brother was working on the Jeep. He confided in his brother. He told his brother the secrets of the Majestic of Purple Mountain. His brother refused to believe in the mysteries of the Majestic. He told him that the Jeep was ready and that they would leave the mountain and never return. Mike convinced him that he needed to play "Taps" one last time and that he would leave after that.

The sun was nearly set and the acting Greenskeeper assumed his position on the flagpole pedestal. He looked to the eighteenth green and saw only three figures. He wondered where Doug was. Then he saw him, standing by the White Oak near the eighteenth green.

As the sun set that day, the acting Greenskeeper played "Taps" on his long bore Native American six hole flute made of walnut. As he played, he watched three players fade into glory. There was no sign of Doug to be found, anywhere.

The former acting Greenskeeper walked back to the cabin. He was surprised to see his old friend had arrived, finally.

"I sure am glad to see my apprentice! How have you been, Mike!" the Greenskeeper said while sitting on the stairs of the cabin.

"I have been better. You look better than when I last saw you in that hospital bed. I hope you are feeling better now. You have a day to rest before getting back to work as the greenskeeper," Mike said to him in a tense tone of voice. This was highly unusual for Mike but this was a highly unusual situation.

John started, "how did you know about that, it was supposed to be—,"

Mike interrupted, "secret? Your good friend Doug took me to see you."

"He did. Did he?" the Greenskeeper commented.

"Yes, and then he asked me to take care of Jessica and tell her that her dad was, killed in action in Afghanistan, a few months ago!" Mike maintained.

"Being the greenskeeper is not always an easy thing, you know. But sometimes, it is the challenges in life that make us stronger. Jessica will be cared for. However, you have the responsibility of telling her someday but not now. The records are sealed for twenty-five years and Doug will be listed as Missing in Action, presumed dead. The government will not confirm his death for at least twenty-five years and maybe not even at that time. This is a hard teaching but it is the truth," the Greenskeeper declared.

"Hard teaching? Is it?" Christopher spoke up, as he entered the discussion.

"How is that Jeep coming along?" the Greenskeeper asked him, hoping to change the subject.

"Sounds like a trick I would use to change the subject from a topic I didn't want to discuss. The Jeep is complete and we will take it home today. Just in time for school.

I have watched you and Samson work with Mike over the past several months. He has grown so much and I am so proud of him. Samson, despite his linebacker appearance, is actually quite harmless. Sure he played along with all of the 'Final Foursome' nonsense but he didn't take it over the top.

Now you on the other hand, have gone way over the top here. He will have nothing to do with telling Jessica anything about her father. Ever! That is not his responsibility. It belongs to someone else, not him," Christopher declared as he came to the defense of his brother.

"I am truly sorry for the manner in which I left a few months ago. I should have told you both. Maybe things would be different if I had," the Greenskeeper said sadly.

"I really didn't like you. Then I liked you a whole lot. Then I didn't like you again and now I really don't like you anymore. These stories, of the Final Foursomes, were all fine at first. They were an adventure for Mike. But now they are too close to home and too real for him to deal with. Don't you see?

I followed you two a few times. I didn't see anything. There is nothing to see because they are not real. Sure I heard you talking to these soldiers. You even had him believing and talking to them. You can keep doing this Final Foursome thing but he can't. It is really too bad that you took something noble that the Minutemen guys, like Caleb, were doing and turned it into a mockery," Christopher declared.

"But they are real. Remember, 'blessed is he who does not see, yet believes'," the Greenskeeper reminded him.

Christopher continued, "I am not sure where you have been. You come back here all banged up and saying that it is all a 'secret' and you can't tell anything about what happened or where you went. Fine. Now we are leaving! Believe this, when we leave this mountain you won't see us again!"

Christopher declared, as he took Mike by the hand to lead him to the Jeep.

"Goodbye Mr. John. Take care of the Majestic of Purple Mountain and Jessica because I can't do it . . . it is too much," Mike uttered in a small voice, as he went away with his brother.

"Goodbye my apprentice," said the Greenskeeper. He sat on the stairs and watched them drive away then he limped into his cabin.

And so ended the epoch of the acting Greenskeeper of the Majestic of Purple Mountain.

Chapter 41

The once roaring fire was now nearly burned out. On the hearthstone, only embers remained of the two logs that John had placed on the fire earlier. The room had gradually cooled and now that coolness had become noticeable.

Michael noticed the coolness before he opened his eyes. How did the fire burn down so quickly he thought to himself? The measurement of the passage of time had always intrigued him. Sometimes he believed, that time was measured by watching the changing seasons, the changing tides, the rising and setting of the sun, and also by the acts of a Republic, a city, or a person. Tonight he thought, it is measured by the burning of logs.

"How long have we been sitting here?" Michael asked his old friend John. Michael was sitting on the couch in the living area of the cabin of the greenskeeper.

"Long enough for the logs to burn away and become just embers," he replied from his position in the chair that sat perpendicular to the couch. John wondered how much Michael remembered of their trip through the memories of that one season, in the year nineteen hundred and eighty-seven. He was soon to find out.

"My how time has slipped away from us tonight. It seems like I arrived only a short while ago and now the hour is late." Michael said to him, as he stretched and began to fidget.

"I would agree. Before you go, have you considered opening the envelope?" John inquired of him looking at the table where the envelope lay in wait of opening.

Michael began, "There is a time and a season for all things under Heaven. However, I believe the time and season for that letter and its opening has passed. I am deeply sorry, for there was a time when I dreamed of breaking its seal and accepting its challenge despite the cost. There was a time, when I stood at the base of the Hillary Step and saw the mountain top within reach. I was a child then and thought, as a child, and dreamed, as a child. Now I am a man and think, as a man, and act, as a man. Oh, that I had the faith to open it. Oh, that I had the faith of a child. I have given this much consideration, as the logs burned, and have determined that it should remain as it is."

After a long pause, John reached for the heart shaped handle on the drawer of the table in front of him. He gently pulled it open and placed the letter back in the drawer and closed it. He then stood erect and offered his hand to Michael saying, "I am a man of my word and I appreciate your thoughtful consideration. I have faith, that there is yet a future for the greenskeeper of the Majestic of Purple Mountain. I know it in my heart. Now, my former apprentice, you may leave."

Standing up, Michael took his hand into his own and gave a firm handshake. Then he stepped close and gave his former mentor a warm embrace. He hoped that John would recognize the coming change in season and embrace it. Then he backed away and headed out the cabin door. Still, deep within his heart, he dreamed of being the greenskeeper but his mind told him otherwise.

He walked down the stairs, and into the darkness of the night. It was only a short distance to the Jeep. On his way, he noticed a faint light behind a grove of trees. He was curious, and followed the dim glow of the light. As he turned down the path, he saw an old barn. It looked familiar, as if out of a dream that was long ago forgotten. He walked up to the closed barn doors and stood by them silently. A shaft of light extended to the ground as it emanated out from between the barn doors. He opened the doors and went in.

He walked into the open area of the barn. The barn was nearly empty except for a few tool chests and a work bench. He went over to the work bench. On the table were a few scattered tools, an old soda bottle and a service manual for a 1941 Willys MB, written in braille. He looked around and saw a set of stairs that led to a loft area.

He ascended the stairs of the loft and they creaked and groaned. It was as if they had not been used in a quarter century. Dust rose around his feet as he made his way upward, step by step. As he arrived at the top of the stairway, he noticed the chain of a light pull. He purposefully pulled the chain and the lights came on. What he saw, looked like a small art studio. There was a small table with various art supplies, brushes and paints. Then he noticed them. They were standing there in silent solemn obscurity.

There were eighteen wooden easels. There were nine on the north side of the loft and nine on the south. They were arranged in the shape of a heart. A white sheet, pure as majestic mountain snow, covered each easel and the rectangular object it protected. He walked amongst the heart of them, without uncovering them, wondering what was behind each veil. He touched them and they pulsated. It was as if he were feeling the pulse of the mountain. They were soft to the touch and warm. He could feel their warmth on his finger tips.

Walking behind them, he pulled the sheets off of four of the eighteen easels. The sheets drifted silently to the floor. He stood behind them for quite a while before he summoned the courage to walk before them. Standing before them, he thought of Picasso. It was as though Picasso had painted the dreams of a child. Dreams of castles and kingdoms, knights and emperors, dragons and damsels, dogwoods and daisies were painted on each canvas in front of him. Like cherry tree blossoms in a spring valley breeze, the images softly swirled in his childlike mind. He dared not uncover the remaining paintings. He carefully covered the paintings, pulled the chain and descended the stairs.

    He closed the barn doors and walked the short distance to the Jeep. He found it just where he had left it. He jumped in the seat, turned the ignition switch and started it right up. As he turned on the lights, he could barely make out the green tint of the paint. He never liked the color, but Christopher insisted that it had to be kept original. It had to be kept just the way it would have been in the year 1941. He turned the Willys 1941 MB Jeep around and began his descent from the mountain on the 'you-ee', just as he had come. It was the second time this Jeep had been driven down this mountain. With his heart, he remembered everything. Misty mountain tears ran down his face and he was moved by the majesty of the moment. If faith the size of a mustard seed could move a mountain, perhaps such faith could move his heavy heart. Oh that it were true, he thought.

    He thought of his time mowing the sixteenth hole, the Lincoln. He remembered the words Lincoln spoke, 'a house divided against itself shall not stand'. A season of decision was upon him and a short season it would prove to be.

    It was only a while later when he pulled into Worthington. It was now Saturday, April 21, 2012, and early in the morning. He needed to get some sleep. The parade was to begin at noon. It was going to be another long day.

Chapter 42

"General Anson, Sir!" said Tiger the great horned owl as he landed in the branches of the White Oak. "I am returning from my second watch, Sir!"

"Tiger, please report," I said. Earlier in the evening he had reported the information about the proposed mining project. He was returning with information from his second survey of the evening.

"Sir, Michael has left the mountain after spending several hours in the cabin of the greenskeeper. A vehicle arrived at the clubhouse at about zero four hundred hours. I believe it was the newest member of the Minutemen Management Group, Deborah. She exited her vehicle and went into the offices. I noticed another vehicle headed up the mountain and I believe it was driven by Joshua," Tiger reported.

"Good work, Tiger. Now please get some rest. We have a challenging few weeks ahead of us and I will need you at your best," I told him. We were in the formative planning stages but I knew that for our plans to be successful we would need every resource operating at optimum levels.

Now, I was going to listen in on what was happening at the clubhouse, so early in the morning. Deborah was the newest member of the Minutemen Management Group and it was unusual for any of them to arrive this early in the morning.

"Joshua, please come in," Deborah said, as she sat at her desk inside the clubhouse offices, "thank you for coming to meet with me so early but this is an extremely urgent matter."

"I am glad that you brought me in on this situation. How may I help?" he said as he stood in the doorway to her office.

Deborah said, "please come in and have a seat. I have a story to tell you. However, first I have a few questions."

"Go right ahead and ask," he said taking a seat near her desk.

"I understand that you have a TS III (top secret level three) clearance and SIGINT (signals intelligence) clearance as well?" She asked.

"Yes, that is correct. As a retired Judge Advocate, I still have them. Is there an issue?" he said with concern.

"Actually, I have a story to tell you," she began, "what I am about to tell you has been classified for nearly a quarter century. Do you see that picture on the credenza over there?" she asked.

"Yes," he said as he took it into his hands.

"The individual at the center left of that picture is a soldier named Doug. He was a Green Beret and was assigned to my unit. He was in the unit that was part of my first command. Our operation was in the spring of 1987. He was my first operational loss.

Under NSDD 166, we were assigned to deliver and train the Mujahideen, Afghan freedom fighters, in the use of FIM 92 heat-seeking Stinger missiles (SAMs). The Soviets' had developed counter measures to the original SAMs. We were there to train them on the use of an advanced missile that was designed to overcome this issue.

In addition, there was an imbedded journalist with our unit. His name was John. He was there as part of an assignment to document and record, for the historical record, our special forces operations and their role in helping the Afghans obtain victory over the Soviet Union. His observations and recordings and all operational details would be held secret for a period of twenty-five years, by directive from the NSA (National Security Agency) and DIA (Defense Intelligence Agency).

We were operating in the Chapri Forest, in what we thought was Afghanistan. However, our guide, Atash from the Khogiani tribe, unknowingly had led us into an area that was Pakistani territory. During this incursion, we encountered two Soviet Mi-24, Krokodil, attack helicopters. The Afghans called them Shaitan-Arba or Satan's Chariots. We took one of them out with a Stinger. But we were not so fortunate with the other. It was equipped with a heat dissipater and flares and evaded the other Stinger we fired.

This Mi-24 was equipped with a fuel-air explosive device. When the pilot deployed it, it went off target and missed most of our unit. However, Doug and John were in the blast radius. In an act of gallantry, Doug shielded John from most of the blast. Doug was mortally wounded and died before we got to him. John was severely wounded by the fire and the shock wave. We carried them over the boarder and called in an air evacuation.

Due to the sensitivity of the situation, being in Pakistan, another layer of secrecy was added to the mission. Doug would be declared 'MIA status unknown' after being lost during a training mission off of the coast of Nikumaroro Island in the South Pacific. His family would be kept in the dark about the truth.

I protested. I believed his family deserved to know the truth. He was deserving of a Medal of Honor, a fact that even my commander acknowledged. When I lost that battle, I proposed the following plan: that his remains would be placed into the Tomb of the Unknown Soldier at ANC (Arlington National Cemetery). There he would be guarded by his army brothers from the Third United States Infantry, The Old Guard. Upon declassification of the mission, his remains would be returned to his family for a proper burial at ANC. However, his time in the Tomb of the Unknown Soldier would forever remain classified. This plan was refused. However, it did not end there.

A supportive member, of the Joint Chiefs of Staff, proposed an alternative plan. Doug, at that time, was the only U.S. casualty of the conflict and the president was aware of this fact. Also, the president was staunchly opposed to the Soviet Empire and had great admiration and respect for the sacrifice that Doug had made for his unit and his country. This plan would require the support and approval of the Speaker of the House of Representatives and the Majority leader of the Senate.

The plan, with the unwavering support of the president, was approved and implemented in the summer of 1987. Since then, Doug's casket has been kept in Washington's Tomb beneath the Crypt of the U.S. Capitol. It has been encased within the Lincoln Catafalque. It was to be kept there until such time as Doug's service, to his country, could be revealed and his proper burial could take place. However, his temporary internment in the Crypt of the Capitol, within the catafalque, would remain a secret for the ages.

Now this is where we come into the picture. Doug was the father of Jessica, the Mayor of Worthington. It is more complicated, still. John, in our story, is none other than the greenskeeper of the Majestic of Purple Mountain.

Monday, May 7, 2012, at 8:21 PM, is the twenty-fifth anniversary of the start of the mission. Finally, he would be returned to his family for a proper burial and the information would become declassified. However, the current geopolitical climate will not allow for declassification of the details of that operation. Instead, they are being sealed for another twenty-five years.

This is where I need your help." Deborah declared.

"What is it that I can help with?" Joshua asked. He noticed a small box on her desk. It was a box containing a Purple Heart.

"There is support within the army leadership for Doug to be awarded a Medal of Honor. However, the secrecy of the mission presents a problem. I have proposed an unconventional solution. I proposed that a Medal of Honor be awarded to an 'unknown soldier of the Cold War Era'. Doug would be this soldier and he would be buried at ANC in a grave marked 'Unknown Soldier'. This action will require an act of Congress. I know, that is a tall order. With Support from the army leadership and the current president we might be able to make this plan work.

Caleb, as a Medal of Honor recipient, has attended every presidential inauguration and inaugural ball since President Truman. He has met every president since Harry Truman was in office. If he would contact the president and talk with him it wouldn't hurt our cause. He could also lobby former presidents for their support.

I have not spoken with John about the operation, since I visited him in Germany just after the event. He was awarded a Purple Heart for his injuries. I am aware that the army leadership has contacted him to validate the account of the incident.

This still leaves us with a huge hurdle, the Congress. The only person I know with any amount of influence on Capitol Hill is a big problem for us. Alexander Garnet, CEO of Axis Energy, is the only person I can think of that might have the type of access, to the leadership of Congress, we need," she stated.

"That is an ambitious plan, I must say. The timing is right though with the twenty-five year anniversary approaching. I will speak with Caleb and I am sure he will support your plan. Garnering the support of Red is another matter. That will take a miracle. However, miracles have been known to happen on this majestic Purple Mountain. Who knows, maybe we will see another one when your proposal is approved," he concluded.

"Thank you. This is important to me and I am sure it will help Jessica in her grieving process, as she goes through the rest of her life. If the plan is approved, I am sure that she will never know that it is her father who is the unknown from the Cold War," she stated.

"As this plan takes shape, I am sure the details will work themselves out. Is there anything else?" he asked?

"Yes, there are two things," she told him to his surprise.

"Please continue. How may I assist?" Joshua asked.

"During the latter years of my commission, I served in SIGINT (signals intelligence). It is something that I live and it has a tendency to carry over into my private life. I mean to say, I always have my ears to the rails.

A few months ago, I began to consider your offer to join the MMG. At that time, I began to hear chatter about the Majestic. This chatter was disturbing to me and I began an effort to vet the information.

During the process, I explored various counter measure options. I implemented the development of a secret plan, without your knowledge or approval. This plan has been pushed beyond the development stage and is ready for immediate implementation. My worst fears were confirmed, during this process. It was only a few days ago that I learned the full extent of the plans to destroy the Majestic of Purple Mountain. A mining project is planned for this section of the mountain. It is called MTR and stands for mountain top removal. It is a brutal assault on nature and is virtually unstoppable once it has been proposed by a mining company.

Over the past several months, historical information regarding the families that the MMG has assisted was gathered. This information was cross-referenced against the lists of Final Foursome groups. The resulting list of families was considered our target group. Contact information has been assembled for this group and is ready for deployment. We have prepared a letter that asks for their support in protecting this mountain. We have named this group, the Friends of Purple Mountain.

I take complete responsibility for my actions and will accept any punishment that is due me. However, I ask that you consider the plan without delay. Upon approval, I ask that it be implemented as soon as possible and that the letters be released immediately," Deborah declared.

"We only recently learned of these plans ourselves. I was told you were aggressive and assertive. Apparently, my intel was right on. This is exactly the reason that we decided to invite you into our midst. I applaud your efforts. I approve the plan. However, please include me in any future plans you may have before you decide to act on them," he said with a smile. "I thought you said, 'two things' didn't you?"

"Yes, I did," she responded.

"Please tell me there are not three?" he said.

"No, sir. There is one last issue that will require the use of your legal background," she began.

"Finally, you left something for me to do! Now, what is it that you need to know?" he questioned.

"It has been said that from a legal perspective, we can't stop Axis Energy from their mining goals. However, I don't believe in legal absolutes and I don't believe in defeat either. So, this is what I am thinking . . . " Deborah began her request.

Chapter 43

It was approximately seven-thirty in the morning on Saturday, April 21, 2012, when a rather unusual automobile rolled into Worthington.

"Does anyone know how to fix a car around here?" Tootsie called out into the garage. She was an older woman, probably around ninety. However, she thought that ninety was the new seventy. Over the years, she kept herself in good physical condition. Nothing about her was average, except for her height and body mass index. According to her, she had a one hundred year warranty and she planned on using all of it.

"We sure do ma'am. What do you got out there?" the mechanic on duty replied before he stuck his head out to see the car. "OH MY . . ., OH MY. . ., Samson, you gotta come and see this one!"

"All right kid, I will be out there in a minute. What is the big deal anyway?" Samson replied. Samson was known to frequent the garage scene from time to time. It is said, that he is good with those Jeeps.

"Samson! Get out here!" the mechanic repeated, "we got a real Automobile out here today!"

"Don't tell me what it is! You know the routine," Samson reminded him. He liked to play the guessing game with Samson. Samson would touch, smell and hear the car. He had been known to taste one if necessary. But he couldn't see them with his eyes for he was a blind man. However, his vision was better than most.

"Ma'am, this is Samson and I am the mechanic on duty. We will help you with this car and find out what is happening with it. But first, see, Samson here needs to identify it. No, Don't tell us what kind of car it is. You see, Samson will identify it. Once he knows what it is, he will tell us what is probably wrong with it," the mechanic told her, "is that OK with you?"

"Fine, Mr. Mechanic. I doubt he will be able to identify this one though. Most people that can see it, can't identify it! Oh, and don't touch my car with that stick!" she warned them.

Samson came out, to the front of the garage, where the car was sitting and placed his hands upon it. He walked from fender to fender along the side of the classic saying, "yes, her four door body is painted two-tone green. There is a light green three inch tall stripe that runs horizontally along the body of the car. It is just a few inches below the top of the doors but does not extend onto the hood. Her curved fenders are connected by a flat running board and are painted black. She has nice smooth curves." He continued to talk, as he walked around the back of the automobile, "the tan convertible top is down, folded and covered, the horizontally split bumper is chrome clad," he said. He then walked along the drivers side of the coach touching it, saying, "wooden steering wheel, rolled buff leather bench seats, split horizontal windshield with a tubular chrome clad frame." He stopped at the front of it and lifted the hood, saying, "chrome valve covers and a green engine block." He closed the hood and stepped back, saying, "spoked wheels, narrow tires and one

fine and dandy 1926 Duesenberg Model A Phaeton," he proclaimed.
"Yes, Sir! He done it! He done it again!" the mechanic said.
"How did he know all of that? He is not blind? Is he?" Tootsie questioned.
"A boy named Michael told me about this one, a few years back. He said it was in Kansas though," he confessed.
"So how did you come by this gem?"
"I purchased it from a classic car dealer in northeastern Oklahoma. His car lot was on an old stretch of Route 66 that used to run through that part of the state. He said he bought it, for cash, from Mr. Duesenberg himself. If you believe that sort of thing." Tootsie replied not believing what she had heard from Samson.
"How on earth did you find it out there?" Samson asked.
She began, "that is a story that will take a while to tell. How much time do we have before this car is ready to go."
"Probably, two weeks!" Samson snickered.
"Now that you have introduced yourself to my car, how about a formal introduction?" she asked avoiding the repair discussion at this point in the conversation.
"Ma'am, yes. Pardon us please, in all of the excitement we forgot that," the mechanic said. "My name is Barney and I am pleased to meet you ma'am."
"Barney, the mechanic, I am pleased to meet you," she told him, "my name is Leona, but my friends call me Tootsie."
"Tootsie, my name is Samson," he said as he extended his hand to her, "I am pleased to meet you. That is one fine automobile that you have there. Well, except for it being broken down. But, it isn't anything that we can't fix. Right Barney?" Samson asked him in jest.
"Right! We can fix it. But fix what?" he asked.

"Just what is it that is wrong with this car?" she asked them. "I am on my way to Arlington, Virginia and I need to get there soon."

"Define soon!" Samson asked.

"At my age, in the next two weeks is soon enough. I am in no rush to get anywhere, fast!" Tootsie told them.

"What you have is an alternator problem. We will have to pull it out and send it up state to have it rebuilt. Alternators were a problem on this model. They were a problem on 1941 Jeeps too." He told her.

"Well, how long will that take?" Tootsie demanded.

"Like I said, about two weeks, give or take a few days," Samson told her. "Looks like it works into your schedule then?"

"Anywhere to stay around here? Also, is there anything to do around here?" Tootsie inquired.

Samson responded, "There is a bed and breakfast just down Main Street and there is a parade today! Beyond that, who knows what a day may bring?"

"Well, send off that alternator. Then have someone get my bags over to that bed and breakfast. I don't want to miss the parade. What time does it start?" Tootsie asked.

Samson pulled the bags from the car, "We will get these to the bed & breakfast and get started on the repairs. The parade starts at noon. You are welcome to sit with me. I will be watching from the reviewing stand at the old courthouse."

"That will be acceptable. Now, let's get moving!" she commanded in a soft tone of voice.

Chapter 44

He is late, she thought, as she sat in her Mayoral office. A small fire burned on the hearth stone. She knew he liked a small fire. Then she heard the sound of familiar footsteps down the hall and suddenly a light rap on the door. It sounded, knock . . ., knock knock knock, . . . knock.
"Come in," she said warmly while instantly forgetting about the tardiness of his arrival.
"Sorry for being a little late. That old Jeep didn't want to move as fast I did this morning," he said while looking at the clock showing quarter past eight.
"Things move a little slower when you reach the age of seventy-one, I hear," she replied.
He entered the room and stood by the fireplace warming his hands, "I like a small fire in the morning. Well actually anytime, if I think about it much," he turned toward her and put his hands behind him keeping them by the fire. "Thank you for meeting so early today. I must apologize for not showing last night at the fundraiser. Something urgent came up that I needed to attend to. Work, you know."
"I know, Red sent you up the mountain to talk with John the greenskeeper. How is he these days. My, it has been years since I have seen him," she disclosed.

"He is good, I think?" Michael struggled with words and turned back to face the other fire in the room. It is getting hot already he thought. How will I tell her, he thought.

"Why did Red send you up there to talk with John?" she inquired.

Still facing the fire, "I quit asking those 'why' questions some time ago. However, what I was doing up there I will answer. I was delivering a business proposition on behalf of Axis Energy. It seemed to go well. I think he is considering it."

She being ever the lawyer, began to have a prosecutorial air in her questions, "What 'business proposition' were you delivering?"

"A unique opportunity to get in on something at let's say, 'the ground level', if you will," he replied vaguely.

"You are a challenge, you do know this don't you? Would you just give me a straight answer? Mr. vice president of public relations, please turn around. I want to see your bright face as you relate with this public," she quipped.

"Talk? More like 'witness badgering' from a seasoned prosecutor! I will report you to the mayor of this town!" he shot back as he turned to face her. He paused for a long moment and considered his next move, "How about if we start over? I go out and then knock and then walk in again. Then instead of heading to the fire, I will come and sit by your desk?"

"Agreed," she said looking down at some official papers on her desk.

Then she heard a rap on the door. It went, knock . . ., knock knock knock, . . . knock. She got up from her desk and went to the door. She stood leaning against it, smiling. Then another series of five knocks. Then she lightly rapt back, 'knock, knock' in quick succession. It was something they had done a thousand times before, if they had done it once. The door opened and there he was.

"May I enter?" he asked.

"Of course. Please do come in. Have a seat," Jessica said to him. The reset from the prior conversation had occurred in her mind and the former conversation went up in the air like smoke in the fireplace.

"Do you remember the day we first met?" Michael asked her from the chair next to her desk.

Laughing, "Where did that come from?"

"I am being serious. Please, humor me with this for a while," he pleaded with his piercing bright blue eyes.

Sitting back in her chair, "it was a Monday, June 8, 1987, that is what I would call our first official meeting. Although, we had seen each other before that day, we really didn't see each other before that. I am rather official these days by the way."

"I remember, it was our last day of school. You were sad and lonely and sitting by yourself during the longer than usual recess. You were sitting in the grass between the playground and the school when I came over to you. Strands of your long wavy auburn hair were swirling gently around your face. Your father had left on a deployment. We talked, as we looked for a four leaf clover. The grass was emerald green and matched your soft eyes," he recalled.

"As I recall, your pudginess, the blue eyed squire, that is you, talked about Purple Mountain and about castles and kingdoms, knights and emperors, dragons and damsels, dogwoods and daisies. Your stories cheered me up. Neither of us found that lucky clover either," she said as her eyes betrayed her speech. She unconsciously looked down to the lower left drawer of her desk. That was the drawer where she kept 'damsel's dreams'. That is where she kept that one clover, the one with four leafs. It was pressed between two sheets of wax paper and was dated using a purple colored crayon.

"Luck was with me that day and I didn't need a clover to prove it. I found a friend," he revealed to her, that which she already knew in her heart.

"Timing was never our strong suit. We meet on the last day of school and then summer break. I didn't see you at all that summer. No, not once!" she stated as she swiveled in her chair and leaned back to look at the ceiling.

"All true, I must admit," he confessed, as he looked at her swiveling in her chair. "I worked the entire summer up on that mountain with my brother Christopher and John the greenskeeper."

"I know. Then school started again. Squire Pudginess, had grown up a little over the summer. He was more like a junior Knight than a pudgy little squire. As I recall, he became my protector, my knight in not so shiny armor. More like my knight in Jordache jeans. Yeah, I like that. Jordache jeans, yes, they were in style back then," she maintained still slowly swiveling in the chair. It was as though she were on a merry-go-round.

I remember, "With your dad gone and all, I felt like I could help. I wanted to keep you safe. So, that is what I decided to do."

"I remember, and except for a few brief periods, you never stopped," she continued, "we were together all through high school. Then the scholarships we both had, from Axis, sent us to the University of Virginia. As if that were not enough, I got a law degree and you, your MBA. Again at the same schools," she recalled.

Michael continued, "Then we both ended up at Axis. You as legal counsel and me as a public relations representative.

We both worked hard, feeding that dragon! As Mr. Garnet would say, 'feed the dragon', meaning keep the mining activities going at all costs. We did just that. You and I both advanced in the organization. By the year 2006, we were both at the director level.

I worked on enhancing the corporate image. I led the charge when it came to corporate posturing, branding, focus groups and political correctness. You worked on legal strategy. You crafted one of the most important legal precedents the mining industry had seen in decades. Sure, it took a while to work through the system. Make no mistake, it was your doing.

We were busy building careers and had settled our work loads down to manageable levels. We were at the VP level, both of us! I was responsible for promoting a 'positive corporate' image to the public and for helping make the company profitable. You were responsible for keeping us all out of jail.

Just about the time our paths were crossing at Axis, you were gone. You left and ran for Mayor, of Worthington, and here you sit," Michael recounted as he leaned back in his chair and stared at the ceiling. "You are so right, our timing was never good."

"Why are you here Michael?" she asked, "this trip down memory lane has been wonderful. However, now it is time to return to reality. We have responsibilities to carryout."

"Jessica, perhaps our timing is finally good," he stated simply.

"How so?" she asked with a hint of curiosity.

"We are in positions to help the people of this community. We can work together, to help bring this community back from the brink of economic destruction.

Axis Energy needs your support. With your support of the MTM project, we can restart our local economic engine, put people back to work, and provide a framework for sustained economic growth. We have both worked hard and now find ourselves in positions where we can effect positive change," Michael suggested without subtly.

She replied, "I thought that was it. Red wouldn't tell me last night but I knew it. There have been murmurings for some time now of a MTR (Mountain Top Removal) project. It is a difficult decision and I am not sure how I am going to come down on it."

His public relations skills went on autopilot, "Jessica, think about the benefits to the community. Think about what MTM (Mountain Top Mining) will bring in terms of jobs, security and in sustainability? Think about how this will help so many people find peace of mind. People and businesses are struggling out there. Opportunities like this just don't come along these days. Not any more. Axis Energy is here to help this community."

"By removing a majestic mountain and replacing it with a shopping mall and a business park? What about John the greenskeeper. What will he do?" she responded.

"I offered him a job with Axis and a place to live too. It is all set. Everything is taken care of. We just need your support on this," he stated softly.

'What is so important about my support?" she questioned him.

"Red wants the full support of the zoning commission. He says that it will 'look good' that way," Michael declared.

"Sometimes we don't get everything we want. Not even Red," she claimed.

"Jessica, I needn't remind you that you and I have been extremely successful at what we do. In part we owe it to him. He paid for our college education.

Now, we find ourselves the victims of our own success. Your legal mind has made this whole exercise, of getting local zoning approval, basically unnecessary. As for my role, I am good at selling this stuff. I am the best doggone 'dragon feeder' there ever was. I will convince these people that this MTM project is good for them. They will buy it because Red wants it that way. In time they will forget the beauty of that majestic Purple Mountain. Yes, they will have a job to go to and money to spend. They will be secure and happy.

However, there is another way to do this. Axis can go through the courts. Sure, it will get ugly. Sure, it will cost a lot in lawyer's fees. And make no mistake, Axis will prevail. We, you and I, helped make that possible.

There is nothing we can do to stop this. Even if we both opposed this project and fought it tooth and nail, we would fail. It is a futile fight. Only hardship and pain are waiting for us at the end of that road.

So, let's take the easy road on this one. That is the only road that I see. Let's help the people do this right. If they believe they can stop it, they will try and fail as miserably as we would. Let's not let them go down that road.

I need your leadership on this one. I need your support. The people need your leadership and support," Michael declared as he looked at her with his blue eyes.

Jessica's steely green eyes, were like floodgates, holding back a river, swollen with years of tears, "I caddied there once, at the Majestic of Purple Mountain. I carried the clubs for my father. We teed off in the afternoon. We had the greatest round going, ever! Then a storm came and we had to wait for it to quit raining before we could finish. We were on the eighteenth fairway when the sun set. I wanted to finish the round with him!

With the faith of a child, I asked for a second sunset that day. Then the miracle happened. We watched the sun reappear in the sky and set again! We watched, as the greenskeeper played "Taps" in faithful solitude. It was beautiful. No we didn't finish that day. I still have the scorecard," she reached down and pulled out a clear plastic bag with the scorecard and the clover and laid it on the desk, "I always dreamed of him coming back to finish this with me. But then the training exercise accident and his going MIA put an end to those dreams, mostly.

What happened that summer after we first met? Where did that squire who dreamed of castles and kingdoms, knights and emperors, dragons and damsels, dogwoods and daisies run off to? The knight he became was not the one he started off to be.

Stories about the Final Foursomes make their way down that majestic and mysterious mountain. Some believe it is an honorable thing, others a hoax, others a joke and some believe it is real. What if it is real? Do we deny others the right to believe in the unbelievable? Were we to save it, would my father come? Would Christopher come? Should we destroy it, we will never know. Do we destroy something sacred for the security offered by a few more shillings in our coffers?

If there is a faith that can call the sun to a second setting in one day, is there a faith that can keep a mountain from being moved?" I need time to think on this and you need to go. Now.

Jessica spun around in her chair so that she faced away from Michael.

Michael stared at the scorecard and the clover laying on her desk The dreams of a damsel were laid bare before him. How could he not tell her of her father's visit to the Majestic, he thought. His thoughts, if they could be painted on canvas, would look as if Picasso himself had painted them.

With his heart, he longed for dogwoods and daisies, dragons and damsels, knights and emperors, castles and kingdoms.

With his hands, he opened the door and the vice president of public relations for Axis Energy quietly left the office of the mayor of Worthington.

Chapter 45

"Samson, these are wonderful seats for viewing the parade," Tootsie told him as they made their way across the platform of the viewing stand and into their seats. A viewing stand had been erected in front of the old court house.

Samson, pointing down the street, said to her, "The parade route will start from the south end of Main Street and proceed north until it passes by us and ends just over there."

They could hear the beating of drums, the sound of the fifes and the bugles. A Fife and Drum Corps, from Williamsburg, was marching in the parade today. Their sounds elicited the sweet smell, of patriotism, in the mind of Samson, as he heard their warm ups. He thought of the sounds he had heard years ago one summer. Echoes of the fife and drum. Echoes of a wood flute playing "Taps" at sunset. Despite his hard appearance on the outside, being a large man, he was soft on the inside. His heart broke for those friends that he had lost in battle so long ago. His heart was strengthened however, by the thoughts of their sacrifice and their gallantry. His heart was steadfast in its support for the Majestic of Purple Mountain. He would give his life for her, if that was necessary to save her.

"Good morning, Ms. Mayor," Red said as he came to the viewing stand. He took a seat, in the second row, sitting directly behind where Samson and Tootsie were seated.

"Good morning, Mr. Garnet," she replied cheerfully. Jessica was still trapped in thoughts about her earlier discussion with Michael. Then the thoughts of her father entered into her mind. The thoughts were overwhelming. She wondered about the others that were like her. What did they think during this time, she wondered. Was it as difficult for them, as it was for her. She knew that those in pain needed to hear a strong voice giving them comfort. She was prepared to do just that, once the parade ended. For now, she would continue in her inward struggle. However, she was experienced at masking her true feelings. "Wonderful day for a welcome home parade, wouldn't you agree?"

"Indeed, I would. It is always a privilege and an honor to welcome home our war heroes," Red commented. In the world of masking feelings, Jessica was a mayor of a local municipality. However in that same world, Red was the emperor of a vast empire. Red perfectly masked his feelings of loss regarding his parents, and other family members that had been killed so long ago. To him, it was as if they had been killed while they were in a parade of their own. They were bringing home one of our own, only to be thwarted at the entry gates. He pondered these things in his heart. It was nearing the time of year to remember such things but not quite yet.

On Memorial Day each year, he visits the cemetery where his parents, aunt, uncle and cousin are buried. He bought one hundred copies of the Worthington Times dated May 27, 1953, and he keeps them in his office in a glass bookcase. Each year he takes a copy of the paper and leaves it in front of one of the grave sites. Each year he relives the experience of the loss. He has never accepted their deaths. Nearly a half century has past and he has an inventory to last another half century. He quietly contemplated cleaning out the bookcase. He wondered if he could summon the courage, to cast them out. He watched the crowd and wondered what demons danced in the hearts and minds of those that have experienced loss. He wondered if there were some like himself, that held on and wouldn't let go. Perhaps, he thought, this year I will let them go. He thought, I will take every remaining copy and leave them at the grave site. This year I will do it, he thought.

There was another option on his mind. Perhaps it was time to read the letter that he had received from the Greenskeeper in the spring of 1987? He had never opened it. He was convinced it was from his uncle, or at least that is what he would be led to believe. What did the letter contain? Just as with his parents, he had never accepted the loss of his uncle. He still had the necklace he had given him. He still had that Babe Ruth baseball. The one from when Babe visited St. Margaret-Mary school back in 1945. The ball with the silver sparkle sealed securely within the crystalline case. What was that sparkle anyway, he silently contemplated. Alexander knew it was time. A season of change was upon them all, here in Worthington. Neither side of the mountain could avoid it this time. These burdens were too great upon him. He had to choose this year.

Red automatically refocused his thoughts on the mining project that was to be publicly announced after the parade.

"Hello, Red," Michael said as he took a seat next to him on the viewing stand.

"Michael, good morning," Red said as Michael sat down.

"Hello, Jessica. It is good to see you again today," Michael said, as he leaned forward to talk with her. Jessica was sitting a row below him.

"Michael, good to see you again so soon," Jessica replied.

Still leaning forward Michael said quietly, "we need to talk again soon. I have more to add to our discussion."

"Sure, we will talk again later. I am sure," she replied knowing that they were kingdoms apart.

"Good," Michael replied as he sat back in his seat. He surveyed the crowd quickly. He was trying anything and everything to keep Christopher out of his mind. Christopher was so close to coming home. Just another day and he would have made it out of Iraq. He would be marching in this parade. Instead, Michael sat symbolically with those that have experienced the loss of a loved one during military service. Just to his side was Red and in front of him, Jessica sat. All three, feeling the same pain of loss, yet each dealing with its aftermath differently.

Michael, of the three, knew better. He had been the acting greenskeeper of the Majestic of Purple Mountain. In one season, back in 1987, he experienced the gallantry of a hundred soldiers that had given their lives in honor; he watched as they faded into glory. He heard their stories and they are all still in his memory. He knew these stories needed to be shared. A great gift had been given to him. The gift was to help people find peace and closure. The kind of peace and closure he desired to have with his brother Christopher. Was it too late now? If he were to revive the stories and write them would there be anyone left to read them? Were there any addressees standing in the crowd today? He couldn't bear the thought of meeting one of them face to face and not telling them. So, he would stay away he thought. The thought of the unwritten and unsent letters, from his season as greenskeeper, haunted him.

How was he to tell Jessica about her father? From her, he could not stay away. A quarter century had passed without her knowing the truth. Nothing was simple in this case. There were other considerations. Military secrecy had to be maintained. Oh, that twenty-five years had passed and he could tell her. However, that was still a few months away or so he thought. What would happen, if the mountain were to be brought down and then she were told? Would she ever forgive him for not allowing her to know?

Once again, he realized why it was that he left the mountain. It was all too hard for him. He feared he had not the faith to do it. He desired to have the heart of a greenskeeper but did he have it? It was as if he were standing at the base of the Hillary Step staring at the snow covered summit. Did he have the courage to attempt the ascent, he wondered. Decisions were being pressed upon them by forces they could not control.

The parade was beginning. Units from each branch of the military were represented. Soldiers young and old, black and white, male and female all participated. Some units marched with precision and were in full dress, while others marched with less precision and were in combat fatigues. Flags were waved, cheers were given and bands played patriotic songs in honor of our returning heroes. It was a grand event and well attended. There was a sense of pride mixed with sadness and hopefulness. Pride in a job well done; sadness for those that had fallen during battle; and hopefulness that we would meet with them again, someday.

The parade ended almost as quickly as it had begun. People along Main Street cheered and waved flags but in the square the willows weeped, the marigolds mourned and the crocuses cried. Life would return to a sense of normalcy, once again, for the families of the returning soldiers. Spouses and parents returning to their family settings would bring joy. However, would anything ever be normal again for the families where their soldier did not return? What of them? How would these find closure and peace?

The mayor prepared for her post parade proclamation. She addressed the parade crowds knowing that she was all that stood between the end of the parade and the life that was to follow.

A podium was set on the reviewing stand. However after taking the microphone, she descended the stairs. She would speak from their level and identify with their plight. Although she had months of advance notice, there was no prepared text, no TelePrompTer, no speech writer giving advice, no focus groups tracking approval. This address would be from her heart. It would come from the daughter of a soldier and the mayor of a town with soldiers.

"Dear Citizens, friends and family:

I ask us to bow our heads, in a moment of silence, for those that have fallen on the battlefield.

We are gathered here today, as a people, to give honor to our soldiers that are returning from war. We thank you for your gallantry in battle. We thank you for your fidelity to our Republic. We applaud you, for your dedicated service to the country you love, its citizens and your fellow soldiers. Your service is of the highest calling and we are grateful. We welcome each of you home today.

The war we fought was honorable and the cause was just. We acknowledge that war causes wounds that require healing. This is true for the soldier and for their loved ones as well. As a people, let us work together to bind our wounds and find peace. We acknowledge that war causes losses worthy of remembrance. Let us endeavor to always remember those that gave, in the words of Lincoln, 'their last full measure of devotion'. Let us strive to bring hope and healing to the families of these that have fallen. I ask each of us to grieve, with our brothers, while they grieve. I ask each of us to mourn, with our sisters, while they mourn. I ask each of us to dance and rejoice, with our brothers and sisters, when our grieving and mourning have ended and we have embraced the acceptance of our losses. Time heals no wounds but working together, over time, we can purpose to heal our broken and our brokenhearted. Working together, there is nothing we can't do.

To those that have sacrificed, so much for our country, we salute you.

May God bless you and may God bless America.

Thank you."

With her speech delivered, the crowds broke and made their way home. The welcome home parade was over. With that, the daily parade of life, with all of its complexities and contradictions, would begin again.

The viewing stand cleared out quickly, except for a few lingering guests.

"Ms. Mayor, the zoning commission has scheduled an emergency hearing for Monday, May 7, at 3:00 PM. At that time, they will consider a proposal from Axis Energy to gain preliminary approval of a Mountain Top Mining project here in Worthington," her trusted assistant told her.

"I figured that was coming and it didn't take long," she said.

"As Mayor, remember, your vote is only needed as a tie breaker. There has not been a tie breaker vote needed in over a quarter century," her assistant reminded her.

"That number seems to be rather common these days," she commented.

"What number? A tie breaker?" she asked.

"No, a quarter century," she remarked as she headed out into the remaining crowd.

"Ms. Mayor, may I have a moment of your time," he asked as he gently grabbed her arm from behind.

Her eyes opened wide upon seeing his face. It was as if Moses had come down the mountain. His hair was now white as snow, "of course Mr. John, let's have a seat on that bench over there." They sat on the bench that sits on the town square. The bench is the one she typically uses for her Friday lunch meetings with the townspeople.

"That was a wonderful speech you just delivered," he told her.

"Thank you. That is kind of you," she replied holding the elder man's hand in her own.

"Do you believe in what you say? Or is it just politics for you?" he cut right to the heart of the matter.

"It is as I say and I meant all of it. Of course, living it out is always the difficult part. There are lots of hurting people out there that need healing. Somehow, we will find a way to help them," she declared.

"I hear that you still have an unfinished scorecard from the year 1987 and that you need to finish caddying the round," he probed.

"I have held it for nearly a quarter century and it is time to let it go," she confessed.

"Not if you believe in that speech, you won't," he claimed.

"How is that, I don't understand?" she said to him.

"I am one of the people you talked to. You said, 'for us to work together to find peace', so lets work together," he insisted.

"Interesting. What do you propose?" she asked.

He asked her directly, "what would bring you peace?"

"Simple. Knowing," she stated.

"Knowing what exactly," he asked.

"Knowing what happened to my dad. Knowing that he wanted to come back and finish what we started. Knowing that his faith came to fruition and he found peace. Knowing that we will meet again in Heaven. Is that too much to ask," she confessed.

"In most cases, yes. However, knowing those things are my speciality. The Majestic is a mysterious and wonderful place and above all, provides peace to those that have faith. You should come and visit some time soon," he encouraged her.

"I will come soon then," she told him.

"We will work together. It is decided," he stated, "I must ascend the Mountain. A Final Foursome is set to play soon and I must be on the fist tee when they arrive." As he pointed to the mountain, she looked in that direction. She thought of the second sunset and the miracle that happened that day so long ago.

She turned to thank him for coming to the parade but he was gone. She sat on the bench, reliving the parade, and the mighty forces behind it. She looked into the hearts of her people and wondered what she could do to help them find peace. We will work together, she thought.

Back on the viewing stand, Red and Michael were talking.

"Michael, you are prepared for your two o'clock press conference?" Red asked fully knowing that he was prepared.

"Yes, Sir. It is, as you would say, 'time to feed the beast'. I will tell the people of all of the wonderful benefits of this MTR (Mountain Top Removal) project—"

Red interrupted him, "Michael, it is MTM, MTM, MTM! Mountain Top Mining not MTR. Do not say the word 'Removal'. That word does not work well in focus groups. That word does not feed the beast. Are you having second thoughts about this?" Red insisted. In his usual display of displeasure, he grabbed his belt at the waist and began to twist his trousers side to side while pulling them up and down at the same time.

Michael not responding to the outburst, but nearly laughing at the sight, continued on autopilot, "I will tell them how it will provide jobs in this weakened economy. I will tell them how this project will restart our local economic engine. I will tell them how this project will provide a framework for sustained economic growth. I will remind them of how Axis Energy partners with this community. I will remind them of the commitment we have, at Axis, to the sustainability of environmental resources. I will remind them that only through working together can we overcome our current economic challenges."

"Yes, that is what they need to hear," Red was saying as he walked away from Michael and descended the stairs of the viewing platform, "Yes, working together we will 'feed the beast' ... "

Michael headed down off of the viewing platform He was the last to leave. As he did, he looked down the street, as if he were expecting Christopher to come marching home. However, the street was empty and the parade was complete. He saw a glimpse of a W200 Dodge Power Wagon driving down main street. It reminded him of the times John had taken them home. Like the parade, the season of the Power Wagon was over. That was a quarter century ago. Michael turned his thoughts to the press conference, as he turned his body and walked in that direction.

Red walked down Main Street to where his coal black sedan was parked along a side street. He noticed a large truck double parked beside it. He approached with a sense of timidity.

"Have you opened that letter you were sent?" a still small voice called to him from inside the truck. The vehicle was a W200 Dodge Power Wagon.

Red stood just behind the drivers door of the W200 and between the two vehicles. It felt as if he were standing between two kingdoms. He could see inside the cab. There was a man in there with hair as white as mountain snow. He knew it was the greenskeeper of the Majestic of Purple Mountain that was calling to him.

Red was moved by the still small voice, "no," he confessed, "it remains unopened after a quarter century. I have it locked away in my desk, at the heart of the Axis Energy Corporate Headquarters."

The W200 pulled away with a loud roar of the engine. It turned on to main Street and was gone from his sight. Red was left standing next to his coal black sedan, contemplating his empire. What was he to do with the letter? He reached to feel the necklace beneath his shirt and it warmed his hand when he touched it. It was the necklace with the garnet stone attached. It was given to him by his uncle Charles before he left for Korea. It was meant as a symbolic gesture. It was a promise that his uncle would return. However, Charles was killed in the last moments of the Battle of Pork Chop Hill and he never returned. Perhaps his return was in another form? He came in the form of a letter but Red was angry that Uncle Charles hadn't come back as he had hoped.

The parade and the following address from Jessica were weighing heavy on his heart. He thought of the words, 'time heals no wounds', and knew the truth of them. He wondered if that still small voice he had just heard whispering, from the cab of the W200, were the words of someone 'working together' to help bind old wounds? Could the Greenskeeper be so audacious, as to seek him out to help heal him? This, despite the knowledge the Greenskeeper had regarding Red's plan to destroy his majestic Purple Mountain. Perhaps the Greenskeeper cared more for the one man than the majestic Mountain itself?

He turned and ran his hand over the smooth coal black surface of his sedan. It was cold to the touch. It was as if his senses summonsed his spirit. Instantly, he thought of the smooth black granite sarcophagi that were in the old cemetery at the edge of town. The ones he visited each year at this time. For the first time he made the connection. The Axis headquarters building was a sarcophagus of its own. In it were buried his dreams, hopes and fears. Most of all, his heart was buried within its cold black granite walls. He opened the door and nearly entered the cold coal black sedan. However, during the parade something happened. He caught a glimpse of a person whom he thought was his great nephew. Red had not spoken with him in years. He closed the door of the sedan and purposed to find his great nephew. Red followed the path of the Greenskeeper. He walked up to Main street and disappeared around the corner, leaving the cold coal black sedan behind.

Chapter 46

It was four o'clock and time for the emergency meeting of the partners of the Minutemen Management Group. This meeting had been called by Joshua. It was in response to the information he had received from their newest member, Deborah. They were meeting in the clubhouse of the Majestic of Purple Mountain.

"I call this meeting to order," Joshua stated. In attendance were Samson, Caleb, Gideon and Deborah. He continued, saying, "each of you have been briefed on our strategy, secretly developed by Deborah, to disrupt and destroy the plans that Axis Energy has for this Mountain. I ask for a vote signaling your support of this plan."

"Aye," Caleb declared.

"Aye, Aye, Aye!" said Samson in a low growl. It was lower than his usual low growl.

"Aye," Gideon declared.

"Aye," said Deborah.

"Then the Ayes have it," Joshua declared, "Deborah, I believe you have a summary of your findings and a tactical plan prepared. Please go ahead," Joshua said.

She began, "Over the past several months, historical information was gathered regarding families assisted by the MMG. This information was cross-referenced against the lists of Final Foursome groups.

The resulting list, of over two thousand families representing all fifty states, is our target group. Contact information has been assembled for this group and is ready for deployment.

We have prepared the following letter. It will be sent to our allies, the Friends of Purple Mountain. It is our hope, that once the letter is read, our allies will come to the aid of the Majestic in its hour of need. The letter reads as follows:

> Dear Friend,
>
> In the course of life, our paths have previously crossed. It is with sadness that we report to you that the Majestic of Purple Mountain is under siege. Many of our local supporters, although fighting valiantly, fear that the battle may be lost already. Our opponent is strong and well resourced.
>
> In an effort to obtain victory over this adversary, we are calling on the help of our allies. We seek neither money, nor any material resource.
>
> We ask that you make haste and come to Purple Mountain. We ask that you come and encourage the faithful who are defending this Mountain. Bring the letters that you received from this mountain and its greenskeeper, for the pen is mightier than the sword. Bring your stories of how gallantry, fidelity and service acted together to conquer many an enemy thought to be unconquerable.
>
> We have planned our final assault for Monday, May 7, 2012, at 1900 Zulu. We ask that you join with us and respond in this hour of need.
>
> Good luck and Godspeed,

Sincerely,

the Minutemen

This is our plan of attack. We will rely on the stories, of those that have been touched by Purple Mountain, to touch the hearts of our towns people and the hearts of those on the zoning commission," she concluded.

"Deborah, I ask that you proceed with the request for assistance from our allies," Joshua declared.

"Yes, Sir. We will send these letters immediately via the United States Post Office. We do not have the approval to use various electronic means of distributing this information. So in the same manner they received their original correspondence from the greenskeeper, they will receive correspondence from us. Each of these letters has been handwritten and wax sealed with the official seal of the Minutemen," she declared resolutely.

"May God bless our efforts to defend the honor of this majestic mountain. This meeting is adjourned," Joshua declared."

the Majestic of Purple Mountain

Chapter 47

The hour was approaching nine o'clock in the evening and a strong mountain breeze was blowing. My branches were gently swaying.

"General Anson! It is I, Tiger, too-too tooooo too-too duty, I am reporting early today, sir!" said the great horned owl.

"Tiger, my dear Tiger! It is an honor to have you under my service," I replied.

"General, when I last left you, you were devising a plan to help rescue this great mountain. Have you any orders for me," Tiger asked expectantly.

"Yes, in fact I have," I told my faithful warrior, "When I was a much younger tree, there was a battle fought on this mountain. A young soldier took refuge behind my girth when his position was fired upon. The bullet lodged in my trunk and the soldier escaped without injury," I began.

"General, that is a wonderful story but how does it relate to our situation?" Tiger respectfully questioned.

"After the war, that soldier returned here. He received a Badge of Merit during his time of service. Instead of keeping it himself, he in turn awarded it to me. He stuffed it into a leather pouch, burrowed a small hole into my side, just by the bullet wound, and inserted the pouch into the hole. He dressed my wounds, spent the night, and left the next day. He never returned after that.

Now, I prepare to lay down my medals. Your mission, is to fly to Kite park. There you will capture a kite, with its string attached, and bring it here to me. Once we have it, we will tie part of the string to my highest branch while leaving three score feet for the kite to fly. With the free end of the string, we will attach it to the burr in my bark where the bullet is lodged within me.

When the next storm blows in, we will launch the kite into the sky. My hope is that it will be struck by lightning. The resulting current will run down the string and expose my old wound and the Badge of Merit hidden within me.

I am sure that the greenskeeper will notice my distress and find the medal in the process. It is my hope, that it will be used to convince the public that the stories of Purple Mountain are true and that there is much mystery on this majestic mountain. It is my hope, they will be persuaded to spare this mountain and extend its seasons," I explained.

"But General, this is an extremely dangerous plan. Many trees, not approaching your stature, when touched by lightning never recover. Their wounds are fatal. These trees are not used for furniture, as honorable as that may be. They become mere firewood stock to be burned," he asserted with respect for the General and his gallant plan.

"Remember, this is a majestic mountain and full of mysteries that we can't understand. This plan is not up for debate. I need your bravery more than ever. The Major General himself, when facing his gravest hour during the Revolutionary War, penned the two words, victory or death, upon a piece of paper. Sacrifices must be made to save this mountain and all that call it home. This is a dangerous mission and only you and I will participate in it. Monk, will not be part of our operational plan, this time. Your regular night watches are hereby suspended. Now, make haste and retrieve the kite that will be best suited for implementing this plan. You have a few days time in order to search one out. When you have captured one, bring it to me and we will proceed as planned. Good luck and Godspeed, my friend," I commanded.

"Yes, Sir. You can count on me Sir," Tiger replied as he flew off into the night. He thought of his great respect and admiration for the General. He thought to himself, although the General was not the tallest, most beautiful, or largest tree in the wood, there was not another tree with greater would than Anson, the White Oak of Purple Mountain.

Chapter 48

The date was Saturday, May, 5, 2012, and the zoning hearing was three days away. The days passed by quickly as the zoning hearing approached. There were a few feature articles in the Worthington Times regarding the benefits of MTM to the community. There were a series of advertisements as well, newsprint, billboards and radio spots were featured. The opinions were many but the town seemed nearly equally divided. Despite the efforts of the Public Relations department of Axis, the project lacked the overwhelming support that management had desired. Red placed the blame squarely upon the shoulders of Michael.

It was later in the evening than Jessica, the mayor, wanted it to be. The activities of the day had kept her long but she was finally on her way to the mountain. She had an appointment to keep with the greenskeeper. She had sent word to him earlier in the week that she would be visiting him on Saturday evening, after his duties were complete for the day. She wasn't sure what they were going to talk about but she knew that they were going to work through this together. By her reckoning of time, she would be there within the hour. She looked forward to finding some sense of resolution with her MIA father and finally finding peace.

It was early in the evening, and the greenskeeper was tending to his nightly duties. On this evening, he penned his letters earlier than normal. Also, he had completed the scorecard for the Monday Final Foursome group. He placed the scorecard at the center of his desk. On top of it was laid a single envelope. It was addressed to 'the greenskeeper of The Majestic of Purple Mountain' and was sealed on the back with a wax seal.

The reserve library was unusually tidy. Everything was stowed in its proper place. It was as if the greenskeeper was planning for an extended period of being away. The last time the area was this spotless was when he had gone to Afghanistan back in 1987. His affairs were in order on that occasion. This occasion was similar, although not exactly the same. He returned from that trip.

He thought about the teachings of his old friend, the White Oak. The White Oak was a wise tree and he knew the texts of the ancient scrolls. In them it was said 'there are appointed seasons, a time to live and a time to die, a time to mourn and a time to dance, a time to laugh and a time to cry'. The greenskeeper knew his seasons were near their end. However, he had great faith that there were yet many seasons for the Majestic of Purple Mountain. He had been a faithful servant and now he was being called home.

Earlier in the evening, after the playing of "Taps" a storm blew in from over the mountain. It was unusual that a storm developed from the east. Like a Blitzkrieg was its assault. It came with mighty power and speed. Its mighty blasts lit the sky and its thunder shook the ground. In an instant, the mighty storm passed but the damage was done. During the storm, a magnificent bolt of lightning landed somewhere close to the cabin. He determined to investigate it, after his evening duties.

With his duties complete, he put a few logs on the fire in the reserve library and exited the room. A sliver of light, from the fire, would give away the secrecy of the room for only a few hours but that would have to be enough. While standing at the front door, he took one long last look at the cabin and its contents. Then he walked away. He traveled down the path that led to the eighteenth green. He went, to the place, where he thought the lightning strike had touched the earth.

He could smell the remnants, of a heated battle, in the twilight air. He approached the White Oak and what he saw broke his heart. On the ground, lay a giant limb from the massive oak yet smoldering. The White Oak, with a massive split in its trunk, had taken a direct hit from a magnificent bolt of lightning. Just as twilight was fading to black, he noticed something odd on the ground under the ancient and majestic tree. It was a small leather pouch laying close to the trunk of the tree. He sat down by the trunk of the tree, leaning against it. He looked at the pouch that was laying on the ground. Next to it was an oak leaf cluster composed of a twig with four bronze colored leaves and three acorns. He carefully grasped the pouch with his left hand. Then the Greenskeeper gently opened the leather pouch. Within it, was a purple cloth cut into the shape of a heart with the word 'merit' sewn into it. The Greenskeeper held it to his left breast.

John lamented, "Oh, that the world would have seen the gallantry of this unique tree and how God uses all of his creation to accomplish His purposes. You were a most faithful tree my friend, Anson, The Great White Oak of Purple Mountain."

Over the years, John was witness to thousands of first tee pinning ceremonies. Each of them were presided over by the Major General, George Washington. John witnessed thousands of acts of gallantry, fidelity and service. He saw soldiers live and he saw them die. Their faces flashed in front of him.

They appeared as sketches drawn in a sketch book. If the images were viewed in a Mutoscope, it would take fifty of them to hold all of the images he had sketched.

He had written thousands of letters to the families of these soldiers. He could see them, in his minds eye, as their mourning turned into dancing and as their crying turned into laughter. These memories and visions gave him great joy.

He had faithfully played "Taps" at sunset, every day, during his epoch, as the greenskeeper of the Majestic of Purple Mountain. In his thoughts, he watched thousands of souls on the eighteenth green fade into glory. The images, of the thousands of purple hearts and the stories they represent, flashed across his memory one last time. It was as if he were walking through a grand art gallery, a gallery of gallantry. Each story had been painted by a master and they hung on the walls for as far as he could see. Then he had a vision of a vast rotunda. On its circular wall were painted eighteen, never ending, green images. Then an image of a Jade jewelry box entered his heart. Carved into its surface was a dragon whose tail contained twelve gemstones of Sardius, Topaz, Carbuncle, Emerald, Sapphire, Jasper, Ligure, Agate, Amethyst, Chrysolite, Beryl, Onyx. The inside of the box was lined in Alabaster and had a majestic image carved into the lid. The last image, in his heart, was of a singular Jade gemstone.

Tears of joy ran down his face, as he wept beneath the White Oak. Then he smiled and breathed his last breath. The greenskeeper of the Majestic of Purple Mountain died.

And then the majestic mountain cried out, "The Greenskeeper is dead. Long live the Greenskeeper!".

Just then, a group of eighteen Snowy Owls swooped in, from The Great White North, and landed in the midst of the White Oak. These were male owls and had solid snowy white feathers. Their beaks and talons were curved and black as coal. Their bright yellow eyes pierced the darkness. It was as though God himself had sent in eighteen angels to watch over the now sleeping greenskeeper.

She arrived at the cabin of the greenskeeper. It was dark, except for the flicker of the light of a fire that was set in the fireplace. The light came through the windows and open doorway, dimly lighting the front porch. She called out to him but got no answer. The heavy wooden cabin door was standing wide open. She thought it odd, that he wasn't there this late in the evening. She contacted Michael and relayed the situation. He would be there within the half hour.

She gingerly entered the cabin through the open doorway. It was sparsely adorned, she thought, but the craftsmanship throughout made it strikingly beautiful. Despite the solitude and darkness, the cabin felt comfortable. She was deeply concerned for her old friend. While waiting, she stoked the fire with a few logs. He would want it burning when he returned, she thought. Where was Michael?

Michael took the shortest route possible and drove the Jeep up the 'you-ee', again. His mind raced, as he pushed that old Jeep as hard as it would go. What had happened to his old friend? His hands were on the wheel and in his heart he dreamed of dogwoods and daisies. Then the mountain spoke with him, in a language he had learned twenty-five years earlier. As he looked about, tears descended from his cheeks as the Jeep continued its ascent of the mountain.

When he arrived at the cabin he met Jessica, who was standing on the porch.

"Where could he be? We had a time setup . . . Sure, I was a little late. He should have been here—," she said.

"I don't know. It is a big mountain. There was a storm earlier. I saw it roll in from the east. Unusual for one to come

from there. Maybe he went to check on the clubhouse," Michael supposed.
'How do we get there?" Jessica asked.
Michael taking her hand said, "this way. I know the way."
They hurriedly walked down the path that led to the clubhouse. Michael had walked it a thousand times. He already knew. He knew it all, even before he arrived at the cabin. The mountain had already told him the news. It was in the misty mountain breeze and it was in the raindrops falling from the leaves of the trees. Even the wildflowers, along the path to the clubhouse, seemed to bow their heads out of respect for his passing. They would find him together and face whatever lies ahead, together. Together they would bind their wounds.
"Look, up there—," Jessica stopped walking, "what are those? They are beautiful. So many of them too. What ever could they be doing up here?"
"They are Snowy Owls, from the north. They have been seen as far south as Ohio but not in Virginia for some years now. How unusual," Michael said.
"Below the tree! There! John! John!" she called to him running. Michael caught up with her just as she realized John was gone. The greenskeeper had died.
They collapsed into the arms of each other. He looked into her steely green eyes and the flood gates gave way. A river of tears, twenty-five years in the making, flowed from her eyes. She wept for John, she wept for the mountain and she wept for her dreams but not for her father. It was uncharacteristic of her to cry or show emotion, for she was strong. Michael remained composed and consoled her.
They stayed with him, until the coroner arrived. Michael asked her to follow the coroner and get John safely back to town. He would stay, close up the cabin and drive the Jeep

back to town. She agreed and descended the mountain following the lifeless greenskeeper. She continued to weep until the river of tears, twenty-five years deep, receded into its proper banks.

Chapter 49

Michael stood under the split White Oak for some time, listening to the mountain weeping over its losses. Jessica and the coroner had long left the mountain. The Snowy Owls remained in the tree, as if guarding a tomb. He found the leather pouch and the Badge of Merit, laying on the ground, in the place where John had died. He pondered their origin as he walked back to the cabin.

"Hoo-hoo hoooooo hoo-hoo,' called Tiger, from a tree that was near the White Oak. He heard nothing, only silence. He was afraid to approach his friend because of the eighteen Snowy Owls.

'Hoo-hoo hoooooo hoo-hoo,' called Tiger again, still in a soft voice. He heard nothing, only silence.

'Hoo-hoo hoooooo hoo-hoo,' called Tiger again, still in a soft voice. Again, he heard only the sound of silence. Then, Tiger flew away saddened by the death of his friend but determined, to make a difference, in this great and seemingly hopeless battle.

The cabin was nearly dark when Michael entered it. The logs, on the hearth stone, were still glowing but they were not emitting much light. It reminded him of another time, just a few weeks earlier, when the logs had nearly burned out on the hearth stone. He looked around the room and it was familiar and comfortable. He went over to the table, in front of the couch and chair. It is the table with the heart shaped drawer pulls. He stood motionless before the table. Then he sat in the chair. It was the chair of the greenskeeper. There was that drawer, right in front of him. It seemed to be calling to him. He reached for the heart shaped drawer pull, paused, and pulled it open.

Nothing. An empty drawer was all he found. His heart sank. He dreamed of dogwoods and daisies. Michael remembered what he had been told, so long ago, 'you keep greens with your hands but you are a greenskeeper from your heart'. He thought of the summer of 1987. He thought of Samson, the Jeep, dragons and damsels, kingdoms and castles, the Major General and all the golfers in the Final Foursomes. The scorecards! Yes, the scorecards he thought. Where had he put them?

The bookcase! He knew exactly where to look. They were stuffed between Melville's, *Moby Dick*, and Dickens', *A Christmas Carol*. He found them! These were the records of every player, in a Final Foursome, during his time as the acting greenskeeper. He had recorded their names, scores and dates of play. He also noted the names of the caddies as well. They were in excellent condition. He held the scorecards tightly to his left breast with his right hand.

As he backed away, from the bookcase, he noticed a sliver of light. What was that, he thought? A light, emanating from under a bookcase, in the hallway? He pushed the bookcase, in front of him, gently to one side. As it slid to the side, a hidden room was revealed! As he entered the room, the bookcase slid shut behind him.

The inside of the cabin never seemed to fit the outside dimensions. The inside seemed smaller somehow. That had troubled him. Now he knew the answer. A secret room occupied the space!

His eyes searched the room quickly. Michael saw a fireplace, desk, bookcases and more bookcases, big books and bigger books. He saw a humidor, used to store those nasty cigars that the Babe would bring. Placing the scorecards down, on top of the humidor, he continued to search the secretive room he had just discovered.

He went to the bookcases first. His eyes darted from side to side, as he searched them. His eyes drank them in, like a thirsty man in the desert finding a pool of fresh water. He saw one labeled the *Book of Merit*. It looked ancient but well preserved. He pulled it down and held it in his hands. Dare he open it? With his left hand he cradled it at the spine and he grasped the edge of the cover with his right. It opened to the first page.

He read the first few inscriptions:

"May 3, 1783

Sergeant William Brown of the 5th Connecticut Regiment.

Sergeant Elijah Churchill of the 2nd Continental Light Dragoons

June 10, 1783

Sergeant Daniel Bissell of the 2nd Connecticut Regiment"

This was the original *Book of Merit*! It was thought to have been lost to the ages. These were the writings of the Major General himself, George Washington! What a treasure! He carefully placed the book back on the shelf and noticed books and books titled *Book of Merit*. He recognized the wars, World

War II, Korea, Vietnam, Iraq and Afghanistan among the many others.

He noticed another bookcase. This one held tall and skinny books. Each book had a year written on its spine. They were sequentially ordered running from left to right with the oldest years on the top shelf of the bookcase. The first year was 1972. His eyes searched frantically, yes, there it was. He pulled it down. On the front cover was written: Sketches of Purple Mountain the year 1987.

He opened it and leafed through the first few months. From the coldness of January through April's thaw he turned the pages. On each page was a detailed pencil sketch of a Final Foursome player and their caddie. A date was noted at the top of each page. The name of the player and caddie were written near the bottom of each page. He sighed a heavy sigh. It was the kind of sigh that says, 'I know what is coming'.

Then he turned the book to Saturday, May 2, 1987. On that page, at the bottom there were two names written into the records. The names were Christopher and Michael with a notation 'my apprentice' written beneath the name of Michael. The sketch was of two boys peering into the woods with a half eaten apple laying on the ground between them. It looked like a Norman Rockwell print. He turned the pages and soared with Barnstorming Biplanes, ran the bases with Babe Ruth, danced with Fred Astaire, and painted with Pablo Picasso. He turned more pages and smelled the sweet smells of dogwoods and daisies and heard the rumbling of a 1941 Willys MB Jeep.

Finally, like an earthen dam holding back a rain swollen river, his steely blue eyes couldn't hold back the flood of tears he held inside. Then a majestic flood, a quarter century rising, spilled over and swept down his face. The flood carried away the debris of a broken heart. It carried away the pain, the doubt and the fears of all of those years. Michael, the greenskeeper of the Majestic of Purple Mountain, wept. After a flood of tears had receded, a new landscape began to appear.

After a time of waiting, he placed the sketch book back on the shelf. He turned and saw a desk in the midst of the room. He went over to the desk and sat in the chair. In the center of the desk was a letter. It was addressed to 'the greenskeeper of the Majestic of Purple Mountain'. This was the letter he was looking for earlier. The letter in the drawer of the table with the heart shaped handle. The letter he refused to open a quarter century ago and only a few weeks ago, as well. He wept, as he held it to his chest. After composing himself, he found a letter opener on the desk.

He turned the letter over and placed it on the desk in front of him. He took the letter opener and like a surgeon with a scalpel he carefully began his incision. The old wax seal remained intact as he skillfully slid the blade beneath it. He opened the flap and gently pulled the letter from the envelope.

Dear Michael,

You have the heart, to be the greenskeeper of the Majestic of Purple Mountain. In some mysterious manner, this majestic mountain chose you. It is your responsibility, to either accept or reject the call it has made on you. Remember, you keep greens with your hands but you are a greenskeeper from the heart.

The stuff has been willed to you. The Dodge, the paintings and drawings, the Cabin and barn (were deeded to me some time ago) and contents are all yours.

There is fresh coffee in the canister. Go on now and make some, as it is going to be a long night.

With Love,

John, the former greenskeeper of the Majestic of Purple Mountain

There it was. John had known all along that he wouldn't open it until now. He had a way with writing letters. They touch the hearts of the intended reader, in a way that only the reader could fully understand. Michael wept again and again.

Michael put the letter to the side. He looked around the old wooden desk admiring its craftsmanship. Then he saw the scorecard. It had been under the letter that he had just read. He gently grasped it with his left hand and held it. The names and faces of all of his Final Foursomes, the ones from his time as acting greenskeeper, flashed across his mind.

He focused on the scorecard in his hand. He knew one of the names on the card by heart. He had cried enough for one night. He would reserve his tears of joy for another day. He wondered in his heart, did the disciples cry tears of joy, as they watched doubting Thomas place his fingers into the nail scarred hands of the Master? Such answers may never be known.

What was he to do now? On the desk, in front of him, were the fountain pen with a heart shaped breather hole and the inkwell made from old rag granite. He opened the drawer of the desk and found the paper and envelope stock. In another drawer were wax supplies and the signet stamp.

He looked across the room, to where he had laid the scorecards. The scorecards from his time as acting greenskeeper. What was he to do? He walked over to the fireplace and put on two new pieces of firewood. Then he walked over to the humidor and gathered the scorecards. He brought them back to the table in the midst of the room. He carefully sorted them into sequential date order with the oldest dated cards placed on the top of the stack.

He looked intently into the fire. He remembered the sweet smells of dogwoods and daisies. He remembered the patriotic melodies of the fife and drum. He remembered their faces, and their gallantry, fidelity and service. He remembered their sacrifices and their stories. He began to write them down in the form of letters to loved ones. In his heart he rejoiced. In this kingdom there were no beasts to feed. In this kingdom, he was a knight with a pen as his mighty sword. And he battled long into the night.

Chapter 50

Jessica had a vision.

"Daddy, did the dragon defeat you? Is that why you didn't come home?" Jessica asked him, as a child would ask.

"Oh, Jessica. No. The dragon of death was defeated long ago by a Majestic King who died for his people, the people he loved, but now he lives forever. He has prepared a new home for us," her father told her.

"How do we get there?" she asked.

"Only through faith in the Majestic King who died but now lives," he told her.

Daddy, "what does that kind of faith look like?"

"It looks like the kind that keeps majestic mountains from being moved by mighty dragons," he told her.

"Tell me about this new home," she asked him.

"It is beautiful beyond imagination, it is like a jade jewel box adorned with twelve beautiful stones. Inside the Jade box, there is a Great White Tree who lives forever," he told her.

"Daddy, I know I will join you there someday. But can I see you before then?" she asked.

"Yes, you will find me, and all of the other knights of the kingdom, holding up the White Castle that sits on the Purple Mountain. You can always visit me there, enter through the heart at the center of the scarlet staircase," he assured her.

And then he was gone. She was not afraid, for she knew the faith of which he spoke.

Chapter 51

It was the early afternoon of May 7, 2012, the day of the zoning commission public hearing. This hearing had been called nearly two weeks earlier, at the request of the commission, based on a proposal for Mountain Top Mining submitted by Axis Energy. It was a hastily called hearing but not out of order. The hearing was set to begin at three o'clock in the afternoon and was to be held, at the Worthington Elementary School, on Jericho Street.

    On the other side of the mountain, Red prepared for the hearing. Like an emperor controlling a vast economic empire, he had prepared his legions for the ensuing battle. At stake in this battle, he believed, was the continued prosperity and longevity of his company. A few months earlier, he directed his legal team to prepare a filing with the state Environmental Protection Agency. Using case law, inspired by a former Axis lawyer, their filing would unquestionably gain immediate approval. Upon gaining the support of the local zoning commission, in essence the people, Red planned to give final approval of this filing. Despite their approval being an unnecessary technicality, he desired their submission to unconditional approval. However, there were doubts, as emperors of empires sometimes have. Alexander hid them, like a thief hiding stolen treasure from the emperor. From his conscious mind, he hid his doubts well and hid them deep. Thieves always return for their treasures, in the stories of emperors and empires.

Red made his final preparations for the hearing. He was uneasy as he had not heard from Michael, the vice president of public relations, in several days. This was unusual behavior for his apprentice. He knew Michael as a faithful servant and held the uneasiness of the moment in check. As he made his final preparations, he thought back to the parade that was held in town a few weeks earlier. Thoughts of his uncle Charles came into his mind. He could almost hear his uncle calling his name, 'Alexander'. He thought of the recent encounter he had with the greenskeeper. What was it that inspired the greenskeeper to reach out to him? He expected a lecture or a threat from him perhaps. He didn't expect a question about a quarter century old letter. Why would he even think it hadn't been opened? He knew that John had died and he thought about the implications.

Unconsciously, Alexander unlocked the drawer. It was as if his childhood had been stolen by the emperor and was locked away within this vault. He examined the contents, an aged letter sealed with a wax seal and a necklace with a garnet stone attached. He loosened his tie and unbuttoned the top button of his shirt. He carefully lifted the necklace and placed it around his neck and covered it with the shirt. He buttoned his shirt and straightened his tie. Then he lightly lifted the letter. He held it to the light but his heart couldn't penetrate its seal. So, he placed it within the coal black briefcase sitting beside the desk. Alexander exited the room consciously leaving the desk drawer unlocked. In the world of emperors and empires, thieves seldom close the vaults after they have removed the treasures from within them.

Red was ready for the hearing. His transportation, for this endeavor, was the black Dragon. He would swoop in from the east and strike like a Blitzkrieg. It was a short flight to Jericho. He unconsciously looked at his wrist watch. Alexander saw the three spinning celestial faces, of the watch, nearing a personal apogee and with it, the fullness of time. Red saw the short hand, on the blue face of the watch, was just past the number fourteen. Red unfastened the watch and turned it over revealing the side with the white face. The small hand was between the Roman numerals II and III. Red refastened it to his wrist with the blue face hidden. Then he reckoned with it, as he waited and brooded.

Jessica walked past the town square on her way to her office. The crocuses were no longer in bloom and the willow trees seemed weepier. She thought of the parade and wished her father would have been marching home with them. She thought of her conversation with John and their plans, to help her find peace. She turned the corner in front of the old courthouse and walked along the side street. She entered her office and it was cold. There was no fire in the fireplace on this day.

The zoning commission hearing weighed heavy on her heart. Her mind raced with thoughts. Was Michael right in his thoughts? Was it inevitable that Axis would have its way? Were I to choose to support MTM, I would, undoubtedly, save the people from economic peril. But at what cost? Do I destroy something sacred for a few more coins in my Coach? These ideas swirled like stars in her head.

The passing of the greenskeeper weighed heavier on her heart. He was a gentle and caring man and there were not many like him. As mayor, she heard the rumors about him and the Final Foursomes. She wanted to believe. It did not go unnoticed, by her, that childlike faith was the inspiration behind the Novaya Zemlya, the second sunset, that evening twenty-five years ago. The last time she saw her father was that night. She still had the unfinished scorecard. She pulled it from her desk and slipped it into her Coach purse. Oh, where was that childlike faith now?

The still unknown status of her father weighed heaviest of all on her heart. Was he truly lost in a training exercise? Where was her father now? These questions haunted her spirit.

It was as though the weight of the world were upon her. She cried out silently, to God, and asked, why have you forsaken me? Jessica wept. After a time, the mayor left her office, crossed the street, and headed to the zoning commission hearing. It was a long road to Jericho.

Members of the Minutemen Management group met on the patio of the clubhouse. Their names were Joshua, Caleb, Samson, Gideon and Deborah. They missed their friend John deeply. However, the time for grieving was not now. From this strategic location, they could survey the course and the concepts they were fighting for. There was a fire in their eyes. The current struggles had reminded them of their days in battle. Although this battle was not quite of the same significance, as their prior endeavors, it was still about honor. Their brothers and sisters, who shed their blood defending our land, had been honored on these golfing grounds.

The names of Caleb and Joshua elicited thoughts of leadership mixed with faith. In biblical times, they were spies that saw the land of milk and honey. They had overcoming faith and advised the people to take the land. However, the people lacked faith and wouldn't listen to them. Years later, they led a people out of the wilderness and into that promised land.

The names of Deborah, Gideon, and Samson elicited thoughts of the Judges from biblical times. Great warriors were they. Their greatest battle, however, was waged in leading their own people. They led their people away from idolatry and into the spiritual truth of the living God. For the people had strayed and their hearts were far from the Lord.

Each member wore camouflage fatigues of colors appropriate to their branch of service. Their battle clothes had no distinguishing markings, only a United States flag affixed to the upper sleeve just below the shoulder. Each one wore name tape, sewn above their right jacket pocket.

There was, as of yet, no response from the letters the Minutemen had mailed to their allies. Unsure of the support from their allies, they were prepared to fight with the resources they had available. They believed that their cause was just and that this mountain and the peace it provided was worth defending.

Michael joined them on the porch of the clubhouse.

"I want to thank each of you for your support of my being the greenskeeper of the Majestic of Purple Mountain," he said with gratitude, "and I want to thank each of you for defending this mountain!"

Michael pulled Joshua aside and said, "We are a go for Operation Scarlet Staircase."

"We are prepared for the operation. Once we have secured the mountain, we will implement the plan," Joshua advised.

Michael and Joshua rejoined the group and they prayed for wisdom, courage, faith and strength. Then, the Minutemen loaded up into the W200 Dodge Power Wagon and followed Michael, who was driving in the 1941 Willys MB Jeep, down the mountain via the 'you-ee'. It was as though the mountain was cheering them on to victory. The wildflowers waved, chrysanthemums clapped and the hydrangeas hollered while the sunflowers sang a long forgotten patriotic song.

When they reached the road, at the bottom of the mountain, the driver of the Jeep halted. The W200 pulled up alongside of it and paused a long pause.

"What is that coming down the road?" Gideon asked from inside the cab of the W200.

Then Samson spoke, "Eleanor the Gray, Sally the White, Cobra the Black and Boss the Red, it is the Four Horsemen." He knew each of them from their unique sound, as they sped by them.

"What?" said Gideon, "All I see is four Ford Mustangs with tinted windows."

"The Four Horsemen are a Mustang enthusiasts club. They are probably on their way to a car show," Deborah said.

"Thats right, yes, all four were Ford Mustangs. Eleanor is a 1967 Shelby GT500; Sally is a 1987 GT convertible; Cobra is a 2003 SVT Terminator; Boss is a 2012 Laguna Seca," Samson observed.

"Well that is enough proof for me and enough horse power too. I think we will let them lead the way!" Joshua said, as he quickly pulled the W200 out onto the road and hit the gas pedal. The Jeep pulled out behind them and they both followed the Four Horseman into town. It was as if they were headed into the battle of the apocalypse.

As they approached town, the Horses pulled up and turned into Thelma Mae's Roadside Diner, for this was not their battle. There was an antique car show being held there. Inside the diner, Thelma Mae saw them coming.

"Elwood," she called to her cook, "puts four chickens in that frier. The Four Horsemen is here and they gonna devour the place! They will pic that chick to the bone! Hurries up now!" for it is a well known fact, that Thelma Mae has the best fried chicken in town.

They pressed on without their escort. When they arrived at the Worthington Elementary School, on Jericho Street, the gates were locked. They had arrived too early.

Joshua, in an act of faith, decided to drive around the block and toot the horn of the W200, while doing so. It would be a parade he thought. The Jeep followed. Then a white Ferrari with Delaware plates 'NELSON' joined in behind them. As they drove they made the first left past the school onto Red Road. Then they proceeded until the next intersection where they made a left onto White Way. They followed it until making a left onto Blue Boulevard. At the next intersection they were back at Jericho Street. They made another left and started the process again. As they drove in front of the school, the gates were still locked. One trip complete, Joshua thought to himself.

As the three vehicles passed the school, a white 1963 Harley Davidson with Pennsylvania plates and a white 2006 Dodge Charger with New Jersey plates joined in behind them honking. They all made the first left on to Red Road with horns honking. Then they all proceeded until the next intersection where they made a left onto White Way. They followed it until making a left onto Blue Boulevard. At the next intersection they were back at Jericho Street. There they made another left and started the process again. As they drove in front of the school, the gates were still locked. Two trips complete, Joshua thought, to himself.

As the five vehicles passed the school, a white 2012 Chevy Suburban with Georgia plates and a white 1964 1/2 Mustang with Connecticut plates joined in behind them honking. They completed the parade around Jericho Street again. As they drove in front of the school, the gates were still locked. Three trips complete, Joshua thought to himself.

As the seven vehicles passed the school, a white 1954 Corvette convertible with Massachusetts plates and a white 2009 Chevy Camaro with Maryland plates joined in behind them honking. They completed the parade around Jericho Street again. As they drove in front of the school, the gates were still locked. Four trips complete Joshua thought.

As the nine vehicles passed the school, a white 1960 Ford pickup with South Carolina plates and a white 2012 Dodge SRT Viper GTS with New Hampshire plates joined in behind them honking. They completed the parade around Jericho Street again. As they drove in front of the school the gates were still locked. Five trips complete Joshua thought to himself.

As the eleven vehicles passed the school, a white 2008 Dodge Challenger with Virginia plates and a white 1969 Pontiac GTO Judge with New York plates joined in behind them honking. They completed the parade around Jericho Street again. As they drove in front of the school the gates were still locked. Six trips complete, Joshua thought to himself.

As the thirteen vehicles passed the school, a white 1955 Ford Thunderbird with North Carolina plates and a white 1957 Chevy Bel Air convertible with Rhode Island plates joined in behind them honking. When viewed from above, it was as if the thirteen white stars of the Betsy Ross flag were circling around the the ancient city of Jericho. They completed the parade around Jericho Street again. As they drove in front of the school, the gates came down and Joshua led the people into the Jericho entrance of the school.

It was approaching 1900 Zulu and their allies were still coming!

Chapter 52

When he parked the Jeep in the parking lot he saw her. He knew her silhouette from twenty-five years away. She was standing in the grassy field of the school near the spot where they had played as kids. He ran to her.

"Michael, what were you doing?" she asked as her auburn hair swirled in the valley breeze.

"Oh, that," he said pointing to the parade route, "we were just killing some time before the start of the hearing. The gates were. . .," he noticed she had lost interest in what he was saying.

"Michael, the hearing is about to start. What are we going to do?" she pleaded with him.

He thought for a long second, "A wise person once told me–, 'you speak for the people with your mouth, but you lead them with your heart," he advised her. Although it wasn't exactly the quote, it had the same spirit.

"Who told you that?" she questioned, "this is not the time to be funny."

He looked down at the green grass and it was about the color of her eyes. He couldn't even look away and not think of her or see her, somehow. As he looked down, he saw a four leaf clover. He bent down and gently plucked it out.

"Do you remember the first time you met me? Your 'real' first time meeting me?" he asked.

"Michael, we don't have time for this!" she said abruptly.

"Jessica, just trust me on this one. Give it a try, please," he urged her.

"OK. When I came here, early I might add, I looked all over for that exact spot. I think we are standing in that exact spot right now–,"

"That is good, now think about how you knew it was this spot," he urged her.

"Michael, what does this have to do with the hearing? We have important business and this is not–"

He interrupted, "Just work with me on this for one more minute. It is important, really. One more minute, then we will both walk in there and do this hearing," he pleaded.

"OK. What now?" she asked.

"Think about how you knew this was the spot. Close your eyes and think back to that time in 1987," he watched, as her green eyes disappeared behind her eyelids, "what do you see . . . What do you smell?" he encouraged her.

"I see . . . dogwood trees," she said with her eyes still closed, "and I smell . . . daisies, yes, yes, dogwoods and daisies, they are just a little ways over there," she said softly while opening her eyes and pointing to the dogwoods and daisies that were nearby.

In actuality, she wasn't sure that this was the exact spot. But she knew that the season was right and that the place was near. This place was near to her heart. She remembered the dogwoods and daisies in bloom near the school that year and also the ones at the Majestic. She had seen them both as had Michael. She, too, dreamed of dogwoods and daisies but would never admit to such a thing.

"Jessica, I have dreamed for years about the dogwoods and daisies. Don't you think it is time for us to smell them again, together?" he asked of her with his steel blue eyes shining, "we were always better together than apart."

"Michael, you have to go in there. You work for Red. You have to go 'feed the dragon' remember? You lectured me just a few days ago about it. Have you forgotten? We both have our duties," she said plainly.

"Jessica, things have changed for me. I have not forgotten, quite the contrary, I have remembered! I remembered the dogwoods and daisies, dragons and damsels, knights and emperors, castles and kingdoms!

I am no longer the dragon feeder for the emperor. I am a knight that writes, at night. Yes, that pudgy little squire, that became a dragon feeder, is now a knight! I know it sounds a little crazy," he said.

"Have you lost your mind?" she asked him, in a serious tone with hands placed on her hips.

"No. I finally found it! I quit working for Red. I mailed in my resignation today," he told her with a smile.

"You have lost it!" she stomped while turning completely around.

"Jessica, I am headed back to the Majestic. I have a duty, to perform, up there," he told her, while looking into her eyes, "and you are headed in there to perform yours!"

"What are you talking about! Talk straight with me. No more allegory stuff. Just say it!" she demanded with a tilted head.

"I am the greenskeeper of the Majestic of Purple Mountain. There is more and you must know. I know you and I have known you. You met me here but I saw you there. . ., on Purple Mountain," he said pointing to the mountain above, "the time you caddied for your dad. I know, don't say it, I should have told you long ago.

Anyway, I saw you that day. I was hiding behind the White Oak tree by the eighteenth green.

Then the most amazing thing happened. I saw you, with childlike faith, call the sun to rise in the West and set again! A miracle! A miracle I tell you! That miracle is legendary in this town, although you have never taken credit for it.

I know that you have the kind of faith, that it will take, to keep a mountain from being moved! Not just any mountain but Purple Mountain! I knew it all along but I was afraid. Afraid of everything. But no more. Now I have found peace and you will too!

We are out of time but there is so much more I have to tell you! When you are finished here come to the Majestic and meet me by the eighteenth green. I will be out in the fairway waiting for you. Don't be late! You must be there, today, twenty minutes before sunset.

Now, go in there and do your duty!" Michael hugged her and led her by the hand toward the school.

"So, let me get this straight. You said, 'we are better together than apart', but now we are going in two different directions. Do I have this right?" she asked with a grin while walking with him.

"Just a little while longer. Have faith. The next time I see you we will finish this and we will not part again!" he promised her as he climbed into the Jeep, "remember, twenty minutes before sunset, at the eighteenth. Be there!"

As he drove away, she pondered what he had said. Now there were two men she longed to meet on the eighteenth, at the Majestic of Purple Mountain. She looked at the old scorecard that she had in her purse. When would peace come? She wanted to cry but there was no time for that. Jessica composed herself and entered the building. There was a mountain to save.

Chapter 53

The black Dragon, from the eastern empire, skimmed over the top of Purple Mountain with mighty speed and power. It carnivorously circled high above the white castle of the western kingdom, as if stalking its prey. But in mid-flight the Dragon saw a vision. The Dragon saw a White Oak tree protected by eighteen snowy white owls. Behind the tree was a knight, with a flaming javelin, standing guard over the kingdom. The Dragon feared the knight with the flaming javelin and vowed never to return.

The flight to Jericho Street lasted only a few brief minutes. During the flight, Red noticed a line of cars approaching the city. It looked odd and caught his eye. They were still a long distance away. Red would arrive, for the meeting, with only a few minutes to spare. He didn't like to spend time with the common people or most any people and planned his agenda accordingly. The Sikorsky S-92 black Dragon helicopter landed on the playground of the elementary school. It was an impressive sight to behold.

The gymnasium was a place for local meetings of this type. Especially, when they were expected to be well attended. Many teachers and parents alike, encouraged their school aged children to attend such meetings. They believed that it was good for children to witness the functioning of the government.

The stands along the side of the gym were pulled out as if there were going to be a basketball game. There were additional seats that were setup on the floor. There were rows of chairs set in the middle of the gym floor. There was a center isle that ran from north to south that divided the gym in half. There were eleven rows of chairs in total and ten chairs in each row. So, there were fifty-five chairs on the east side of the gym floor and fifty-five chairs on the west side floor.

The stage, at the north end of the gym, was set. It sat three feet higher than the gym floor. A table with seven chairs and seven microphones was setup on the stage for the six zoning commission members and the mayor. The chair, of the mayor, sat exactly in the middle of the stage. It was as though half of her seat was on the east side and half on the west side. No one knew for sure, as no exact measurement was made. The mayor is not a voting member, of the commission, unless there is a tie vote.

There was a microphone setup halfway between the stage and the floor seating. It sat on a tablecloth covered table. The design, of the table cloth, was a print that outlined all fifty states of the Union. The tablecloth had been leftover from the school play held a few weeks earlier. The table was placed on the center dividing line between east and west. Looking from above, it was as if the Republic was divided from east to west. The people, addressing the commission, would face them as they spoke. This was the designated place for the people to redress their grievances.

If the seating tendencies of the people were indicative of their loyalties, then the west siders were in serious trouble. The most recent polling of the town revealed a split populace. Sometimes, the pollsters and pundits get it wrong.

There were only five people sitting on the west side of the gym. They were all sitting in the front row of the floor section.

Each was dressed in camouflage fatigues and had a flag patch on their shoulder. They looked small. However, they had faith as their ally and they had a secret plan. It was as if David was facing off against Goliath.

Red entered the school through a back door. He found his way, into the gymnasium, where the meeting was being held. He was almost the last person to arrive for the hearing. He scanned the room for his servant, Michael, but did not see him. He waited as long as he could wait and took a seat in the front row of the east side floor seating section.

The zoning commissioners filed in. It was like watching the judges of a high court take their places, at the bench, before the hearing of a case. As they filed in, the crowd rose to their feet.

To open the proceedings, a school age child, led the reciting of the Pledge of Allegiance. Most people recited the pledge from rote memory. Although, some people reflected upon the meaning of the words they had recited.

"We call this special session of the zoning commission into order. Today we will hear the petition of Axis Energy. They are seeking zoning approval for mountain top mining operations on the west side of Purple Mountain. More specifically, the property currently known as the Majestic of Purple Mountain.

Our process is as follows. Representatives of Axis Energy will make an opening statement and that will be followed by a period of time set aside for public comment. Upon completion of public comment, each zoning commission member will vote on the motion to approve the zoning change requested by Axis Energy. A simple majority vote is needed for approval. In the case of a tie vote, the mayor will cast the tie breaking vote," the mayor declared, as she read from the script.

"Will the representative of Axis Energy please step forward for your presentation," the mayor announced while looking at Red.

Although Red was surrounded by an overwhelming amount of people, the one person he needed in the room wasn't in the room. Where was Michael, he thought? His vice president of public relations was missing in action. What was he to do now?

"Will the representative of Axis Energy please step forward for your presentation," the mayor announced, a second time, while looking at Red. She smiled a polite smile. It was the smile of a skilled politician working the crowd. She thought of the words Michael said, 'you have your duty and I have mine', now she was performing her duty. Her duty was to the people, not Red.

"Will the representative of Axis Energy please step forward for your presentation," the mayor announced, a third time.

The crowd murmured while they waited.

Chapter 54

Michael drove as fast as he could to get back to the mountain. He arrived minutes before the ceremony, on the first tee, was to begin. He parked the Jeep outside the cabin. He ran into the cabin and directly into the secret room of the greenskeeper. He needed the scorecard. After grabbing it, he ran out of the cabin. He ran past the White Oak with the eighteen Snowy Owls still standing watch. He ran past the clubhouse, across the patio, down the heart shaped staircase, and past the flagpole pedestal. He wasn't too late was he?

As he neared the first tee, he could hear the sounds of the Fife and Drum Corps. As he rounded the last corner, he could see the Major General standing at attention on the first tee. The Ceremony was set to begin.

Then he saw him. Christopher! It was Christopher! He held back the tears of joy, not yet he thought. The ceremony. He must wait until after the ceremony. Michael, focused his thoughts on the ceremony. Somehow, he kept the last images, of the Iraq incident, out of his mind. Then, he focused his heart upon his brother.

Christopher's dress uniform was tightly pressed. Everything about his uniform was in order, just as Christopher would have it. He looked just as Michael had pictured him, since he lost him in November. Although, there was something different. There was peace about Christopher that surpassed his understanding.

Christopher was standing at attention, alone at the bottom of the stairs. He was unaware of Michael's presence. The other golfers, in the Final Foursome, for this day, withdrew upon their own request. They believed that this was a day for brothers and that their day would come at another time. It was a moving gesture, from those that had already sacrificed so much. Michael would be sure to make a special notation on the scorecard and in the *Books of Merit*.

Christopher began his ascent of the stairs. As he set foot on the tee box, the Fife and Drum Corps began to march in place and play the tune 'Chester' the anthem of the Colonial Army. When Christopher stopped two paces into the tee box, he was facing to the west. This placed him just across the tee box from the Major General. The Fife and Drum Corps were to the left of Christopher.

"Christopher, Staff Sergeant, United States Army, 1st Cavalry Division, please step forward," the drum major commanded as he issued a silent signal to the snare drummer to cease the drum roll. "For unusual gallantry during the Iraq War, in November, two thousand and eleven; for extraordinary fidelity; and for essential service; you are hereby awarded the Badge of Military Merit. Your name and regiment will be enrolled in the *Book of Merit*."

"Well done, Christopher," Major General Washington proclaimed, as he stepped forward. He reached into his coat pocket and removed a small purple heart shaped cloth. Embroidered in white was the word MERIT surrounded by eighteen embroidered leaves, nine on either side, connected by a thin line resembling a branch. He pinned the badge above the left breast pocket of his uniform. Christopher saluted and stepped back at attention. As Christopher stepped back the drum major sent another silent signal and the drum corps began to march in place.

"At ease soldier. You are hereby dismissed," Major General Washington commanded. Then he pivoted one hundred and eighty degrees and began to march his way toward the woods. The Fife and Drum Corps pivoted ninety degrees and began to march toward the woods. As they marched, they were playing 'Yankee Doodle'. Into the woods, went the Major General and then the corps disappeared into the woods as well.

"Christopher! Christopher! Christopher!" Michael screamed as he ran up the stairs of the first tee.

Christopher smiled and turned to greet his brother, Michael. As he did, his clothes changed into those of a golfer with the Badge of Merit still pinned to his breast.

It was a mystical majestic moment on the grounds of Purple Mountain. The brothers embraced among tears of joy. It was like watching doubting Thomas plunge his finger into the nail scarred hands of the Master. The brother who, twenty-five years removed, said that there were no Final Foursomes was now among their membership. Michael wept.

"Michael, I am sorry—," Christopher started before being interrupted.

"No, No, No! You are my brother! And you are here! We must celebrate! There is so—" Michael began to say as he was yet interrupted by another.

"Much I have to explain to each of you!" John the former greenskeeper of Purple Mountain said as he ascended the stairs. In their joyful celebration, they had missed his appearing.

He was dressed in pure white. The dress of a caddie. The dress of a servant. He was the caddie selection of Christopher.

"It is you! It is really you!" Michael screamed. He embraced his beloved friend.

"Michael, Michael, your faith has set you free. Look around you. It is as you asked, during our trip through your memories, just a few weeks ago. Your brother is here, I am here and this mountain has not been moved!" John reminded him.

"But I was so wrong! I could always see the Final Foursomes. But, after I found out about Jessica's father being killed in Afghanistan, I couldn't handle the pain. Also, I was angry that you left us. It was all so messy. I told Christopher that I couldn't see anything of the Final Foursomes. I lied and I ran from this mountain. I ran from what I knew in my heart was right.

Then destiny poured like grains of sand, through the hour glass of time, and twenty-five years passed. I became the dragons' caretaker, working at Axis. The dragon was Axis Energy and its economic empire. I fed the dragon by working for Red as his public relations vice president.

Then Christopher went off to war. I went to Iraq, to bring him home from the war. Then I watched, from the Hanging Gardens of Babylon, as his name was added to the *Books of Merit*. Christopher died as I watched. I returned home, discouraged and defeated. Upon my return, I was instructed to destroy this mountain and all that was on it. I nearly did.

Now I stand before you, my brother, and this mountain and I am ashamed of my actions. I was a traitor and a liar and have no right to see things, as majestic and mysterious as these," Michael confessed and wept bitter tears.

"Michael, Michael, God has forgiven you! You turned your heart to Him and He has set you free! As I said, look around you! Rejoice!" John proclaimed.

"You know, during all of those days back in 1987, there was one thing we never finished," Christopher asserted.

"What could we not have done up here! The Greenskeeper had us doing everything for him that summer? We moved tees around on tee boxes, checked green speeds, mowed the rough and raked the sand traps. We even restored a Jeep! What could we not have done up here that there was to do?" Michael asked him.

"Golf!" Christopher replied, "Now caddie, tell me about the Majestic of Purple Mountain! Oh, and hand me my driver," he said.

Thus John began to tell them everything about the Majestic of Purple Mountain. As they began to walk down the fairway, with John talking to the two brothers, it was as if they were walking on the road to Emmaus.

John said, "From the first tee through the eighteenth green, she is perfection. The tee boxes present an altar like appearance, elevated and ornate, with their smooth horizontal surfaces exposed to the heavens. The fairways, like an emerald sea with long rolling waves of shimmering color, flow effortlessly into deep pools of jade. Engagingly exquisite, she is, with each green presenting a paradox of beautifully difficult design. Meticulously manicured throughout are the grasses, trees, shrubs and plants each adorning the course as a jewel set in its mounting. Honor her, as you would your mother, and you will have many seasons.

Now about this first hole. The player with an indomitable spirit will score well on this invincible hole. It measures four hundred yards from the gold tees and is a par four. The hole is practically straight from tee through green. The fairway is generally sloped from right to left. There is a level landing area two hundred and thirty yards out and on the right side of the fairway. Hitting the landing area leaves the golfer with a level approach shot into the green. Missing that landing area is costly to the player. If he is left of the target he will face a side hill lie. If he is long he is faced with a downhill lie."

The three of them walked down the fairway of the Washington hole. Christopher had kept the faith. Now his faith was being brought to fruition as he played the Majestic. Michael would treasure this memory, of his brother playing the Majestic, in his heart for the remainder of his life.

At the same time, John explained the mysteries of the Majestic of Purple Mountain to the newly appointed greenskeeper. However, one mystery defies explanation. It is the mysterious miracle of faith.

The remainder of the afternoon was to be the remembered by Michael as the Greenskeeper's walk of love.

Chapter 55

The crowd at the zoning commission hearing was waiting and murmuring. Red was waiting and wondering. Wondering where his faithful servant Michael was. Red was furious with Michael and wasn't concerned about Michael or his whereabouts. His only concern was that he wasn't here to support him.

Jessica continued to look at Red. As she began to lean into her microphone and microseconds before she spoke, Red jumped from his chair.

Red walked over to the microphone and hastily unhooked it from its stand. He turned and faced the crowded gymnasium. As he addressed the crowd, he tended to look at the five people that were sitting alone on the west side of the gym. They were the Minutemen. He knew of them. He couldn't quite understand how they were able to smile in the face of certain defeat.

Although he was an executive of a mining empire, he didn't have a silver tongue. He pick-axed his way through his impromptu presentation. He told the people that this project would bring them, in his words, 'economic independence, freedom and security'. This project would take care of their needs as a community. He detested presentations and especially this one. Michael would have made Axis look better and that mattered a great deal to Red. He thought, perception was everything and truth was not important. Except for the truth that he had already won this battle. He finished speaking and sat down.

"Thank you, Mr. Alexander Garnet. The commission appreciates your views," Jessica announced. "Now, this is the time we have reserved for public comments. We ask that those who come to speak, first announce their name and their address. This is a time for comment only. Neither the commission, nor Axis Energy representatives will answer any questions. Please come forward now," she said with expectancy, as she looked toward the Minutemen. It was as if she were calling them into action.

The five Minutemen, Joshua, Caleb, Samson, Gideon and Deborah who were sitting on the west side of the gym, in the front row, remained seated and silent. Although, they were smiling.

Jessica made a second call for comments, "public comments are welcome at this time. I will give this another minute and without any further discussion, we will take our vote."

The gymnasium was silent and still. For fifty-seconds it remained that way, until there was a still small voice that whispered from the back of the gymnasium, "My name is Tootsie. I am from the great state of Delaware!"

The stunned crowed all looked to the doorway, underneath the worn basketball hoop, at the end of the gymnasium opposite the stage. They saw an older woman walking down the center isle of the floor seating section. If you asked her, she would say 'I am ninety going on seventy'. She had a simple elegance about her. She was dressed modestly with a blue blouse and khaki pants. She was wearing a white satin sash that had the word 'Delaware' written on it in large purple letters. It was the type of sash a sixth grader might wear in a school play about our fifty states. Every eye was upon her, as she walked up to the microphone to redress the commission. When she arrived, at the microphone, she stopped and adjusted her blouse and sash.

"I object!" Red yelled, as he stood to his feet. He grabbed his belt at the waist with hands on either side of him. He then, in one motion, twisted his trousers while he pulled them up and down slightly. It was an awkward sight, "She has no standing here! She is from Delaware. She is not a—"

Samson, the Minuteman, interrupted him, as he could hold back no longer, "Excuse me Sir. My name is Samson. I have fought along side my countrymen. We have fought, in foreign lands, to protect the land we love. I have watched soldiers give their lives for the rights that we hold most dear. One of those rights, is the right of our citizens to petition the government for a redress of grievances. She has every right to address this commission."

The crowd watched the exchange with interest. The meeting that appeared to be nearly over, was just beginning.

"She will have the right to speak. However, comments must be related to the mountain top mining proposal we are discussing," Jessica declared.

Red and Samson sat back down in their seats.

She stood resolute before the microphone, "My name is Tootsie, I am from Delaware. My sister, Helen, was killed in action, in April 1945, in Hanau, Germany. She was a Staff Sergeant in the U.S. Army Nursing Corps. In 1987, I received this letter from the greenskeeper of the Majestic of Purple Mountain," She was holding a letter in her hand and removed its contents saying, "there were two letters in the envelope. One described the purpose of the letters and the other was a letter to me, from my sister."

The crowd gasped in unison!

"I will now read her letter, as written by the Greenskeeper.

> Dearest Tootsie,
>
> It is on the occasion of our mother's passing that I write you. You see, there were things I couldn't tell you until she had gone. I know it sounds childish but we all have things we don't want our mother's to know.
>
> You were insightful as a child. I am not sure, how you knew, what you knew but you knew it. It was true that grandfather and I had been barnstorming with Amelia Earhart back in 1926, over those golden Kansas wheat fields and above the future Route 66. We had to hide this from mother, you, and basically everyone else. Mom would not have been pleased. She hated me flying with even grandfather.
>
> Well, I wanted you to know. Grandfather received a letter from a Mr. Duesenberg some time later. It included two photographs that will prove you were right all along. You will find them in grandfather's study. They are hidden within the peppermint pipe box. I loved the sweet smells of peppermint. Oh, one last thing. Take a look at the stamp on the Duesenberg letter. It was always fun flying inverted, you know!
>
> Until we meet again,
>
> Love
>
> Helen"

The crowd began to sit nearer to the edge of their seats. It was as if they were interested in hearing this story.

"I found the peppermint pipe box tucked away in mother's things. I loved that smell. Anyway, I found the Duesenberg letter in the peppermint pipe box," she said as she pulled the letter from her purse.

"In it were two old photographs. One is of Helen, standing with Amelia Earhart, in front of the Canary and the Jenny my grandfather owned. The other is of my sister standing in front of a 1926 Duesenberg Model A Phaeton. She is wearing the same clothes as the ones in the other photograph," she paused while holding the photographs up in the air for the commissioners to see.

The crowd remained on the edge of their seats, waiting for her next words.

She placed the pictures on the table and they covered the state of Kansas. Then she held up the Duesenberg letter, "please take a close look at this stamp. It is an Inverted Jenny 1918 twenty-four cent U.S. Postage stamp. The stamp was a misprint and only one hundred were ever put into circulation.

A few years ago, I was offered one million dollars for this stamp. I told the gentleman that I wasn't interested in selling, but he insisted. Finally, I told him that I wouldn't sell it even if he were to offer me the world. I wouldn't sell the memory of my sister for a million dollars, nor would I exchange it for the world.

How the greenskeeper of the Majestic of Purple Mountain knew these things is a mystery. That he knew them is not. For those of you that might be skeptical, I understand. I was skeptical once too. If you like, step outside and look in the parking lot. You will see a 1926 two tone green Duesenberg parked out there. I drove it here a few days ago . . . Yes, it was the day of the parade. I was passing through town on my way to visit Arlington National Cemetery but had car trouble. The boys at Barney's Garage fixed it for me. Oh, I have talked too long so let me wrap this up . . .

Now I ask each of you, will you exchange the majesties of your Purple Mountain for monetary gain?

One more thing," she said as she turned and looked to the rear of the gymnasium, "it is going to be a long afternoon," she declared. At the rear of the gymnasium was a long line of citizens. Each was wearing a red, white or blue shirt, khaki pants and a white or red colored satin sash. Each held a letter, with a broken wax seal, addressed from the greenskeeper of the Majestic of Purple Mountain.

As she left the microphone, she placed her letters, even the Duesenberg with the inverted Jenny stamp, on the table over the state of Delaware. As she went to her seat, she shook the hands of the Minutemen. As she did, they consoled her over the loss of her sister. Samson blushed, as he felt the air move from the wink of her eye, as he pinned her with a Friends of Purple Mountain medallion. After passing by Samson, she turned into the second row of the west side floor seating section. She sat in the chair that was closest to the center isle.

The crowd whispered and their faces lit up. A few of them silently slipped out of their seats and went and sat on the west side of the gymnasium. They sat in the grandstands, out of respect, leaving the floor seating open for those still standing and waiting to redress the commission.

Then the Greenskeeper's parade of the letters began.

Chapter 56

It was 3:15 PM, on Monday, May 7, 2012. Mr. Hughes was sad that he couldn't attend the zoning commission hearing. He could see the Elementary School from his school office window, as it was only about a mile away from the Worthington High School. However, he had a duty to his students. It was the appointed time for the Worthington High School Marching Band to begin their spring practices.

Mr. Hughes assembled the students in the band room for a quick meeting before the start of spring drill practice season. These were the students that would be returning for the 2012 marching season, in the next school year.

He addressed the seventy-six students of the Worthington High School Marching Band. It was an informal address, "students, students, let's get started, as we have lots of work to do. The music that we have selected for our 2012 marching season, next fall, will be familiar to each of you. It is the music we performed for the Worthington Elementary School play a few weeks ago. The performance for our 2012 marching season is called 'America the Beautiful'. We will march to the following songs, 'Chester', 'Yankee Doodle Dandy', 'A tribute to the Armed Forces', 'The Star Spangled Banner', 'God Bless America' and will finish with 'America the Beautiful'. This performance is the most challenging performance any Worthington High School Marching Band has ever attempted. I have faith, that with hard work and practice, lots of practice, we will bring home victories during our marching season competitions next year.

Don't be fooled, 'America the Beautiful', is a beautifully difficult performance. It will challenge your skills as a musician and as a marcher. However, you have an advantage. You already know the music. These are the songs we performed in the elementary school play. I remember a few students grumbling when we decided to help them with their play. But now we can use what we did for them to help us with our upcoming marching season.

During practice tonight, we will play the music that we already know. However, we are going to begin working on our marching movements. There won't be many tonight, but we will have at least one movement for each song. As always, we will continue to add movements, over the next few weeks, until we have the entire footwork for the performance mapped out.

This is an aggressive schedule but I have faith in each of you and your abilities as musicians and marchers.

Now, I need the section leaders of the Color Guard, Woodwinds, Percussion and Brass to assemble your members and head out to the practice field.

One last thing before you go. Remember, to play from your heart!" Mr. Hughes concluded. He watched the students file out of the band room.

He went into his office. He had a surprise for his students. At the end of the practice, the students would be treated to a performance of 'America the Beautiful', by members of the University Marching Band. The University Band used 'America the Beautiful' as their performance during the 2011 marching season. They were set to arrive at about 7:30 PM, near the end of practice.

The University Band occasionally performs for high schools, in this type of setting. They believe in giving back to their community. It is their hope, that their performance tonight might inspire the students to carry on, despite the difficulty of the performance that has been selected for them. They already know that the rewards are greater than the sacrifices made to attain them.

Mr. Hughes and Mr. Shatto, the band director of the University Band, had served together in the U.S. Marine Corps. They were band brothers. Mr. Hughes had spoken with him earlier in the day and knew that they were already on their way to Worthington.

Mr. Hughes left his office with a smile and headed to the field of competition. The thoughts of the zoning commission hearing were no longer on his mind, as he had a band to lead.

Chapter 57

It was 3:17 PM at the Worthington Elementary School and the zoning commission hearing continued. Tootsie had just taken her seat in the second row of the floor seating section. There were now a total of six people seated in the west side floor seating section of the gymnasium. The east side of the gymnasium was nearly full of people, while there were only a few people sitting in the bleachers on the west side. There was a long line of people waiting to redress the commission.

Through the open windows of the gymnasium the soft sounds of music drifted in. It was the sounds of the high school band performing their warm-ups prior to the start of band practice. The sounds would be imperceptible were it not for the complete silence in the room.

The Greenskeeper's parade of letters was beginning. There was a long line, stretching out of the gymnasium, of people wearing red, white, or blue shirts and khaki pants, waiting to speak to the commission. Each person was wearing a white or red sash with the name of a state written upon it in purple lettering.

The next person redressed the commission.

"My name is Danny, from Pennsylvania. My father Jack, was killed in action at Pearl Harbor, 12/7/1941. He was a Seaman Apprentice in the U.S. Navy," then he read the letter from the Greenskeeper. When he finished reading, Danny laid his letter on the table, over the state of Pennsylvania and filed past the Minutemen. As he passed them, he was greeted by each member of the Minutemen. He shook hands with Joshua, who said to him, 'we are sorry for your loss'. He shook hands with Caleb, who said to him, 'we grieve with you, but not without hope'. He shook hands with Deborah and Gideon. When he got to Samson, Samson pinned a Friends of Purple Mountain medallion on the white sash draped over his blue shirt. The medallion was placed just over his heart. As he went through the line, he thought he recognized one of them. He took his seat in the second row of the west side floor seating section, next to Tootsie.

Then he realized where he had seen one of them. He remembered seeing Caleb in Shanksville, in mid-September 2011. Caleb, had gone to Shanksville in the aftermath of September 11th. He was there to help. He helped counsel people that came to town, stricken with grief, over the events of that day. The local V.F.W. hall offered counseling services, free of charge, to those that were in need.

The school music teacher heard the sounds of 'Chester' drifting in through the window, as the Minutemen silently comforted Danny before he took his seat.

The school history teacher heard the sounds of 'Chester' drifting into the room. Chester, he knew, was the battle hymn of the American Revolution. He thought of a verse of that old hymn, something about generals fleeing from beardless boys. Strange, he thought.

An unnamed and shrewd commission member saw that the town supported the mining project. From the beginning of the meeting, he was counting votes based on the floor seating section alone. The east side section represented support for the mining project and the west side section represented those opposed. When the hearing began the vote was 55 East and five West. He was in favor of the project, for now.

It is interesting how the same people can look at a similar set of circumstances and see different things.

The next person redressed the commission.

"My name is David, from New Jersey. My uncle, Donald was killed in Action on 2/7/1970, in Vietnam. He served in the U.S. Army and was a Corporal," then he read the letter from the Greenskeeper. When he finished reading, he laid his letter on the table, over the state of New Jersey and filed past the Minutemen. As he passed them, he was greeted by each member of the Minutemen. He shook hands with Joshua, who said to him, 'we are sorry for your loss'. He shook hands with Caleb, who said to him, 'we grieve with you, but not without hope'. He shook hands with Deborah and Gideon. When he got to Samson, Samson pinned a Friends of Purple Mountain medallion on the white sash draped over his blue shirt. The medallion was placed just over his heart. As he went through the line, he thought he recognized one of them. He took the third seat in the second row of the west side floor seating section.

As he sat, he remembered. He remembered seeing Gideon during the aftermath of the December 2000 nor'easter. Gideon was there handing out fleece blankets at a local shelter. It must have been him, he thought to himself.

The next person redressed the commission.

"My name is Sharon, from Georgia. My brother, Troy was killed in Action on 1/3/2010, in Afghanistan. He served in the U.S. Air Force, 10th Air Support Operations Squadron, and was a Senior Airman," then she read the letter from the Greenskeeper. When she finished reading, she laid her letter on the table, over the state of Georgia and filed past the Minutemen. As she passed them, she was greeted by each member of the Minutemen. She shook hands with Joshua, who said to her, 'we are sorry for your loss'. She shook hands with Caleb, who said to her, 'we grieve with you, but not without hope'. She shook hands with Deborah and Gideon. When she got to Samson, Samson pinned a Friends of Purple Mountain medallion on the red sash draped over her white blouse. The medallion was placed just over her heart. As she went through the line, she thought she recognized one of them. She took the fourth seat in the second row sitting next to David.

As she sat in her seat it came to her. She remembered seeing Gideon during the 2008 floods. She remembered seeing him handing out cold drinks to those that were filling sandbags.

The next person redressed the commission, as sounds of 'Chester' drifted in the room.

"My name is Shirley, I am from Connecticut. My husband, Wally was killed in action, during the battle of Pusan, on 9/2/1950 in Korea. He was a Lance Corporal in the 1st Marine Division of the U.S. Marines," then she read the letter from the Greenskeeper. When she finished reading, she laid her letter on the table, over the state of Connecticut and filed past the Minutemen. As she passed them, she was greeted by each member of the Minutemen. She shook hands with Joshua, who said to her, 'we are sorry for your loss'. She shook hands with Caleb, who said to her, 'we grieve with you, but not without hope'. She shook hands with Deborah and Gideon. When she got to Samson, Samson pinned a Friends of Purple Mountain medallion on the red sash draped over her red blouse. The medallion was placed just over her heart. As she went through the line, she thought she recognized one of them. She sat in the fifth seat of the second row and on the isle.

the Majestic of Purple Mountain

As she sat in her seat, memories swirled in her spirit. She remembered seeing Samson passing out clothing to victims of Hurricane Bob in 1991. He was working with members of the local Salvation Army.

A loud "OohRah" came from the crowd.

The next person redressed the commission.

"My name is Vickie, I am from Massachusetts. My grandfather, Deron was killed in action during the Tet Offensive, in Vietnam, on 8/15/68. He served in the 82nd Airborne Division of the U.S. Army as a Staff Sergeant," then she read the letter from the Greenskeeper. When she finished reading, she laid her letter on the table, over the state of Massachusetts and filed past the Minutemen. As she passed them, she was greeted by each member of the Minutemen. She shook hands with Joshua, who said to her, 'we are sorry for your loss'. She shook hands with Caleb, who said to her, 'we grieve with you, but not without hope'. She shook hands with Deborah and Gideon. When she got to Samson, Samson pinned a Friends of Purple Mountain medallion on the white sash draped over her blue blouse. The medallion was placed just over her heart. As she went through the line, she thought she recognized one of them and took her seat in the third row directly behind where Tootsie was seated.

Then she remembered. She remembered seeing Joshua, at a local soup kitchen in the days following the Great Barrington Tornado of 1995.

The next person redressed the commission.

"My name is Pete, I am from Maryland. My Father, Kyle was killed in action on 8/22/65, in Vietnam during Operation Starlight. He was a Gunnery Sergeant, 1st Marine Division, U.S. Marine Corps," then he read the letter from the Greenskeeper. When he finished reading, he laid his letter on the table, over the state of Maryland and filed past the Minutemen. As he passed them, he was greeted by each member of the Minutemen. He shook hands with Joshua, who said to him, 'we are sorry for your loss'. He shook hands with Caleb, who said to him, 'we grieve with you, but not without hope'. He shook hands with Deborah and Gideon. When he got to Samson, Samson pinned a Friends of Purple Mountain medallion on the white sash draped over his blue shirt. The medallion was placed just over his heart. Then he sat in the third row next to Vickie.

He was moved by the moment. He remembered a time when the pastor, of his local church, came and prayed with him after the death of his father.

In the silence between speakers, some in the crowd noticed soft music in the background. It was as if an old forgotten patriotic hymn was being played.

The next person redressed the commission.

"My name is Becky, I am from South Carolina. My son, Paul was killed in action on 1/23/1991 during the Gulf War. He was a Private in U.S. Army with Old Ironsides," then she read the letter from the Greenskeeper. When she finished reading, she laid her letter on the table, over the state of South Carolina and filed past the Minutemen. As she passed them, she was greeted by each member of the Minutemen. She shook hands with Joshua, who said to her, 'we are sorry for your loss'. She shook hands with Caleb, who said to her, 'we grieve with you, but not without hope'. She shook hands with Deborah and Gideon. When she got to Samson, Samson pinned a Friends of Purple Mountain medallion on the white sash that was draped over her blue blouse. The medallion was placed just over her heart. She sat in the third row beside Pete.

She was moved by the moment. She remembered a time when local church members brought food to her after the death of her son. It was a time of great stress for her and that simple act of kindness helped her in her hour of need.

    The next person redressed the commission.

    "My name is Edward, I am from New Hampshire. My father, George was killed in action on 9/9/1943, in Italy during operation Avalanche. He was a Private 1st Class, U.S. 5th Army, U.S. Army," then he read the letter from the Greenskeeper. When he finished reading, he laid his letter on the table, over the state of New Hampshire and filed past the Minutemen. As he passed them, he was greeted by each member of the Minutemen. He shook hands with Joshua, who said to him, 'we are sorry for your loss'. He shook hands with Caleb, who said to him, 'we grieve with you, but not without hope'. He shook hands with Deborah and Gideon. When he got to Samson, Samson pinned a Friends of Purple Mountain medallion on the red sash that was draped over his white shirt.. The medallion was placed just over his heart. Then he took his seat in the third row.

    He was moved by the moment. He remembered a time when local church members brought clothing to his home in the summer of 1944. A single mother and her five sons were in great need of them. Although it was a single act of kindness, it was remembered over a half century later.

    The next person redressed the commission.

    "My name is Gary, I am from Virginia. My sister, Melody was killed in action on 12/9/2003, in Iraq. She served as Petty Officer 1st Class, U.S. Navy," then he read the letter from the Greenskeeper. When he finished reading, he laid his letter on the table, over the state of Virginia and filed past the Minutemen. As he passed them, he was greeted by each member of the Minutemen. He shook hands with Joshua, who said to him, 'we are sorry for your loss'. He shook hands with Caleb, who said to him, 'we grieve with you, but not without hope'.

He shook hands with Deborah and Gideon. When he got to Samson, Samson pinned a Friends of Purple Mountain medallion on the red sash draped over his red shirt. The medallion was placed just over his heart and he sat down in the remaining empty seat of the third row.

He was moved by the moment and remembered a time when his bible study class members came and prayed with him, in early December of 2004. It was a time of deep sadness for him and they grieved with him but not as ones without hope.

The next person redressed the commission.

"My name is Alan, I am from New York. My father, Phillip was killed in action on 1/29/1945, aboard the USS Serpens, during World War II. He served as a Fireman in the U.S. Coast Guard," then he read the letter from the Greenskeeper. When he finished reading, he laid his letter on the table, over the state of New York and filed past the Minutemen. As he passed them, he was greeted by each member of the Minutemen. He shook hands with Joshua, who said to him, 'we are sorry for your loss'. He shook hands with Caleb, who said to him, 'we grieve with you, but not without hope'. He shook hands with Deborah and Gideon. When he got to Samson, Samson pinned a Friends of Purple Mountain medallion on the white sash draped over his blue shirt. The medallion was placed just over his heart. As he went to his seat he thought one of the Minutemen looked familiar. He sat in the fourth row directly behind Vickie and along the center isle.

As he sat, he remembered. He remembered seeing Joshua in the days after 9/11/2001. Joshua was handing out cold water bottles to people on the streets of New York City. Joshua had set up a small tent on a street corner near where the pictures of missing family members were posted. People were thirsty and Joshua was there for them at their time of need. The next person redressed the commission.

"My name is Jeff, I am from North Carolina. My Cousin, Joey was killed in action on 2/3/1952, in Korea. He was a Private 2nd Class in the U.S. Army, 1st Cavalry Division," then he read the letter from the Greenskeeper. When he finished reading, he laid his letter on the table, over the state of North Carolina and filed past the Minutemen. As he passed them, he was greeted by each member of the Minutemen. He shook hands with Joshua, who said to him, 'we are sorry for your loss'. He shook hands with Caleb, who said to him, 'we grieve with you, but not without hope'. He shook hands with Deborah and Gideon. When he got to Samson, Samson pinned a Friends of Purple Mountain medallion on the white sash draped over his blue shirt. The medallion was placed just over his heart and took his seat in the fourth row and sat next to Alan.

He was moved by the moment and listened to the soft sounds of the music drifting in through the open windows of the gymnasium.

The next person redressed the commission.

"My name is Denise, I am from Rhode Island. My niece, Elizabeth was killed in action, in Afghanistan, on 10/23/2002. She was a private 1st Class, in the 4th Marine Division of the U.S. Marine Corps.," then she read the letter from the Greenskeeper. When she finished reading, she laid her letter on the table, over the state of Rhode Island and filed past the Minutemen. As she passed them, she was greeted by each member of the Minutemen. She shook hands with Joshua, who said to her, 'we are sorry for your loss'. She shook hands with Caleb, who said to her, 'we grieve with you, but not without hope'. She shook hands with Deborah and Gideon. When she got to Samson, Samson pinned a Friends of Purple Mountain medallion on the white sash draped over her blue blouse. The medallion was placed just over her heart and she took her seat in the fourth row sitting next to Jeff and directly behind Becky.

She reflected on the moment. Thirteen letters had been read aloud revealing the secrets of long silenced soldiers. Through the act of laying down a letter, each was picking up something greater. Each person was picking up a fresh sense of faith. In her spirit, she knew there were greater mysteries remaining to be revealed on this majestic Purple Mountain. In a combined act of courage, these Friends of Purple Mountain were demonstrating individual acts of faith. She smiled, as she thought about her courageous niece.

The people in the audience were taking notice of the Greenskeeper's parade of letters.

The school music teacher had been listening to the soft sounds of 'Chester' floating in through the open windows. It was the faint sounds of the Worthington High School Marching Band. They were practicing for the next marching season. The band was practicing for the performance of 'America the Beautiful'. The song 'Chester' is the introductory song of the performance. From the sound of it, the band was struggling but they continued to play on.

The school history teacher had been watching the unfurling events of the hearing. When he looked, at the west side floor seating of the gymnasium, from his seat high in the bleachers, he saw an interesting sight. On the west side, he saw five Minutemen standing in front of the thirteen original colonies of the United States of America. In his mind, he saw the beginnings of the United States flag appearing on the floor of the gymnasium. There were thirteen white stars.

There were red and white stripes and a rectangular blue area resembling the union of the flag.

The Worthington Postmaster looked at the table where the speakers were leaving their letters. He saw a pattern developing. Letters were coming to Worthington from the eastern seaboard.

An unnamed commission member was keeping tally on the vote. A quick survey revealed that the West had picked up 13 votes. During the public comments, the East had lost 18 votes. The grandstand section on the west now had at least 20 people seated within it. There had been none seated there at the start of public comment. This seemed odd to him but not alarming. He still supported the mining project. However, he determined to keep a closer watch on the votes as the hearing progressed.

In the distance the music changed. The rally call of 'Chester' gave way to the sounds of 'Yankee Doodle Dandy'. The marching band was practicing the next set of steps in their performance of 'America the Beautiful'.

The sounds of 'Yankee Doodle Dandy' were faintly drifting inside the gymnasium. It is a favorite of young children and many of them took notice of it being played. Some, even began to whisper the words.

Chapter 58

It was now past 4:30 PM and the zoning commission hearing was in full swing. People were engaged in listening to the stories of those who had come from the East Coast of these United States.

Some, in the room, noticed the soft sounds of music stirring in the valley breeze. It was a familiar hymn, 'Yankee Doodle Dandy' and the presence of music became more noticeable as the evening drew on.

Public comment continued and the parade of the Greenskeeper's letters continued.

The next person redressed the commission.

"My name is Rob, I am from Vermont. My brother, Adam was killed in action on 1/18/1968, in Vietnam. He was a Petty Officer 3rd Class in the U.S. Navy," then he read the letter from the Greenskeeper. When he finished reading, he laid his letter on the table, over the state of Vermont and filed past the Minutemen. As he passed them, he was greeted by each member of the Minutemen. He shook hands with Joshua, who said to him, 'we are sorry for your loss'. He shook hands with Caleb, who said to him, 'we grieve with you, but not without hope'. He shook hands with Deborah and Gideon. When he got to Samson, Samson pinned a Friends of Purple Mountain medallion on the red sash draped over his white shirt. The medallion was placed just over his heart and he sat in the fourth row next to Denise.

As he sat down, he noticed the music drifting in through the windows.

The next person redressed the commission.

"My name is Kay, I am from Kentucky. My nephew, Tyler was killed in action in the Gulf War on 1/24/1991. He served in the 1st Calvary Division of the U.S. Army," then she read the letter from the Greenskeeper. When she finished reading, she laid her letter on the table, over the state of Kentucky and filed past the Minutemen. As she passed them, she was greeted by each member of the Minutemen. She shook hands with Joshua, who said to her, 'we are sorry for your loss'. She shook hands with Caleb, who said to her, 'we grieve with you, but not without hope'. She shook hands with Deborah and Gideon. When she got to Samson, Samson pinned a Friends of Purple Mountain medallion on the red sash draped over her red shirt. The medallion was placed just over her heart and she sat down in the fourth row next to Rob.

As she sat down, she was moved by the moment. She remembered how Tyler's wife had been diagnosed with breast cancer four years after Tyler's death. It was a difficult time for everyone in her family. She remembered how her church reached out to them. During treatments, they helped with providing meals. This allowed Kay to spend more time tending to the needs of Tyler Jr. He was about six years old at that time.

In the distance the song changed. The band had now moved on to playing another hymn. The new song that drifted into the room was a 'Tribute to the Armed Forces'. The band was now playing the official fight songs of the various branches of the United States Military.

It seemed, as if the meeting were picking up momentum.

The unnamed commission member noted that the West now had 20 votes and the East had 35. Although, the West was picking up votes the East still had the advantage. The East still seemed stronger than the West.

As the next person redressed the commission, the faint sounds of the hymn 'Anchors Aweigh' were rolling in like waves, through the open windows of the gymnasium.

"My name is Stephanie, I am from Tennessee. My cousin, Henry was killed in action on 10/23/1983, in Beirut. He served as a Petty Officer in the U.S. Navy," then she read the letter from the Greenskeeper. When she finished reading, she laid her letter on the table, over the state of Tennessee and filed past the Minutemen. As she passed them, she was greeted by each member of the Minutemen. She shook hands with Joshua, who said to her, 'we are sorry for your loss'. She shook hands with Caleb, who said to her, 'we grieve with you, but not without hope'. She shook hands with Deborah and Gideon. When she got to Samson, Samson pinned a Friends of Purple Mountain medallion on the white sash draped over her red blouse. The medallion was placed just over her heart and she took her seat in the fifth row along the center isle.

She was moved by the moment. She remembered the time just following his death. Upon his death, Henry's daughter Juliet was left parentless. Stephanie adopted her. Juliet was the person who drove Stephanie here to this hearing.

As the hymn, 'The Army Goes Rolling Along' quietly countermarched through the open windows of the gymnasium, the next person redressed the commission.

"My name is Allison, I am from Ohio. My husband, Dale was killed in action, in Grenada, on 10/25/1983, during Operation Urgent Fury. He served as a private in the 2nd Battalion 75th Ranger Division, of the U.S. Army," then she read the letter from the Greenskeeper. When she finished reading, she laid her letter on the table, over the state of Ohio and filed past the Minutemen. As she passed them, she was greeted by each member of the Minutemen. She shook hands with Joshua, who said to her, 'we are sorry for your loss'. She shook hands with Caleb, who said to her, 'we grieve with you, but not without hope'. She shook hands with Deborah and Gideon. When she got to Samson, Samson pinned a Friends of Purple Mountain medallion on the red sash draped over her white blouse. The medallion was placed just over her heart and she sat in the fifth row next to Stephanie.

As the next person redressed the commission, the faint sounds of the 'Marines Hymn' seemed to be coming from the halls.

"My name is Andrew, and I am from Louisiana, where you come as you are and you leave different. My son, Arthur was killed in action, on 12/22/1989, in Panama during Operation Just Cause. He served as a Lance Corporal in the 1st Marine Division of the U.S. Marine Corps," then he read the letter from the Greenskeeper. When he finished reading, he laid his letter on the table, over the state of Louisiana and filed past the Minutemen. As he passed them, he was greeted by each member of the Minutemen. He shook hands with Joshua, who said to him, 'we are sorry for your loss'. He shook hands with Caleb, who said to him, 'we grieve with you, but not without hope'. He shook hands with Deborah and Gideon. When he got to Samson, Samson pinned a Friends of Purple Mountain medallion on the white sash draped over his red shirt. The medallion was placed just over his heart and he sat in the fifth row beside Allison.

The next person redressed the commission.

"My name is Kimberlie, I am from Indiana. My nephew, Hubert was killed in action, on 10/4/1993, in Somalia during

Letters from the Greenskeeper

the Battle of the Black Sea. He was a Specialist in the 3rd Battalion, 75th Ranger Regiment of the U.S. Army," then she read the letter from the Greenskeeper. When she finished reading, she laid her letter on the table, over the state of Indiana and filed past the Minutemen. As she passed them, she was greeted by each member of the Minutemen. She shook hands with Joshua, who said to her, 'we are sorry for your loss'. She shook hands with Caleb, who said to her, 'we grieve with you, but not without hope'. She shook hands with Deborah and Gideon. When she got to Samson, Samson pinned a Friends of Purple Mountain medallion on the red sash draped over her white blouse. The medallion was placed just over her heart and she sat down next to Andrew and directly behind Rob.

A new hymn seemed to fly in from the wild blue yonder, as the next person redressed the commission.

"My name is Kevin, I am from Mississippi. My friend, Clyde was killed in action, in Bosnia, on 5/12/99. He was a Technical Sergeant in the U.S. Air Force," then he read the letter from the Greenskeeper. When he finished reading, he laid his letter on the table, over the state of Mississippi and filed past the Minutemen. As he passed them, he was greeted by each member of the Minutemen. He shook hands with Joshua, who said to him, 'we are sorry for your loss'. He shook hands with Caleb, who said to him, 'we grieve with you, but not without hope'. He shook hands with Deborah and Gideon. When he got to Samson, Samson pinned a Friends of Purple Mountain medallion on the red sash draped over his red shirt. The medallion was placed just over his heart and he took his seat in the fifth row along the isle.

The music drifting in was changing and the school children took notice. Many of them stood to their feet and put hand over heart, as they heard the first notes of the 'Star Spangled Banner' playing.

At that exact moment, Jessica, the mayor, called for a short pause in the meeting. It would resume in ten minutes. Everyone in the room immediately stood to their feet. They had been absorbed in the hearing and had lost track of time. All took the opportunity to stand and stretch their legs for a few minutes. The loud commotion drowned out the faint sounds of the anthem playing in the valley breeze.

It was as if everyone had stood up for the playing of the 'Star Spangled Banner' out of instinct.

Chapter 59

The zoning commission hearing had resumed after its short ten minute break.

When the people returned. Those from the west side floor section returned to their original seats. A few people, who had been sitting in the east side floor section moved over and into the bleachers of the west side.

The mood of the people was changing, as were their opinions about the mining proposition before the commission. People were helping one another climb the bleachers, offering hands of support where there were no railings. The atmosphere was congenial, optimistic, energetic and most of all, contagious. It was as if the people were singing a new song.

All who had been sitting, in bleacher seats before the break, returned to bleacher seating. But, many had switched sides moving from east to west.

The shrewd commission member took a quick vote tally when the people returned to their seats. It was a narrowed margin for the East. The East now had 30 votes compared to the 25 of the West. He looked to the grandstands also. To him, their votes did not count. However, by the looks of it, nearly half of the audience was now sitting on the west side. This was not good news for the supporters of the mining proposition. The next few speakers may turn the tides in this battle, he thought.

In the gymnasium, the history teacher sat near the top of the west side bleachers. From his vantage point, it looked as if a United States flag was appearing, on the west side floor seating area below. He saw rows of red and white stripes and a blue union. Then he counted twenty-five white stars. The Friends of Purple Mountain Medallions, worn by each person seated on the west side floor section, were fashioned in the shape of stars. He thought, I must be out of my mind, and returned to listening to the proceedings.

In the distance the 'Star Spangled Banner' played.

The parade of the Greenskeeper's letters continued.

The next person redressed the commission.

"My name is Jennifer, I am from Illinois, the Land of Lincoln. My son, Salvatore was killed in action, in 1994, in Yugoslavia. He was a Master Sergeant in the U.S. Air Force," then she read the letter from the Greenskeeper. When she finished reading, she laid her letter on the table, over the state of Illinois and filed past the Minutemen. As she passed them, she was greeted by each member of the Minutemen. She shook hands with Joshua, who said to her, 'we are sorry for your loss'. She shook hands with Caleb, who said to her, 'we grieve with you, but not without hope'. She shook hands with Deborah and Gideon. When she got to Samson, Samson pinned a Friends of Purple Mountain medallion on the white sash draped over her red blouse. The medallion was placed just over her heart and she took her seat in the sixth row along the center isle and directly behind where Stephanie was seated.

The sounds of the 'Star Spangled Banner' rocketed through the open windows of the gymnasium. Many, in the crowd, had taken notice. They heard the Worthington High School Marching Band practicing in the background. They had missed their opportunity to stand but they did not miss the playing of National Anthem. It turned their hearts toward home.

The Worthington Elementary School music teacher knew that the 'Star Spangled Banner' hymn was the centerpiece and turning point of the performance that the high school marching band was practicing. From the sounds of it, they were perfecting it but it wasn't quite perfect yet. She thought, they must be working extremely hard at this part of their performance. She said a quick prayer for them. She asked God to lead their every step.

The sounds of the 'Star Spangled Banner' shot through the open windows of the gymnasium.

The next person redressed the commission.

"My name is Christy, I am from Alabama. My uncle, Roger was killed in action, in the Battle of Iwo Jima, on 2/23/1945, in World War II. He served as a Hospital Corpsman in the U.S. Navy," then she read the letter from the Greenskeeper. When she finished reading, she laid her letter on the table, over the state of Alabama and filed past the Minutemen. As she passed them, she was greeted by each member of the Minutemen. She shook hands with Joshua, who said to her, 'we are sorry for your loss'. She shook hands with Caleb, who said to her, 'we grieve with you, but not without hope'. She shook hands with Deborah and Gideon. When she got to Samson, Samson pinned a Friends of Purple Mountain medallion on the red sash draped over her white blouse. The medallion was placed just over her heart and she sat in the sixth row next to Jennifer.

The sounds of the 'Star Spangled Banner' burst through the open windows of the gymnasium.

The next person redressed the commission.

"My name is Johnny, and I am from Maine. My dad, Patrick was killed in action, on 6/27/1952, in Korea. He served as a corporal in the 2nd marine Division, U.S. Marine Corps," then he read the letter from the Greenskeeper. When he finished reading, he laid his letter on the table, over the state of Maine and filed past the Minutemen. As he passed them, he was greeted by each member of the Minutemen. He shook hands with Joshua, who said to him, 'we are sorry for your loss'. He shook hands with Caleb, who said to him, 'we grieve with you, but not without hope'. He shook hands with Deborah and Gideon. When he got to Samson, Samson pinned a Friends of Purple Mountain medallion on the white sash of his red shirt. The medallion was placed just over his heart and sat beside Christy in the sixth row. Seated directly in front of him was Andrew.

The music stopped and the Anthem's call had been sent. The crowd sat in silent reflection.

Chapter 60

There was a brief pause in the zoning commission hearing being held at the Worthington Elementary school. The next speaker had yet to approach the microphone.

The shrewd commission member knew the numbers were not good for the East. There were 27 people sitting in the east side floor seating section. During the playing of the National Anthem, he didn't notice the defections to the West. There were now 28 seated in the west side floor seating section. They numbered one more in number than those who were seated in the east side floor seating section. Sometimes just one more is enough, he thought.

The Worthington Postmaster looked at the table where the speakers had placed all of their letters from the Greenskeeper. What he saw was that about half of the country had hand-returned letters to Worthington. Each letter contained an original postmark from Worthington. If the forensics team, at the police station, were to dust the letters for fingerprints they would surely find those of the postmaster on each of them. Tears streamed down the face of the postmaster.

In the crowd, there were more seated in the west side bleachers than were seated in the east. There was a great movement from within the crowd. It was as if a great battle had been won. It was as if the flag had been raised over Iwo Jima. Yes, an important battle had been won. However, the war was not over yet. The crowd determined to fight on but with renewed confidence.

The Worthington Elementary School music teacher already knew that prayers had been answered. In her heart, she knew the next song to be played. It is the longest song of the performance being practiced by the high school marching Band. Tears streamed down her face.

The Worthington Elementary School History teacher looked again at the west side floor seating section. He wasn't the only one to notice that a flag, not yet complete, was unfurling before their eyes. There were red and white stripes and stars sitting amongst a blue union. People were moved to tears. It was as if that tattered flag, from Fort McHenry, had been laid out on the gymnasium floor for them to see.

A long retired veteran of World War II relived stories of how America defeated the Axis powers. In an instant, his mind relived American battles in foreign lands against the fierce opponents of Germany, Italy and Japan. He also relived the rebuilding of Europe, under the Marshall Plan, in the aftermath of such devastation. He remembered meeting former soldiers, of the Empire of Japan. He visited Japan, in 1995, some fifty years after wars end. He knew the battle for this mountain was complete. However, there would need to be a time of healing. He trusted that people of good faith would find a way work it out.

The pastor of a local church sat in the bleachers of the west side of the gymnasium. He saw the Judges of ancient Israel, Deborah, Gideon and Samson calling a straying people back to the true faith. He saw Joshua and Caleb, great men of biblical times, leading a people by faith. Yet, all five of them demonstrated a compassion for people that was contagious.

It is interesting how people see the same set of circumstances and come to different conclusions. However, on this occasion, the majesties of God's divine plan did not go unnoticed by the people of faith that so loved this Purple Mountain and its mysteries.

People, from across this great land, were assembling. By the mercies of God, they were becoming an unfolding union of people laying down burdens and binding wounds. Some wounds were old and scarred over, while others were fresh and yet bleeding.

Then all of creation, within earshot of the Worthington High School Marching Band practice field, heard the voice of God calling to them through the Nations' lullaby.

The song 'God Bless America' drifted through the gymnasium. As it played, a people of faith were moved to tears of sorrow and joy and of hopes and fears.

A parade the likes of which had never been seen in Worthington, or anywhere else for that matter, was developing. The parade of the Greenskeeper's letters continued.

As the next person redressed the commission, the song 'God Bless America' drifted through the gymnasium.

"My name is Thomas, and I am from Missouri. My brother, Harry was killed in Action on 10/4/2003, in Afghanistan. He served as a Private in the 3rd Marine Division of the U.S. Marines," then he read the letter from the Greenskeeper. When he finished reading, he laid his letter on the table, over the state of Missouri and filed past the Minutemen. As he passed them, he was greeted by each member of the Minutemen. He shook hands with Joshua, who said to him, 'we are sorry for your loss'. He shook hands with Caleb, who said to him, 'we grieve with you, but not without hope'. He shook hands with Deborah and Gideon. When he got to Samson, Samson pinned a Friends of Purple Mountain medallion on the red sash draped over his white shirt. The medallion was placed just over his heart and he took his seat in the sixth row sitting next to Johnny.

"My name is James, I am from Arkansas. My son Felix, was killed in action, on 3/22/2004, in Afghanistan. He served as an Airman in the U.S. Air Force," then he read the letter from the Greenskeeper. When he finished reading, he laid his letter on the table, over the state of Arkansas and filed past the Minutemen. As he passed them, he was greeted by each member of the Minutemen. He shook hands with Joshua, who said to him, 'we are sorry for your loss'. He shook hands with Caleb, who said to him, 'we grieve with you, but not without hope'. He shook hands with Deborah and Gideon. When he got to Samson, Samson pinned a Friends of Purple Mountain medallion on the red sash draped over his red shirt. The medallion was placed just over his heart and he took his seat in the sixth row along the isle.

"My name is Sean, I am from Michigan. My son Isaac, was killed in action, on 2/27/2005, in Afghanistan. He served as a Sergeant, 4th Marine Division, U.S. Marine Corps.," then he read the letter from the Greenskeeper. When he finished reading, he laid his letter on the table, over the state of Michigan and filed past the Minutemen. As he passed them, he was greeted by each member of the Minutemen. He shook hands with Joshua, who said to him, 'we are sorry for your loss'. He shook hands with Caleb, who said to him, 'we grieve with you, but not without hope'. He shook hands with Deborah and Gideon. When he got to Samson, Samson pinned a Friends of Purple Mountain medallion on the white sash draped over his red shirt. The medallion was placed just over his heart and he took his seat in the seventh row along the center isle. Seated directly in front of him was Jennifer.

"My name is Elisha, I am from Florida. My brother Manuel, was killed in action, on 5/3/2004, in Iraq. He served as an Airman 1st Class in the U.S. Air Force, 6th Security Forces Squadron," then he read the letter from the Greenskeeper. When he finished reading, he laid his letter on the table, over the state of Florida and filed past the Minutemen. As he passed them, he was greeted by each member of the Minutemen. He shook hands with Joshua, who said to him, 'we are sorry for your loss'. He shook hands with Caleb, who said to him, 'we grieve with you, but not without hope'. He shook hands with Deborah and Gideon. When he got to Samson, Samson pinned a Friends of Purple Mountain medallion on the red sash draped over his white shirt. The medallion was placed just over his heart and he sat in the in the seventh row beside Sean. Sitting directly in front of him was Christy and seated in front of her was Allison.

"My name is Megan, I am from Texas. My daughter, Lydia, was killed in action, on 4/18/2005, in Iraq. She served as a Corporal in the 1st Armored Division, U.S. Army," then she read the letter from the Greenskeeper. When she finished reading, she laid her letter on the table, over the state of Texas and filed past the Minutemen. As she passed them, she was greeted by each member of the Minutemen. She shook hands with Joshua, who said to her, 'we are sorry for your loss'. She shook hands with Caleb, who said to her, 'we grieve with you, but not without hope'. She shook hands with Deborah and Gideon. When she got to Samson, Samson pinned a Friends of Purple Mountain medallion on the white sash draped over her red blouse. The medallion was placed just over her heart and she and took her seat in the seventh row sitting next to Elisha. Seated directly in front of her was Johnny and seated in front of him was Andrew.

The sweet song continued to caress the ears of those that were open to listening. Many people sitting in the east grandstands were moved in their spirit. In response, with childlike faith, they left the east grandstands and headed to the west grandstands.

"My name is Paige, I am from Iowa. My daughter, Lindsey, was killed in action, on 8/4/2011, in Afghanistan. She served as a Seaman in the Explosive Ordinance Division 12, of the U.S. Navy," then she read the letter from the Greenskeeper. When she finished reading, she laid her letter on the table, over the state of Iowa and filed past the Minutemen. As she passed them, she was greeted by each member of the Minutemen. She shook hands with Joshua, who said to her, 'we are sorry for your loss'. She shook hands with Caleb, who said to her, 'we grieve with you, but not without hope'. She shook hands with Deborah and Gideon. When she got to Samson, Samson pinned a Friends of Purple Mountain medallion on the red sash draped over her white blouse. The medallion was placed just over her heart and she and took her seat in the seventh row sitting beside Megan. Seated directly in front of her were Thomas, Kimberlie, Rob, Edward and then Sharon.

"My name is Abbie, I am from Wisconsin. My great uncle, Harold, was killed in action, on 2/7/1967, in Vietnam. He served as a Master Sergeant in the 2nd Marine Division of the U.S. Marine Corps," then she read the letter from the Greenskeeper. When she finished reading, she laid her letter on the table, over the state of Wisconsin and filed past the Minutemen. As she passed them, she was greeted by each member of the Minutemen. She shook hands with Joshua, who said to her, 'we are sorry for your loss'. She shook hands with Caleb, who said to her, 'we grieve with you, but not without hope'. She shook hands with Deborah and Gideon. When she got to Samson, Samson pinned a Friends of Purple Mountain medallion on the red sash draped over her red blouse. The medallion was placed just over her heart and she filled the last remaining seat in the seventh row. Directly seated in front of her were James, Kevin, Kay, Gary and Shirley.

The Worthington Postmaster and many in the bleachers looked at the table where the speakers had placed all of their letters from the Greenskeeper. Each wondered when letters from the Western states would arrive. Like the wife of a soldier, they were waiting in expectation for news from their loved ones. But above all else, they wanted their loved ones home.

"My name is Chloee, I am from California. My niece, Rachel, was killed in action, on 1/7/2012, in Afghanistan. She served as an Airman Basic in the 1st Fighter Wing of the U.S. Air Force," then she read the letter from the Greenskeeper. When she finished reading, she laid her letter on the table, over the state of California and filed past the Minutemen. As she passed them, she was greeted by each member of the Minutemen. She shook hands with Joshua, who said to her, 'we are sorry for your loss'. She shook hands with Caleb, who said to her, 'we grieve with you, but not without hope'. She shook hands with Deborah and Gideon. When she got to Samson, Samson pinned a Friends of Purple Mountain medallion on the white sash draped over her red blouse. The medallion was placed just over her heart and she took her seat in the eighth row along the center isle.

"My name is Shaun, I am from Minnesota. My son Ray, was killed in action, on 9/27/2006, in Afghanistan. He served as a First Sergeant, 1st Marine Division, U.S. Marine Corps," then he read the letter from the Greenskeeper. When he finished reading, he laid his letter on the table, over the state of Minnesota and filed past the Minutemen. As he passed them, he was greeted by each member of the Minutemen. He shook hands with Joshua, who said to him, 'we are sorry for your loss'. He shook hands with Caleb, who said to him, 'we grieve with you, but not without hope'. He shook hands with Deborah and Gideon. When he got to Samson, Samson pinned a Friends of Purple Mountain medallion on the red sash draped over his white shirt. The medallion was placed just over his heart and he sat down beside Chloee in the eighth row.

"My name is Mya, I am from Oregon. My sister, Erica, was killed in action, on 8/18/2006, in Iraq. She served as a Senior Airman, U.S. Air Force," then she read the letter from the Greenskeeper. When she finished reading, she laid her letter on the table, over the state of Oregon and filed past the Minutemen. As she passed them, she was greeted by each member of the Minutemen. She shook hands with Joshua, who said to her, 'we are sorry for your loss'. She shook hands with Caleb, who said to her, 'we grieve with you, but not without hope'. She shook hands with Deborah and Gideon. When she got to Samson, Samson pinned a Friends of Purple Mountain medallion on the white sash draped over her red blouse. The medallion was placed just over her heart and took her seat in the eighth row and sat beside Shaun.

"My name is Jaeonna, I am from the wheat fields of Kansas. My daughter, Amber, was killed in action, on 7/15/2007, in Afghanistan. She served as a Seaman Recruit, U.S. Navy," then she read the letter from the Greenskeeper. When she finished reading, she laid her letter on the table, over the state of Kansas. As she did, she noticed the Duesenberg picture and it seemed familiar to her. Then she and filed past the Minutemen. As she passed them, she was greeted by each member of the Minutemen. She shook hands with Joshua, who said to her, 'we are sorry for your loss'. She shook hands with Caleb, who said to her, 'we grieve with you, but not without hope'. She shook hands with Deborah and Gideon. When she got to Samson, Samson pinned a Friends of Purple Mountain medallion on the red sash draped over her white blouse. The medallion was placed just over her heart and she sat down in the eighth row beside Mya.

"My name is Riley, I am from West Virginia. My cousin, Horace, was killed in action, in April 1983, in El Salvador. He served as a Seaman in the U.S. Navy," then he read the letter from the Greenskeeper. When he finished reading, he laid his letter on the table, over the state of West Virginia and filed past the Minutemen. As he passed them, he was greeted by each member of the Minutemen. He shook hands with Joshua, who said to him, 'we are sorry for your loss'. He shook hands with Caleb, who said to him, 'we grieve with you, but not without hope'. He shook hands with Deborah and Gideon. When he got to Samson, Samson pinned a Friends of Purple Mountain medallion on the red sash draped over his red shirt. The medallion was placed just over his heart and he was seated in the eighth row along the isle.

"My name is Jesy, I am from Nevada. My friend, Gene, was killed in action, on 1/25/1991, in the Gulf War. He served as a Sergeant 1st Class, 82nd Airborne, U.S. Army," then he read the letter from the Greenskeeper. When he finished reading, he laid his letter on the table, over the state of Nevada and filed past the Minutemen. As he passed them, he was greeted by each member of the Minutemen. He shook hands with Joshua, who said to him, 'we are sorry for your loss'. He shook hands with Caleb, who said to him, 'we grieve with you, but not without hope'. He shook hands with Deborah and Gideon. When he got to Samson, Samson pinned a Friends of Purple Mountain medallion on the white sash draped over his red shirt. The medallion was placed just over his heart and he sat in the ninth row along the center isle.

"My name is Gray, I am from the fruited plains of Nebraska. My sister, Lauren, was killed in action, on 7/5/2010, in Afghanistan. She served as a Corporal, 2nd Marine Division, U.S. Marine Corps.," then he read the letter from the Greenskeeper. When he finished reading, he laid his letter on the table, over the state of Nebraska and filed past the Minutemen. As he passed them, he was greeted by each member of the Minutemen. He shook hands with Joshua, who said to him, 'we are sorry for your loss'. He shook hands with Caleb, who said to him, 'we grieve with you, but not without hope'. He shook hands with Deborah and Gideon. When he got to Samson, Samson pinned a Friends of Purple Mountain medallion on the red sash draped over his white shirt. The medallion was placed just over his heart and took his seat in the ninth row sitting beside Jesy.

"My name is Eleanor, I am from Colorado. My grandson, Travis, was killed in action, on 4/5/2007, in Iraq. He served as a Private, 1st Cavalry, U.S. Army," then she read the letter from the Greenskeeper. When she finished reading, she laid her letter on the table, over the state of Colorado and filed past the Minutemen. As she passed them, she was greeted by each member of the Minutemen. She shook hands with Joshua, who said to her, 'we are sorry for your loss'. She shook hands with Caleb, who said to her, 'we grieve with you, but not without hope'. She shook hands with Deborah and Gideon. When she got to Samson, Samson pinned a Friends of Purple Mountain medallion on the white sash draped over her red blouse. The medallion was placed just over her heart and she was seated next to Gray in the ninth row.

"My name is Raymond, I am from North Dakota. My brother, Samuel, was killed in action, on 8/6/2008, in Iraq. He served as a Specialist, 25th Infantry Division, U.S. Army," then he read the letter from the Greenskeeper. When he finished reading, he laid his letter on the table, over the state of

North Dakota and filed past the Minutemen. As he passed them, he was greeted by each member of the Minutemen. He shook hands with Joshua, who said to him, 'we are sorry for your loss'. He shook hands with Caleb, who said to him, 'we grieve with you, but not without hope'. He shook hands with Deborah and Gideon. When he got to Samson, Samson pinned a Friends of Purple Mountain medallion on the red sash draped over his white shirt. The medallion was placed just over his heart and he took his seat in the ninth row sitting next to Eleanor.

The shrewd commission member gave up on tallying votes. In his heart, he knew that he would vote his conscience despite the will of the people. Somehow, the up coming election cycle was not included in his calculations.

"My name is Cleta, I am from South Dakota. My mom, Sarah, was killed in action, on 10/20/2007, in Afghanistan. She served as a Seaman Apprentice, Naval Security Force, U.S. Navy," then she read the letter from the Greenskeeper. When she finished reading, she laid her letter on the table, over the state of South Dakota and filed past the Minutemen. As she passed them, she was greeted by each member of the Minutemen. She shook hands with Joshua, who said to her, 'we are sorry for your loss'. She shook hands with Caleb, who said to her, 'we grieve with you, but not without hope'. She shook hands with Deborah and Gideon. When she got to Samson, Samson pinned a Friends of Purple Mountain medallion on the red sash draped over her red blouse. The medallion was placed just over her heart and she took her seat in the ninth row along the isle.

"My name is Willis, I am from Montana. My great granddaughter, Amanda, was killed in action, on 09/22/2004, in Iraq. She served as an Airman Basic, U.S. Air Force, 1st Special Operations wing," then he read the letter from the Greenskeeper. When he finished reading, he laid his letter on the table, over the state of Montana and filed past the Minutemen. As he passed them, he was greeted by each member of the Minutemen. He shook hands with Joshua, who said to him, 'we are sorry for your loss'. He shook hands with Caleb, who said to him, 'we grieve with you, but not without hope'. He shook hands with Deborah and Gideon. When he got to Samson, Samson pinned a Friends of Purple Mountain medallion on the white sash draped over his red shirt. The medallion was placed just over his heart and took his seat in the tenth row along the center isle.

"My name is Anna, I am from Washington. My niece, Heather, was killed in action, on 9/24/2008, in Afghanistan. She served as a Senior Chief Petty Officer, U.S. Navy," then she read the letter from the Greenskeeper. When she finished reading, she laid her letter on the table, over the state of Washington and filed past the Minutemen. As she passed them, she was greeted by each member of the Minutemen. She shook hands with Joshua, who said to her, 'we are sorry for your loss'. She shook hands with Caleb, who said to her, 'we grieve with you, but not without hope'. She shook hands with Deborah and Gideon. When she got to Samson, Samson pinned a Friends of Purple Mountain medallion on the red sash draped over her white blouse. The medallion was placed just over her heart and she took her seat in the tenth row sitting beside Willis.

"My name is Vincent, I am from Idaho. My daughter, Whitney, was killed in action, on 4/24/2009, in Afghanistan. She served as a Staff Sergeant, 1st Armored Division, U.S. Army" then he read the letter from the Greenskeeper. When he finished reading, he laid his letter on the table, over the state of Idaho and filed past the Minutemen. As he passed them, he was greeted by each member of the Minutemen. He shook hands with Joshua, who said to him, 'we are sorry for your loss'. He shook hands with Caleb, who said to him, 'we grieve with you, but not without hope'. He shook hands with Deborah and Gideon. When he got to Samson, Samson pinned a Friends of Purple Mountain medallion on the white sash draped over his red shirt. The medallion was placed just over his heart and he sat down beside Anna in the tenth row.

"My name is Sophie, I am from Wyoming. My husband, Jason, was killed in action, on 7/9/2010, in Iraq. He served as a Private, 3rd Marine Division, U.S. Marine Corps.," then she read the letter from the Greenskeeper. When she finished reading, she laid her letter on the table, over the state of Wyoming and filed past the Minutemen. As she passed them, she was greeted by each member of the Minutemen. She shook hands with Joshua, who said to her, 'we are sorry for your loss'. She shook hands with Caleb, who said to her, 'we grieve with you, but not without hope'. She shook hands with Deborah and Gideon. When she got to Samson, Samson pinned a Friends of Purple Mountain medallion on the red sash draped over her white blouse. The medallion was placed just over her heart and she took her seat in the tenth row sitting next to Vincent.

"My name is Charlie, I am from Utah. My wife, Jamie, was killed in action, on 6/1/2011, in Iraq. She served as an Airman Basic, 3rd Wing, U.S. Air Force" then he read the letter from the Greenskeeper. When he finished reading, he laid his letter on the table, over the state of Utah and filed past the Minutemen. As he passed them, he was greeted by each member of the Minutemen. He shook hands with Joshua, who said to him, 'we are sorry for your loss'. He shook hands with Caleb, who said to him, 'we grieve with you, but not without hope'. He shook hands with Deborah and Gideon. When he got to Samson, Samson pinned a Friends of Purple

Mountain medallion on the red sash draped over his red shirt. The medallion was placed just over his heart and he sat in the remaining open seat of the tenth row beside Sophie.

"My name is John, I am from Oklahoma. My mom, April, was killed in action, on 10/4/2004, in Iraq. She served as a Lance Corporal, 4th Marine Division, U.S. Marine Corps.," then he read the letter from the Greenskeeper. When he finished reading, he laid his letter on the table, over the state of Oklahoma and filed past the Minutemen. As he passed them, he was greeted by each member of the Minutemen. He shook hands with Joshua, who said to him, 'we are sorry for your loss'. He shook hands with Caleb, who said to him, 'we grieve with you, but not without hope'. He shook hands with Deborah and Gideon. When he got to Samson, Samson pinned a Friends of Purple Mountain medallion on the white sash draped over his red shirt. The medallion was placed just over his heart and he took his seat in the eleventh row along the center isle.

"My name is Hannah, I am from New Mexico. My fiancé, Fredrick, was killed in action, on 3/30/1969, in Vietnam. He served as a Private 1st Class, 3rd Marine Division, U.S. Marine Corps.," then she read the letter from the Greenskeeper. When she finished reading, she laid her letter on the table, over the state of New Mexico and filed past the Minutemen. As she passed them, she was greeted by each member of the Minutemen. She shook hands with Joshua, who said to her, 'we are sorry for your loss'. She shook hands with Caleb, who said to her, 'we grieve with you, but not without hope'. She shook hands with Deborah and Gideon. When she got to Samson, Samson pinned a Friends of Purple Mountain medallion on the red sash draped over her white blouse. The medallion was placed just over her heart and she took her seat in the eleventh row sitting beside John.

"My name is Amelia, I am from Arizona. My nephew, August, was killed in action, on 1/7/2012, in Afghanistan. He served as an Airman 1st Class, U.S. Air Force, 19th Airlift," then she read the letter from the Greenskeeper. When she finished reading, she laid her letter on the table, over the state of Arizona and filed past the Minutemen. As she passed them, she was greeted by each member of the Minutemen. She shook hands with Joshua, who said to her, 'we are sorry for your loss'. She shook hands with Caleb, who said to her, 'we grieve with you, but not without hope'. She shook hands with Deborah and Gideon. When she got to Samson, Samson pinned a Friends of Purple Mountain medallion on the white sash draped over her red blouse. The medallion was placed just over her heart and she sat next to Hannah in the eleventh row.

The Worthington Elementary School History teacher and most in the gymnasium looked again at the west side floor seating section. What they saw had not been in existence since 1/2/1959 but was created on Independence day of 1912. There, before their eyes, were red and white stripes, a blue union and forty-eight stars. A sixth grade student yelled, 'look a forty-eight star flag!' and the people saw a nearly completed Republic.

"My name is Olivia, I am from Alaska. My husband, Angelo, was killed in action, on 12/05/2007, in Iraq. He served as a Seaman Apprentice, U.S. Navy," then she read the letter from the Greenskeeper. When she finished reading, she laid her letter on the table, over the state of Alaska and filed past the Minutemen. As she passed them, she was greeted by each member of the Minutemen. She shook hands with Joshua, who said to her, 'we are sorry for your loss'. She shook hands with Caleb, who said to her, 'we grieve with you, but not without hope'. She shook hands with Deborah and Gideon.

When she got to Samson, Samson pinned a Friends of Purple Mountain medallion on the red sash draped over her white blouse. The medallion was placed just over her heart and she took her seat in the eleventh row sitting beside Amelia.

"My name is Stephen, I am from Hawaii. My brother, Jacob, was killed in action, on 1/27/2012, in Afghanistan. He served as a Private, 1st Marine Division, U.S. Marine Corps.," then he read the letter from the Greenskeeper. When he finished reading, he laid his letter on the table, over the state of Hawaii and filed past the Minutemen. As he passed them, he was greeted by each member of the Minutemen. He shook hands with Joshua, who said to him, 'we are sorry for your loss'. He shook hands with Caleb, who said to him, 'we grieve with you, but not without hope'. He shook hands with Deborah and Gideon. When he got to Samson, Samson pinned a Friends of Purple Mountain medallion on the red sash draped over his red shirt. The medallion was placed just over his heart and filled the remaining open seat in west side floor seating section.

The shrewd politician saw only two people remaining on the entire east side of the gymnasium. They were seated in the front row of the east side floor seating section. He knew one of them intimately. The other he did not know but they were seated side by side. During the parade of letters, the long forgotten faith of a people was awakened. The people were silent but they couldn't have spoken louder.

The Worthington Postmaster looked at the table where the speakers had placed all of their love letters from the Greenskeeper. What he saw brought tears to his eyes, for it was a vision of the near future. He saw letters that had been brought to Worthington from sea to shining sea.

The Worthington Elementary School history teacher saw what every good student of history should see as they looked upon the gymnasium floor. A complete Union! An unwavering flag of red white and blue with fifty stars. It was attached to a mast made of five Minutemen. The states were seated in order of their birth into the Union from eldest to newest. The parade of the Greenskeeper's letters had shown the people that we are individuals yet a people and we are states and yet a Union. When a person is in need we come to their aid, likewise when a state is in need other states band together and come to their aid in the hour of peril.

The Worthington Elementary School music teacher knew the next song in the performance. Many in the audience were silently anticipating the playing of a majestic hymn. The music teacher knew they would have to wait. This final act of the performance included something unexpected for the students. Their first few times through the marching footwork would have to be made without instruments. There would be a period of about fifteen minutes of silence from the marching band.

The Minutemen remained standing in an act of faith. Except for the brief recess, they had been standing to greet everyone from Tootsie to Stephen and from Delaware to Hawaii. The firmness of handshakes Stephen received were just as firm as those offered to Tootsie. They showed deference to all and partiality to none. The patriots had dreamed of victory but the war was not yet won.

The music stopped playing.

The parade of the Greenskeeper's letters ended, as do all parades.

Or so it seemed.

Chapter 61

At four hours, this was the longest zoning commission hearing in the history of Worthington and it wasn't over yet.

The mayor addressed the people, "I want to thank all of those that addressed both this commission and the people, with your thoughts and insights. It truly has been an inspiring evening. We will close public comments at this—"

The mayor had been interrupted by a still small voice saying, "wait." It originated out of the east side of the gymnasium but no one saw who had said it. There were not many options to choose from though.

"Hoo-hoo hoooooo hoo-hoo," came the call of a Great Horned Owl through the open windows. It was as if God was speaking through all of his creation on this evening. Even the animals of the kingdom were listening, some thought. Never before had such sights and sounds been seen at a simple zoning commission hearing.

The mayor made one last plea, "This is the last opportunity, if you have something to say, please come and don't delay," she called softly.

Something stirred in the room. A fresh valley breeze seemed to flow through the gymnasium but its source was unknown. It didn't come through the windows nor from the halls. It was almost imperceptible but was noticed by those with faith. For each sensed it in their soul.

Something stirred in the front row of the east side floor seating section. A man reached into his coal black briefcase and pulled out a letter. Not just any letter. This letter was postmarked in Worthington and was postmarked May 1987. The exact day of the post mark had worn off years ago. The back of the envelope was sealed with a wax seal. The man heard the last call for public comment and he was responding in faith.

He stood to his feet and began to walk. Every eye in the gymnasium was upon him. He walked between the east side bleacher section and the floor seats toward the end of the gymnasium where the Greenskeeper's parade of letters had begun. Then before he exited the gymnasium he stopped and paused a long pause. He looked at the face of his wrist watch. Alexander saw the small hand pointing to the Roman numeral VII. Red unfastened the watch and turned it over exposing the side with the blue face and celestial images. As he refastened it, time reckoned with him. As he looked into Deus' dial, he understood that the celestial measurements were at apogee and with it the fullness of time had come.

And then he decidedly pivoted one hundred and eighty degrees and started walking down the center isle. He was walking the path of the Greenskeeper's parade of letters. He was wearing a coal black suit with gold pinstripes, a white Amosu bespoke shirt and a solid red tie. He held a letter in one hand and he held his other hand just below his neck touching his chest ever so slightly. His head looked down, as if he were watching his feet take every step along the long path to the microphone. As he looked down, it was as if there were sawdust on the floor. He thought it may have been thrown down before the hearing to keep people from slipping on the wood floor of the gymnasium.

He stepped up to the microphone, with the entire city of Worthington watching. He looked at the table in front of him. There were fifty letters laid bare before him. Over the last four hours, he had a front row seat as these letters arrived from the various states of this great land. Each with a personal story of gallantry and fidelity that inspired a servant attitude in others. These letters of love were laid out like a map, of this great Republic, detailing the people that so loved it. It was a grand design for binding our wounds in the aftermath of conflict and strife. Each letter represented precious blood spilled for this Republic on the field of battle.

Each letter had a name inscribed upon it. Each letter had a date inscribed upon it. Each had been sealed, in sometime past, with a wax seal. All were penned by the same fountain; the fountain with the heart shaped breather hole; and in the same hand; the hand of the greenskeeper.

The letter in his hand was no different from the others in size, or ink color, or weight, or quality of paper. The letter he held so tightly, in his hand, was nearly indistinguishable from the others. Except for one thing, the name on the outside of the envelope was his name.

Then he spoke his name, not his nickname or any other type of name. "My name is Alexander Garnet, I am from Worthington, Virginia. My uncle, Charles, was a corporal in the U.S. Army's I Corps, 7th division. He was killed in action during the Battle of Pork Chop Hill on July 11, 1953," he said with a silver tongue.

"I received this letter twenty-five years ago from the Greenskeeper of the Majestic of Purple Mountain. After hearing the public comments, I felt compelled to come. To come and join in this grand parade where we, as a people, face the mortality of our loved ones and ourselves. I felt compelled to join with you in unraveling these great mysteries of life. What happens to us when we die? What happens to the living when their loved ones are departed? How do we find peace? I came here tonight to move your beloved and majestic Purple Mountain. Instead, each of you have bound together, as a people of faith, and have moved a mountain of purple off of me. I thought I had riches, like the Phoenician kings of Tyre, until I heard the stories of your riches. Your riches are pure and of an incorruptible type. They are part of your heritage, your legacy, and the fabric of your lives.

However, there is one purple that we share. Each person, in the Greenskeeper's parade of letters, has a loved one that has spilled their precious blood for us. Like knights fighting for a majestic kingdom, they spilled their blood. They spilled it for our hopes, our dreams, and our freedom from tyranny in all its forms. But most of all, they spilled it out of love.

What I am holding in my hand, may well be the last letter to ever walk in the Greenskeeper's parade of letters. I doubt that any, who have been so blessed, as to have such a majestic letter as this, would hold it so long without revealing the riches held within it. I don't like being any, anymore.

The night has been long and I appreciate your patience with this old man before you. I was not always like this. I lost my parents at a tender young age and my beloved uncle Charles as well. It was a devastating blow to a young boy. These are not idle excuses, as I am sure each of you know. Perhaps tonight, I have taken those first few steps toward finding peace.

I have said enough. Let us hear the Greenskeeper's words to a man, that was once dead to the mysteries of life and its glorious riches, but has been made alive through the sacrifices of others. Let us hear the words of a knight who felled the dragons of death with his mighty fount." He opened the letter as everyone watched and listened. He began to read it aloud.

Chapter 62

"My Dearest Nephew Alexander,

Life is like baseball. Sometimes you strike out. Life threw you a curve and you didn't see it coming. Both life and pitchers are like that. Darn pitchers! Just keep swinging. Don't be afraid to strike out.

Back in 1945, Babe Ruth came to that old school of mine, St. Margaret-Mary. We played baseball with him all day. He taught us more in a day than I ever imagined possible. It was a grand time. He was near the end of his seasons in life. Yes, life like baseball has its seasons. We play and play and don't recognize their passage and we look back and the seasons are gone. Gone like a Ruth ball over the fence. I hate when seasons end!

This is where baseball has the advantage over life. It is immortal. Well, at least in our hearts it is. Who wants a season to end without knowing of its return? Especially when it comes to baseball!

Oh, one last thing. That 'Ruth' ball that I gave you has a story. The Big Bambino knocked it over the fence. It went five hundred and fifty feet from home plate. It ended up in a cave of some sort and it covered the ball with some silvery white powder. I cov-

ered the entrance to the cave and planned on telling you about it but it just slipped my mind. You come from a mining family, so have them take a look at it. Who knows, maybe it will make you rich some day? Remember, the most valuable riches are the ones that no amount of money can buy. Store up those kind, for no one can take them from you or destroy them.

I gotta go now. Remember, just keep on swinging.

Bring that necklace I left with you, the one with the garnet stone, when we meet next, ok?

Love,

Uncle Charles"

Chapter 63

There was not a dry eye in the entire gymnasium at the end of the Greenskeeper's parade of letters.

Alexander, after reading the letter, stood motionless before everyone in the room. With one hand he held the letter and his other hand was gently rested on his chest just below the neck. Then he began to fold his letter and reinsert it into its envelope. When he finished he placed the letter in his left shirt pocket, the one nearest his heart.

Then he loosened his tie and unbuttoned the top button of his shirt. From within his shirt he pulled out a garnet stone attached to the chain. It was the stone that his uncle Charles had requested that he bring to their next meeting. The people let out a collective sigh. Alexander was touched by this gesture.

Then the last person seated on the east side floor seating section of the gymnasium rose to his feet. He walked three steps forward and turned ninety degrees and walked four more steps to position himself at the side of Alexander.

Then the man standing next to Alexander spoke, "There have been lots of parades lately. The one we have witnessed tonight has been the most majestic parade I have witnessed during my lifetime.

A few weeks ago, many of us attended a welcome home parade for our Iraq war soldiers. That parade and what it represented set the stage, in part, for this one tonight.

I have lived in Worthington my entire life. I am a quiet man and not given to much company. What would you expect for someone that studies rocks for a living, as I am a professor of Mineralogy at Western Virginia State Community College.

It had been twenty-five years since I had last spoken with my great uncle Alexander. I could have easily reached out to him over the years. However, I chose otherwise, as did he, until the parade a few weeks ago.

After the parade had finished, I returned to my home. Minutes later, there was a knock on my door. A knock on my door is unusual, I will admit. However, this knock sounded twenty-five years in the making.

When I opened the door, there stood my great uncle Alexander. What he did next surprised me. He rushed in and hugged me with the biggest hug. I invited him in and we talked for a short while. Then he surprised me again.

He asked me if I could give him a ride home. He said he had car trouble after the parade. So, the man who needed nothing asked me for something. I agreed and we went to the east side of Purple Mountain. We went to the Axis headquarters building, the Monolith.

He insisted that I come with him to his office. I initially refused, although politely. However, I sensed a change in him and, being intrigued, I eventually agreed. We went into his office. There he took off his coat, loosened his tie and unbuttoned his top shirt button. He exposed a necklace. It is the same one that he his wearing right now. It is the necklace with the garnet stone mentioned in the letter.

We talked for a while and I looked out the window for a time. When I refocused, my uncle Alexander was holding the letter from the Greenskeeper. He was rubbing the postmark with his index finger.

Then I saw it. There was a baseball encased within a sealed crystalline cube. The quality of the crystal case was so dazzling that I went in for a closer inspection. When I did something unusual happened, again.

My uncle Alexander tossed it underhanded to me. It was like a second baseman flipping the ball to the shortstop at the beginning of a double play. I nearly dropped it. As he threw it, he told me to keep the ball. He wanted to thank me for my hospitality and for my bringing him to his office. The crystalline case alone was extremely expensive, not to mention what it contained," he expressed, as he pulled something out of his right side jacket pocket.

"This is the Ruth ball that was mentioned in the letter–" a collective sigh filled the room. After composing himself, he said, "wait, it gets better. I kept it under protest expecting to return it to him in a few days. However, over the next few days I noticed something about the ball. It was almost imperceptible to the eye due to the crystalline case it was enclosed within. I noticed an iridescence!

I am pleased to inform all of you tonight, that after a spectral analysis we have confirmed the source of this iridescence. It is the iridescence of Indium! Indium is an element designated with the symbol 'In' and it is number 49 on the atomic scale. Its primary use is for computer touch screens and it is an extremely rare and valuable metal. Additionally, this find is unbelievably rare. It is pure Indium. There has never been a confirmed pure Indium mine discovery on the planet, ever! A pure Indium mine might be worth billions!

Were it not for the Greenskeeper's parade of letters, I suspect that my uncle would have never opened his letter. The source of the Indium would have remained a mystery for all of time.

When I had the ball analyzed, a few collectors got wind of a Ruth ball and called me. I didn't return their calls. I wouldn't sell this ball for the entire world. It was a gift from my great uncle's uncle and is priceless to me.

One more thing, I have a favor to ask of each of you. I suppose it will be alright, since we are all family now. I ask that you forget the location of the Indium as will I and my uncle. That mine, if it exists, should remain part of the mystery and richness that is Purple Mountain. Thank you," he concluded. Then he embraced his uncle.

The entire gymnasium erupted into celebration.

Alexander walked toward the Minutemen. These were the individuals he had come to defeat. He shook hands with Joshua, who said to him, 'we are sorry for your loss'. He shook hands with Caleb, who said to him, 'we grieve with you, but not without hope'. He shook hands with Deborah and Gideon. When he got to Samson, Samson pulled a pure white silk sash from his pocket and placed it over the head and shoulder of Alexander. Then he pinned a Friends of Purple Mountain medallion on the sash just above his left breast.

When Alexander and his great nephew looked around the room there was not an empty seat on the west side of the gymnasium, anywhere.

Joshua and Caleb stood up and stepped forward, while the other Minutemen remained seated. The two most prominent seats of the west side floor seating section would be occupied by the former enemy of the West. This during the all important vote on the motion before the hearing. Joshua and

Caleb sat on the floor in front of Alexander and his great nephew.

The two most prominent leaders of the Minutemen were sitting with their backs exposed to their former enemy. However, they were without concern. They were brothers now. Their families were all interconnected by the stories of the blood of fallen soldiers. There now existed a sacred covenant of trust amongst these people, where there had been none, on this Majestic Purple Mountain.

"Thank you," the mayor said, "it is time for a vote. However, I ask our audience to remain silent during the voting.

Commission on the matter of Mountain Top Mining approval how say you? Please answer yes to approve and no to disapprove."

The audience was totally silent in anticipation of victory.

The mayor said, "I will call roll," she began the roll call.

"No," said Mr. Gold when he was called; "No," said Mrs. Ruby; "No," said Mr. Diamond; "No," said Mrs. Faith; "No," said Mr. Hope; "No," said Mrs. Love.

Just as Mrs. Faith cast the deciding vote, the marching band struck up the tune 'America the Beautiful' and its sound was heard clearly throughout the gymnasium.

Jessica stated, "The request by Axis Energy for a zoning change related to Purple Mountain is denied!"

In her heart, she had joy. People had banded together in faith and saved Purple Mountain. Maybe, she thought, she would finally get to play that last hole with her father. There would be plenty of time for celebration later and she remained composed, in outward appearance. She began to pack up so she could leave and head up the mountain.

One would expect a celebratory atmosphere. However, that was not to be.

Every person in the auditorium, stood to their feet. Then the people softly broke out in song. Tears streamed down the faces of many as they listened to the sounds of that old hymn. Together they would strive to perfect their performance of it. That perfecting will take a lifetime.

The songs of the republic played through their hearts over the past four hours. It was as if the marching band were calling them to sing the old forgotten hymns of a Republic, of a people, and of a Purple Mountain.

They sang for a time and the meeting adjourned.

It was 7:15 PM and there was an unusual light valley breeze in the air.

Chapter 64

The zoning commission hearing had just adjourned. However, one last announcement was made, by the elementary school music teacher. She said, "the University Marching Band is in town for a performance of 'America the Beautiful'. It will begin soon over at the high school football field." The people were excited and a parade of cars began making their way to the high school. With the Spirit filled valley breeze, the music would be heard up and over the peaks of the majestic Purple Mountain.

Jessica was the last person left in the gymnasium. She was doing her normal duties of making sure everything was closed up and in order. Then she looked at the clock. She was running late! Michael said to be there twenty minutes before sunset. Sunset was at 8:21 PM tonight. She headed for her car but was stopped by Alexander.

"Jessica, don't you think we should be going?" he called to her gently.

"Going where, Mr. Garnet?" she replied.

"To the Majestic of Purple Mountain and call me Alexander, please," he stated simply.

"How did you know I would be going there?" she asked.

"I just knew it in my heart. Please have a little faith in me. I know I am new at this, but I am working on it. The Sikorsky S-92 is waiting on us," he said as he took one last look at the elementary school gymnasium floor. It was as if he had hit the sawdust trail. He bent down and scooped up some sawdust into his hands and left the room. When he got outside he exposed his palms to the heavens and watched the sawdust fly into the Spirit filled valley breeze. He waited on Jessica before heading to the Sikorsky.

Jessica heard a loud rumble from the last car leaving the school parking lot. It was plated in Delaware and had the letters NELSON on the license plate. It was a white sports car, but she didn't catch the make.

Jessica met Alexander and they ran to the waiting Sikorsky. It sat ready, with rotors spinning, near the spot where she and Michael had decided to fight for Purple Mountain and the people they so loved. They jumped into the cabin and the Sikorsky lifted off in flight.

"How long of a trip is it to the clubhouse?" she said as it flew them directly over the marching band practice field. Then the Sikorsky banked in a sweeping turn and headed straight up the mountain.

"It flies 190 miles per hour at max speed. It will take us there quicker than any car you could have taken. We will be there soon," he said with a smile.

"Alexander, that was a beautiful statement you made in there. The people were moved by your act of faith in opening that letter and reaching out to your family recently. What, may I ask, besides everything we saw tonight, inspired you do it?" she politely asked him.

"As I sat there I saw a living demonstration of faith. I thought about a local majestic mountain moment. It is one that has circulated for years. It seems, as local legend has it, a girl with childlike faith once prayed to God that the sun would set a second time in one day. She did this, the story goes, so that her father could finish a round of golf. It inspired me to think that if God would respond to the request of a child about a golf round, then he might just respond to me," Alexander said as he saw the Majestic of Purple Mountain come into view through his window.

"So, what did you ask for?" if I may ask.

"Sure, I asked some time ago. Yes, It was just in the days following the parade. I asked that God would move a mountain of purple for me. Trust me, I know what is involved in moving mountains. It takes a monumental effort to move a mountain. But this mountain was immovable in my eyes. It felt as if I were the victim of my own success. I felt for a time, that despite every effort of mine, the exercise would prove to be futile," he confessed to her.

"What did you do?" she asked.

"I asked Him to send me someone who could show me what childlike faith looked like. I wish I had been there to see the sun set twice in a day. What a glorious sight it must have been! But I wasn't. So I thought, if I could just get a glimpse of what that kind of faith looked like, then I could use it to move that mountain of purple I spoke of.

God responded loud and clear at the hearing. He sent the Greenskeeper's parade of letters. Had John not sent those letters, I suspect we would be having a much different conversation at this moment. It required a whole parade of those letters and the lives they represent, to inspire me to open the one I had kept all those years. I am glad that John could see those Final Foursomes. Had he not, I would have never dealt with the loss of my uncle," Alexander said as they were on their final approach into a landing on the eighteenth fairway.

Jessica saw the Majestic of Purple Mountain as she had never seen it before. She was high above it and she could see the flagpole pedestal where the unwavering flag waved. This being the same flagpole where the Greenskeeper once stood in faith and waited for the sun to rise in the west and set again. Her spirit was moved as she thought about the legend that inspired Alexander, to act in childlike faith, to have his mountain of purple moved.

And it came to pass that miracles related to this majestic mountain continued to happen. By faith, a group of God's creation banded together, for a short time, to keep the Majestic of Purple Mountain from being moved. Moreover, as a result of faith, in action, a mountain of purple was moved.

In her mind, moving the mountain of purple was the more important miracle. For God is more interested in saving the souls of men than in saving the mountains of His creation in their natural beauty. He sacrificed His son for man and not for mountains. He raised His son that man would have everlasting life through belief in Him. For what purposes He razes mountains she was unsure. Could it be that the threat of razing caused people to respond in faith and accomplish His plans for mankind? Such questions are too mysterious for they approach the unfathomable mercies of God in His plans for mankind and His creation.

A man had been changed during the Greenskeeper's parade of letters. She wondered how many others were changed on this occasion. She was sure there would be purple mountains in Heaven and equally as sure that there would be no mountains of purple in that perfect place.

The valley breeze, being moved by the Spirit, was soon to carry the sweet melodies of the hymns of a nation.

The Sikorsky landed directly in the middle of the eighteenth fairway and about eighty-seven yards from the eighteenth green. Jessica hugged Alexander and thanked him for the lift and stepped out the door and walked away from the rotor wash. The Sikorsky lifted straight into the air. It flew away by circling above the flagpole pedestal one time in a counterclockwise direction before peeling off and heading east over the purple peaks of the majestic mountain. It looked as if the Sikorsky had turned back the hands of time and disappeared in the process.

Jessica stood in the exact spot where she and her father had been rained out twenty-five years earlier. Thoughts of a lifetime passed in front of her like soldiers on parade.

When she was young, she often thought of his soldiering in allegorical terms. When she thought of him soldiering, she thought of him as a great knight fighting for a mighty kingdom. She remembered that he once said that he was a knight that threw flaming javelins at dragons. It was a sweet childhood memory that she cherished. She often wondered, in her youth, if a dragon had defeated him in battle despite his gallantry and faithfulness. For she thought there were powerful dragons in the kingdoms of the unknown. As she grew older, these thoughts faded as she thought more mature thoughts.

As an adult, she accepted the hard realities of her father's status; Missing In Action, presumed dead. She was a woman of faith but she still didn't like the sound of the words 'presumed dead'. It wasn't that she liked Missing In Action much better but at least that was more hopeful in her mind.

She remembered her last discussions with her father, as families of fallen or missing warriors often do. She remembered him telling her of his faith while they walked on this majestic Mountain.

She thought about Alexander's three questions about the 'great mysteries of life' during his address to the commission. He asked: 'what happens to us when we die?; 'what happens to the living when their loved ones are departed?'; and 'how do we find peace?'

She thought about her father's answers to these questions that were rooted in his faith. He said that 'our faith in Jesus' would allow us into heaven upon our death. He said that our family could trust God based on the evidence that supported the scriptures. He said that having faith in the knowledge of these things would bring peace.

She was at peace with her father because she believed these things. However, she hoped above all hopes that she could finish that one round of golf they had shared as father and daughter.

The faith of a people had kept this mountain from being moved. Perhaps, such faith could turn back the hands of time and allow her hopes, of seeing her father again, to come true.

She felt the Spirit filled valley breeze flow through her hair and it lightened her burdens. It was as if they were carried away, into the whispering winds.

Just then, she felt a tap against her foot. When she looked down a golf ball was laying beside her foot. She stood motionless looking down at the ball and wept in joyful expectation!

Chapter 65

The people of Worthington were assembling at the high school football field. It was an impromptu assembly of the people in response to the sweet sounds of the Republic heard during the zoning commission hearing. The people had been moved by the Greenskeeper's parade of letters. There were a parade of cars headed into the parking lot and streams of people flowing into the grandstands. It was as if God, in his unfolding plan, had orchestrated the entire evening including a Spirit filled valley breeze to carry the music up the mountain.

The Worthington High School Marching Band had finished their drills for the evening and they were waiting for the University Marching Band to take the field in battle. Their first afternoon of spring drills had gone unexpectedly well. Some of the students talked about how well they had already memorized their footwork. It was a difficult performance but the students were perfecting it as a group, in this their first practice. However, their music was as solid as gold.

The University Marching Band was coming off an award winning season. They had also used 'America the Beautiful' as their program. They had nearly perfected the performance last year and now they would perform it before these aspiring band members. The band had won awards for their marching skills as they had flawless footwork on the field.

However, there was a problem. Life is like a marching band, sometimes you must march to the beat of a different drummer. Somehow, the trailer with the band instruments was empty! Yes, empty. They were left at the University and there was no getting them here now.

As word went through the crowd that the performance was being cancelled a person had an idea. She had blown into town from Kansas where their state motto is, 'To the stars through difficulties'. She knew that they could work together and save the performance.

Jaeonna, from the wheat fields of southern Kansas, the part of Kansas where barnstormers used to fly in the 1920's, had an idea. Her plan, although difficult, was yet possible. The Worthington Band would play the music from the end zone bleachers while the University Band marched on the field.

Jaeonna, presented her plan to the band directors. They decided it would challenge both bands and that it would build character. Most of all, the music would be played and the performance would run as scheduled.

The band section leaders and drum majors were brought in on the plan and they accepted the challenge. When the band members found out, they were equally challenged and believed it was a good idea.

The high school band sat in the end zone bleachers with their instruments raised to attention. Mr. Hughes called to them saying, 'from the heart'. The band started playing.

As the University Band took the field their director urged them to 'march from their hearts'. The University Band members took the field without their instruments. However, their color guard did have their equipment with them. They had their rifles, sabers, and flags of red, white, and blue.

The valley breeze, being moved by the Spirit, was soon to carry the sweet melodies, of the hymns of a Republic, through the grandstands, beyond an awakening city, and up a majestic Purple Mountain.

The performance started with the song 'Chester'. As the high school band played from the end-zone, the University Band began to march. The people saw a marching band, without instruments, playing music! The University band members acted as if they had their instruments in their hands and were playing them. For instance, drummers sticks beat on nonexistent drumheads, trombone players arms slid imaginary slides, and trumpet players fingers pressed on nonexistent keys. Also remember, that the end zone bleachers were not in the field of vision for grand stand viewers when they looked across the field. It was a ghostly sight.

As 'Chester' played, a history teacher, in the grandstands, thought of the American Revolution. In his minds eye, he saw a fife and drum corps making the rally call to Minutemen and militias. Images of beardless boys being led into the battles of Lexington and Concord flowed thru his mind, as he watched the ever moving drill team powerfully toss rifles and sabers into the air. He saw images of the Major General, George Washington, as he looked at the drum major leading the band in their performance. He saw a patriot army, being perfected, right before his eyes.

As 'Yankee Doodle Dandy' played, the people in the grandstands started to get into the act. They were clapping and singing along to the bright beat of a well known tune. Children stood and marched in place. A World War II veteran had visions of James Cagney and Joan Leslie marching in his head. The history teacher, in his mind, saw Captain Washington marching along on the field with the band. In this moment, it was fashionable to march and sing.

As 'a Tribute to the Armed Forces' played, the crowd became even more energetic. Those with affiliations to the various military branches stood as the battle song of their individual branch army, navy, air force or marines was played. As these individuals stood, those that were seated clapped and offered other signs of gratitude, to those standing, that had served them with such honor.

As 'The Star Spangled Banner' began, everyone in the grand stands stood to their feet. With every hat off and every hand held over heart, the people sang the anthem of our nation. The history teacher thought back to the unfurling flag he saw on the floor of the elementary school earlier in the evening. Tears streamed down his face, as his mind carried him to a battle scene from the War of 1812 at Fort McHenry.

As people sang, a wonderful fireworks display began over the peaks of Purple Mountain. Fireworks gallantly streamed over the top of the mountain and red rockets glared, as bombs were bursting in the air. The fireworks were being launched from the Axis Mining company headquarters on the east side of Purple Mountain. Alexander Garnet had an inventory of fireworks that were going to be used at a company picnic later in the year. He thought it would be better to use them tonight. He was a changed man and the timing was flawless.

A pastor from a local church was in the grandstands with his family. He thought about the last stanza of the anthem. He thought about how the people of a nation, that put their trust in God, had been sustained over the ages. Going back to the first settlements of this country, people came to this land for religious freedom. Tears streamed down his face as he watched the color guard on the field in front of him wave a star spangled banner of red, white, and blue.

As 'God Bless America' played everyone in the grandstands stayed on their feet. The people kept on singing! People in the grandstands had come from all across this land. Olivia from Alaska reflected on the events of the past several weeks. She had been called here by the Minutemen to help them defend an ideal that they so loved. That ideal was America and the principles of freedom and liberty. Principles that people had given their lives to defend. These Minutemen rallied a nation to defend the honor of those that had given their lives to defend it. Many a person in the grandstands, reflected on how God had blessed them and their nation.

Yes, people from this land had responded. People like, Charles from Utah and Paige from Iowa sang a song to the land that they love. People like, Chloee from California and Shirley from Connecticut sang a song to the land that they love. It was as though people were singing, to their home sweet home. Many of them were a long way from home but they felt at home just the same.

As 'America the Beautiful' began to play the crowd remained on its feet. Eleanor from Colorado thought about the heritage of this song. Katherine Lee Bates took a train ride to Colorado Springs. What she saw on that trip inspired her to write a poem 'Pikes Peak' and from that poem a most beloved hymn emerged.

Willis, from Montana, with tears streaming down his face, reflected on the song as he attempted to sing the words but couldn't. He thought of his beloved great granddaughter Amanda who had given her life in Iraq. Amanda loved the beautiful spacious skies of Montana, he thought. They had inspired her to reach for the sky and she later joined the U.S. Air Force. He felt the Spirit filled valley breeze on his skin as he thought of his great granddaughter flying in the clouds.

He was moved by the moment, as a national lullaby soothed his scarred spirit.

Jaeonna, from Kansas, with tears streaming down her face, reflected on the song as she attempted to sing its words but couldn't. She thought of her daughter, Amber who was killed in Afghanistan while serving in the U.S. Navy. She thought of the amber waves of grain she had seen on her family farm in the state of Kansas as a child. She felt the Spirit filled valley breeze blowing through her amber colored hair. She was moved by the moment, as a national lullaby soothed her scarred spirit.

Hannah, from New Mexico, with tears streaming down her face, reflected on the song as she attempted to sing its words but couldn't. She thought about her fiancé Fredrick, who was killed in Vietnam. He had a strong connection with his jarhead Marine buddies. They were a brotherhood, she thought. He was a good man and she missed him. She felt the Spirit filled valley breeze blowing over her skin. She was moved by the moment, as a national lullaby soothed her scarred spirit.

Rita, from Rhode Island, with tears streaming down her face, reflected on the song as she attempted to sing its words but couldn't. She thought about her beloved nephew Peter, a U.S. Coast Guard pilot, who had given his life while attempting to save others from the stormy seas off the New England coast. Peter loved the outdoors and the oceans. He had served off the California coast before his move to the New England area. He served from sea to shining sea, she thought. Rita missed him dearly. She felt the Spirit filled valley breeze blowing over her skin. She was moved by the moment, as a national lullaby soothed her scarred spirit.

Raymond, from North Dakota, with tears streaming down his face, reflected on the song as he attempted to sing the words but couldn't. He thought of his grandson Samuel who gave his life in Iraq while serving in the U.S. Army. Samuel was a true patriot, he thought. He felt the Spirit filled valley breeze on his skin, as he thought of his grandson living out his patriot dreams. He was moved by the moment, as a national lullaby soothed his scarred spirit.

By the end of the playing of the song 'America the Beautiful' there was not a dry eye in the grandstands that night. The faithful felt the Spirit filled valley breeze blowing over their skin. They were moved by the moment, as a national lullaby soothed their scarred spirits.

People had assembled from across this great land. They had been called to this place to defend a Purple Mountain. The Purple Mountain was going to be moved and they were called here to defend it and the principles it represented. They had come to defend honor, virtue, courage and heroism, gallantry, fidelity and service. In the process, these people were moved in their spirit. A flood of emotion washed over those that had come from sea to shining sea. A people had come together and in the process of saving a mountain from being moved they were moved by a mountainous display of patriotism. People were gathered and they were binding wounds. Some wounds were old and others were fresh and yet bleeding. Together, a people of faith were finding peace in the midst of the storms and struggles of life.

The majesty of the American experience was put on display that night. Although, this particular performance of 'America the Beautiful' would not be recorded in annals of American history, it would forever be recorded in the souls of those that attended.

It is interesting that a group of people can witness the same performance and walk away from it inspired in different ways. It was as if there were layers of harmony in the Spirit filled valley breeze that night.

America the Beautiful is beautiful indeed.

Chapter 66

The Greenskeeper's walk of love was nearing perfection. The three of them, John, Michael and Christopher had walked the course the entire afternoon.

Christopher was having an excellent round. Early in the round, Christopher began to carry his own clubs. He realized that Michael needed time with John to learn the mysterious ways of the greenskeeper of the Majestic of Purple Mountain. He had been generously rewarded, during his round, for his faithfulness to shot planning on the southern arm of course. Similarly, he had been equally rewarded for his gallant and aggressive play over the first eight holes of the northern arm. It was a faith filled round and it was nearly complete.

They were standing on the tee box of the eighteenth as Christopher hit his final drive. Splitting the fairway, with a perfectly long and straight drive, the ball gently landed and rolled down a slope out of their view. Christopher began to walk as Michael and John talked.

"Michael, our walk is nearly complete here on Purple Mountain. My walk is complete, and now I am going to where she is waiting for me. We will meet again, when you come to where I am going. Remember, you are a greenskeeper from the heart. Now go to your brother and rejoice with him while there is yet time!"

Michael looked down the fairway for his brother. When he looked back, John was gone. He wondered who John was talking about when he said 'she' but the thought quickly left him. Michael smiled and ran to his brother's side and they walked together one last time.

"Christopher, when did you first see them? The Final Foursomes?", he asked.

"When we saw the sun rise in the west, twenty-five years ago, I felt them calling me. I watched John stand steadfast in his faith until the sun rose in the sky. It inspired me, to be worthy of someone playing such song as he did and with such faith. I can't recall if I saw them but I at least saw shadows of them. And now here I am as one of them." he declared.

"I saw them for the first time on that day. Then I saw them in their full glory as they played their rounds here as members of the Final Foursomes. I watched from the flagpole pedestal as they passed into glory off of the eighteenth green. I loved hearing their stories and wanted to be a part of that. Then the incident with Jessica's father and we left here. You know the story," Michael said.

"Let that one go, will you! All has been forgiven. Remember? It will all work out. You did the right thing in the end. Now you are the greenskeeper! So, be the greenskeeper and go play "Taps" or something that greenskeepers do!" Christopher said with a smile.

As they came to the crest in the fairway Michael saw her. He knew her silhouette from twenty-five yards away! She was standing next to the ball that Christopher had just hit. Michael wondered if she had seen it. He ran to her calling, "Jessica! Jessica! Jessica!"

She heard him but she didn't move. She was looking at the golf ball at her feet and hoping beyond hope. Michael arrived at her side and quietly stood by her.

He understood the magnitude of the moment on this Purple Mountain. Moments like these are a rare thing in this life. Moments when faith, hope and love combine and the majesties of God are glimpsed.

Chapter 67

As Michael stood by Jessica, a Spirit filled valley breeze carried with it a song. It was 'Chester' the battle cry of the Republic.

Then another noise, that sounded like the far away gallop of a horse, was coming from the direction of the eighteenth tee box. They turned and stared down the fairway. What they saw amazed them.

Cresting over the hill, was the Major General, George Washington, riding on his white horse! It was as if the Major General answered to the calling of 'Chester' that was drifting in the air!

"Whoa, Nelson!", the Major General said as he stopped the horse right in front of them. He dismounted and said to Christopher, "soldier, tend to the horse".

Christopher had just walked up. He dropped his golf bag and ran over to Nelson and took his reins into his hands and led the horse to the side of the fairway.

"Soldier, come out!" the Major General commanded, as he looked into the woods toward the White Oak.

Then they heard a rustling from within the trees that lined the fairway. What they saw thunderstruck them. It was as if a knight with a flaming javelin appeared. He stepped out from within the trees. The knight laid down his weapon and continued his walk toward them.

Tears of joy, flowed from Jessica's jade green eyes and down her face. It was her father!

"Soldier, attention!" the Major General commanded as Doug walked up to them, "soldier, I have heard that you feared them not and that you trusted in God. Additionally, when the battle was most fierce you laid down your life for another soldier. For unusual gallantry, demonstrated during the battle of Chapri Forest, in 1987, I hereby award you the Badge of Military Merit. Well done Doug," the Major General said as he pinned the badge to the left breast of Doug's uniform, "your acts of gallantry and fidelity will be recorded in the *Book of Merit*."

The Spirit filled valley breeze carried a new tune up the slopes of the majestic mountain. It was the sounds of 'Yankee Doodle Dandy'.

Then the Major General motioned for Michael to join him over by Nelson, on the far side of the fairway.

"I understand that you are the new greenskeeper?" he asked.

"Yes, sir!" Michael replied.

The Major General was tapping his feet to the rhythm being carried in the air, as he placed his arm over the shoulder of Michael, "son, when I heard that song at the opera it was a disappointment. It is so much better out here in the open air! The way it was meant to be played.

This is a field ceremony. We have them occasionally. It is more intimate than our first tee ceremonies. Anyway, I worked it out with the Minutemen and we are suspending the Final Foursomes and the first tee ceremonies for a fortnight. Sorry, two weeks. That is effective immediately. Also, there is need to play "Taps" tonight, as the band has you covered. They are playing a special tune tonight in the place of "Taps". Spend some time over the next few days with the family we have here in town, ok? Anyway, I hear you have a Yankee Doodle Sweetheart and you are her Yankee Doodle Boy?

John and I were good friends and I hope we will be as well. One more thing. Your left taillight is out on the Willys. It is interesting what you notice while being in a parade. You might want to fix it before we head down to ANC in a few days," he said.

He walked over to his horse, Nelson. He mounted the horse and rode toward the sweet sounds of an old battle cry that was floating in the air. It looked as if he went to town riding on a pony.

A few yards away, Jessica held an old score card in her hand. It was the one she had kept for twenty-five years. In her heart, she always believed that this moment would arrive. She had childlike faith. Now it was time to watch, as her father exercised his last measure of faith.

"Let's finish this!" Doug said to her, "what club do you recommend, caddie?"

"There is a slight left to right breeze, the pin is at the back, we are eighty-seven yards from the hole and it is a club uphill," she had thought about this shot for years, "a hard pitching wedge," she recommended.

"I have been looking at this shot for twenty-five years, and have studied it from every angle imaginable , and that is the only club that will work here," he said.

Doug addressed the ball and looked up the fairway at the pin. Then he looked down at the golf ball he was about to strike. This shot required faith. As he swung his club in faith, he saw the ram in the thicket, and the faith that stayed the hand of Abraham from plunging a knife into the heart of his only son. Doug possessed that kind of shot saving faith. His final round would be complete soon.

Jessica had waited a quarter century to watch this one swing of the club. She recalled the walk she had on these hallowed grounds twenty-five years earlier. It gave her comfort to recall her father's legacy of faithfulness. However, to see this shot required a faith of her own. When she watched her father's faithful flowing swing, it was as if Jonah, after three days in the belly of a whale at the bottom of a jade sea, was spit onto the shore. Jessica possessed shot seeing faith.

Christopher had played the course with unusual gallantry and faithfulness. He had positioned himself well for this one last, but all important, shot. He desired to finish strong. There was a time in his life when he had to make a choice. At the crossroads in his life, the Greenskeeper challenged him to become 'Christ bearing'. He decided to change that instant. His life was forever different. Now because of that one choice, and the many choices that flowed from it, his path led him here to the place where true faith is perfected. As he swung his club in faith, he saw doubting Thomas putting his fingers into the nail scarred hands of the Savior. Doug possessed shot saving faith.

Isn't it interesting how three different individuals, of the same faith, chose three different stories that point to their individual faith in one Savior.

The Spirit filled valley breeze carried with it a majestic song about a beautiful banner.

The four of them walked the final yards of the eighteenth fairway. As they did, the sounds of the 'Star Spangled Banner' flew threw the air. Over the peaks of the mountain there were fireworks. Doug and Christopher had fought their battles with gallantry and fidelity. They were proven true in their hour of calling and their faith was proving true in its hour of calling. When they reached the green, they could see the flagpole pedestal. On the pedestal, an unwavering flag waved. It was as if these warriors saw the McHenry Flag flying by the dawns early light.

The Spirit filled valley breeze carried with it a majestic song about a beautiful blessing.

They stood by their country at a time of need and gave their precious lives in defense of it and its principles. There were tears of joy as Doug and Christopher laid down their Badges of Merit on the fringe of the green. Each of them knew, that to enter the next kingdom, it took faith in the sacrifice of one greater than themselves, it took faith in the one who had sacrificed everything and died, and yet lived again.

Jessica and Michael stood near the eighteenth green. They watched Doug, Christopher and John fade into glory, as the sun slipped below the horizon. They went into glory, in the same manner, as all of others had gone before them.

Just at that moment, Michael and Jessica felt a gentle Spirit filled wind swirl about them. It was the most pleasant wind either had experienced. The Spirit in the wind comforted their sorrow filled souls and fanned the flames of faith that burned deep within each of them. Their heavy hearts were made light and their spirits were lifted by what the Spirit imparted. The Spirit filled wind swirled about them for a time, times and half time. Then the wind ceased, as suddenly as its arrival had occurred, but the Spirit remained within them. They stood in solemn silence at the fringe of the eighteenth green on a now silent and still majestic Purple Mountain.

Michael and Jessica heard a faint noise from behind them. The noise was soft and sounded like the beating of wings. They were led by the Spirit to follow the sound. They walked a few paces down the path that led to the cabin and they were stopped by a majestic sight. They were looking directly at the White Oak. Underneath this tree is where Michael had stood twenty-five years earlier when he saw Jessica for the first time. Underneath this tree is where Jessica found John and where John found the heart filled pouch just before he died. The tree was dead, having been split by a lightning strike. But God, who is rich in mercy, had a plan.

They looked at the tree and counted seventeen Snowy Owls perched throughout its massive branches. Then from around the back of the tree they heard the beating of wings. As they looked at the tree, a single Snowy Owl appeared in their sight. It was flying about the tree in a counterclockwise direction. It appeared from the left side of the tree. As it flew, its wings were just a few inches from the leaves of the tree. It was flying about the lowest part of the canopy of the tree. It disappeared from view as it rounded the right side of the tree.

Then they heard a slight increase in the sound of the beating wings. The rhythm had not changed only the depth of the sound. As the Snowy Owl appeared again, in flight, from behind the tree, it was joined by another Snowy Owl. This Snowy Owl emerged from the right side of the tree and flew in a clockwise direction. Its flight path was similar to that of the first but was slightly higher up the canopy. As the two white Owls crossed the center vertical axis of the tree, Michael and Jessica heard another slight increase in the sound of the beating wings.

Then two more Snowy Owls appeared from behind the tree with one appearing from the left and the other from the right. They too flew with their wings just inches from the leaves of the tree. The sound of the beating of wings increased again and again. It continued to increase until there were seventeen Snowy Owls, in flight, circling about the tree. Their wings beating in unison as they circled the tree. The Owls were spread out evenly across the canopy of the tree when viewed from top to bottom. From a distance, it looked as if the tree had been covered by a large white spinning cone. Gabriel, the arch-owl, perched upon the apex of the tree. It looked as if he were directing them. He rotated his head two hundred and seventy degrees clockwise and then back to center. Then he rotated it in the same manner in a counterclockwise direction before turning it back to center. The seventeen Snowy Owls circled the tree for a time, times and a half time. Then they began their slow ascent.

In unison, the Snowy Owls changed their pitch. They began to fly in an upward direction while maintaining their conical formation. It looked as if Gabriel, now ascending, was lifting the spinning cone straight up and off of the tree. As the cone was lifted, a majestic transformation was revealed to them.

The leaves of the tree had become alabaster in color and glistened in the twilight. The trunk of the tree now looked as if it were a mighty column made of Yule Marble. Its intricately carved surface resembled the bark of a tree. Where the trunk of the tree had once been split, there was a now dark scar. The resurrection was complete and The Great White Oak of Purple Mountain was alive again!

Then the Snowy Owls broke formation, and flew away from The Great White Oak, who was dead but now lives. The Snowy Owls separated, with an Owl flying to each of the eighteen holes of the Majestic. They were flying the path of the Greenskeeper's walk of love. The path that Michael had walked with John earlier in the day. When they finished flying the Greenskeeper's walk of love, the Snowy Owls converged upon the flagpole pedestal. They began to circle the flagpole. After each complete rotation around the flagpole a single Snowy Owl broke formation and flew directly to the north. After eighteen rotations, the final Snow Owl headed north. They flew in a straight line and their wings all beat in unison. These mysterious birds had completed their mission and were never seen again on Purple Mountain.

As the last of them disappeared from sight, another bird soared in the northern sky. As it soared, its flight path took the shape of a continuously spinning circle approaching the mountain. It looked as if the eagle was riding on a great wheel in the sky. The eagle after a time, times and half time landed in the midst of The Great White Oak.

Michael and Jessica watched these events unfold before them and their spirits were lifted yet again. They turned and walked back down the path a few paces and stopped when they reached the center of the eighteenth green.

Chapter 68

Tiger, the great horned owl of Purple Mountain, was perched in a tree that was in the yard of Mr. Loche, the town jailor. Earlier in the evening both Tiger and Mr. Loche had been assembled with the townspeople at the zoning commission hearing. Tiger, during the meeting, was perched outside the elementary school in a large dogwood tree. Mr. Loche attended the hearing and sat on the east side bleachers of the gymnasium at the start of the hearing.

Mr. Loche went to the meeting expecting the usual uneventful governmental meeting. Although the meeting was widely talked about in the community, he expected that few, if any, people would attend. He supported the mining initiative and thought it would be good for the local economy. However, in his heart, he loved Purple Mountain and its sights, stories and most of all living within its solemn shadow.

When he arrived, at the meeting, he was surprised by the large number of people in attendance. He wasn't surprised by the seating arrangements. He thought that most were like himself. This was a time to think with your wallet and not the time to think with your heart. He and the residents of Worthington watched intently, as the meeting unfurled before them.

When he heard Red speak he thought that the meeting would come to a quick conclusion and end with the commission voting to approve the zoning change requested by Axis Energy. However, that thought was quickly put to rest as the 'Friends of Purple Mountain' began to tell their stories by reading their letters. He was particularly moved by the story told by Tootsie. He had seen the two toned green Duesenberg in town and wondered where it had come from. He listened in amazement as the parade of letters passed through his heart. Somewhere between Delaware and Hawaii, he knows not where, his heart changed and his thinking about the zoning request changed with it. Yet, there was something even deeper within him that was awakened. It happened when he witnessed the transformation of Red Garnet.

The people of Worthington knew this man. They knew his story. Red lost his family at a young age. In response, he had determined to become a rich man to fill the void within him. We all have voids that need filling and what we chose to put in them defines who we become. Red indeed became an extremely rich man and an extremely powerful man. However, he became an extremely reclusive rich and powerful man with a void in his life that couldn't be filled by earthly riches. For earthly riches can't fill the voids that exist in the hearts of man.

Mr. Loche, during the evening, was most moved when Alexander Garnet addressed the people. The rhetorical questions Alexander articulated cut him to the heart. Mr. Loche had been searching for answers to those same questions. As jailor, he knew the plight of the prisoner. During his time as jailor, he had released thousands of prisoners when their sentences had expired. He saw the joy on their faces as they once again experienced freedom. He also knew that there were prisons without bars or doors. He realized that he was tired of living in such a place as that and his heart changed. As he exited the meeting, he had a new found hope in his heart. Before going to hear the band play, he stopped by his home. While there, he opened the door to the bird cage that hung in the living room of his home. Then he opened a window and quietly exited the house through the front doorway without uttering a word.

As Mr. Loche walked from the porch of his house to the sidewalk, he saw a great horned owl land in one of his trees. He loved living in the solemn shadow of Purple Mountain with its God given sights and sounds. He stopped and looked directly at the majestic animal. The owl slowly turned his head one hundred and eighty degrees and exchanged glances with Mr. Loche. Then Mr. Loche continued on to the sidewalk and walked toward Worthington High School. It was a beautiful evening for a short walk.

Before the owl could call to his friend within the house, she came flying out of the living room window. It was Monk, the Quaker Parrot and his dear friend. She joined him in the tree.

"Tiger, it is good to see you. Can you believe it? I am free! Free as a bird I tell you! I am not sure what got into Mr. Loche but he just took the door off of my cage and opened the window. Strange things are happening in this town! I am so glad you are here. What are you doing here anyway and why do you look so sad?" she asked him.

"You-you yooooou you-you haven't heard have you?" he replied sadly.

"Heard what? I haven't been able to get away in a few days now. I planned to be out tomorrow but it seems I am out a little earlier than I thought. It is so beautiful out here. I haven't seen the sunset from outside that house since winter. I am not sure I remember what one looks like. OK. What is going on. What don't I know? Tell me," she said.

"General Anson is dead. He was killed, by a lightning strike, trying to save us and the mountain. I told him that it would end that way but he wouldn't listen to me. He was more than a general to me he was my friend. Although he wasn't the tallest tree, or the largest tree, or the most beautiful tree, he was the most gallant and faithful tree in all the world. I miss him so-so soooooo so-so much," he confided in her.

"I am so sorry Tiger," she said. Then she sat with him for a time, times and half time before she continued, "he was my friend too. He loved us and that mountain. Will you take me to see him? We need to hurry because I don't like to fly at night. I will go even if you don't! However, I would really like it if you came with me. I want to sit in his branches one last time before he is gone forever," she said.

"I have not gone back there in days. I am not sure he is still there. They may have cut him down already and carried him away– but I am willing to take you there. I am not sure what we will find but we will find it together," he said as he dropped from the branch and took to flight.

They flew directly toward Purple Mountain. Their flight path took them over Worthington High School and the cemetery at the base of Purple Mountain. As they flew, they saw an eagle soaring in the sky above Purple Mountain. Tiger and Monk landed in a tree that was near their friend Anson but not close enough to see him. They sat silently in the tree for a while. Then the eagle joined them.

"My name is Isaiah. I am the messenger of the King. I am here to tell Anson, The Great White Oak, that the King has granted his request. Why is it that you look so sad?" he asked them.

"Whaaa whaaaaaa-a-a-aarrk", Tiger shrieked in an Owl language. After composing himself he said, "Anson is dead and his request died with him. I saw it with my own eyes. When I left him, the Snowy Owls were with him. They are said to be angelic creatures and are believed to carry away the departed spirits to the North. That is why we are so sad," Tiger said to the Bald Eagle.

"The King keeps his promises! The Snowy Owls served their purpose and have indeed returned to the North. However, your friend lives and this mountain will not be moved! Go and see for yourselves!" he encouraged them.

"It can't be true! No tree comes back to life after sustaining a trunk splitting lightning strike of the type that struck Anson. You and the King that sent you must be mistaken. Although, in my heart I wish that what you said were true," she replied.

"I will go and look. I want to believe that what you say is true. Please stay here with my friend until I return," Tiger said as he flew off toward his friend.

Tiger flew the short distance to where Anson should be. When he came to place where his friend should be, he couldn't believe his eyes. He saw a Great White Oak where is friend Anson used to have his roots planted. This Oak had Alabaster leaves that glistened and a brilliant white trunk with a dark scar. Tiger was a brave owl and flew directly into the midst of The Great White Oak and landed on one of its branches. When he landed, it was difficult for him to balance. His talons would not penetrate the bark of the branch. He managed to balance himself.

"Tiger, my dear friend Tiger!" a soft and familiar voice called out.

"Hoo-hoo hoooooo hoo-hoo is calling my name?" Tiger uttered as he nearly fell off of the branch.

"I am Anson, The Great White Oak of Purple Mountain, who was once dead but now lives forever," he replied.

"General! You are alive!" Tiger replied elatedly.

"Tiger, my dear friend Tiger! I once was your general but now I am your friend. The old way of things has passed and the new has come. I have much to tell you–"

"How is this possible? You were dead!" Tiger asked. His footing was now more secure.

"There are great mysteries on this mountain, Tiger. Now, go and tell Monk what you have seen and bring her here," he said to him.

"She won't believe it! Isaiah, the messenger of the King, told us you were alive. She is with him now," Tiger replied.

"Bring her here and have her place her wing in my side and look upon my trunk with the healed scar. When she does this, then she will believe," he said.

Tiger flew straight back to his friend Monk. He told her what he had seen and heard. She didn't believe him. Her heart wanted to believe but her head knew better. She was an intellectual bird above all else and her reason could not reconcile the message her friend had delivered. So, she went with Tiger to see her old friend Anson one last time.

When she arrived where The Great White Oak stood, she was amazed. She went into the midst of the tree, to the special place Tiger had mentioned. She saw the healed scar and she placed the tip of her wing into the side of the living tree, into the place where the badge of merit had been. She fell to the ground and said, "My friend you are alive!" In that moment her heart confirmed what her intellect couldn't reconcile. She was filled with joy.

"My friends, now go and tell everyone, animal and plant alike, on the mountain that I live and that this Purple Mountain has been saved," he asked them.

Tiger and Monk flew away with joy in their hearts. They told everyone on the mountain that the mining project was dead and that Anson, The Great White Oak of Purple Mountain, is alive.

Chapter 69

The Spirit filled valley breeze carried with it a majestic song about a Majestic Purple Mountain.

Jessica and Michael walked south, from the center of the eighteenth green, toward the flagpole pedestal. It was an eighty yard walk. Each was pondering the amazing things they had witnessed over the past few hours, few weeks and the last twenty-five years. This was the spot where the Novaya Zemlya had happened twenty-five years earlier. On that day, they had witnessed a miracle as the sun rose in the west after having already set. Now, twenty-five years later they had witnessed even greater miracles.

In an outpouring of support from around this nation, people from all fifty states in the Union, converged to save this majestic Purple Mountain from being moved. This outpouring of faith had changed the man, Red Garnet, who had been determined to destroy Purple Mountain. Instead, a mountain of purple was moved off of him and Alexander Garnet was now a changed man.

After faithfully waiting twenty-five years, Jessica was rewarded. She was allowed to witness her father's completion of that unfinished round from 1987. Michael was rewarded as well, as he witnessed both Doug and Christopher complete their faithful and gallant rounds at the Majestic of Purple Mountain.

As Jessica and Michael approached the entry way to the flagpole pedestal, Michael stopped her. Michael stood in the entry way to the flagpole pedestal looking directly east. Forty-eight yards in front of him was the heart shaped stair case that led up to the patio of the clubhouse. The brilliant white Clubhouse was beautiful, in the twilight, with the peaks of Purple Mountain set behind it. Above Purple Mountain was an ever increasing field of appearing stars, as the eastern sky succumbed to the darkening night sky.

Jessica stood five feet away from the entrance to the flagpole pedestal, facing directly west, looking straight at Michael. Behind Michael, she saw the flagpole pedestal. Beyond it, she could see the darkening Mountain slope sliding down toward town. On the horizon, she saw the final glimmers of light from a sun that had already set. In the southwest sky, she saw Venus shining brightly.

"Remember when I said that, 'we are better together than apart?', I meant every word of it. Now, you are going to stand there as I walk backwards and stop just beneath the flagpole," he told her.

"Are you crazy? What are you doing?" she said with a smile.

"Yes, I am crazy! But stay there. Trust me on this, this is going to be good!" he said as he began to walk backwards. He took nine two foot steps backwards until his back was against the flagpole and he stopped.

"You have lost it, haven't you?" she said to him as his bright blue eyes shined, like the Logan Sapphire, in the twilight.

With his back touching the flagpole he said, "Now, walk to the entry way of the pedestal and stop."

"OK," she said as she took a few steps forward and stopped. She continued to look at him.

"Good!" he said, "Jessica, you have a story to tell me. We have known each other for twenty-five years but do we really know each other? Don't answer that!

You have just witnessed your father complete his journey of faith and finish his round at the Majestic. In a way, you have been stuck in the year 1987 until just a few minutes ago. Now I must walk you back to me.

Now, place your left hand on the railing to your left," he gently called to her.

She placed her left hand on the railing as he had instructed her, "Now what?" she asked him as she turned her head to the right and looked directly at him.

He continued, "Now I want you to keep your hand on the railing while you start walking," he watched as she started walking around the inside perimeter of the flagpole pedestal in a clockwise direction. "Now, I want you to tell me about your life in the days just following the announcement that your dad went M.I.A., in the summer of 1987."

While walking intermittently, "In the summer of 1987, I was told that my dad went M.I.A. I didn't believe it. So, I created a world where I could see him. When I was six or so, I used to think of him as a mighty knight who fought dragons. I talked with him about this and he played along with me. He told me he was a knight who hunted flying dragons with a flaming javelin. During that summer, I dreamed that he was in a far away kingdom. I dreamed that he fought against flying fire breathing dragons using a flaming javelin.

Then I met you! You were a pudgy little kid with crystal blue eyes. I added you in to the story because my knight needed a squire. So you became, Michael, the pudgy little squire. I invented many adventures for us," she continued to walk and he continued to look directly eastward while listening intently.

"When we started school after that summer, you had grown out of being squire pudgy and had become a junior knight. I continued to invent stories over the next several years, but eventually I put these childish stories away," she said as she stopped walking. She was now standing a few feet inside the opening of the flagpole pedestal 15 feet directly in front of Michael. She turned ninety degrees and was facing due west and looking directly at him.

He continued, "Now, take two steps toward me."

"What are we doing?" she protested firmly while taking her steps.

He continued, "Now turn to your left ninety degrees and start walking. I want you to walk a perfect circle around this flagpole keeping 12 feet between you and it at all times. OK?"

"All right," she said, as she started walking.

"Now, start with our high School days and tell me what you were feeling during those days," he encouraged her.

"It was the year 1997, our graduation year. A year when a girls dreams are supposed to come true. But not for me . . .," she paused and wept. "My dad was gone! No dad . . .," she paused and wept, "for homecoming court! No proud dad . . .," she paused and wept, "posing with me for our pre-prom pictures! I was extremely angry . . .," she paused and wept, "I was graduating high school and my dad was still M.I.A. . . .," she paused and wept, "I know that I took out my pain on you. I was mean to you. But you were there for me and you listened to me and helped me. But I was still angry . . .," she paused and wept, "no matter what I did, the anger wouldn't go away," she said as she stopped. She was standing directly between Michael and the opening of the flagpole pedestal. She was standing directly 12 feet in front of him.

"Now turn and face me and take two steps toward me," he encouraged her.

She stood there for more than a few seconds, then she pivoted ninety degrees and took two steps in his direction and smiled. She now stood nine feet directly in front of him.

"Now, turn left–,"

She interrupted him, "And walk a nine foot circle around you," as she began to walk.

"Tell me about your college days and early work career," he said.

"We both graduated Worthington High School with honors and were awarded full ride scholarships, from Axis Energy, to attend the University of Virginia. We were together and we were good. We graduated at the top of our respective classes. I was in prelaw and you were in the school of business. I thought if I could be good enough he would come," she completed one revolution at nine feet and continued to walk.

"It didn't bother me when my dad didn't come for graduation. I knew there was yet another one to come. He would surely be home by then! So I went to law school while you earned your MBA. I was disappointed when he didn't come to law school graduation. But I knew there would be other events in the future that he could still make. So, I worked hard and earned a position at Axis Energy as a staff attorney," she completed another revolution at nine feet and continued to walk.

"I worked hard at Axis and so did you. I became deputy general counsel and developed astounding legal positions. But still he didn't come. So, I decided that I would go into public service. I thought that maybe he would come for my election celebration . . . or my inauguration ceremony . . . But he didn't come . . .," she stopped talking and walking. She stood nine feet directly east of him. With tears rolling down her face she turned to face him and she took two steps toward him. Then she paused six feet in front of him. She then turned to her left and walked around him.

"Then I was depressed. I hid from you and everyone. I hid myself in my work as mayor. It worked for a while and I hid my depression well. I served others needs and that relieved some of the pain that I felt. But it didn't take it away for long," she said as she completed one revolution at six feet.

"Then the mountain top removal project was proposed. It broke my heart . . ." she said as tears continued to flow from her green eyes, "I didn't want to have to be the one to decide the fate of our majestic Purple Mountain. However, it was my duty if it came down to it. People needed work. I knew that they did. It was my legal work that helped decide a court case that seemed to give the mining companies and Axis unlimited power. This majestic Purple Mountain was falling down and it was all my fault. Just a few weeks ago, you came to my office and we talked. For the first time in years we really talked. Sure, the subject matter could have been better. Sure, our timing was bad. Was it ever good? But we talked," she said as she completed her second revolution at six feet.

"However, I wanted my dad to come back here and play that last shot . . . That last shot we couldn't take twenty-five years ago, even though we saw a miracle that day. Earlier today, in desperation and with childlike faith, I prayed for another miracle and put that old score card into my purse. Then I went to the zoning commission hearing," she said, as she completed the third revolution at six feet and stopped directly to the east of Michael. Then she turned and faced him and took two steps toward him with her eyes locked onto his soft blue eyes. She was now standing three feet directly east of Michael who was still standing with his back to the flagpole.

She paused a long pause and turned her body to the left and started walking around the flagpole in a clockwise direction, "Then we met in the field outside of the elementary school. You had changed and were so excited. You believed we could win this battle and save this majestic Purple Mountain. So, you left and told me to meet you here," she said as she made her first revolution around the flagpole and continued circling.

"Then the zoning commission hearing at the school happened. It was amazing! People came from everywhere to support this Purple Mountain and the people who love it for its majestic purposes. The beauty of the unwavering spirit of America was put on display in the elementary school. It was a beautiful sight to behold, as a people bound both old and fresh wounds. This display of faith lifted my heart to heights I thought were no longer possible. The parade of the Greenskeeper's letters inspired the citizens of Worthington, Alexander Garnet and least of all me. The response was so overwhelming, I didn't even have to cast a vote," she said as she continued to circle him from three feet out.

"The meeting ended so fast. Then Alexander flew me here in the Sikorsky. It was as if he dropped me right back where my dad and I left off twenty-five years ago. And there he was, my dad! No longer M.I.A., I knew what had happened to him after all of these years. There was no 'training accident'! My dad was killed in action in 1987 during an incursion into the Chapri Forrest of Pakistan while training Afghan freedom fighters. He gave his life to save John. He walked patriot's path and died in gallantry. Then, I was given a gift. I was allowed to see him finish that round! I witnessed his shot of faith! I know where he has gone and someday I will join him there. I was so happy!" she said as she stopped directly east of Michael.

She turned and faced him directly, "We witnessed the resurrection of the The Great White Oak of Purple Mountain.

Then, we came here to the flagpole pedestal and I have been doing circles ever since . . ." she said to him.

Michael said to her, "Close your eyes, take two steps forward and wait twenty-five seconds before you open your eyes," he proposed.

She took two steps and started counting backwards from twenty-five, "twenty-five, twenty-four, twenty-three . . . two, one," then she opened her eyes and he was gone!

Chapter 70

Immediately after the zoning commission hearing, the Minutemen assembled in the parking lot at the place where the Dodge W200 was parked. It was a time for celebration but the celebration would have to wait. Operation 'Scarlet Staircase' was now being put into motion. Assembled at the Dodge were Joshua, Caleb, Samson, Gideon, Deborah and Tootsie.

Joshua briefly addressed the Minutemen, "Ladies and gentlemen, we acted in faith, having gallantry and fidelity as our allies. Then according to the mercies of God and with the help of our friends from across this great nation, our Majestic Purple Mountain has been saved. Not only that, but together we bound wounds and consoled the families of those that have paid the supreme sacrifice for our freedoms. This will be a day that is long remembered in the history of Worthington, Virginia. I commend each of you for your efforts in securing this victory and to God be the glory.

As much as this victory is deserving of celebration, the current moment does not provide for such an opportunity. As each of you know, operation 'Scarlet Staircase' has been authorized and partially implemented. It is an honor to serve with each of you again. I pray that this operation will be as successful as our last. Please load up in the Dodge and we will discuss our plans as we drive. As I call your name, please report on the current mission status," Joshua declared. They loaded up and pulled out of the parking lot of the elementary school and on to Jericho Street.

"Samson, report," he commanded.

"Yes, Sir. Logistical planning and support update. The clubhouse patio area has been readied for the operation. Seven ceremonial flags of purple and white, bearing the crest of the Majestic of Purple Mountain, have been hung between pillars of the west front of the clubhouse. Each flag measures six feet wide by twenty-seven feet long. Ceremonial banners of purple and white cover all windows of the clubhouse from the ground level and up. Purple and white banners, each measuring ten feet in length, have been hung along the western railings of the patio. Ceremonial flags of purple and white, each bearing the crest, each measuring ten feet wide by sixteen feet long, have been hung between the pillars on the basement level of the building. These items have all been pre-positioned but they are yet to be unfurled. Each item has a radio controlled release mechanism. Upon receiving the command, we will unfurl the flags and banners.

One hundred chairs, fifty on the north side of the patio and fifty on the south side of the patio, have been assembled. The first row of chairs are set eighteen feet to the east of the western patio railing and are centered from north to south. There are ten rows of chairs with ten chairs in each row and the rows are spaced three feet apart. Each chair is covered with a solid white linen chair cover that reaches to the ground. Each chair back has a nine inch wide purple satin sash tied around it with the bow in the back position.

At the north and south ends of each row are candelabras. Each candelabra has nine stems with a rose shaped candle holder at the end of each stem. There are two concentric rows of four stems and one stem in the center. The outer most and lowest row holds purple candles. The base of the inner most row of candles is equal, in height, to the top of the candles seated in the outer most row. The inner most row holds white candles. The center stem holds a jade green candle and the base is equal, in height, to the top of the inner most row candles. Each candle is nine inches in length and six inches in width. The center candle of each candelabra stands nine feet above the patio floor when seated properly. Each candelabra is made of cast iron and is painted coal black in color. The center post of each candelabra is nine inches in diameter and resembles the old fashioned lamp posts that adorn the Worthington Town Square.

To the east of the seating area, there are two tables. One table sits on the north side and one sits on the south side. Each table is eight feet long by six feet wide and is covered with a white linen tablecloth. The table skirt is made of linen and is purple in color. A jade green ribbon, nine inches wide is draped along the front edge of the table and is connected to the table at the ends and center with green bows. The table on the south will be used for the buffet line. The table on the north will be used for a cake table.

The dinner is being provided by Thelma Mae's catering. We will be served the finest fried chicken strips in all of Virginia, cheese squares, fruit and biscuits. The cake is fashioned after the clubhouse. It is iced with white frosting and adorned with purple rosettes. Affixed to the sides of the base level of the cake are shortbread cookies with each made in the shape of a soldier. From a distance, it looks as if the soldiers are holding up the cake.

We have secured the participation of eighteen members of the Worthington Symphony Orchestra. They will perform from the southwest corner of the patio. They will perform Mendelssohn's Wedding March, Pachelbel's Cannon in D.

Major, Handel's Finale and Bach's Trumpet Voluntary and other classics into the evening.

We have secured the required materials for the 'scarlet' phase of the operation as well. I saved this comment for last. We have, literally, a ton of red rose petals! Each of our one hundred guests will be trained and is partly responsible for the dispersing operation. Each person will be provided with a purple or white basket containing twenty pounds of petals. The purple basket holders will cover the northern staircase and the white basket holders will cover the southern staircase. It takes forty pounds of petals to cover a flight of stairs! The timing of this part of the operation is critical and must be coordinated with our surveillance team.

That is the report, Sir," Samson reported.

"Excellent work Samson. Your attention to detail is duly noted. Gideon, report," he commanded.

"Yes, Sir. Surveillance report. Our surveillance team will be stationed on the roof of the clubhouse. We will operate on visual signals only sir. We will not have access to audio. We have developed signals for this operation and have communicated them to our field operative and the members of this unit. Again, timing during the 'scarlet' phase of this operation is critical. We are ready, Sir," Gideon reported.

"Fine work Gideon. Caleb, Report," Joshua commanded.

"Yes, Sir. Tactical plans have been developed and personnel have been deployed. The tactical plan has six distinct phases. During the pre-proposal phase we need to position an operative in the base of the flagpole pedestal. To do this we will use the hidden tunnel that runs between the clubhouse and the base of the pedestal. During the proposal phase, we will wait for final approval on the operation. Once acceptance of the proposal has been confirmed by Gideon's team, we will launch the post-proposal plan into action. We will have approximately five minutes to execute this phase of the operation. During this phase, we will bring our field operative to the clubhouse using the hidden tunnel and we will execute the 'scarlet' operation and flag and banner deployments. Additionally, Deborah will deploy Jadeyn during this phase. I understand that her foster parents are already on their way here to bring her to us. During the procession phase, our pre-positioned field operative will escort the subject up the path to the clubhouse. They will ascend the southern staircase and stop when they reach the top of the heart shaped staircase. There she will meet with our field operative that has just come from the flagpole pedestal. During the ceremony phase, I will officiate. Finally, during the post ceremony phase we will celebrate with them!" Caleb reported.

"Caleb, that is a tight tactical package. Deborah, report," Joshua commanded.

"Yes, Sir. Contingency planning sir has been on going. Conditions have been favorable thus far for this operation. We were prepared to commence with the operation regardless of the outcome of the zoning hearing. However, our victory there has given us momentum going into Operation 'Scarlet Staircase'. I have listened intently to the unit leader reports and I am in total agreement with their assessments. However, there is one flaw in our plan. It is a detail that we overlooked during our planning phase for this operation. Although this detail will not influence the outcome, it will make the operation a greater success, should we be able to include it," she reported.

"Deborah, thank you for your assessment. What is the detail that we missed?" Joshua asked.

"We forgot to include a wedding dress!" Deborah reported.

The Dodge Power Wagon was at the service entrance to the Majestic of Purple Mountain. As they looked up the mountain, they could see fireworks exploding. The display was coming from the east side of Purple Mountain. Joshua pulled in and headed up the mountain.

"Don't you worry now honey! I got this one covered," Tootsie chimed into the discussion, "I have been in town for a few weeks now and I notice things. I noticed how those two have looked at one another. It was obvious to me. I asked Samson about them and their history. That confirmed what I already knew in my heart about them. Then Samson told me about Operation 'Scarlet Staircase'. I asked him for the tactical and logistical plans. I came to the same conclusion honey. No dress! So, I took it upon myself to purchase one. I guessed at her dress size. After I purchased it, I gave it to Samson in a sealed box and asked him to store it at the clubhouse for me. I told him we would be needing it soon. So, have your pre-positioned operative person take it with him when he makes the switch with Michael, and Jessica will have her dress! She can change in the stairway of the flagpole pedestal and make her entrance from there," Tootsie declared.

"Tootsie, you deserve the Presidential Medal of Freedom for that!" Joshua declared as the Dodge Power Wagon rolled to a stop in front of the clubhouse. As they pulled up, they could see Michael and Jessica walking toward the flagpole pedestal from the eighteenth green. Operation 'Scarlet Staircase' was still a go.

As they piled out of the Dodge, a black helicopter appeared above the mountain top and was headed directly for them. It landed to the east of the clubhouse and a person stepped out. He was dressed in a blue suit with white pinstripes. He approached them, as the helicopter retreated to the other side of the mountain.

"I understand we are having a wedding tonight? I have known Jessica since she was in high school. I have known Michael even longer than that. I helped put her through college and law school. She even worked for me for a time. She is the closest thing to a daughter I will ever know. I would be honored to be the one to walk her down the isle and give her away at this ceremony," Alexander Garnet said.

"How did you know?" Joshua asked.

"Who doesn't know about these two? The whole town knows! Probably the only person that doesn't know at this point is—,"

"Jessica!" everyone said in unison and laughed!

"Everyone, we have an operation to conduct. Mr. Garnet, please work out the details with Caleb. Please remember to wear your dress uniforms for the ceremony. Now, good luck and godspeed!" Joshua commanded.

"Alexander, before you go may we talk for a minute?" Deborah asked.

"Of course, how may I help you?" he responded.

"There is no time now to discuss the details, however, there is a delicate and urgent political matter in Washington D.C. that you may be able to assist us with. Could we talk after the ceremony?" Deborah asked him.

"Deborah," he said as he reached for her hand, "I am sure we can have this, as you say, 'delicate and urgent political matter' distilled down, into its essential elements, before we finish our short walk over to the other side of the building. Once we do, I will place a call to my team in D.C. and we will begin working on it tonight," he stated plainly as they began to walk and talk.

"Mr. Garnet, may I call you Alexander?" she asked.

"Yes, of course. Deborah, after the events of today we are almost family!" he replied.

"Alexander, there is a bill working its way through Congress and it needs the bipartisan support of the Congressional leadership. This is what we need . . ." she continued as they walked westward. Alexander was briefed before they reached the patio and he had a plan worked out before they parted ways five minutes later. Alexander would contact his lobbyists in D.C. before the ceremony started and they would have a status report drafted and sent back to him before the end of the evening.

Alexander caught up with Caleb who was standing about ten feet away from the western edge of the patio, "Caleb, I understand that I am to receive my orders from you. Is that correct?" he asked him in a respectful tone.

"Yes and we are glad to have you working with us on this operation," Caleb said as he looked out toward the flagpole pedestal, "there is a tunnel that runs from under the clubhouse out to the flagpole pedestal. At the end of the tunnel, there is a spiral staircase. It is inside the pedestal. Access to the pedestal surface is made through a floor tile. There is an automatic lift used to lift a floor tile on the western edge of the pedestal. The lift is operated by a switch that is affixed to the staircase railing and it is located about six feet from the top of the staircase. Just flip the switch and the floor tile will raise slightly and slide away. The stairs will then lead you right up and on to the surface of the pedestal. Michael will give three sharp taps on the flagpole and that will be your signal to open the floor access panel. Remember, timing is everything on this mission. Now, I will walk you to the elevator and set you on your way. We need to see Samson about that wedding dress, on our way. Don't forget to take the dress with you!" he instructed Alexander.

"Aye, Aye, Captain! I always wanted to say that!" Alexander said with a smile and they headed toward the clubhouse.

Caleb sent Alexander on his way with the wedding dress in hand. Then he met with the other members of the team in the cantonment area. It was time for everyone to retreat to the locker rooms and change into their formal dress uniforms.

The Minutemen went into action. Gideon took up his position on the rooftop awaiting the signal. Samson and Tootsie were completing a final logistical inspection. Joshua was working to see that the arriving guests were pointed in the right direction. Caleb was working with the guests and preparing them for their participation in the 'Scarlet' deployment.

The operative, Michael, was currently standing on the flagpole pedestal with his back against the flagpole and facing east. The subject, Jessica, was standing about twelve feet in front of Michael.

Deborah, was talking with Jadeyn about her role in the operation. When she finished, Jadeyn went and stood near the railing of the porch. She wanted to watch Michael and Jessica. This allowed Deborah an opportunity to talk with the foster parents.

"Thanks for bringing her to this event," Deborah continued, "losing her parents at six years of age is terribly difficult. After losing her Mother in a training exercise in the South Pacific it must have been extremely heart wrenching to find out that her father had been killed in an automobile accident? I can't imagine. But I know someone who might understand," Deborah said to them.

"She has adjusted well and is doing better than we expected. She is a resilient young lady who, despite her circumstances, has continued on with life. Who is it that you have in mind?" the foster mom asked her.

"Jessica, the bride, lost her father when she was eight years old. He too, was declared missing in action. He has never been found. She knows what it is like to be a fatherless young lady. I understand that there are only distant relatives in this situation and that she will need a home. We just might have an opportunity here. Jadeyn has been brought here, at this moment in time, for a purpose. I am sure of that. Let's talk about this again later in the evening," she said to them.

Everyone was in their proper place. The chairs, tables, candelabras, food, rose petals, banners and flags were all readied for final deployment. The members of the symphony were seated with instruments at the ready.

All eyes were placed upon Gideon. Everyone was waiting for him to give the signal for the post proposal operations to begin. Operation 'Scarlet Staircase' was in play.

Chapter 71

Jessica stood, at the base of the flagpole, in disbelief. She couldn't believe that Michael was gone! She decided to close her eyes, count to five, take a deep breath and then reopen them. She did exactly that and he was still not there! Then she happened to look down.

"Will you marry me?" Michael proposed. He was on bended knee looking directly up and into her green eyes. Her eyes were open so wide, it was if he were looking into the Gachala Emerald. Her knight in shining armor had finally arrived! In his hand, he was holding an open ring box. The ring was made of 24 carat gold and a heart shaped diamond was suspended within its tension setting. It was colorless, flawless and more importantly, not weightless. He waited patiently for a response as did the entire operational team.

Jessica paused a long pause, "Someone once told me 'we are better together than we are apart' and 'that if I met him on this mountain twenty minutes before sunset, we would never part again'. I am beginning to believe him. With my hand, I accept the ring you offer to me. With my heart, I accept the life you offer me!" she said as she extended her left arm and hand to him. As he placed the ring on her finger, she gently touched his head with her right hand. Michael stood to his feet and embraced Jessica. He was careful to keep her looking westward until the post proposal operation was complete.

Gideon gave the signal and the post proposal plans were set into motion. The banners were unfurled by Samson at the push of a button. Caleb, put operation 'Scarlet' in motion. Purple and white buckets filled with red rose petals were spread over the heart shaped staircase. The orchestra readied for playing and Deborah led Jadeyn down the path toward the flagpole pedestal. When they reached the half way point, Jadeyn told Deborah that she would walk the rest of the way alone. Jadeyn was now standing just a few feet to the east of the pedestal entrance.

Five minutes had passed and Michael tapped three times on the flagpole.

"Jessica, I need you to trust me one last time. When I say go, I want you to turn and face the clubhouse. Whatever you do, once you turn and look do not look back this way!" Michael instructed her.

"You are quite demanding. OK. I agree to your terms," she said happily.

"Go!" he said as he let go of her. As she turned, he quietly walked to the western edge of the pedestal where the floor had opened. He quickly traded places with Alexander. Michael held out his arms and slid down the spiral staircase and headed through the tunnel to the clubhouse. He reached the elevator shaft in ten seconds. He changed into his prepositioned tuxedo as the elevator ascended. In a few seconds, he would be standing at the western edge of the patio at the top of the northern staircase. Caleb, in full military dress whites, would be standing on the patio between the staircases.

As she turned, she couldn't believe her eyes! How did he do it! Her eyes scanned the clubhouse first. The clubhouse lights illuminated the building and the peaks of Purple Mountain were visible in the twilight sky directly behind it. She saw purple and white banners and flags and draperies everywhere she looked. She heard the symphony playing. And there it was, the scarlet staircase from her visions as a child. The heart shaped staircase was transformed. It was completely and entirely covered in red. Tears filled her eyes. Then she saw her. It was a flower girl. She was smiling and the girl's bright green eyes looked like pools of jade. She looked at the clubhouse again and there he was. How did he get up there? If he is up there, then who is standing with me here? She turned and saw a familiar face.

"Jessica, it would be an honor to escort you to the clubhouse!" Alexander said to her. Alexander was wearing his blue suit with white pinstripes, a white Amosu bespoke shirt, a purple and white striped bow tie and loafers without socks.

"How . . ., what . . ., who . . ., Oh, I am so underdressed for this! Did he not think about that! What are we going to do?" she asked him, grinning.

"Jessica, if you would like, there is a wedding dress for you to wear. It is hanging and waiting for you. It is about half way down the spiral staircase. Just walk over there and you will find the opening for the stairs. Be careful as you go down. I will wait here until you return," he told her with a fatherlike smile on his face. "You know, Michael was always good at planning these types of special events for me at Axis. Maybe I won't fire him after all."

"You can't fire him, he quit! The resignation letter is in the mail." Jessica said as she headed down the spiral staircase. The wedding dress was beautiful and fit her to perfection. Jessica, reemerged and took her place at the right arm of Alexander. "It will be an honor to have you escort me!" she said to him as they began the short walk to the clubhouse. As she touched his arm, she felt the luxuriousness of his suit coat jacket. It was the finest material she had ever touched. She asked him about it and he replied, 'it is just a suit'. As they began to walk, the symphony started playing Mendelssohn's Trumpet Volley.

Leading the way on the path, was Jadeyn. As she walked, she laid down red rose petals. Set against the white stone of the path, the petals looked like drops of blood. As they approached the staircase, Jessica noticed something. It was a heart shaped engraving embedded within the wall in the alcove underneath the stairs. It was about the size of Lecture VI of *The Common Law* printed in folio. She made a note to return later and investigate, as this was not the proper time.

She and her escort, ascended the southern scarlet staircase and stopped when they reached the last step of the staircase. She was amazed with the setting. The candelabras were glowing in the darkness and every chair was filled. There were both familiar and unfamiliar faces in the crowd. To her left she saw a familiar face. It was that of Michael.

"Who gives this woman to be married?" Caleb asked.

"I give her, my name is Alexander Garnet and I am her friend," he responded as he walked Jessica the final few steps to meet Michael.

Caleb was a U.S. Navy Captain. He had been Captain of the USS Canberra, CAG-2, a Boston class ship. As Captain he was authorized to perform weddings. He was dressed in his full navy whites. His jacket was full length. The shoulder boards had one gold star and four gold bars. The five buttoned jacket was closed at the neckline. Each round button was golden in color and had an embossed image of an eagle holding, within its talons, an anchor. The perimeter of the button was adorned with thirteen miniature stars. Above the right breast pocket was a black name plate. Above the left breast pocket was a surface warfare breast insignia. It looked like a wing. Laying across the wing were two crossed swords with a shield in the center. Below the insignia, medals were pinned to his jacket.

However, there was one medal that was not pinned to the jacket. This medal was worn about the neck. A light blue ribbon stretched around his neck and the medallion hung down and covered the top most button of his jacket. There was a metal bar at the top of the medallion that bore the word 'VALOUR' and a blue ribbon with thirteen white stars was hung from it. Hanging from the ribbon was a Tiffany Cross. In the center of the medallion was the Seal of the United States. Surrounding the Seal are the words 'UNITED STATES NAVY'. The center section of the medallion has a circular shape about the size of a U.S. Silver Dollar. There are four triangular sections that extend from the center of the medallion. They are located at the twelve, three, six and nine o'clock positions on the medallion. Each contains the image of an anchor. The Tiffany Cross is the rarest of all Medals of Honor. As a Medal of Honor Recipient, Caleb, may wear his uniform at his pleasure. He is also entitled to military transport and barracks accommodations in keeping with his rank. Additionally, he has been invited to each Presidential Inauguration and Inaugural Ball since receiving the award.

Michael and Jessica were now standing before Caleb and they were facing the west. Caleb was positioned at the center of the staircase and about six feet to the east of the patio wrought iron railing. These were the railings with the heart shaped centers.

Caleb began the ceremony, "We are gathered here, as friends and before God, this evening for the wedding of these two individuals. Marriage is a sacred institution and was established by God who saw that man should not live alone. Marriage is a lifetime covenant between a man and a woman.

Michael, do you take Jessica, as your wife, in seasons of plenty and in seasons of wanting, in seasons of happiness and in seasons of sadness, in seasons of health and in seasons of sickness, loving her, willing to give your life for her, until death do you part?"

"I do," Michael responded gently, yet steadfastly.

Caleb continued, "Jessica, do you take Michael, as your husband, in seasons of plenty and in seasons of wanting, in seasons of happiness and in seasons of sadness, in seasons of health and in seasons of sickness, loving him and respecting him, until death do you part?"

"I do," Jessica softly and gently responded.

Caleb resumed, "It is traditional that these two exchange rings at this point in the ceremony–" Michael interrupted him, stepped forward and whispered to him. "Due to the unusual timing of this ceremony, the exchanging of rings will be a private matter handled at a later time.

By the power vested in me by the government of the United States of America and its Navy, I pronounce you husband and wife! You may kiss the bride!" Caleb announced.

Everyone in the crowd stood to their feet and cheered. The Worthington Symphony Orchestra members began to play Katherine Lee Bates' America the Beautiful. After their kiss, Michael and Jessica proceeded to the food table and encouraged their guests to follow. Michael and Jessica mingled with their guests, thanking them for their support, while they listened to sounds of the symphony. It was a grand setting for a wedding.

Michael and Jessica then performed the traditional cake cutting ceremony, as the familiar melody of 'Amazing Grace' was drifting in the Spirit filled air. However before they ate the first piece of cake, Michael did something unusual. He took one of the shortbread figures, lining the base of the cake, into his hands. He broke it into two pieces and gave one to Jessica while keeping the other. Then he poured two glasses of red wine, one for each of them. Then they each ate the cookie and drank a drink of the wine. Many others followed them, in this unusual yet beautiful ordinance.

As the evening progressed, the people gathered for this event shared their lives, their stories, their hopes, and their dreams with the newlywed couple. It was a truly grand evening for all that were in attendance.

During the course of the evening, Jessica and Michael spoke with Jadeyn, the flower girl. She touched their hearts. They instantly developed a deep connection with this young girl. After she left the reception, Michael and Jessica sought out her story.

Jessica, with Michael at her side, finding Deborah said, "Deborah, I understand that you arranged for Jadeyn to participate in our wedding. I want to thank you for including her. She was one of the highlights of our evening. She was most unexpected, in an evening filled with the unexpected! How did you come to know her and how did you arrange for her to be the flower girl?"

"Jessica and Michael, first I want to congratulate you on your marriage and I wish you much joy in your lives together. If two people ever belonged together, it most certainly is the two of you!

As for Jadeyn, tragedy has visited her on several occasions. She is a resilient and resolved little girl despite her circumstances. You see, she is parentless and being without close relatives she has been placed in a foster situation. Her foster parents are wonderful people and I have known them for years. But, she will eventually need a home and a family. This will not be easy. Her father was killed recently in an automobile accident. Her mother is a Navy Seal. About a year ago, during a training exercise off of coast of Nikumaroro Island in the South Pacific, she was lost and declared Missing In Action, status unknown. Until that issue is resolved, she will remain in foster care. It is our hope, that someone will take her in and raise her in a family setting. She deserves that, all children deserve that. We are praying about it and we are working on it," Deborah conveyed to them.

"A 'training exercise off of the coast of Nikumaroro Island in the South Pacific' where have I heard that before?" Jessica said with a smile. Only hours ago, she would have been devastated at hearing the word 'Nikumaroro'. She would not have shown it but the feeling would have come. However, things were different now. Things were much different now. She had grieved for her father and she knew that he was in Heaven. Now she was prepared to help others, who being like her, had experienced the loss of a parent to the unknown.

"She will live with us," Michael said,"here on this majestic Purple Mountain with its jade green golf course. She will live here. I am sure of it. Isn't Joshua a retired military lawyer or judge or something like that? I am sure he can help get us started in this process. She needs a family and a mother who can identify with her situation. Who better than Jessica because she once lived it?"

"I don't know what we will have to do, but we will do whatever it takes to make her home with us," Jessica stated.

"Exceptional! I will start working on it tonight. I am sure that this will be a long road but I am confident that the trip down this road will be a good one! I am excited about this and I am sure her foster family will agree with me. We will talk more tomorrow?" she advised.

The evening wound down, the symphony was silenced and the guests went on their way. Jessica and Michael stayed and helped with the cleanup efforts. Working together, over the course of a few hours, the facility was returned to its pre-ceremonial state. During this time, Michael and Jessica talked with each of the Minutemen. Plans for the next few days were developed. These included a course tour for the Friends of Purple Mountain, funeral plans for John and a trip to Arlington National Cemetery. The newlyweds thanked the Minutemen for their efforts in saving the mountain and for planning and executing operation 'Scarlet Staircase' with gallantry, fidelity and service.

Michael and Jessica were the last people at the clubhouse that evening. After everyone had gone, they went and stood at the top of the scarlet staircase and looked westward.

"When did you know that you loved me?" Jessica asked him.

Michael looking fifty-three degrees to his right said, "When I first saw you standing over there."

"That was twenty-five years ago. Are you sure?" she asked him.

"Absolutely. There has never been anyone that captivated me like you have. Never. I knew I would never find anyone for me that was as perfect as you. So, now that I have answered, what about you? When did you fall in love with me?" he asked.

"I would have to say it was when you were somewhere between a squire and a knight. Over the years, I hoped you would be the knight that I was looking for and I always wanted it to be you! I just knew it would be you!" she said.

"My life changed forever that summer. It changed me in ways that I am only now beginning to see and remember. I worked with John for about a month and met many killed in action soldiers, as they played in Final Foursomes. He taught me what it was to be the greenskeeper of the Majestic of Purple Mountain. Then he left and I was made acting greenskeeper. While Christopher restored that Jeep, Samson and I restored the stories of stilled and quieted spirits. Then the visions began. They came to me in dreams and I wasn't sure what to do with them. These visions flowed out of me and onto canvas, as I painted each one that summer. I found them recently. I found them in the loft of the barn. It was the night that I came to tell John that I was going to destroy his majestic mountain. He knew better. He knew this mountain wouldn't be moved. In a way, it was my heart that was moved. When I saw John and those pictures again, it was as if my stilled soul had been stirred by those quieted spirits.

Your father came here late that summer. It was during my time as acting greenskeeper. He asked me to watch over you and to tell you that he was gone. However, I couldn't do it. I couldn't tell you. I could watch over you, I promised him that, but I couldn't tell you that he was gone. It was too much for me and I left this majestic Purple Mountain and the honor of restoring the stories of stilled spirits.

Instead, when we grew-up, I went and worked for Red and Axis Mining. There, I fed the dragon and I fed it well. I was a skilled communicator and I helped make Axis successful. So successful, in fact, that I nearly destroyed all of this," he said as he pointed out to the grounds of the Majestic.

"Then I went to bring Christopher home from Iraq and I lost him. Then within a few months, I lost John. After that, I wasn't going to lose this mountain or you. I decided to have faith that things would work out. I decided, that we could, against all odds, somehow save this mountain. Most of all, I wanted us to be together. In my heart, I knew that is what I had to do.

Now, here we are. Our Purple Mountain has been saved and we are together!" he concluded.

"Isn't it amazing what a little faith can do? If, faith the size of a mustard seed can move a mountain, can such faith keep a mountain from being moved? It would appear that it did just that. It seems that a mountain of fear and doubt was moved from off of your heart. I am glad for that. Over the past few days, you have a peace about you that I have not seen in twenty-five years. I hope to always see it.

Now, about my father. I understand your reasoning but you should have told me. However, I forgive you for not telling me. I thank you for sticking by me through the years. I hope you will forgive me for the way I treated you during times in our past? I am sorry for that.

The past is behind us and our future is out there," she said as she pointed to the grounds of the Majestic of Purple Mountain. "We both have been given a gift. We have the ability to restore the stories of stilled spirits. We have the honor of doing this as a team. I am dropping out of the race for mayor. There are more important endeavors in life for me now. We will work here on this mountain together as husband and wife."

Michael and Jessica walked the short walk from the clubhouse to the cabin of the greenskeeper, their home. The time was just after midnight and a waning gibbous moon, shedding its light, was on the rise above the peaks of Purple Mountain. Neither of them had ever seen the cabin in such a setting. The cabin was lit only by the moon and the stars. It was quiet and still. It was as if the mountain was still grieving over the loss of John.

They entered the darkened interior of the cabin. Michael led her into the reserve library. He sat her in a chair at the desk and he started a small fire on the hearthstone. Soon the room was illuminated with a fire's faint glowing.

"We will have no secrets," Michael told her. He proceeded to show her everything he had found in the reserve library. He showed her the *Books of Merit*, the sketch books, the humidor with the Cuban cigars, the letter and envelope stock, the wax and seal and the fountain pen of the Greenskeeper. However, he had not uncovered all of the mysteries of the Greenskeeper.

"Michael, what is this?" Jessica asked him as she opened the bottom left hand desk drawer.

Chapter 72

Jessica sat at the desk of the Greenskeeper, in the reserve library of the cabin, listening and watching as Michael revealed the secrets contained within it. As he talked, she followed his every movement with her viridescent eyes. The room was dimly lit by the yellow and blue flames of the glowing fire. When Michael finished, she noticed that he hadn't opened one of the desk drawers. It was the drawer on the bottom left hand side of the desk. She decidedly reached for it and placed her hand on its handle.

The bottom left hand desk drawer was difficult to open. It was as if the drawer had not been opened in years. She lifted the drawer slightly, pulled gently and it opened. Her eyes grew wide as the contents of the drawer were revealed by the light of the gibbous moon streaming through the window of the dormer above. The desk area was basked within its light. She gently lifted the object with both hands and held it, suspended in the air, out in front of her eyes. By this time, Michael was kneeling beside her. His eyes grew wide also. They were both amazed with the object.

She slowly lowered the Jade box to a position just above her lap. It was about eight inches long by six inches wide by four inches deep. They looked at the carving on the lid. It was an intricately carved body of a dragon in profile view. The head of the dragon was located in the upper right section and its body stretched across the surface of the lid. The tail of the dragon curved from the left edge back toward the center of the lid and then dropped over its side. The tail then stretched around the box in a counter clockwise direction. She slowly lifted the box to eye level. There was one stone, of Sardius, set within the tail before the tail wrapped around the corner of the box. She slowly rotated the box a quarter turn in a clockwise direction. As she did, the stones radiated shards of ghostly gibbous light. On this side of the box, the tail had three equally spaced stones of Topaz, Carbuncle and Emerald. She then turned the box a quarter turn in a clockwise direction revealing another set of three stones within the tail of the dragon. These stones were of Sapphire, Jasper and Ligure. Each stone again casting off the glow of ghostly Gibbous light. She turned the box another quarter turn following the tail of the dragon. On this side were stones of Agate, Amethyst and Chrysolite. She rotated the box again, following the tail as it wrapped around the box. She was now looking at the front of the Jade box and the last two stones on the tail were of Beryl and Onyx.

She then lifted the box above her head and slowly rotated the box. As she did, they watched as shards of ghostly gibbous light danced about the walls of the reserve library. It was the final performance of the dance of the dragon's secrets. Neither of them spoke a word. The only sound in the room was the occasional crackling of the small fire on the hearthstone.

After a time, times, and half time she lowered the box and placed it in her lap. They looked at the carved image of the dragon for a time. It was a majestic image. The Jade box was familiar to each of them, as each had seen it in a dream. Then they pondered the Jade box. What mysteries were hidden within the Jade box protected by the dragon with the tail of twelve stones? What mysteries may be explained were they to disturb the dragon from its sleep? Each wondered of its origins and contents.

Michael watched as she gently grasped the lid. From his view point, the head of the dragon lined up directly with the hearthstone in the background. It looked to him as if the dragon were breathing fire.

Jessica paused a long pause and then slowly lifted the hinged lid. When opened, the lid stood at a ninety degree angle to the box below. The inside of the box was Alabaster lined. The inside of the lid contained, at its center, a carved image of a Great Oak Tree with a dark vertical scar on its trunk. Its canopy stretched from side to side filling the top half of the lid surface. One area was absent of leaves and it looked as if a branch were missing from the canopy.

The dragon had indeed been protecting secrets. For within the box, were items of the type worthy of protection. Contained within the Alabaster lined Jade box were a picture, a folded news clipping, an envelope, two medallions and two golden bands.

An aged black and white photograph, with yellowing edges, was of a family. The photograph was of a man with his arm hung over the shoulder of woman who was holding an infant. The couple appeared to be filled with joy. The news clipping was written in a foreign language and contained a picture of a damaged ancient citadel. It had a handwritten date on it of January 1968 and the word Huê. There were two medallions, one in shape of a star and the other was heart shaped. The star medallion, made of linen, had sixteen points, a green dragon ran the length from top to bottom. The medallion was surmounted by an oval center of light blue, within it was foreign writing, and it was surrounded by a thin red band. The other medallion was a Purple Heart made of metal.

In addition, there were two bands of gold with one being slightly larger than the other. Finally, there was an envelope with two names written upon it. The names written on it were Michael and Jessica.

Jessica reached into the Jade box and removed the letter. She then handed it to Michael. Both pondered its contents but they both knew the authorship. The handwriting gave it away. It was their letter from the Greenskeeper. At that moment, its contents were as mysterious as its origins. How had he known, to write to them, they wondered.

As Michael opened the envelope its wax seal crumbled and fell in pieces on to the wooden floor. He carefully lifted the letter from the envelope and unfolded it. Still kneeling at her side, he prepared to read the words that John had written to them. Then he began reading the letter.

"September 1987

Dear Michael and Jessica,

Life, like this Majestic Purple Mountain, will remain a mystery until the end of the ages. When the ages end, and they will end, the author of life will explain everything to us. For now, we see life as through a darkened glass but then we shall see it as through crystal. Until then, maintain your childlike faith. It will serve our mountain and those that depend on it well. For we know, that the author of life works all things for the good of those that love him. We also know that He has prepared, in advance, good works for those that have received the gift of grace.

In what follows, I will attempt to explain the mysteries of the life, loss and love of this one greenskeeper. Hopefully, these stories will touch your hearts and *inspire each of you to continue in the work that we have begun here.*

In 1966, I was twenty-four years old and working as a freelance writer in Vietnam. I was a war correspondent. While there I met Jade. We met during a worship service being held in an underground house church. Although the Catholic church was tolerated, Protestant denominations were not. Jade was of Vietnamese royalty and became a Christian at a young age after hearing missionaries preach the gospel. We fell in love and she disavowed her heritage to marry me, a foreigner. Her family was not pleased. However, her great-grandmother was sympathetic to our position and supported us in secrecy. She gave us the Jade box as a wedding gift. She said that we could sell it and use the proceeds to escape from the country and start a life in the States. Jade would not part with it and I would not abandon war writing. We chose to stay.

Life was difficult for us but it was filled with joy. We lived on the outskirts of Huê, in what you would consider a hut. We were happy, healthy and in love. Money was tight and stories were difficult to sell but we found ways to survive. Then we had a son. He was beautiful and we loved him with all our hearts.

In late January of 1968, on information I received from a friend, I left the village for a short time to cover a developing story. After being lured away, the Tet Offensive began. Jade and my son were in the city of Huê, celebrating the new year with great-grandmother when the attack began. They took shelter in the Citadel of Huê along the Perfume River. The Vietcong and the North Vietnamese Army, in a surprise attack, captured the Citadel at 0800 on January 31, 1968. Due to the fierceness of the battle, I was unable to reach Huê until mid-February. When I arrived, our village had been destroyed. My sources told me of the mass killings of civilians that were perpetrated by the VC and NVA. They also told me of their belief in a capture and kill list that was maintained by the VC. The VC were determined to kill members of the royal family and others. It was later determined that the VC executed over six thousand civilians during the Massacre of Huê.

I searched frantically for Jade and my son for days. There was no word on their whereabouts. Finally, a source told me to head south down the Perfume River about eighteen kilometers. There, he told me, I would find my family.

I traveled by boat, under the cover of night, until I reached the wharf of the Tomb of Gia Long. This was the ancestral burial grounds of Jade's family and it was known for its beauty. It sits at the base of a small mountain. In legends, it is guarded by fourteen blue dragons and fourteen white tigers. It was the last place where I wanted to look.

When I arrived, I ran up the staircase of the four dragons, and directly into the center courtyard. My heart will not allow me to see again what I saw in that moment. In that moment, I came to know the sting of death. I buried them there, in an unmarked tomb, among her ancestors, after a silent and solemn ceremony. Then I grieved, but not as one without hope. For we know that the author of life has an eternal plan. He has taken away the sting of death and he *will raise those, who believe in him, to eternal life on the last day.*

I returned to the village where we had lived and began the painful process of healing. I helped bury the dead in the days that followed. Her grandfather was so moved, that he awarded me the 'Order of the Dragon of Annam' for being of useful service to the Emperor. The award was first given in 1886 and had been discontinued in 1945. We never spoke of Jade or our son.

Over the course of the next few years, I helped people grieve. As a community, we slowly rebuilt homes and lives despite being in a war zone. I continued to write about the war. I quit freelance work, and joined a news service. They became disenchanted with my war reporting and called me home to the States in 1972.

Somehow this Purple Mountain found me in 1972. Despite having no experience, Caleb hired me on as greenskeeper the first day he met me. I don't know how, but he knew my story. He knew of my loss and of my response to its sting. He knew my heart. As for me, I felt a connection with this mountain instantly.

The first afternoon I was here, I walked the Greenskeeper's walk of love. I walked the entire layout of the Majestic of Purple Mountain. As I did, this mountain spoke to my weary soul. The Majestic, with its jade colored grasses and adornments, comforted me. In a mysterious way, it was as if Jade were here with me. I treated the Majestic as if it were my wife. I loved this course and cared for it. In return, it blossomed and practically maintained itself. This gift from the author of life, provided a unique opportunity for service.

On my first day as greenskeeper, Caleb told me of the Final Foursomes concept. I agreed to participate in any way I could. I saw my first Final Foursome that day and I played "Taps" at sunset for the first time. That evening, I penned the first letters from the greenskeeper and made the first entries into the Books of Merit and the sketch books. From that day, I never looked back. My calling was to help those, that had experienced the sting of death, find peace.

Since the course required little maintenance, I was given the gift of time. I used that time to do something unusual. I began to paint. I have painted each member of every Final Foursome that has ever played the Majestic of Purple Mountain. My studio, was in the loft of the barn. I painted every day of the week except on Sundays. On Sundays, I took the paintings into the Gallery of Gallantry and hung them there on display. Over the course of time, there became too may paintings to display. There are a few paintings in storage for every one painting that is displayed. The Books of Merit will serve as a guide for you to locate any painting that you may need to access. The Gallery of Gallantry is nearby. In your hearts you already know of its location. Jessica's father once told her of its location.

Recently, it was my pleasure to meet both of you. I knew that day it would be the two of you that would replace me. Jessica, with her childlike faith, called the sun to rise again in the west and it did. In the process, she made it possible for me to retain the ability to see the Final Foursomes.

Michael, you were like a son to me. Had my son lived, I pictured him as having your spirit. As I soon discovered, Michael had the gift of vision. Not only could he see the Final Foursomes, he saw visions of the past, present and future. He painted eighteen visions on canvas, over the past few months, and left them in the loft of the barn. I will store them with the other paintings and put them in the proper places at the proper times.

What I didn't know when I met the two of you, was the pain that the two of you would bear in the wake of Doug being declared Missing In Action. However, the author of life works all things to the good of those that love him. This is a hard teaching, as each of us can attest to. As Michael knows, I quit asking the 'why question' some years ago. But, we know the teaching is true. Perhaps, our pain motivates us to help those who suffer also? As we help others grieve, we too grieve with them but not as ones without hope.

By the time you read this letter, my season as greenskeeper will have passed. Your season is now beginning. Treat the Majestic with honor, as if it were your mother, and you will have many seasons. Remember, you keep greens with your hands but you are a greenskeeper with your heart.

The gold bands were our wedding rings. I am sure you will find them useful.

Lastly, if you grieve for me, grieve not as ones without hope. For we know that the author of life has prepared a place for us in Heaven. Remember, in that place there will be no more crying, nor mourning,

> *nor death. We shall meet again. I will be waiting for you under the tree of life along the banks of the crystal clear river. Until that day, keep the faith and may the author of life keep you in his grace.*
>
> *With love,*
>
> *John,*
>
> *The Greenskeeper of the Majestic of Purple Mountain"*

Michael folded the letter and placed it back in the envelope. He then lifted the gold bands and gave the larger one to Jessica. In the sight of God, they exchanged rings. Then he removed the Purple Heart medallion from the box and placed it on the desk.

Together, they placed the envelope, the picture, the news clipping and the Order of the Dragon of Annam back into the Jade box and closed it. Jessica, placed the Jade box back in the desk drawer where she had found it.

The night would be long but they knew exactly where they needed to go and what they needed to take with them. Michael gathered some of the needed items and Jessica gathered the rest of them. In silence, they left the reserve library and then went out the cabin door. They were headed to the Greenskeeper's Gallery of Gallantry.

Chapter 73

The gibbous moon, casting off its ghostly light, was perched high in the night sky as Michael and Jessica walked the short walk from their cabin to the clubhouse. The first rays of the sun were hours away, there was yet time to prepare for the day ahead. As many newlyweds do, they were operating off of adrenaline. There would be time for sleep another day.

"So, you know where we are going? I was here all that time in the summer of 1987 and I never knew there was a Gallery of Gallantry!" Michael said to her.

"You were full of surprises earlier. Now it is my turn! Follow me, I have a few surprises of my own," Jessica told him with a smile. She led him across the patio of the clubhouse and then down the stairs of the heart shaped staircase. When they reached the bottom she stopped. "Over the past twenty-five years, I have had a recurring dream. Part of it came true earlier tonight when I saw the 'scarlet staircase'. The red rose petals were beautiful! They were more beautiful than the ones in my dream. However, there was more. In my dream, my father said that I would find a door at the center of the scarlet staircase. I looked for it earlier, as I made my way from the flagpole pedestal. I didn't see a door but I did see something. Still, I don't understand," she remarked as they stood at the landing area of the staircase looking eastward back toward the clubhouse basement.

"It must be here! Let's take a closer look under the staircase," he told her as they walked under the stairs. The basement wall was recessed about ten feet behind the staircase. There was just enough ghostly light being cast off of the gibbous moon to see underneath the stairs. The wall was made of solid sandstone but had a small visible vertical crevice at the center. As they walked closer, they noticed a carving in the sandstone wall. Upon closer inspection, it was an intricately carved shape of a heart and filled a two foot square section of the wall at about eye level. At the center of the heart carving was a small heart shaped notch. It was split at the center by the crevice and was about fifty-four inches above the floor. "I thought we might need this!" he said as he pulled the Purple Heart medallion from his pocket. It was the one that he had taken from the Jade box. He held it up to the notch in the wall and it was a perfect match.

"Grab my hand," he said as they inserted the medallion into the notch. They backed up a few steps and looked at the heart within a heart. The purple medallion's center seemed to radiate a soft glow against the white sandstone. Then it began. They watched as the medallion began to turn in a clockwise direction and recess in one continuous motion. When the medallion was turned completely upside down, the spinning and recessing motion abruptly stopped. Then there was a muffled sound, it was as if a gun were fired at close range behind a solid wall. It startled them both and they backed up a few steps more. As they did, they watched in amazement as the wall began to open, splitting at the crevice.

They had not noticed that there were two sections of wall in front of them. The walls separated at the center and slowly slid away. What remained, behind the sandstone wall were two solid brass doors. Each door measured eight feet high by six feet wide. Each door had nine square panels of equal size.

The surface of each panel contained an image. On the southern door were the images of the nine holes of the southern arm of the Majestic of Purple Mountain and those of the northern arm were on the other door. It was the history of the construction of the Majestic of Purple Mountain. The door handles were made of solid brass and fashioned in the likeness of flag sticks. Each flag, at the top of the flag stick, had the crest of the Majestic of Purple Mountain engraved in it. Michael grabbed the handle of the northern door and Jessica the handle of the southern. Together, in one motion, they opened the doors of the Gallery of Gallantry. They paused a long pause, and together walked into the darkness behind the doors.

As they walked in, lights began to flicker on throughout the cavernous gallery. The gallery was much larger than the footprint of the clubhouse and patio area. The ceilings were eighteen feet high and the floors were inlaid with Minton tiles. There was a large ornate entry area with carved sandstone walls that led to an arched open doorway. They walked and stood in the archway. Then they walked in. There was a large square shaped room at the center of the gallery. Openings were at the corners of the walls as there were no doors. Along the outer sections of these walls were glass display cases. The cases were empty. Within the square shaped room was an inner chamber. Its walls were made of Yule Marble and there were twelve doorways cut into it. The Minton tiles on the floor, at the center of the inner chamber, seemed to emit light. They did not enter into the chamber, for they were not yet ready for its secrets. They decided to explore the other parts of the gallery first.

To the north and northeast there were a series of chambers and the same was true to the south and southeast and far east sections of the structure. Paintings, hung from floor to ceiling, adorned the exterior and interior walls of the chambers. These were not just any paintings. Each painting was that of a soldier. Then Jessica remembered what her father had said in her dream. It looked as if these soldiers were holding up an original copy of the capital of the United States, the building above them. In her dream, knights were holding up a white castle. These were the paintings that John spoke of in his letter. There were thousands of them. Jessica and Michael wept at the sight of the soldiers that had sacrificed their lives in defense of the land they so loved. John had painted each soldier that had graced the grounds of the Majestic and played in a Final Foursome. He poured his life into this work and did so out of love.

As they walked through the chambers, Michael remembered some of the soldiers. He had met them during the summer of 1987, while working with John. Some of the paintings included the image of the caddie that was selected by the soldier. Some paintings depicted the soldier in a battle scene and others depicted the soldier in dress uniform. Each painting was as unique as the individual it depicted.

Jessica and Michael located a vast storage area that lined the perimeter of the north, east and south most outer areas of the gallery. Paintings were stored on shelves from floor to ceiling. The shelves were labeled with dates and the paintings were alphabetized for each date. The *Books of Merit* would serve as a key to locate a stored painting.

There was precious little time to waste if they were going to accomplish their goal before sunrise. Their plan was to locate the paintings related to the soldiers that were represented by the letters that were read during the Greenskeeper's Parade of Letters. After the commission hearing, Jessica had collected the letters. Alexander brought them to the wedding ceremony and left them with her, as she had left them in the Sikorsky earlier.

Over the course of the next several hours, they located each of these paintings. After locating all of the paintings, they hung them on the outer walls of the center section of the gallery with their corresponding letters placed below them in the display cases. There were twelve paintings hung on the north and south walls and thirteen hung on the east and west walls. In all, there were fifty of these paintings. After hanging the paintings and placing the letters in the glass display cases, it was time to explore the inner chamber of the gallery.

With a humble spirit, they entered the outer part of the inner chamber through the opening at the northeast corner. They walked around the perimeter of the inner chamber in a clockwise direction. The walls faced north, south, east and west. The walls were three feet thick and helped support the building structure above. Each wall had three doorways equally spaced and sized. The doorways were nine feet in height and above each doorway were twelve gemstones of equal size and type. The stones were of the following type Sardius, Topaz, Carbuncle, Emerald, Sapphire, Jasper, Ligure, Agate, Amethyst, Chrysolite, Beryl and Onyx.

They entered the inner chamber through the center door on the east side wall. Within the inner chamber there were eighteen paintings arranged in a circular formation. Each painting stood on an easel. Located nine feet behind each easel was a carved pillar, of Yule Marble, that stretched from floor to ceiling. The pillars formed a circle having a diameter of fifty-four feet. As they walked in the doorway they stopped in front of the eastern most easel. They looked at it in amazement and moved to the next painting to the left.

The paintings on the easels were in cubist form and resembled Picasso paintings. Michael knew these works, for they were his works. These were the eighteen visions of the Acting Greenskeeper of the Majestic of Purple Mountain.

The painting they were viewing was that of a Ram in a thicket. This was the ram that stayed the hand of Abraham and was later sacrificed in place of his son. They walked to the next painting on the left. The painting was of a Red Dragon destroying a school with its mighty tail. The next painting was of Dogwoods and daisies and it made them both smile.

The next painting brought Jessica to her knees in tears. Michael wept with her as they looked at a knight with a flaming javelin. It was the image of her father that they were viewing. After a time of grieving, they moved to the next painting. The image was of two flying dragons with hammer and sickle tattoos. Again tears flowed down their faces as they pondered the meaning of the painting before them.

As they continued their viewing, the next image was of a dragon with a tail of twelve stones. Wrapped within the protection of the tail was a Jade box. The image brought tears of joy seasoned with sadness. The next image painted was that of white tigers and blue dragons protecting a Long tomb. They grieved for their friend John and his loss but not as ones without hope.

The next image painted was that of a sea serpent with a knight in his belly. The serpent was sitting at the bottom of a jade sea.

The next painting was that of a Great White Oak surrounded by angelic winged beings. They were now standing in front of the western most painting looking eastward. Beyond the painting and behind the pillar was the inner circle. As they moved past the Great White Oak painting they could see an image that was inlaid within the Minton tiles on the floor. It was the image they had seen on the inside of the Jade box earlier in the evening.

The next easel held a painting of gray, white, black and red horses. As they continued their circular path, the next painting was of thirteen stars circling the walls of Jericho. Michael smiled as he remembered the trip he and the Minutemen made to the zoning commission hearing.

A damsel in the claws of a smiling dragon was the next image to be viewed. Jessica smiled as she thought about how Red Garnet had been transformed by the Greenskeeper's Parade of Letters.

The next image painted perplexed them more than any other. Perhaps there will always be unexplained stories related to this majestic and mysterious mountain. The image was of a flying tiger perched in a tree. It was watching a winged monk whose wing was caught in a tree. It must mean something they thought.

The next painting was of knights who looked as pillars holding up a great castle. They smiled as they thought of the joy, mixed with a little sorrow, that the Greenskeeper's paintings would bring to the hearts of the people that saw them.

The next easel held a painting of black monoliths with four red roses and one white rose. As they continued to walk, the next painting was painted in 'Indium white' and looked like pillars of creation.

The next painting was that of a one toothed black dragon. The dragon had a tail made of multicolored bands, fifty-one in all. The dragon was flying over thousands of little white stones laid out in intricate patterns.

The final painting was of a white sarcophagus protected by an eternal guard.

They had completed viewing the eighteen images and were standing with their backs to the center doorway of the eastern wall of the inner chamber. They walked six feet forward and were standing three feet in front of a Yule Marble pillar. There were eighteen pillars in all. Each pillar was three feet in diameter. These pillars would become known as the 'Majestic Pillars of Faith'.

They stepped to their left and came to stand in front of the next pillar. This was the only pillar with words carved into it. Into this pillar were carved the words 'Council of God before the creation of the world'. No other markings could be found on this pillar.

The next pillar was carved with images from the six days of creation. The wedding of Adam and Eve in the garden of Eden followed on the next pillar. Following the wedding pillar was the pillar of the fall of man. Into this pillar was carved the forbidden fruit and a serpent with a smooth tongue.

Into the next pillar was carved the promise of God. This promise of God was displayed as a rainbow wrapped around the pillar from ceiling to floor.

Into the next pillar was carved the image of the birth of a promised son. The next pillar was of blood on a doorpost and followed by a pillar with an image of a mountain and two stone tablets with ten commands of God.

The next pillar was of faithful spies looking at the land of milk and honey. The next pillar was of three judges of Israel. These were a blind man, a woman and a man with a fleece.

They continued to circle the inner chamber. The next pillar contained the image of a boy, a sling and a stone, and a mighty giant.

The following pillar was of a virgin with child and of a baby in a manger. The next pillar was of a wedding feast and depicted the changing of water into wine. On the following pillar was the raising of Lazarus from the dead and depicted a savior that wept.

On the next pillar was carved an image of three crosses standing on a rocky hillside. On the pillar that followed was carved the image of an empty tomb.

They walked to the next pillar. On this pillar was carved the trumpet call of God and depicted the battle of Armageddon where the smooth tongued serpent was defeated.

The final pillar of faith depicted a new Heaven and Earth for the old had passed away. A great city falling out of Heaven and onto Earth was carved into the pillar. The city looked as if it were an alabaster box surrounded with twelve gemstones of Sardius, Topaz, Carbuncle, Emerald, Sapphire, Jasper, Ligure, Agate, Amethyst, Chrysolite, Beryl and Onyx.

Having completed their viewing of the Pillars of Faith, Michael and Jessica were again standing with their backs to the center doorway of the eastern wall of the inner chamber. They walked to their left passing nine pillars and then they stopped. When they stopped they turned and faced eastward. They then walked forward nine feet and were now standing within the circumference of the pillars of faith. On the floor beneath them was an intricately designed image contained within the Minton tiled floor. The image was of Heaven. The Tree of life filled the largest part of the heavenly depiction upon the floor surface before them. The tree stood as if on the banks of a crystal river. The mighty trunk of the tree extended eastward before them and the canopy of the Tree, whose leaves were white as snow, filled the eastern half of the floor area. The image seemed to glow as if it were giving off light. They were amazed at the sight of it.

Michael and Jessica stood in the inner chamber, admiring its beauty, for a time, times and half time. Then they slowly stepped backwards in a westward direction, until they exited through the center doorway of the western wall of the inner chamber.

Their inaugural visit to the Greenskeeper's Gallery of Gallantry was now complete. As they exited through the brass doors, the lights began to flicker out. They returned to the cabin and marveled at what they had seen. The first rays of the sun would come in a few short hours and with it a new epoch would begin at the Majestic of Purple Mountain.

Chapter 74

The date was May 8, 2012, and it was the morning after the zoning commission hearing. The townspeople of Worthington would not soon forget the events that transpired the evening before. Nor would they forget the events of the day that followed. Sometimes, unusual circumstances call for unusual responses. Miracles, like gold dust lining the streets, are rare occurrences in life. Collective recognition of the miraculous, like a gold paved street, is nearly never seen on this side of Heaven. These are only seen in dreams. However, dreams were becoming reality in Worthington it would seem.

Worthington, seemingly overnight, became a new city. There was a new sense of optimism in the hearts of the people and it was contagious. The spirit of fear that had once filled the hearts of the people was gone. People believed in miracles again and they were beginning to believe in themselves as well. Despite the poor economy, many of the local businesses closed for the day or operated with minimal staffing levels. The schools and local government offices were closed as well. In the wake of the events of the prior evening, people couldn't wait until the weekend to see the Majestic of Purple Mountain. People were headed up the mountain to see what mysteries existed there. Many had never been there before and others had not been up the mountain in years. The faith of a people had been restored and a mountain had been saved. Perhaps, the mountain and its mysteries would somehow save them.

On the mountain, the Minutemen were assembled and ready for action. Joshua addressed them, "As you know, the Majestic of Purple Mountain has been closed to play for the next two weeks. However, this does not mean that we are closed for other operations. From the looks of it, this will be a day long remembered in the annals of the Majestic of Purple Mountain. Not only are the Friends of Purple Mountain coming to visit with us but many of our townspeople are already on their way here. For many of them, this will be their first time visiting with us. For others, it will be their first visit in years. Regardless of their circumstance, each person that comes here today will see the majesty of this unique place. Our people are awakening to new possibilities and there is a spirit of optimism amongst the people that has not been seen in years. This precious mountain, and its majestic purpose, has been saved and now this mountain will help save a people.

Throughout the day, we will conduct tours of the course. I will cover holes one through four. Samson and Tootsie will cover holes five through nine. Caleb will handle holes ten through twelve and Gideon will take holes thirteen through fifteen. Finally, Deborah will lead them through the final three holes of the course. Please take time to explain the setup of the hole, the challenges it presents and flora and fauna that surround it.

News of this mountain and its mysteries has been spread far and wide in just a few short hours. We know that there are people on their way here from across the region. This will be a day long event. Also, there are a few surprises for you. First, there will be music on the patio beginning as the tours start and will run throughout the day. We will be graced with the

University Band, the Worthington High School Band, the Worthington Symphony and members of 'The Old Guard' marching band will be here as well. We are truly blessed to have someone like Mr. Hughes. He spent hours contacting people last night to arrange for this musical tribute. Please thank him when you see him.

Additionally, there will be a unique tour beginning at 1500 hours. I promise that this will be something to remember. Michael and Jessica will lead this tour. Our last course tours will end about a half hour before that tour begins. Please meet here on the patio.

Finally, there will be public viewing, of our friend John, later today in the rotunda. This viewing will begin at 1900 hours. I expect each of you to be dressed and ready to participate, as we are serving as the honor guard. Members of the Third United States Infantry, The Old Guard, are standing watch over him currently. There will be a changing of the guard ceremony at 1950 hours. Please assemble in the office area of the clubhouse at 1930 hours for a weapons inspection. Tonight we will carry the 1766 Charleville Infantry Musket with the button style ramrod. Let's make him proud.

Once again, it is an honor to serve with each of you. Let's show them the Majestic of Purple Mountain and let them experience the mystery that it is."

It is not known how many people came to the mountain that day. However, it was more than anyone could have ever dreamed. Every Friend of Purple Mountain, who had answered the call of the Minutemen and had come from within the four corners of the continental United States, Alaska and Hawaii stayed in town after the hearing. They were the first guests to arrive on the mountain that morning. They helped keep a mountain from being moved and now they would be moved by the mystery and majesty of that same mountain.

These were the first to participate in the course tour that came to be known as the Greenskeeper's Walk of Love.

Joshua began the Greenskeeper's Walk of Love on the first tee. He was dressed in Regimentals that were reminiscent of those worn by George Washington in 1789. He wore a blue coat, buff pants, black boots, and his grayish black hair was pulled back into a short pony tail. In the air, the sweet sounds of patriotic music could be heard. It was the sounds of 'The Old Guard Fife and Drum Corps'. Joshua explained the Final Foursome concept with them. He also explained the origins of the Badge of Military Merit and the Purple Heart medal.

As he led them over the first four holes, of the course, he told them of the challenges that each hole presented the golfer. He explained the fidelity that one must possess to effectively play the front nine of the Majestic. He pointed out the Carolina Cherry trees, the Dogwoods and Daisies, and the Pampas grasses with their plume like flowers. He walked them through the mysterious shade of Southern Red near the fourth tee and then showed them the Magnolias that lined the fourth hole.

Samson and Tootsie led the next leg of the Greenskeeper's Walk of Love. They led them through holes five through nine on the southern arm of the course. They showed them the rose colored blossoms of the Crab Apples of the fifth and the Yellow Jasmine vines of the sixth. They continued by leading them through the fragrant wood smells of the Juniper trees of the eighth and finished the tour of the front nine by showing them the Tea Olive shrubs that lined the ninth. Then they walked them through the mysterious shade of the Northern Red Oak that stands along the path to the tenth hole. They then handed them off to Caleb.

Caleb, wearing his complete Naval Officer's uniform, began the first leg of the tour of the northern arm of the Majestic of Purple Mountain. He explained the gallantry that is required to complete the back nine of the Majestic. As he led them, the sounds of 'Anchors Aweigh', the fight song of the United States Naval Academy, could be heard as it seemed to wash over them. He led them past the Hollies, Redbud trees and then past the Nandina Oriental shrubs that lined the twelfth hole.

Gideon took the group through the next set of holes. As he led them, the sounds of the song 'God Bless America' drifted in the air. He led them through the mysterious shade of the Water Oak that stood between the twelfth green and the thirteenth tee. He led them through the Chinese Firs, the white flowered Firethorns and the Azaleas that adorned the course like jewels in a crown.

Deborah and Jadeyn had the honor of bringing the visitors through the finishing holes. As Deborah led them, the soft strains of patriotic hymns could be heard in the air. She explained the legend of the Lincoln hole. She walked them past the Golden Bell flowers behind the sixteenth green. She doted on the White Dogwoods, with their distinctive white flowers, that lined the seventeenth fairway. Then she showed them the Camellia Flowers that were in bloom around the eighteenth tee. As they walked down the fairway of the eighteenth, she stopped them as they were about eighty-seven yards from the final green. She explained the kind of faith that is required to hit the perfect shot into the final green of the Majestic and the kind of faith that is required to view such a shot.

When they arrived at the final green, Deborah told them of the legend of the Novaya Zemlya, the second sun rise. She also told them about the tradition of playing "Taps" at sunset and the faithfulness of John, the former greenskeeper of the Majestic. She explained how he had kept that tradition during his seasons. Deborah and Jadeyn then led the group to the clubhouse.

Deborah and Jadeyn talked while on their way to meet the next group of visitors at the sixteenth tee. Jadeyn expressed to her how the trees and plants spoke to her. She told her that they had told her a secret. The secret was that her mother would be coming to the Majestic and that her mother would stay here until she could play the course. The plants told her how Jessica's father had done the same thing but that he had finished playing recently and was in Heaven now. Jadeyn did not expect to see her mother but she expected to feel her presence when she came. Deborah treasured these things in her heart and reassured Jadeyn that what she heard was true. Deborah planned on telling Jessica and Michael about this little talk they had.

The course tours continued as the townspeople of Worthington and others from throughout the region came to the mountain. The Minutemen led tours, of the Majestic of Purple Mountain, inspired the people. People were inspired by the majesty of the mountain and by its beauty. People also took notice of the beauty of the clubhouse. It was as if they had seen an early photograph of the Capitol of the United States. People were also inspired by concept of the Final Foursomes. Most believed that the Final Foursomes were an honor to those selected and many believed that John had seen them play their rounds. Some believed that the players existed only in the mind of John and that he was a man with an honorable mission. Yet a small few in number, still did not believe. An even smaller few believed him to have been insane. These small few would soon have yet another opportunity to believe. However, no one believed that the Final Foursome concept was a dishonor.

The last tours of the course finished at 1430 hours, just as expected. On the patio of the clubhouse, the Worthington Symphony was beginning to play. The time was approaching for the next tour to begin. This first tour would become known as 'The procession through the Greenskeeper's Gallery of Gallantry'.

Michael and Jessica addressed the people, who were standing in the patio area, and prepared them for the tour. Then they led the people down the heart shaped staircase. As the people descended the stairs, the symphony began playing 'America the Beautiful'. The people quietly and respectfully gathered at the bottom of the staircase. Those that had participated in the Greenskeeper's Parade of Letters were allowed by all to move to the front of the line. These would be followed by anyone that had experienced the sting of the death caused by the loss of a loved one in battle. These were followed by the remaining people in the group.

Michael and Jessica, flanked by the Minutemen, pulled open the brass doors of the Gallery of Gallantry. As the doors opened, a Spirit filled breeze flowed out of the gallery and over the people. The breeze ended as quickly as it had begun but everyone assembled felt it pass them. Some felt it as the touch of loved one, some as a cool and refreshing wind over their skin and to others it was just a common movement of the air about them. Isn't it interesting how people can experience the same breeze and feel it differently.

After the breeze past them, Michael and Jessica led the people into the Gallery of Gallantry. The Friends of Purple Mountain were the first to see what mysteries were held within the walls of the gallery. Each immediately found the painting of their loved one and the letter from the Greenskeeper that was displayed in the glass case below it. Fifty paintings, in all, lined the four walls of the center section of the gallery.

Each of these Friends experienced something profound in that moment. Their grief, like that of John, would never completely be healed on this side of Heaven. However, that did not preclude the existence of hope and healing in the midst of deep sorrow. Together they wept and together they bound their wounds. Some wounds were old and scarred over and some were fresh and yet bleeding. People were grieving together and people were experiencing healing. Those that watched recognized the majesty and mystery of the moment. Instinctively, they waited quietly for a time, times and half time, in the entry way to the gallery before solemnly entering.

Four of the Minutemen took up positions at the four corners of the center section. It was as if they were standing guard over the inner chamber of the gallery. Samson stood with Tootsie as she looked at her beloved sister. The painting was of Helen. Behind her image was an image of Amelia Earhart. Behind them, in the picture, was an inverted red 'Jenny' JN-4HT flying into the clouds. In the bottom left corner of the painting was the signature of the painter. It was signed with the name of John. Tootsie smiled and whispered something to her sister. In the glass case below the painting were the letters she brought with her to the commission hearing. These were the letters from the Greenskeeper and the Duesenberg letter with the inverted Jenny stamp. Also, the pictures were in the case as well.

As Tootsie stood looking into the display case, Jaeonna walked by. Jaeonna, was intrigued by the biplane image in the painting and she stopped. She looked at the picture in the case. It was familiar, too familiar. In the picture that featured the Duesenberg, a barn could be seen in the distant background. The barn was only partially constructed. Jaeonna, knew that barn. It was a picture of her family farm in southeastern Kansas. Jaeonna wrapped an arm around Tootsie and wept. Over the next few minutes, she told Tootsie the stories her grandfather had told her of the barnstormers that once visited their family farm in 1926. She told her how Amber, as a child, loved to run through the golden wheat fields of that farm. She then led Tootsie to the painting of Amber. The painting was of a young girl running through amber waves of grain while holding model biplanes in the hands of her extended arms. Both thought joyful thoughts of days gone by.

The people were amazed as they walked through the gallery. There were thousands of paintings adorning the walls. Each had been painted by the former greenskeeper, John. On the walls of this gallery, were the images of the soldiers that had given their lives to protect the land that they so loved. Just as with the letters, how could he have known the details about these soldiers?

Then they discovered the inner chamber. The people were reminded again of the faith of their fathers' and of the faith that founded a nation. The heritage of this faith cannot be stripped away from the founding of the nation but all to often it can be forgotten by its people. They were reminded that there are visions and that dreams do come true on this side of Heaven. Finally, they were reminded that there is hope for life everlasting.

Most came to realize the magnitude of this recent discovery. This gallery not only put on display the gallant acts of gallant soldiers but it displayed the mystery and majesty of the land that those soldiers so loved. Only twenty-four hours earlier, the people were prepared to discard this gift for the sake of a few more dollars and the security of the same. Then this mysterious mountain called out to them in ways that only the faithful were able to understand. The faithful were awakened from their sleep and they helped save this Majestic Purple Mountain. Now this Majestic Purple Mountain would help save them. The possibilities for this mysterious and majestic place were endless. The people treasured what they had found and they began to understand the heart of the Greenskeeper. They were now firsthand witnesses to the healing his faithfulness encouraged. The people began to reexamine their lives and their purposes and they were doing this with a sense of fresh faith.

The procession lasted for hours but there came a time to close the brass doors for the day. Michael and Jessica stood at the doors as the guests filed out. The Friends of Purple Mountain were some of the last to exit. Some of them took their paintings with them. However, all of them left their letters behind. As Michael and Jessica closed the doors, it was as if they saw the Shekinah Glory of God emanating from the inner chamber of the gallery.

It was now 1855 hours and the people were assembling on the patio of the clubhouse. They were gathered for the public viewing of John, the former greenskeeper of the Majestic of Purple Mountain. It was a great gathering of people. People representing each of the fifty states were on hand for this event as well as many local residents and others from around the region. People formed a line beginning at the main entry way into the clubhouse from the patio. This line stretched around the south and east ends of the building and then down the service road. Public viewing began at 1900 hours.

The body of the Greenskeeper, in a flag draped, plain wooden casket, was laying in honor at the center of the rotunda on the second floor of the clubhouse. A single red rose lay on the top of the casket. His casket was laid with the head to the east and the feet to the west. The area immediately surrounding the casket was roped off. An honor guard, from the Third United States Infantry, surrounded the casket. The guards were stationed one at the head, two on either side of the center and two on either side of the casket at the feet. They stood perfectly still about five feet from the casket facing outward. Each carried a M1903 Springfield with a bayonet.

The time came for the changing of the guard. All visitors, out of respect, became still. The Minutemen entered the rotunda from the western doorway in a single file line. Each branch of the military was represented. Each carried a 1766 Charleville Infantry Musket with the button style ramrod. They entered the roped area from the east and each relieved the service member representing their branch of service. The relieved honor guard respectfully and quietly withdrew from the casket area forming a single file line as they exited. The changing of the guard was completed and the entire process lasted about nine minutes. The Minutemen stood guard for the remainder of the public viewing time.

The public entered the rotunda area using the western entrance. The path around the casket proceeded in a clockwise direction. On the sandstone walls of the rotunda were carved notches that held paintings. There were eighteen paintings in all. Nine paintings lined the northern walls and nine lined the southern walls. Carved into the sandstone above each painting were various trees and shrubs. People noticed that the paintings and carvings were images inspired by the Majestic of Purple Mountain. Painted into the dome of the rotunda was an image of an unknown figure. The figure was surrounded by eighteen winged angels. It was as if these figures were looking directly down upon this solemn ceremony.

The last individuals to view the casket were the Friends of Purple Mountain, Tootsie, Alexander Garnet, Jessica and finally Michael. Michael and Jessica entered the area inside the ropes and laid two roses on the top of the casket. As they did, each placed their left hand on the casket and held the other hand to their heart. They stood there for a time, times and half time. Then they clasped hands and Jessica led Michael away from the casket and beyond the roped area.

The guard was changed again, in a solemn ceremony. As the Minutemen slowly and quietly marched out of the room through the western doorway they were followed by the Friends of Purple Mountain, Tootsie, Alexander Garnet, Jessica and then last of all Michael.

The Greenskeeper's procession of life had come to an end.

Chapter 75

It was the early morning hours of Tuesday, May 9, 2012. The earth needed to rotate another eighteen degrees about its axis before the sun would rise. Even at this early hour people were gathering at the cemetery in Worthington, VA. A Great Horned Owl looked on from a treetop as the gibbous moon shone brightly in the western sky. It cast off so much light, that it lit the faces of the people that had assembled for this unusual early morning burial service. Townspeople gathered for the burial of a man that most barely knew. However, they were quickly learning more about him and what they were learning touched their hearts. There were no recorded family members, of the deceased, in attendance that morning. However, the list of friends was growing.

 A long procession of vehicles descended the mountain. They were following a 1967 Dodge Power Wagon W200 Crew cab. Immediately behind the Dodge was a 1926 two tone green Duesenberg. It was driven by a lady in her nineties that acted as if and believed she was in her seventies. This vehicle was followed by a 1976 white Ferrari 512 BB with a Delaware license plate and dark tinted windows. It was followed by twelve white vehicles, one from each state, representing each of the original thirteen colonies less Delaware. Behind those were a line of vehicles plated from the remaining thirty-seven states in the Union. These were the Friends of Purple Mountain.

The cemetery is located near the western base of the mountain. It rests quietly between the town and the Majestic of Purple Mountain but is closer to town. The main road within the cemetery is on its western edge and runs in a north and south direction. From the road, the cemetery is to the east and slopes gently up the mountain.

As they came to the cemetery, the Dodge was the first vehicle to stop. It came to a stop on the east side of the main cemetery road and was facing to the north. Then in a slow progression, each vehicle in the line passed by the Dodge Power Wagon. In the bed of the power Wagon there was a flag draped plain wooden casket. The Duesenberg was the first to pass and it parked immediately in front of the Dodge. The 1976 Ferrari 512 BB, with an expired 1976 bicentennial plate, followed and parked in front of the Duesenberg. It was followed by the next twelve vehicles, each white in color, each following the parking pattern that had been established by the Duesenberg. They were followed by the remaining thirty-seven vehicles. When the vehicles were parked they formed a line of vehicles whose license plates represented each of the fifty states of the Union. The vehicles were lined up in the order in which the states had been admitted into the Union. It looked as if the line of cars, when viewed from the cab of the Duesenberg, stretched from Delaware to Hawaii. Friends had arrived, for this solemn service, from every state in the Union.

In unison, forty-eight driver side doors opened and two motorcycles were dismounted. The fifty drivers took position next to their respective vehicle and each was facing to the south. The car from Hawaii was the first to have its door closed. Then the doors closed in order of the states stretching back to Delaware. When the motorcycles were reached in the line of door closings, they deployed their kickstands. From above, it looked as if a row dominoes were falling one onto the next. Each driver stood beside his vehicle motionless and at attention.

Stephen from Hawaii was the first to move. He pivoted ninety degrees to his right and walked to the western edge of the road perpendicular to his northern facing vehicle. He pivoted ninety degrees to his left to face to the south. Then he began to walk down the road. He stopped when he became parallel with the next standing driver. Then Olivia from Alaska joined him on the road. She walked until she stood three feet to the east of Stephen and then pivoted ninety degrees to her left to face the south. Then the two of them marched in unison until they became parallel with the next driver, Amelia from Arizona. Amelia followed the same pattern that had been established by Stephen and Olivia. As they continued to march, they were joined by Hannah from New Mexico, John from Oklahoma and Charlie from Utah. They formed a line that stretched across the road and was six people wide. In unison, they marched forward and stopped three feet to the north of where Sophie from Wyoming was standing. Sophie followed the pattern established by the other drivers. When she took her position in the procession, she stood three feet in front of and between Stephen and Olivia. They marched forward, in unison, stopping three feet to the north of each driver in the line of vehicles. As they did, each person joining the procession assumed their proper place in the procession. When viewed from above, it appeared as though the stars of the flag of the United States of America were gathering for this procession. When the procession reached the Ferrari, there was no one waiting, so they advanced one car forward. When Tootsie, from Delaware, joined the procession there were nine rows of people. There were five rows of six individuals and four rows of five individuals.

The procession waited as the honor guard silently and solemnly lifted the casket from the Dodge. Then the honor guard, in one continuous motion, pivoted ninety degrees left and stepped forward out of the roadway and on to the grass. The honor guard held their position until the procession of states was behind them. In unison and without command, the members of the procession of the states marched forward until the middle most row was lined up with the honor guard and they stopped. Then in one motion and without command, they pivoted ninety degrees to the left and began marching. They followed the honor guard up a slight hill and to the grave site. The honor guard set the casket above the grave site and stood at attention.

At the grave site, people were already seated. Michael, Jessica and Alexander were seated. Tootsie joined them when she arrived. Then the Friends of Purple Mountain gathered behind them. Behind and around them the people from Worthington, who had assembled earlier, gathered.

Michael delivered a short address as the sun began to rise on the other side of the mountain, "We are gathered here in the shadow of this majestic Purple Mountain that God created. We realize that our lives are as the mist that hangs in the air around the base of this mountain. Life, like a mist on the mountain, is here one moment and gone the next. Look at the beautiful flowers that grow along the mountain side, we like they are beautiful, in our own ways, yet eventually both man and flower wither and fade away. Eventually we all die, our bodies return to the ground and our souls return to the author and giver of life.

What is the duty of man? It is to love God with all of heart, our mind, and our soul and to love others as ourselves.

How is it that we demonstrate this love? We obey the commands of God. We clothe those without clothing, we feed the hungry, we comfort the grieving and we give drink to those that thirst for it. In doing these things, we position ourselves to help others find the bread of life and living water.

May we count our days as blessing and not waste their passing. For who knows the number of his seasons on earth. Some of us have many and others few. Help us to remember, the value of life is not measured in the number of seasons lived; rather its value is measured by the sacrifice given for it. We have been bought with a price. Our redeemer, Jesus, gave his life that we might live. In advance, he has prepared good works that we might walk in them. Give us the faith to walk in them, we ask you. Give us an everlasting hope. Lastly God, we ask that you would guide us in the paths of righteousness.

Our friend has been returned to you. However, we know that death has been conquered by Jesus, the sinless lamb of God, who was raised from the dead. We know, on the last day, at the trumpet call of God, our corruptible bodies we will be raised as incorruptible. Then He will take us to the place He has prepared for us in Heaven. In Heaven there are neither tears, nor mourning, nor death for those things have passed away. Until that time, we have this great hope and we trust in the promises of the author and giver of life.

Now, our friend John belongs to the ages," before returning to his seat, he pulled a wood flute out from under his jacket. It was a long bore Native American six hole flute made of walnut. He then played "Taps", as he had twenty-five years earlier when he was the acting greenskeeper. A light morning valley breeze carried its sounds up the mountain and past the flagpole pedestal of the Majestic.

As Michael sat down, the honor guard began folding the flag that draped the casket. Everyone watched as the flag was folded. It was a contemplative time in the hearts of these Friends of Purple Mountain; Tootsie thought about life; Danny pondered eternal life; David remembered veterans; Sharon prayed to God seeking guidance; Shirley prayed for our nation; Vickie silently recited the Pledge of Allegiance; Pete heard the sounds of military fight songs; Becky recited the twenty-third Psalm; Edward thought of his mother; Gary remembered his father; Alan thought of the God of Abraham, Isaac and Jacob; Jeff thought of eternity and Denise thought about a nation whose trust was placed in God. When the honor guard finished, the flag was tightly folded in a triangular shape. When folded, it resembled the shape of a tricorne hat. The last honor guard member, to hold the flag, inserted three spent cartridges into the final fold and presented it to Michael.

Then an honor guard firing party, consisting of five Minutemen and three others, prepared for a series of three rifle volleys over the grave.

Joshua as commander issued the orders, "Ready. . ., Aim. . ., Fire!"

The infantry men discharged their weapons upon command. When they did, smoke and fire exited out from the gun barrels. The smoke hung in the air before slowly fading away.

As the firing party reloaded, Joshua waited, then he commanded, "Aim. . ., Fire!" weapons were discharged. Again Joshua waited, as the firing party reloaded, then he issued the final commanded, "Aim . . ., Fire!" and the final volley was made.

People filed past the gravesite and consoled Michael and Jessica on their loss. People offered them their deepest sympathies. Alexander was the first to pass through the line and then he quietly slipped away to an older section of the cemetery. After the people had filed by, Michael and Jessica and the Friends of Purple Mountain went to find Alexander. Michael knew exactly where he had gone.

They found him in the older section of the cemetery. The section guarded by the twisted oak trees. Alexander stood in front of the five black granite monuments. Behind him was a stack of newspapers laying on the ground. They were from the May 27, 1953, edition of the Worthington Times. The Friends of Purple Mountain filed past the stack of papers. As they did, each removed a copy from the stack, and quietly gathered behind Alexander. Alexander hadn't noticed their arrival. When he turned, he noticed the newspapers were gone. It was as though the people had carried his grief away with them. The Friends of Purple Mountain filed past him. As they did, they consoled him over his loss. They grieved with him, but not as ones without hope. The Minutemen also consoled him as did Michael and Jessica. Then they left him alone, at the grave site of his family.

As Alexander prepared to leave, he placed a single red rose at the front of each grave, except for the grave of his mother. He placed a single white rose upon her grave. He would return again soon to see the progress on the changes he had authorized to the monuments. He was adding engravings to the surfaces of the monuments. These changes were proper and long overdue. Alexander left the gravesite and headed for the front of the line of vehicles that were parked along the road.

The people of Worthington headed to their vehicles and were the first to leave the cemetery. However, a few of the faithful stayed behind and were slowly moving their vehicles. They began to form a line, parking behind the Dodge Power Wagon. A sense of anticipation floated in the air. Many planned on going to Arlington National Cemetery. An announcement about the trip had been written on the funeral cards. These cards were distributed to all that came to pay their last respects to the Greenskeeper while he was lying in repose.

The Friends of Purple Mountain headed out to their vehicles. Samson headed for the Duesenberg along with Tootsie. Joshua, Caleb, Gideon, Deborah and Jadeyn, found Alexander and walked with him toward the head of the line of vehicles. Alexander, upon completion of the ceremony, had already summoned his transportation.

The black Sikorsky S-92, came thundering down the western slope of Purple Mountain. It landed in the road about thirty-sixty feet in front of the car from Hawaii. Alexander led the Minutemen and Jadeyn toward the Sikorsky.

Michael and Jessica were the last people remaining on the hillside of the cemetery. They watched, as the people prepared for one last procession. Everyone was headed to Arlington National Cemetery. It came to be known as the Greenskeeper's procession to the Path of Patriots.

Jessica's eyes were opened, as she looked at the line of cars. She smiled saying, "Michael, there is your dragon with the multicolored tail of fifty-one bands! Do you see it?"

Michael couldn't believe his eyes! He saw his painting brought to life before them. The Sikorsky was the black dragon. The line of cars was the multicolored banded tail. The first thirty-seven cars behind the Sikorsky were of many different colors. They were arranged in sections with each section looking like a rainbow. The last thirteen cars were solid white in color and were followed by the two-tone green Duesenberg. The scene was just as he had painted it. Except for the tooth of the dragon. Where was the dragon's tooth he thought?

Michael and Jessica descended from the cemetery and headed for the Duesenberg. They joined Tootsie and Samson who were waiting on them. At the head of the procession, the Sikorsky lifted off of the ground with the thunderous sound of a thousand hoof-beats. The black dragon with the multi-colored banded tail began its journey toward the Path of Patriots.

Chapter 76

The procession from Worthington to Washington D.C. would last several hours. Alexander Garnet, using his vast network of connections, obtained approval to lead the parade by Helicopter. His Sikorsky S-92 would fly about 60 yards in front of and 80 yards above the advancing line of vehicles in the parade.

The path of the procession would loosely follow the Appalachian trail. The procession headed northeast on Route 19 and then east on Route 460. The procession then turned northeast on Blacksburg Road. This road led them through the George Washington National Forest.

Michael drove the Duesenberg, with Jessica riding shotgun. In the back seat were Tootsie and Samson. As the last vehicle in the Friends of Purple Mountain section of the procession, they had a unique view. The terrain was both hilly and winding. Michael and Jessica watched as the multicolored banded tail of the dragon waved its way through the virtuous Virginia landscape. They watched from the rear of the procession, as the Sikorsky flew past the north end of Brush Mountain. As it did, it looked as if the dragon had an exposed bottom tooth. About a minute later, the Duesenberg passed by a sign that read: Dragons Tooth two miles ahead. In the hills of Virginia, there is a rock formation on the side of a mountain that has been named the Dragons Tooth. This rock outcropping, is a triangular structure that reaches up from the mountain and toward the sky. They had found the missing tooth of Michael's dragon.

The procession continued northward. It wound its way through the Jefferson National Forest until it reached the Sam Snead Parkway and the Monongahela National Forests. It was as if Sam Snead were leading this group through God's grand golf course. When the procession reached Route 50, it banked to the right and headed due east toward Washington D.C.

Inside the Sikorsky, the occupants were wearing headsets. Joshua, Caleb, Gideon and Jadeyn were listening to music. However on a private channel, Deborah and Alexander were beginning a conversation.

"Deborah, I have just received some outstanding news. However, our arrival at ANC will be delayed about three hours," Alexander was happy to report.

"Alexander, I am excited! Please explain?" she requested.

"My team in Washington D.C. went into high gear after our discussion the other evening. Usually my personal intervention is required in matters of this magnitude. However, in this case it wasn't. It seems that there was quite a bit of pressure being brought to bear regarding this issue. My team tells me that all four former Presidents personally intervened. Each of them personally contacted the House and Senate leadership. I must say, in all my years dealing with congress, I have never witnessed something like this. Needless to say, the issue has been resolved. Congress voted to award the Medal of Honor to an 'Unknown Soldier of the post Vietnam Cold War Era'. As if that were not great news, there is more! We have been invited to the U.S. Capitol! Things are developing quickly and that is unusual for D.C.

I have been informed that the 'unknown soldier' receiving the award will be laying in state in the Capitol Rotunda later today. The Minutemen and the Friends of Purple Mountain have been selected to participate in the procession from the Capitol to Arlington National Cemetery. Before participating in the procession, we are invited to the viewing in the Capitol Rotunda being held from 5:15 PM to 6:15 PM. I must say, this has exceeded my wildest expectations!" Alexander confided.

"Amazing things have been happening lately. We have little time but we have enough time to plan our strategy. We need to get the word out to our friends down there!" she said as she motioned to the line of vehicles following the Sikorsky through the Virginia countryside.

Meanwhile, at the Capitol, preparations were being made. The Speaker of the House and the Majority leader of the Senate authorized operation 'Clean the Catafalque'. During the late 1980's, three soldiers who gave their lives battling the Soviet empire, were secretly and temporarily interred within the U.S. Capitol or on the Capitol grounds. It was hoped, that in time, their sacrifices could be made public. However, after twenty-five years it was determined that their missions and sacrifices would remain classified. It was now time for these soldiers to have a proper burial.

The Sergeants at arms of the House and Senate were informed of the plan as well as the Architect of the Capitol (AOC). Under the plan, they were directed to secretly remove the caskets, that had been secretly stored for the last twenty-five years. The oldest of the caskets was the first to be retrieved. It was to be removed from its hiding place within the Lincoln Catafalque. A second casket was to be removed from its hiding place within the Grotto at the Summerhouse. The third and final casket was to be removed from its secret hiding place within the basement of the Senate. Then, under the direction of the AOC, the caskets were to be transported to Joint Base Andrews and placed into the custody of the 89th Airlift Wing Air Mobility Command.

A selection ceremony was planned to begin at 1525 at a location on the base. A Medal of Honor recipient, from World War II, had been selected to choose one of these soldiers to represent an 'Unknown Soldier from the post Vietnam Cold War Era'. The medal of Honor recipient would signify his selection by placing a white rose on the casket of his choice. He would place a red rose on the others. The caskets, with a red rose, would be entrusted to the US Navy for proper burial. The casket with the white rose would be transported to the U.S. Capitol and placed under the authority of the AOC.

The AOC was responsible for planning the ceremony, to be held in the Rotunda, for this Unknown Soldier. The AOC also notified the United States Capitol Police of the ceremony and the events that would follow.

In cooperation with Members of the Third United States Infantry, The Old Guard, the casket would be moved from the transport vehicle and into the Rotunda of the U.S. Capitol. The Unknown Soldier would receive a burial with full military honors. An honor guard would be assigned to the casket while laying in State in the Rotunda. The Caisson Platoon was charged with moving the casket from the Capitol to ANC. An escort team, casket team, colors team, military band, firing party and a bugler were assigned to this burial. After hours burial services for this Unknown Soldier were specifically approved by the president through an executive order. These were the plans related to the burial of this Unknown Soldier.

Meanwhile, plans were changing. The Sikorsky was preauthorized to land at Reagan National Airport (DCA) but it was redirected to land at Joint Base Andrews. It broke away from the procession about an hour before the procession was due to arrive at ANC. Inside the Sikorsky, Caleb was holding three long stem roses. There were two red roses and one white rose. They would be on the ground at 1515 hours.

The procession of vehicles to the Path of Patriots was about an hour west of the Capitol when the Sikorsky broke away from the procession. When it broke away, the procession was headed east on US Route 50. As it did, the Ferrari at the end of the Friends of Purple Mountain line of vehicles made its move. It pulled into the passing lane and began to head for the front of the line. As it did, the occupant took notice of each vehicle that was in the procession.

The first vehicle that the Ferrari trotted by in the line was driven by Danny from Pennsylvania. He drove a 1963 white Harley Davidson motorcycle. The serial number of the bike was 64FL8304 and at one time it was assigned to the Dallas Police. The next vehicle was driven by David from New Jersey. It was a white 2006 Dodge Charger with a Hemi and had been a standard unmarked police issued vehicle. The 47th vehicle, in the procession, was driven by Sharon from Georgia. She drove a 2012 white Chevy Suburban. The first three vehicles, passed by the Ferrari, were of the type often seen leading dignitaries or other leaders through city streets on their way to and from events. The next vehicle in the line was a white 1964 1/2 Mustang. It was driven by Shirley from Connecticut.

Shirley was preceded in line by a white 1954 Corvette convertible registered to Vickie from Massachusetts. Next in line was Pete from Maryland driving a white 2009 Chevy Camaro. The 43rd vehicle in the procession was a 1960 Ford pickup truck. It was driven by Becky from South Carolina. Her truck was formerly used on her family farm and had been in the family since its first day in use. The next vehicle in line was a white 2012 Dodge SRT Viper GTS. The snake was handled by Edward from New Hampshire.

The 41st vehicle in the procession was a white 2008 Dodge Challenger. It was driven by Gary from Virginia. In the late 70's Gary owned a 1970 Challenger R/T but he fell on hard times and sold it. This car reminded him of the car of his youth but without the troubles that plagued his 70's car. The next car in line was driven by Alan, a judge from New York. He drove a white 1969 Pontiac GTO.

The Ferrari 512 BB continued its run to the front of the line. The next vehicle it ambled past was a white 1955 Ford Thunderbird. Jeff, from Kitty Hawk, North Carolina seemed to be flying along just fine.

A white 1957 Chevrolet Bel Air Convertible was the next vehicle in the procession. It was driven by Denise from Rhode Island. She recently had the car restored and modernized. She replaced the original engine with a Chevy 427 LS3 crate engine. Her new found 640 horses were running along like thoroughbreds at the Belmont Stakes. She loved to watch the ponies run. The 37th vehicle in the procession was driven by Rob from Vermont and it was a silver 1960 Mercury Cougar. Ahead of Rob was Kay from Kentucky. She was driving a 1969 AMC SC/Rambler-Hurst 'Scrambler'. When moving it looked light purple but when parked it was obviously painted red, white and blue. A light blue 1968 Mercury Colony Park Station Wagon was the next vehicle in the procession. Stephanie from Tennessee was at the wheel.

Allison from Ohio, in a light green 1967 Buick GS California, held the next position in the procession. Ahead of her was a silver 1967 Plymouth Belvedere Super Commando 440. It was driven by Andrew from Louisiana.

The next automobile, passed by the Ferrari, was a red 1967 Chevy Camaro Z28. Kimberlie from Indianapolis, Indiana was driving the car she once drove new off of a show room floor. The next vehicle was an orange 1969 Dodge Charger with the number '01', in black, painted on the door. It held the 31st position in the line of vehicles and was driven by Kevin from Mississippi. In front of the Dodge was a yellow 1968 AMX Javelin. It was from the 'Land of Lincoln' and was driven by Jennifer.

In the 29th position of the procession, Christy from Alabama was driving a green 1968 Chevy Chevelle. A blue 1961 Chevy Impala was the next vehicle in line. It was driven by Johnny from Maine. Thomas from the 'Show me state' held the next place in line. He drove an indigo 1970 Challenger R/T convertible that on occasion was known to give him problems. However, over the years he learned to live with the temperamental beast. A 1955 Chrysler 300, in vintage violet, was the next vehicle passed by the Ferrari. James from Arkansas could feel the rumble from the 300 horsepower engine under the hood. The next vehicle in the procession was a silver 1974 GMC Vandura 1500. Sean and his son Isaac bought the van in 1999 and restored it. Isaac had a talent for airbrush painting. An airbrushed U.S. Flag, in varying shades of gray, adorns the sides of the van. The flags fill the entire surface area of each side panels. When viewed from a distance, the vehicles in positions 37 through 25 looked like a supernumerary rainbow. The main arc of the primary rainbow was represented by the cars in positions 25 to 32 and the cars in positions 33 to 37 provided the additional colors beneath the main arc.

Driving in the next position was Elisha from Florida. He drove a violet 1981 Plymouth Reliant K. The next car was an indigo Chevy Caprice and was the 23rd vehicle in the procession. It was driven by Megan from Texas. Things seem bigger in Texas. The 1977 Chevy Caprice was a big car but not as big as it used to be. Paige from Iowa was the next driver in the procession. She drove a blue 1984 Jeep Cherokee. A green 2011 Tesla Model Sx (extended range) held the next spot in line and it was driven silently by Abbie from Wisconsin. Chloee from California drove the next vehicle in the procession. It was a yellow 1983 Chrysler minivan.

The Ferrari, on the bridle, cantered by the 19th vehicle in the procession. It was an orange 1973 Dodge D100 Club cab that was driven by Shaun from Minnesota. The Ferrari continued its cantering as it quickly passed the red 1975 AMC Pacer driven by Mya from Oregon. Next in the line of vehicles and running in 17th position was a silver 1990 Saturn S-Series sedan. It was driven by Jaeonna. She lives, in the shadow of a 12 mile section of old Route 66, on a family farm where Amelia Earhart and a Barnstormer once visited.

In the next position was a red 1950 Indian Chief Black Hawk motorcycle. It was driven by Riley from West Virginia and a graduate of The Citadel, the Military College of South Carolina. He was quite familiar with this scenic trip having ridden through this area many times. An orange 1958 Studebaker President was the next vehicle passed by the Ferrari. As it passed, the Ferrari flashed its headlamps. The Studebaker was driven by Jesy from Nevada. In the next position was a yellow 1959 Cadillac convertible driven by Gray from Nebraska. He loved the fins on the car. Eleanor from Colorado drove the next vehicle and was running in the 13th position. She drove a green 1953 Oldsmobile Rocket 88 convertible. A blue 2005 Mustang GT convertible was the vehicle in front of the Rocket 88. Raymond drove it in from the High Plains of North Dakota. The 11th vehicle in the procession was an indigo Dodge Viper RT/10 Roadster driven by Cleta from the

Black Hills of South Dakota. In front of Cleta was a violet 1990 Corvette ZR-1. It was driven by Willis from Montana 'the land of the Shining Mountains'.

The galloping Ferrari, off the bridle, was closing in on the front of the line. The next vehicle that it passed, holding the 9th position, was a silver 2010 Saturn Sky driven by Anna from Washington. The next vehicle was a violet 2009 Chevy Silverado. It was driven by Vincent from Idaho. An indigo 1999 Ford Excursion, driven by Sophie from Wyoming, was the next vehicle in the procession. It held the 7th spot in the line. The next spot in the line of vehicles was occupied by a blue 2012 Cadillac Escalade Hybrid. It was driven by Charlie from Utah. He was preceded in line by a green 2012 Ford F-150 EcoBoost, holding the 5th position, driven by John from Oklahoma.

Hannah from New Mexico held the next position in the procession. She drove a yellow 2008 GMC Denali. She picked a Denali because of her love for the mountains. Hannah has been a supporter of renaming Mt. McKinley to Mt. Denali but the effort has continued to fall short in congress. Amelia from Arizona held the 3rd position in line. She used her orange 2003 Dodge 1500 SRT-10 to haul her mobile veterinary trailer. She travels her state making 'barn calls' and healing horses along the way. The 2nd car in the procession had made the longest land trek to arrive in Virginia. Olivia drove her red 2011 Chevy Avalanche from the state of Alaska to Virginia. The trip was about 4,500 miles and required seven straight days of driving, one way. She spent nearly $1,000 in fuel, another $700 in lodging and believed the trip to be worth every penny!

Leading the procession was Stephen from Hawaii. He drove a silver 2013 Lincoln MKX crossover SUV with Hawaii license plates. Due an upcoming job change, he recently had his car shipped to the continental U.S. He had driven it, into Worthington, to participate in the Greenskeeper's Parade of letters.

The Ferrari, having trotted, ambled, cantered and galloped by the procession of vehicles, became the leading horse in the Greenskeeper's procession to the Path of Patriots. The Ferrari was leading the procession into Arlington, Virginia on Arlington Boulevard (US Route 50). It was now 1510 hours and they were due to arrive at ANC at 1600 hours.

When the Sikorsky landed at Joint Base Andrews it was 1515 hours. The occupants quickly exited the Sikorsky. After they were out, it lifted off and began its flight back to Purple Mountain. Jadeyn's hair blew wildly as they stood within the rotor wash. Then they were led to awaiting late model black SUV's. They were taken directly to a large hangar operated by the 89th Airlift Wing Air Mobility Command. The SUV's stopped outside of the hangar and the occupants were escorted to the partially opened hangar door. Inside the hangar sat two Boeing VC-25A aircraft. Each had the words 'UNITED STATES OF AMERICA' written across the fuselage and were painted white and blue with a gold stripe running around the fuselage of the plane. These aircraft, when carrying the president of the United States, are known as Air Force One.

Between the two aircraft lay three flag draped caskets. They seemed small when compared to the VC-25A aircraft. However, they seemed large when viewed in the context of what the aircraft represented. Each of these caskets held the remains of an 'Unknown Soldier of the post Vietnam Cold War Era'. An Honor guard accompanied each of the caskets. Inside the hangar all things were perfectly still. It was as if there were an attitude of silence and respect.

The Minutemen, Jadeyn and Alexander were escorted into the building and taken to the place where the caskets were laying. The Minutemen were all in dress uniform and were prepared for the occasion. The group stood in a line and were facing the flag draped caskets that were about eighteen feet in front of them.

In silent solemnity, Caleb unwrapped the roses he had been carrying. He handed the wrappings to Jadeyn. Caleb walked about eight paces forward and he proceeded to select an 'Unknown Soldier'. He placed a white rose upon the middle casket in the group. Then he placed a red rose on the casket to the right and then a red rose on the remaining casket. He then returned to his friends and resumed his position in line.

They watched as the caskets with the red roses were loaded, by a casket team, into one of the VC-25A's. The casket with the white rose was loaded, by a casket team, into a black late model SUV. This portion of the ceremony was complete. As the engines of the VC-25A began to start, the group was led out of the hangar and into awaiting late model black SUV's. As they were driven away, the hangar doors began to open. The VC-25A was headed immediately to Edwards AFB. Within eighteen hours, the soldiers would have a proper burial at sea ceremony. The ceremony would take place upon the deck of the USS Ronald Reagan (CVN-76) deployed in the South Pacific. Their remains, as their brothers manned the rails, would be given to the depths of the sea.

It was 1555 hours when the three black SUV's left the grounds of Joint Base Andrews and headed for the Capitol. Two SUV's carried the living and one carried the dead and all carried modern day heroes. The vehicles were being escorted by members of the US Capitol Police. They were scheduled to arrive at the U.S. Capitol at 1630 hours.

The Greenskeeper's procession to the Path of Patriots continued its drive along Arlington Boulevard. It was being led by a white 1976 Ferrari 512 BB with a rear Delaware license plate that read 'NELSON'. The front license plate contained the Seal of the President of the United States. Arlington Boulevard wraps around the north side of Arlington National Cemetery and connects into Jefferson Davis Highway near the northeast side of ANC. The Ferrari led the procession to the entrance of ANC at Memorial Drive and entered the visitors parking area. It was 1600 hours. After all the vehicles had entered, the Ferrari left the parking area and trotted eastward on Memorial Drive and turned southward on the George Washington Memorial Parkway. As it vanished from sight, it appeared to be galloping toward Mt. Vernon. The 1976 Ferrari 512 BB was never seen again.

Michael led the group to the Arlington Metro subway station. The group included the Friends of Purple Mountain and about two hundred residents of Worthington that made the trip. It would be about a twenty minute ride to the South Capitol station on the blue line. With any luck, they would arrive at the east steps of the US Capitol before 1700 hours.

A U.S. Capitol Police escort led three late model black SUV's down Constitution Avenue. The motorcade came to a stop at the steps of West Front of the U.S. Capitol. It was 1630 hours. The Minutemen, Jadeyn and Alexander stood silently near the steps and watched as a casket team carried an Unknown Soldier up the northern steps and into the Capitol. As the casket team ascended the stairs the flag on the Capitol descended to half mast.

The group walked about half way up the northern stairs and stopped. Then, as a group, they stood on the steps silently looking to the west. They could see the Washington Monument, the Lincoln Memorial, and across the Potomac, on a hillside, they could see Arlington National Cemetery. The group descended the stairs and began their walk around the building. Everyone was to meet, at the base of the steps, on the East Front of the Capitol, at 1700 hours.

Chapter 77

It was a beautiful spring day in Washington D.C., the Capitol of the United States. In the blue sky above, there were widely scattered low hanging Alabaster white cumulus clouds. The temperature was 70 degrees and a gentle Northerly breeze continuously moved the leaves of the Magnolia trees that lined the U.S. Capitol. It was 1700 hours.

A group that included Michael, Jessica, Samson, Tootsie, the Friends of Purple Mountain, and various residents of Worthington and another group that included Joshua, Caleb, Gideon, Deborah, Alexander and Jadeyn converged on the steps of the East Front of the U.S. Capitol. These knew not exactly what was about to transpire but they knew that they would face it together. Everyone noticed the position of the flag. It was positioned at half mast.

It was 1715 hours as the group began to ascend the stairs. Various residents of Worthington were followed by the Friends of Purple Mountain, Alexander, then the Minutemen and Tootsie, Jadeyn, Michael and lastly Jessica. At the top of the stairs they came to the Columbus Doors. These bronze doors stand nearly 17 feet high and weigh 20,000 lb. On the doors, there are eight panels that depict the life of Christopher Columbus. As the group approached, the doors slowly opened revealing the Rotunda area within.

The group quietly entered the Rotunda area through the eastern entryway. As they entered, they noticed a flag draped casket at the center of the Rotunda. The casket was resting upon the Lincoln Catafalque. Surrounding the casket was an honor guard. The honor guard stood within a velvet roped area that formed a circle with a diameter of eighteen feet. The group filed into the room and, in a clockwise motion, walked around the perimeter of the Rotunda. They did this until everyone had entered the room. When everyone had entered, the group formed a complete circle within the perimeter of the Rotunda. Jessica was the last to enter the Rotunda and stood next to Michael and Jadeyn at the eastern entryway. Jessica noticed the Reagan and Lincoln statues. She also noticed the Apotheosis of Washington. It was as if President Washington, surrounded by thirteen angels, was looking down on them from above. Her three most favorite Presidents and those of her father, were attending in spirit, she thought.

Then a figure entered the Rotunda from the western entryway. It was the president of the United States. He approached the roped area and stopped about thirty-six feet in front of it. He then read the following proclamation:

> "As President of the United States, in the name of Congress, I take pride in presenting the Medal of Honor, posthumously, to an Unknown Soldier of the post Vietnam Cold War Era, for conspicuous gallantry and intrepidity at the risk of his life above and beyond the call of duty. Be it enacted by the Senate and the House of Representatives of the United States of America assembled, that the President may award, and present in the name of Congress, the Medal of Honor to the unknown American who lost his life while serving during the post Vietnam Cold War Era, as a member of the Armed Forces of the United

> States of America and who has been selected to lie buried in a grave marked as Unknown Soldier, in the National Cemetery at Arlington, Virginia, as authorized by Section 9 of the national Cemeteries Act of 1973 (Public Law 92-43), Ninety-third Congress.
>
> Additionally, this Medal of Honor, is to be held in trust at the Gallery of Gallantry museum located on Purple Mountain in Worthington, Virginia.
>
> May God have mercy on the soul of this unknown soldier and may God bless America."

Upon finishing his statement, the president paid his last respects to the soldier. On his way out of the rotunda, he presented Jessica with the Medal of Honor and left the Rotunda. As mayor of Worthington, she was responsible for its safekeeping until it could be placed in the Gallery of Gallantry.

Various members of congress entered the Rotunda. House members entered from the south entryway and Senators from the north. Each paid their last respects to the soldier. During this period of time the U.S. Capitol Rotunda was open to the public. Although no public announcement of the event was made, people still came. These also respectfully filed past the casket of the Unknown Soldier.

The residents of Worthington were the next group to pay their final respects. As they left the rotunda each passed by the Minutemen and shook their hands. When they came to Jessica, each gently embraced her. The Friends of Purple Mountain were next to pay their respects to the Unknown Soldier. They filed by the casket in the same order as they had entered the zoning commission hearing. Tootsie was the first in line and Stephen was the last. As they exited the Rotunda each embraced Jessica.

The Minutemen and Alexander Garnet were the next group to pay their respects to the Unknown Soldier. As they left the room, each stopped and embraced Jessica and consoled her. Although unable to articulate it, each was aware that Doug would never return home. Deborah and Joshua were especially moved by the moment. Did Caleb select Doug as the Unknown Soldier, they wondered? They would never know and neither would anyone else. The identity of this soldier would be known only to God.

Michael, Jessica and Jadeyn were the last individuals to pay their respects to the Unknown Soldier. They were allowed entry into the roped area and stood by the casket for a time, times and half time. Jadeyn, placed a single red rose on the casket before the group left the flag draped casket. They exited the Rotunda through the western entryway and descended the southern stairs of the West Front of the Capitol. As they exited, the Columbus doors on the East Front of the Capitol were closed and the honor guard gave way to the casket team. The casket team carried the flag draped casket out of the Rotunda and descended the southern stairs of the West Front of the Capitol. They placed the casket on the caisson. The procession of the Unknown Soldier was set to begin and the time was 1830 hours.

The procession route would take them west down Independence Avenue, SW passing both the Washington Monument and the Lincoln Memorial with its Yule Marble glistening in the light of the late afternoon sun. Then it would cross the Potomac River on the Arlington Memorial Bridge and head straight into Arlington National Cemetery on Memorial Drive. At the end of Memorial Drive the procession would turn right onto Schley Drive. Then they would follow it turning on Sherman Drive and finally come to a stop in front of the Old Amphitheater. The procession of the 'Unknown Soldier of the post Vietnam Cold War Era' would be a four mile journey. Although the walk would last about an hour, to some it would seem as if it were only minutes long. However for some, this walk would seem to last for hours. Isn't it interesting, how people on the same walk experience the passage of time differently.

The procession route was secured by elements of the U.S. Capitol Police. Leading the procession was an eight man Color Guard unit from 'The Old Guard'. From left to right it consisted of an infantryman, a U.S. flag bearer, a U.S. Army flag bearer, a U.S. Marine flag bearer, a U.S. Navy flag bearer, a U.S. Air Force flag bearer and a U.S. Coast Guard flag bearer followed by another infantryman. Each infantryman carried a M1903 Springfield rifle held to their outside shoulder.

Marching behind them were two hundred residents from Worthington, Virginia. They were organized into twenty rows of ten people each. They were followed by the Friends of Purple Mountain. They were joined by Alexander, who had been made an honorary member of their group. They were organized into nine rows. There were five rows of six persons and four rows of five persons. They were followed by the Minutemen who were in dress military uniform and marched in unison side by side. They were followed by Tootsie and Jadeyn. The last civilians in the procession were Michael and Jessica.

Following these were the various other elements of the 3rd Infantry Division, The Old Guard. The Fife and Drum Corps were the first of these. There were thirteen members in all. One drum major carrying an espontoon and wearing a light-infantry cap. One bass drummer, three snare drummers, four each of ten hole fifes and single-valve bugles. Each member wore a black tricorn hat with white trim. Their red coats were lined in blue with lapels, collars and cuffs of blue.

The buttons, on each side of the lapel, numbered thirteen and were of the same size and color as a U.S. Silver Half Dollar. The waist coat was buff white as were the breeches. The corps wore leather shoes with socks pulled to the knee. These uniforms were reminiscent of the ones worn by musicians of the Continental Army in 1781. The Fife and Drum Corps were reestablished in 1960. Since that time, their music has elicited patriotic feelings from many a person who believed they had none left within them. During the course of the procession, they played a total of six patriotic hymns.

They were followed by fifty members of the United States Army Band 'Pershing's Own'. The Army Band marched in silence until they reached the gates of ANC. Once inside, they performed three selections before the procession reached the Old Amphitheater. These were Amazing Grace, The Battle Hymn of the Republic, and God Bless America. Following the band was an escort platoon consisting of eight soldiers and a platoon commander. Each soldier carried, on his right shoulder, an M1903 Springfield with a bayonet.

The caisson platoon followed the band. The caisson platoon consisted of the Lipizzans 'White Horse Team'. These Lipizzans are direct descendants of those rescued by the United States Second Cavalry on April 28, 1945 during "Operation Cowboy" in Hostau, Czechoslovakia. A team of six white horses, each saddled, pulled the black 1918 caisson. The first pair of horses are known as the lead team. They are followed by a pair of horses known as the swing team. The last two horses are known as the wheel team. The three horses on the left side of the caisson have riders and the ones on the right are riderless. The platoon leader rides a matching Lipizzan. He maintains a position to the immediate left of the rider of the lead team. The casket team walks beside the caisson with four soldiers on either side. The casket rides on the flat surface of the caisson with the union of the flag facing the rear. When the Fife and Drums are silent, the clip-clop of hooves can be heard throughout the procession. Directly following the Caisson was a riderless caparisoned Lipizzan horse led by a soldier. There were boots in the stirrups facing in a backwards position.

The riderless horse was followed by a firing party of eight. There were seven infantry men with M1903 Springfield rifles resting on their right shoulders. They were led by a commander.

When the procession reached the Old Amphitheater, the caisson platoon stopped. Everyone watched as the casket team, hand over hand, lifted the casket of the Unknown Soldier from the old wooden deck of the caisson. In unison and in one motion, they turned ninety degrees and marched toward the Old Amphitheater. They carried the casket up the stairs and gently rested it upon the marble dais near the front edge of the stage. Inscribed in the marble were the words 'E Pluribus Unum', the words that appear on our National Seal, and the words that serve as our de facto national motto, 'Out of many, one'. The stage faces slightly southeast and one can see the Pentagon, slightly to the left, when looking out in the distance.

The Old Amphitheater has a quaint feeling about it. It sits in an area that was once a garden tended by a great General. It is a semicircular structure with a small rectangular stage area connecting the two ends. The stage area has columns made of marble and the semicircular structure has columns made of brick. The bricks have been painted white. The white wooden arbor roof of the structure was overgrown with vines. The green leaves on the vines provide shade for both the stage area and the brick pathway that lines the floor of semicircle. Flowers lined either side of the pathway. The center area of the Amphitheater is slightly sunken and its grass covered surface was jade green in color.

The people gathered in the grassy area of the Amphitheater. Circling them were members of the Army Band. They were standing on the brick pathway underneath the vine covered arbor roof. As the Army Band played the 'Star Spangled Banner' the people placed their hands over their hearts and military members saluted. Then the Army Band played 'America the Beautiful' and there was not a dry eye left in the Old Amphitheater. Then the music stopped.

From the stage, Jessica addressed the people, "E Pluribus Unum, it is an action and not just a phrase. It means, many uniting into one. I ask each of you . . . Is this not what we are–? Is this not what we have been–? Is this not what we hope to become–?

We have been given the privilege of honoring this Unknown Soldier. What better way to honor him than to honor the cause for which he sacrificed his life? He gave his life defending our freedoms. He dedicated his life to preserving the rights so eloquently written and defended by our founding fathers. He gave his life defending our unalienable right to life, liberty and the pursuit of happiness. We have been endowed with these rights by a loving and all powerful God. However, maintaining our right to freely exercise these rights requires our commitment to eternal vigilance. What does eternal vigilance look like, you may ask?

>It looks like the mast of the Maine,
>>like nurse in white,
>It looks like an eternal flame,
>>like a Challenger in flight.

>It looks like the barracks of Lebanon,

      like the Serpens lost,
It looks like the forest of Argonne,
      like the Canadian Cross.

It looks like a Confederate battle,
      like a Civil War wound,
It looks like an empty saddle,
      like an Unknown's Tomb.

    It is said, that in Heaven the streets are paved with gold. However on this side of Heaven, the Path of Patriots is paved with eternal vigilance.

    Over the past few days we who were many became as one. We came together and shared the stories of our loved ones who have walked Patriot's Path. We grieved together and we bound our wounds. Some wounds were old and scarred over and others were fresh and yet bleeding.

    Yet, there is another group with whom we need to become one. It is the group whose Patriots have traveled the same path as ours but whose bodies have been given to the ages never to be returned. To these, may this Unknown Soldier become as their loved one who has walked Patriot's Path.

    Spread throughout these hallowed grounds are individual graves whose tombstones are marked as Unknown Soldier. In a few moments, this Unknown Soldier will be taken by his brothers and placed in such a tomb as these. In time, when the ground settles, his tomb will be indistinguishable from the others. His final resting place, although here, will remain a mystery to us until the end of this age. His identity, like the others, will be known only to God. But, when we return here and find a tomb such as this, may we endeavor to remember that Unknown Soldier as a member of our family.

Not far from here, is the Tomb Of the Unknowns. It is the official embodiment of this idea. It has been guarded day and night since the 1930's and visited by millions of mourners over the years. There is a wreath laying ceremony planned for this evening at sunset. I respectfully ask that each of you join with me, in that place, as we pay our respects to those interred there.

We will grieve for these soldiers. But we will grieve not as those without hope. For we trust in the promises of God, the creator and author of life. We know that He has promised eternal life to those who believe in His Son. On the last day, at the trumpet call of God, the dead in Him will be raised incorruptible. In an instant we will all be changed as well. Then we shall meet Him in the air and He will take us to that Alabaster City in the sky. In that place there is no more death, nor mourning, nor tears for the old order of things will have passed away.

Now we entrust this Unknown Soldier to his brothers who will give him to the ages," Jessica concluded. She touched the flag draped casket one last time and left the podium.

The casket team carried the Unknown Soldier to the caisson and slowly loaded it onto the wooden deck. Then his brothers led him down a beautiful tree lined path. It was the Path of Patriots unknown. They proceeded down Meigs Drive and made a left turn on to McPherson Drive. The caisson came to a stop after passing the gravestone numbered 13-8138.

The crowd silently and respectfully departed from the Old Amphitheater. Many headed directly to the Tomb of the Unknowns. However, a few headed in other directions.

Alexander Garnet headed off a short distance to the west. He went to Section One just off of Meigs Drive. He located the tomb of Abner Doubleday and a few paces from it was the tomb of his uncle Charles. Alexander kneeled beside the headstone. As he did, he reached into his shirt and took off the Garnet stone necklace that he was wearing. He pressed it to his lips and then placed it on top of the headstone. After a time, times and half time he stood to his feet and silently made his way toward the Tomb of the Unknowns.

Tootsie also had a stop to make in Section One. She knew the location, for she returned to it annually. She went to the tomb of her Grandfather. His rough cut granite headstone looked like a medium sized boulder that was cut in half. It was four feet wide and three feet deep at the base. It stood seven feet tall and had rounded top. One side was smooth and flat and the other surfaces were rough cut. A nook was carved into one side and a bronze bust filled the space. She thought it remarkable that it looked so much like him. She remembered, as a child, seeing his beard blowing in the wind as he flew about in the Jenny. When she walked to the other side of the headstone she found something interesting. Laying on the ground was a rolled up tobacco leaf. She picked it up and smelled an unusual, yet familiar smell. As she unrolled the leaf, she found three unwrapped peppermint sticks. She loved the smell of peppermint.

She then walked a short distance down McPherson Drive and into Section Twenty-one, the Nurses section. In an alcove of trees, on the side of a hill, stands a granite statue of a Nurse. She loved to visit it because it resembled her sister Helen. Helen never returned home from the war. Tootsie smiled at the statue and started her walk to the Tomb of the Unknowns.

It was nearly sunset and everyone assembled, in silence and respect, on the eastern steps of the Memorial Amphitheater. On the plaza in front of them was the Tomb of the Unknowns. A white sarcophagus made of Yule Marble sits on top of the tomb of the Unknown from World War I. It has four levels consisting of a sub-base, base, dye and a cap. From where they stood, it looked about twelve feet long, six feet wide and ten feet tall. Its neoclassical design and carvings were completed by the Piccirilli Brothers in 1931. The western facing panel has an inscription that reads: 'HERE RESTS IN HONORED GLORY AN AMERICAN SOLDIER KNOWN BUT TO GOD'. On the Northern and southern panels are carvings of three wreaths each. These six wreaths represent the six major campaigns of World War I. On the eastern facing panel is a carving of three Greek figures representing Peace, Victory and Valor. In front of the sarcophagus, on the west side, and laid into the plaza floor were three white marble slabs. Below the slabs are the Unknowns of World War II, Korea and Vietnam. The Unknown of Vietnam was identified in 1998 and he has been reinterred, near his family home, at Jefferson Barracks National Cemetery.

A few feet to the west of the Tomb there was a solitary soldier standing guard. They watched as he solemnly marched from one end of the plaza to the other. The soldier takes twenty-one steps, on a well worn black rubber mat, as he marches from one end of the plaza to the other. As he marches, he passes between the Tombs and the Memorial building. When he stops, at the north end of the plaza, he turns 90 degrees to the east and clicks his heels and he stands for twenty-one seconds. Then he turns ninety degrees to the south, clicks his heels, puts his rifle on his outside shoulder and walks twenty-one steps south to the other end, of the plaza, and there he repeats the process. The soldier's uniform and his M1903 Springfield rifle with bayonet are meticulously maintained and checked, by the platoon leader, before his post. He continued to guard the Tomb, seemingly unaware of their presence, but he was aware.

Caleb was selected to represent the group, at the wreath laying ceremony. Caleb was wearing his dress whites. The same uniform that he wore when he was Captain of the Canberra. He met with the Sergeant of The Guard and the bugler, before the ceremony, in the Memorial building.

Then the ceremony began. The platoon leader approached the center of the plaza from the south. When he reached the center of the plaza he stopped and crisply turned 90 degrees to the west, clicked his heels, and faced the audience that was assembled on the stairs. Then he addressed them solemnly saying, "the ceremony, you are about to witness, is a wreath laying ceremony. It is conducted by the former Captain of the U.S.S. Canberra and Medal of Honor Recipient. I ask that everyone remain standing and silent during this ceremony. All military personnel in uniform will render the hand salute and it is appropriate for all others to place your hand over your heart upon the command of 'present arms'. Thank you." Then he turned clicked his heals and walked on the black mat toward the south end of the plaza where the wreath was waiting upon a wreath stand.

Then the doors of the Memorial building opened and the Sergeant of the Guard led Caleb and a Guard bugler solemnly down the stairs. As Caleb passed uniformed military personnel on the stairs, they offered him, regardless of their rank, a hand salute. As they walked down the stairs, the Platoon leader began to walk toward the Tomb as he held the wreath stand. When the Platoon Leader reached the center of the plaza, he placed the wreath stand just inches to the east side of the black marching mat. Then they all met in front of the Tomb.

Caleb stepped up and lifted the purple and white wreath. It had thirty-eight leaves and twelve berries. Then he slowly walked forward as the Platoon leader walked backwards holding the wreath stand. They stopped at the base of the World War II Tomb and Caleb placed the wreath and stand in that place. Before they could move, a faint noise was heard that came from the west. It was the sound of a seven gun rifle volley. Then Caleb and the Platoon leader returned to stand by the Sergeant of the Guard. As they did, Caleb thought back to another ceremony. It was a ceremony held on the deck of the Canberra in May 1958.

Then the Sergeant issued the command, "Present arms". As he did, the people placed their hands over their hearts and uniformed members of the military saluted. Then another seven gun rifle volley was heard coming from off in the distance.

Then the Guard bugler, standing on the marching mat and to the south of the Tomb, played "Taps" as the sun set below the western horizon. As he finished, a third and final seven gun rifle volley was heard coming from off in the distance. The Sergeant of the Guard then issued the final order, "Order arms" he said.

Upon that command, the Sergeant of the Guard, Caleb and the Guard bugler ascended the stairs and went into the Memorial building. Caleb quickly returned to the stairs and joined his friends.

Underneath a twilight sky, in that moment, the many became as one. Underneath a twilight sky, they grieved for their lost soldiers and for the Unknown Soldiers.

They grieved together but not as ones without hope. After a time, times and half time, in silence and respect, they solemnly departed the Tomb of the Unknowns. As they departed, to live out their lives, there was hope in midst of their hurting hearts.

Although their hearts longed for their soldiers, their souls found peace in the victory provided by the sacrifice of their Savior.

Made in the USA
Charleston, SC
09 November 2012